THE SAVAGE CURTAIN

BY KATHRYN LE VEQUE

KATHRYN LE VEQUE NOVELS

Medieval Romance:

The de Russe Legacy:
The White Lord of Wellesbourne
The Dark One: Dark Knight
Beast
Lord of War: Black Angel
The Falls of Erith

The de Lohr Dynasty:
While Angels Slept (Lords of East Anglia)
Rise of the Defender
Spectre of the Sword
Unending Love
Archangel
Steelheart

Great Lords of le Bec:
Great Protector
To the Lady Born (House of de Royans)

Lords of Eire:
The Darkland (Master Knights of
Connaught)
Black Sword
Echoes of Ancient Dreams (time travel)

De Wolfe Pack Series:
The Wolfe
Serpent
Scorpion (Saxon Lords of Hage – Also related
to The Questing)
Walls of Babylon
The Lion of the North
Dark Destroyer

Ancient Kings of Anglecynn:
The Whispering Night
Netherworld

Battle Lords of de Velt:
The Dark Lord

Devil's Dominion

Reign of the House of de Winter:
Lespada
Swords and Shields (also related to The
Questing, While Angels Slept)

De Reyne Domination:
Guardian of Darkness
The Fallen One (part of Dragonblade Series)

Unrelated characters or family groups:
The Gorgon (Also related to Lords of
Thunder)
The Warrior Poet (St. John and de Gare)
Tender is the Knight (House of d'Vant)
Lord of Light
The Questing (related to The Dark Lord,
Scorpion)
The Legend (House of Summerlin)

**The Dragonblade Series: (Great Marcher
Lords of de Lara)**
Dragonblade
Island of Glass (House of St. Hever)
The Savage Curtain (Lords of Pembury)
The Fallen One (De Reyne Domination)
Fragments of Grace (House of St. Hever)
Lord of the Shadows
Queen of Lost Stars (House of St. Hever)

**Lords of Thunder: The de Shera
Brotherhood Trilogy**
The Thunder Lord
The Thunder Warrior
The Thunder Knight

Time Travel Romance: (Saxon Lords of
Hage)
The Crusader
Kingdom Come

Contemporary Romance:

Sea of Dreams
Purgatory

Kathlyn Trent/Marcus Burton Series:
Valley of the Shadow
The Eden Factor
Canyon of the Sphinx

Other Contemporary Romance:
Lady of Heaven
Darkling, I Listen

Multi-author Collections/Anthologies:
With Dreams Only of You (USA Today bestseller)
Sirens of the Northern Seas (Viking romance)

The American Heroes Series:
Resurrection
Fires of Autumn
Evenshade

Note: All Kathryn's novels are designed to be read as stand-alones, although many have cross-over characters or cross-over family groups. Novels that are grouped together have related characters or family groups.

Series are clearly marked. All series contain the same characters or family groups except the American Heroes Series, which is an anthology with unrelated characters.

There is NO particular chronological order for any of the novels because they can all be read as stand-alones, even the series.

For more information, find it in **A Reader's Guide to the Medieval World of Le Veque**.

TABLE OF CONTENTS

FOREWORD

The battle of Halidon Hill was fought during the second Scottish War of Independence near Berwick-Upon-Tweed, Northumbria, England. It is an interesting and particularly brutal chapter of history when the entire city of Berwick, held by the Scots, was under siege by the forces of Edward III. The city's defenses were placed under the command of Sir Alexander Seton, a Scotsman loyal to the underage King David II, son of Robert the Bruce.

Although Seton led a strong defense, it was a long and bloody conflict that finally forced the Scots to ask for a temporary truce. King Edward agreed to this providing that Seton supplied hostages. Seton did, one being his own son, Thomas. There are conflicting reports that he actually supplied two sons. There was a deadline on this truce, however, and when the Scots refused to surrender the city at the deadline, Edward began hanging the hostages in full view of the city walls. The first one hanged was young Thomas Seton, said to have been somewhere around fourteen years of age. His father and family watched him die.

This event, and many others, culminated in the battle of Halidon Hill, which was a decisive English victory. Berwick surrendered the following day on July 20, 1333.

This is a tale of a love story set within the chaos of a city fallen. In every hour of darkness, there is still hope.

CHAPTER ONE

July 20, 1333 A.D.
Berwick-Upon-Tweed, Northumberland, England

AGAINST THE BLACK of the moonless sky, the fires lingering from the siege could be seen. The last dying embers of the battle blended into the smoky haze that hung heavy in the air. All was oddly still as the inhabitants of the city returned to what was left of their homes; some were ravaged while others were untouched. The citizens had been out in force for most of the day, helping each other, as the city of Berwick tried to resume a sense of normalcy. But that sense was a long way off.

The city walls were in shambles, mostly to the west and southwest where the English had been able to gain ground for launching their massive siege engines. They had also come by way of the sea, battering the city from the east. Day and night, the bombardments from King Edward's forces came strong and steady. There was a seemingly endless supply of Englishmen with which to harass the increasingly weary city. For an entire month, the siege had raged. Now, it was finished.

The aftermath of the siege and surrender was beyond horrific. There were bodies in the streets and the stench of blood mingled with smoke from the dying fires. The Scots holding the city had long since surrendered, fled or died, and the English now filled the city like a great Anglo tide. They crashed upon Berwick's threshold on their mighty warhorses, pouring through gaps in the walls or through the burned gates that had stood strong and proud throughout the siege. Like the mighty hand of God, the English had swept back the savage curtain to reveal the battered and dying city beneath.

At midnight, the smoke from the crushed city was still fresh and pungent. Dogs could be heard barking on occasion or a child crying in the distance but, for the most part, it was eerily still. Edward's advance forces had already moved into the city to secure the strategic points, one being Berwick Castle on the banks of the River Tweed. The castle had become the central command post as groups of English combed the city to secure it for the arrival of the king.

And arrive he did, like a conquering Caesar. Edward was not a pampered king; he had been fighting most of his life and was a warrior before he had been a monarch. Astride his massive Belgian charger, he thundered into the city with a retinue of advisors and senior knights, all of them battle born and bred. Carrying torches through the battered streets, they made their way to Berwick Castle.

Banners flapped in the brisk wind and torches blazed as they thundered down the dark avenues. The castle was well fortified with hundreds of English troops as the king and his entourage arrived and the group made its way into the great hall. Fighting men were everywhere, some sporting impressive battle wounds, as Edward sought the one man in particular that he knew to be heading the room. The Earl of Carlisle, his most faithful subject, had secured not only half the city personally, but the castle as well. Edward's pale eyes sought out Sir Tate de Lara, the commander of his forces.

He was not difficult to locate; Tate had seen the king arrive in the hall and was making his way towards him. De Lara was a big man with the dark coloring of his Welsh mother, the illegitimate son of Edward I and uncle to the current king. He met his nephew in the middle of the smoky, dim hall.

"Sire," he greeted amiably. "You will be pleased to know that the entire city has been secured. Patrols are reporting in from all corners of the city and I am told all things are well in hand. Berwick is finally ours."

Edward seemed older than his twenty-one years; this siege had seen more than its share of hardship and he was already missing some friends in death. He was greatly relieved to see a healthy and sound de Lara, the man he depended on more than any of his other generals. He shook the man's hand thankfully.

"Praise God," Edward muttered, feeling his fatigue but unwilling to show it. "I could have not have done this without you."

De Lara smiled wearily. "I had a good deal of help."

Edward shook his head at the man's modesty. "You, as always, are the catalyst for men to show their true strength." He eyed the group of unfamiliar faces lingering near the hearth; there were women in the mix and he knew them to be hostages. He nodded his head in their direction. "Seton, I presume?"

De Lara's storm-cloud colored eyes drifted to the group huddled near the blazing fire. "Indeed," he replied. "The man and his family. Would you interrogate them tonight or wait until morning? It has been a long day and I am sure you would like to rest."

Edward waved him off. "I have waited a long time for this moment and I shall not be put off by something as mundane as my exhaustion," he began to walk towards the group. "Where is Pembury?"

De Lara followed. "He went out to secure the posts for the night personally. He should be back momentarily."

Edward focused on the hostage group. "Does he know what you and I have discussed?"

De Lara shook his head with some dissatisfaction. "He knows that he will be made commander of Berwick once the city is secured," he made sure to speak pointedly to the king. "Beyond that, I thought it best that you tell him his destiny."

"I told you to do it."

"He will take it better coming from you."

Edward glared at de Lara as they came upon the hostages. But it was a brief scowl, unnoticed by the group before him. Edward was quickly composed into the emotionless, somewhat haughty, monarch as his gaze moved amongst the unfamiliar faces. An odd hush fell upon the room as the king finally confronted his opposition face to face.

"Who is Alexander Seton?" he demanded.

The man standing in front of the group bobbed his head slightly. "I am he."

Edward's gaze fixed on the man; he was older, as he knew he would be, nearly bald but with a powerful body beneath the tartan and mail. Sir Alexander Seton had led the defenses against the English, holding the city of Berwick for several months before finally being forced by the decisive English victory at Halidon Hill to surrender.

The king planted himself in front of Seton, continuing his scrutiny; there was a good deal of confusion in his expression as if trying to figure out a great many things. Without warning, Edward balled a fist and struck Seton firmly on the jaw. The older man went reeling as the women in his group shrieked.

"That was for forcing my hand," Edward growled, daring the man to come back at him. "You made an agreement, Seton. The city was to surrender at the appointed date and you would still have your son. What possessed you to trade your son's life for your stubborn pride?"

Seton rubbed his jaw, eyeing the passionate young king. "You would not understand, my lord."

Edward was growing increasingly livid. "He was a child yet he behaved with more honor than those who call themselves adults," he pointed a finger at Seton. "God damn you for forcing my hand against your brave son. God damn you for sending to death a young man who held out hope until the very end that his father would save him."

De Lara was standing next to the king, his jaw ticking faintly as he watched the exchange; young Edward had spent most of his young life running from Roger Mortimer and his mother, so the man well understood a child's fear and confusion when a parent refused to protect him. It was a painful subject made more painful by the death of Seton's fourteen year old son, a lad that Edward had come to know during his captivity.

Seton had pledged his son as a hostage to ensure that the Scots would surrender Berwick should reinforcements not arrive in time, but the deadline came and went, no reinforcements came, yet Seton did not surrender. Edward was forced to execute hostages as punishment. Thomas Seton had died with a rope around his neck and hope in his heart.

"It did not give my father pleasure to watch my brother die." A young woman standing behind Seton made herself known. "My father's hands were tied; his commanders refused to surrender. Even if he wanted to submit to your deadline, he could not have. His men would not have obeyed."

Edward's focus moved from Seton to the woman behind him; she was short of stature with lush dark hair and eyes of the palest blue he had ever seen. She was a strikingly lovely woman even dirty and disheveled as she was. Edward's attention fixed on the girl.

"Who are you?" he demanded.

Seton turned to look at the girl, his expression bursting with disapproval, but the young woman ignored him and stepped forward.

"I am the Lady Joselyn de Velt Seton," she said with courage. "Alexander Seton is my father."

"Then Thomas was your brother."

She nodded, losing some of her confidence. "Aye," she nearly whispered. "He was my younger brother."

Edward cocked his head slightly. "I was not aware that Seton had two daughters."

Joselyn nodded. "Maggie is my younger sister. I am the eldest of the Seton children."

The king's eyebrows lifted. Then he turned to de Lara with a knowing glance. "Joselyn," he murmured, pronouncing it the way she had; *Joe-zalyn*. He looked back at the young woman. "How old are you, lady?"

"I have seen twenty-two years, my lord."

"Who is your husband?"

"I am not married, my lord."

Edward was shocked. "No husband?" he repeated, incredulous.

"Why not?"

"She has been at Jedburgh Abbey," Seton answered for her. "She has been living by the Augustinian code since she was eleven years of age."

Edward looked at the man as if he had lost his mind. "That," he pointed at Joselyn, "has been meant for the cloister? Are you completely stupid, man? She would command a husband of such wealth and stature as you could not dream of."

Seton looked at his daughter, who gazed back at him with some fear and, as de Lara thought whilst studying her, some chagrin. Before the conversation gained too much steam, a group of knights entered the hall and distracted the focus. Their voices were loud, the sounds of their weapons and mail reverberating off the old stone walls. Edward and Tate turned to the group, as did everyone else in the room. The muscle of the king's forced had arrived.

"Ah, Pembury," Edward grabbed de Lara by the arm and pulled him away from the Seton clan. He gestured to the group of incoming knights, now beginning to cluster around a massive table of food several feet away. "You will tell him now of his destiny. And mind that you leave out nothing."

De Lara was obviously displeased with the command. "You had better ask where Seton's other daughter is before I tell him. If you want the man to marry her, then...."

Edward shook his head. "Forget about Margaret Seton. We have a very lovely and completely viable prospect right here. He will marry Joselyn Seton before this night is through and secure the city with a marriage to the daughter of the defeated Scot commander."

Tate couldn't help it; he grunted with exasperation, running a weary hand over his face. Then he glanced at the Lady Joselyn, standing small but strong next to her father. She certainly was a lovely little thing. There was no use in fighting the king's wishes; once the man's mind was set, there was no deterring him. He sighed in resignation and turned in the direction of the knights now settling in.

"Stephen," he called to the group. "A word, please."

Stephen of Pembury separated himself from the group and headed in de Lara's direction. He was an enormously muscled man standing eight inches over six feet and was easily taller than even the tallest man in the room, de Lara included. In fact, Pembury was a giant wherever he went. With his dark hair, chiseled features and cornflower blue eyes, he cut a striking figure of male virility and power, and had more than his share of female admirers. He was enormously strong, intelligent and obedient to a fault. He had been close friends with Tate for years and the cornflower blue eyes twinkled as he came upon his friend and liege.

"Outposts are set for the night, my lord," he said in a deep voice. "There are four serious breaches in the walls but I have those covered by at least twenty men each. We'll set to repairing them come sunrise but for now I have told the men to rest for the night. 'Twill be the first real rest the men have had in over a month."

Tate nodded. "I do not disagree with you on that account," he told him. "We are all quite weary."

"This has been a long and eventful two days."

"Eventful and bloody."

Stephen wriggled his dark brows in agreement, eyeing the king as the man wandered over to the hearth where a group of unkempt people huddled. The young king seemed particularly weary and pensive, but considering the length and cost of the siege of Berwick, Stephen was not surprised.

"Any further orders from Edward?" he asked quietly.

Tate thought long and hard on that question. Then he crossed his powerful arms, struggling to find the correct words.

"You have known since this campaign began that Edward intended to place you in charge of the military garrison of Berwick," he began.

Stephen began to show the first signs of his fatigue; he rubbed his eyes and took a deep, weary breath. "Aye," he stopped rubbing his eyes and blinked them furiously as if struggling not to fall asleep where he stood. "I have already picked my command team with the approval of the king. Too bad Ken isn't here; I am sorely missing the man."

He spoke of Kenneth St. Héver, their friend and colleague, now on the Welsh Marches keeping the Welsh princes at bay. All three men had served together for the past several years, a powerful trio of knights for Edward's cause, and this was the first instance that had seen them separated. Tate nodded in agreement to Stephen's comment.

"We will unfortunately have to do without him." He eyed Stephen as the man watched the king on the other side of the room. After several moments of struggling to find the correct words to tell the man of his destiny, he finally sighed heavily and faced him. "Stephen, you need to be aware of more directives involving your appointment."

Stephen looked at him. "What are those?"

Tate wisely went with the good news first. "For exemplary service during the siege of Berwick, you have been granted the battlefield commission of Baron Lamberton which includes Ravensdowne Castle near Blyth, just north of Newcastle. The fiefdoms of Bedlington and Blyth are yours. These are rich lands, Stephen. Congratulations."

Stephen suddenly didn't appear too weary. His blue eyes stared at de Lara first in disbelief, then in gratitude.

"I know that area," he said after a moment. "It is indeed wealthy and populated."

De Lara smiled faintly and slapped him on his enormously broad shoulder. "No one deserves this more," he told him softly. "I am proud of you."

Stephen smiled modestly, reaching up to remove his helm. Setting it on the table behind him, he raked his fingers through his damp, nearly-black hair. "I am honored," he said simply. "I would thank Edward personally when he is not so occupied."

De Lara's smile faded somewhat. "There is something more."

Stephen's mood was good, having no reason to believe that any-thing else forthcoming would be met with disapproval. "Good Christ, what more could there be? I am already greatly honored. Anything more will seem excessive."

Tate turned in the direction of the king, now standing at the hearth with a few of his advisors. De Lara dipped his head in the general direction.

"Note the group of captives?" he mentioned to Stephen.

The big knight nodded. "Who are they?"

"Alexander Seton and his family," he replied. "There are three women in the group."

"I see them."

"Note the young one that is standing next to the balding man in the kilt?"

Stephen's eyes fixed on the small figure across the room. "Dark hair?"

"Aye."

Stephen paused a moment, studying the distant figure. "Pretty girl," he commented, turning back to Tate. "Who is she?"

"The Lady Joselyn Seton. Your new wife."

Stephen stared at him. Tate stared back. They just stared at each other. Tate kept waiting for some kind of adamant response but Stephen did nothing more than stare. Stephen was, in fact, inordinately cool and always had been, but this lack of response was calm even for him. After several long moments of mutual staring, it was Stephen who finally broke; he smiled thinly and raked his hands though his hair again.

"I do not want a wife."

"What you want is not at issue," de Lara stated, though not unkindly. "Edward feels that the security of Berwick will be sealed when the new commander of the English forces marries the daughter of the defeated Scots leader. It is a tradition as old as battle itself, Stephen. To marry the daughter of your defeated enemy is to ensure peace. You know this."

Stephen was laughing, though not with humor. He was struggling to refuse, which in any case he knew he could not do. Frustration and disbelief were turning into anger, an emotion he was not particularly familiar with. The man was so cool at times that some had wondered if he had ice water in his veins instead of blood.

"I was a soldier when I walked into this room," he muttered. "Now I am a pawn."

Tate lifted an eyebrow. "Untrue. You have been elevated in rank and status and are a valuable asset to the king. I suggest you look at it that way." He lowered his voice and stepped close to the big man. "Whatever fury you are feeling, be done with it now. You have a directive to fulfill before this night is out and Edward is in no mood for foolery. You are the last man I would expect emotion from, Pembury. Do your duty, as we all must."

The humorless grin on Stephen's face faded as he gazed steadily at his liege. The cornflower blue eyes glittered, shifted, and finally cooled. After a moment, he nodded shortly.

"Of course, my lord," he was back to sounding calm and professional. "The king's will shall be done in all things."

Tate nodded faintly, eyeing Stephen as if to suggest he was not unsympathetic. But that was where it ended; they were knights and they did as they were told. It was the end of a very long and bitter struggle and they were perhaps more edgy than they should have been out of sheer exhaustion. But they were professionals and knew what was expected of them. Together, they moved towards Edward.

The king saw them coming, straightening as he focused on Stephen. Stephen saluted his monarch, a young king he had known since he had been a very young boy.

"Sire," he greeted evenly. "May I extend my deepest gratitude for the honors you have given me. I am humbled by your generosity."

Edward didn't dare look at Tate, fearful that he would see that, somehow, Pembury had been forced into his smooth little speech. He genuinely liked Stephen, a man that was as strong and silent as the grave, yet possessed the most devious sense of humor he had ever seen. When he had been younger, he had been the butt of a few of Stephen's pranks. The man could be merciless but it was all in good fun.

Gazing into the familiar eyes of one of his most powerful knights, he sensed there was not an excess amount of good humor in the man at the moment. He suspected why but he would not back down or change his directive. Sometimes he had to remind himself that he was now the king and these knights he had grown up around were his vassals. They were men he had learned much from, considering them fathers in place of the one he never had. Stephen was one of those men. He secretly hoped the man was not truly upset.

"You deserve nothing less," Edward replied. "I hope that you will be able to inspect your holdings sometime in the very near future, Baron Lamberton."

Stephen genuinely smiled at the sound of his new title. "I know the lay of the land in that area somewhat and it is a rich and populated region."

Edward nodded, the warmth of the moment fading as the unspoken subject of the betrothal hung in the air. Edward cleared his throat softly and plunged into the topic.

"I presume that Tate told you of your new wife," he lowered his voice.

Stephen nodded, but not without a cocked eyebrow. "He did."

"I would have you marry her this night. The Scots must know we mean to dominate them in every way. Rebellion will not be tolerated."

Stephen didn't argue and he didn't question; it would be of no use. It would not change the way of things.

"Does she know yet, Sire?"

"She does not. Nor does her father."

"I presume you will tell them both?"

Edward's reply was to motion to one of the lesser knights standing nearby. When the man came close, the king quietly ordered him to find a priest. Stephen watched the knight jog off, his armor and mail jingling a crazy tune. He looked back at Edward to find the young king staring at him.

"I will tell the father but you tell the girl," he told him quietly. "She is to be your wife, after all. You may as well start to know her immediately."

Stephen almost rolled his eyes but caught himself. Still, the square jaw was ticking with displeasure and Edward was sure he heard a low growl at some point. But the knight nodded obediently.

"The dark haired lass, I presume?" he dipped his head in the direction of the huddling family.

Edward turned around, eyeing the group; along with Seton and his eldest daughter, there was apparently a mother, a grandmother, and two other elderly men in mail and dirty tartan. It was an odd family group. Not so odd, however, when one considered that Seton had lost all three sons in the siege of Berwick. Women and old folk were all he had left, which was something of a tragedy.

"Take the girl somewhere and explain things to her," Edward hissed the order as they turned for the group. "I will keep the family at bay. Once the priest arrives, you will marry her and consummate the marriage immediately. I want no room for error."

It was a harsh command but Stephen didn't flinch. "Aye, Sire."

"Oh... and Stephen?"

"My lord?"

"Congratulations. She is a beautiful woman."

Stephen found a great deal of irony in that statement. He repressed the urge to roll his eyes again. Marching behind the king as they reached the tattered group of rebels, he came to a halt when the king did, a massively silent sentinel bigger than any man any of them had ever seen. He crossed his arms, appendages the size of tree branches.

"This is Sir Stephen of Pembury," Edward announced to the group. "He is Guardian Protector of the City of Berwick, Commander of the King's Forces and a knight unlike any you have ever seen. He is cunning, experienced and possesses strength that would put Samson to shame. If you value your lives, you will obey this man as you obey me. Is this in any way unclear?"

Seton was gazing up at Stephen with a baleful expression; even in defeat, the old man had courage. He had been through hell and lost nearly everything, but still, his inherent defiance had not left him.

"What is to become of my family and me?" his gaze moved back and forth between Stephen and the king. "Are we to hang as Thomas did?"

Stephen returned the hateful stare without emotion; there was no reason to respond to the challenge of a prisoner. But he looked to the king for the reply.

"You will be my guests for the time being." Edward didn't like the way the man was glaring at them. "Your new home will be Alnwick Castle until I can think of a more suitable place. But your daughter has a different destiny."

Stephen took that as his cue. Reaching out, he grasped the petite brunette by the arm and yanked her clear of her family group before anyone could react. Alexander roared in protest as his wife screamed; the commotion brought the knights and soldiers in the great hall to bear, armed to the teeth and prepared to stab the first Scots who tried to cross the line. While the women in Seton's group began to wail pitifully, Seton himself suddenly lost all of his arrogance.

"Please, Sire, I beg you," he was quickly growing panicked. "Not Joselyn. Take me for whatever punishment you choose and I shall gladly submit myself. But leave my daughter alone."

Stephen was already pulling Joselyn across the hall, heading for the main door. He was focused on his duty and ignored the chaos that had erupted. In his grasp, his prisoner was doing very little resisting; instead, she seemed to be trying to calm her kin.

"Da!" she called to the man steadily. "All will be well. Do not fret so!"

Her father tore his eyes away from the young king in time to see his daughter being hauled through the front door by a mountain of a man. Pembury was the biggest knight he had ever seen and he was terrified. Hand on his heart as if to hold in his terror, he looked back to the young king.

"What will you do with her?" he asked in raspy voice.

Edward cocked a fair eyebrow. "Have no fear, Seton," he was not sure he liked this man in the least. "She will not meet the same fate as your son. In fact, you have just met your future son-in-law. You could live to be a thousand years old and never find such an honorable man. Consider yourself and your daughter extremely fortunate."

Seton looked as if he were about to pass out. In fact, that was what his wife did as soon as Joselyn left the room.

CHAPTER TWO

T HE SMELL OF smoke and death was heavy in the air now, just a few moments after midnight, as Stephen pulled Joselyn across the dusty bailey and towards the keep of Berwick. The moon was starting to emerge, just peeking over the northeast hills, and the land was illuminated a soft gray color. Joselyn didn't say a word as the enormous knight pulled her up the steps into the keep and took her into the first room they came to, a small solar just off the main entry. Once inside the cold and dark room, he shut and bolted the door.

He had also let her go by that time. Clad in her tartan and a rough wool garments that were heavy and warm, she pressed herself against the wall as far as she could go while Stephen went to see about a fire. There was very little kindling but he piled it expertly, searching until he found the small piece of flint and stone used to light the fire. He managed to spark a small blaze on the first try.

So far, he hadn't said a word. Joselyn watched him closely, struggling not to show her anxiety. He was big and evil-looking, covered with dark stains that she could only assume to be blood. He wore no helm, his short black hair glimmering weakly as the small fire grew in strength. He blew on it a few times and when he was convinced it was not going to die, he stood up to face her.

It was like looking up at the tallest tree; she had to crane her neck back simply to look the man in the face. Being Scots, she had seen her share of big men, but the English knight before her went beyond even what she had ever witnessed. Along with the black hair, he had a square jaw and straight nose, and the most brilliant blue eyes she had ever seen. They were the color of cornflowers and as he looked at her, they fairly glowed with curiosity, power and perhaps a bit of anger. She couldn't really blame him. But she was very concerned about what he was going to do with her. After several appraising moments, he lowered his gaze and vigorously scratched his scalp.

"As you have been informed, my name is Stephen," he said in a deep voice that seemed to bubble up from his toes. "I am a knight in the service of King Edward, as I also served his father. I am Baron Lamberton of Ravensdowne Castle in Northumbria and will inherit the title of Baron Pembury upon my father's death. I am also formerly a member of the Sovereign Military Hospitaller Order of St. John of Jerusalem, of Rhodes and of Malta. I am therefore an accomplished knight with wealth and status and you, my lady, are to have the honor of becoming my wife."

He looked at her as he finished his sentence. Joselyn stared at the man, digesting his words, her features registering shock, surprise and disbelief in that order.

"Wife?" she repeated, stunned. "But… but I cannot marry."

"You can and you will," Stephen told her, "and before you throw yourself into fits of hysterics, know that this is not my doing, but the king's. He has ordered us to wed to cement an alliance between the rebels and conquerors of this city. To resist, for either of us, would be futile."

Joselyn's pale blue eyes were wide with astonishment. She felt so much shock at the announcement that it was difficult to comprehend. She also felt a great deal of fear and embarrassment, knowing that the reasons behind her resistance might very well negate the deal. They were reasons she'd not spoke of since they had happened. But now, cornered by the big knight who was to be her husband, she found the horrific reasons filling her thoughts. It was making her ill simply to recollect that which she had tried so hard to forget.

"But you do not understand, my lord," she said, her voice quivering. "It is impossible for me to wed."

"Why?"

Her face, even in the dark, flamed a deep, dull red. She knew she must tell him but it was a labor of the greatest strain to bring forth the words.

"Because I have been living in a convent since I was eleven years of age," she replied. "I am meant for the cloister."

"Those plans have now changed."

"But they cannot!" she snapped, banking swiftly when she saw the look on his face. She had a healthy fear of this knight whom she did not know. "Please believe me, my lord, it is nothing against marriage in general. I have never been meant for any marriage."

Stephen inhaled deeply, wearily, and rested his enormous hands on his slender hips. "I understand your commitment to the cloister," he moved towards her slowly. "I, too, was committed to a monastic order but that is no longer the case. Sometimes the needs of country and king overshadow even those of the Church. Surely you understand that."

She moved away from him as he came closer, the tartan falling away from her head. She had cascades of luscious dark hair, slightly curly, giving her an ethereal loveliness in the weak light. For as much turmoil going on inside of him, even Stephen noticed it. With her pale blue eyes, nearly black hair and finely sculpted features, she was an exquisite creature.

"I suspect my reasons for committing myself to the cloister are different from yours," she inched away from him as he drew close. "Perhaps you recanted your vows, but I will not recant mine. My reasons are firm enough that I cannot ever marry."

"Have you actually taken your vows yet?"

She almost lied to him but her truthful nature had her shaking her head before she could think. "Nay," she murmured. "Not yet. I am due to take them after the New Year."

"How old are you?"

"I have seen twenty-two years."

He lifted a dark eyebrow and halted his advance; he could see that she was moving away from him. "If you have been in the cloister eleven years, why have you not taken your vows before now? If you were serious about becoming a nun, then you should have taken those years ago."

She lowered her gaze with uncertainty. "I... that is, the sisters would not let me. Not yet. They said that I still had penitence to do."

"Penitence for what?"

Her eyes flew to him and her breathing began to grow faster and faster. She swallowed, hard, endeavoring to retain her courage to say what she must. But she found she couldn't look him in the eye as she spoke, praying he would understand her words and rush to the king to demand the betrothal be broken. In her deepest humiliation was her only hope that he, too, would be humiliated enough to fight it. *Spit it out, foolish lass!*

"When I was eleven years old, my father took me and one of my brothers on a trip to Carlisle," she spoke barely above a whisper as she sank onto a stool against the wall. "My father went into Carlisle quite a bit on business but it was the first time I had ever gone with him. I remember that my brother and I were so very excited to go to the big city; it was an enormous place with soldiers and people. My father took us to a street with vendors who had goods from all over the world. While my father was attending to business, somehow I wandered away. I remember smelling something sweet and delicious, and I went in search of it. The next thing I realized, someone grabbed me and took me to a grove of trees that was just beyond the border of the street. I tried to scream and to fight, but he was simply too strong. I was only eleven years old, mind you, and no match for the man. He had been one of the many English soldiers I had seen throughout the city. When he finally took me to a place where no one could hear my cries for help, he...."

She suddenly trailed off, unable to continue. Stephen, however, was riveted to her dark head, suspecting with some certainty what she was about to tell him. There was a table in the room and he lowered his big body onto the corner of the table, his eyes fixed on her with sharp intensity.

"Go on."

She was staring at her feet. Her head started wagging back and forth. "Please...."

"Tell me the rest."

She kept her head lowered for the longest time. One big tear fell to the dusty floor, followed by a second. "He... he compromised me."

"He raped you?"

She nodded, once. "My family committed me to the cloister because I was not a suitable marriage prospect being that I was no longer a virgin. I have been there ever since."

"Yet you are here at Berwick with your family during the event of a siege. Why is that?"

She cleared her throat softly as she struggled for composure. "My mother needed me," she said softly. "She has not been well for some time and my father called me home almost a year ago. With the loss of her sons, the madness has only gotten worse."

"After eleven years away, he calls you home?"

"He did."

"Do you not have a sister that could have attended to her also?"

"Maggie is already married and living in York. Her husband would not let her come."

Stephen drew in a slow, steady breath, his eyes still riveted to her lowered head. The story, such as it was, had grown by leaps and bounds. He would not be made a fool of.

"You will forgive me if I do not believe you," he said quietly.

Her head snapped up, her pale blue eyes wide with shock and outrage. "You do not...?" she could hardly grasp what he had just said. "You do not *believe* me?"

"I do not."

She was beside herself. "Must I prove to you that my mother is not well? How would you expect me to do that?"

"I did not mean the story about your mother, although it does ring strange. I mean the story about the English soldier raping you at eleven years of age."

Her mouth flew open with outrage. "Do you think I tell you this horrific story simply to gain your sympathies?"

He was unemotional. "Women will say or do most anything to gain their way. No matter what you tell me, you and I shall be married as soon as the priest arrives."

Joselyn was beyond shocked; it never occurred to her that the man would not believe her. Her shock turned to rage such as she had never known and the fire of the Scots, so inherent to her soul, bubbled up like a great raging beast.

"Perhaps shallow English wenches tell stories that are meant to bleed the heart of sympathy, but I do not lie and I do not weave elaborate fabrications," she seethed. "What I told you was the truth. I should have expected no sympathy from a dishonorable English hound that would hang a young boy and call it justice."

Stephen merely lifted an eyebrow. "I did not hang a young boy. And he would not have been hanged had your father possessed any honor and stuck to his bargain."

"He tried to keep his promise but his men would not listen," she fired back passionately. "Do you not understand this? He wanted to honor the deal struck with the English, to surrender the city on the appointed date, but his men refused to do his bidding. So my father watched as you hanged my little brother, a sweet young lad who had never caused harm to anyone. He watched, weeping, as Thomas was hanged beyond the city walls. He cried his name as my brother breathed his last. Don't you dare accuse my father of a lack of honor; you are hardly worthy to speak the man's name much less judge him."

Stephen still sat perched on the edge of the table, his arms crossed as she fired her speech at him with all the subtlety of an exploding trebuchet. He was, in fact, mildly impressed with her courage. And the more he watched her, the more intrigued he was with her unearthly beauty and inherent strength.

"Then your father is a poor commander," his manner was cool.

"Had he been a capable leader, his men would have done his bidding without question. It simply proves my point that the Scots are savages without honor, your father included. He is a weakling to have allowed his son to be hanged because he was unable to control his men."

She stared at him, so much rage and disbelief in her mind that she could no longer verbalize it. Unable to stomach the sight of him any longer, she turned away from him.

"You contemptible bastard," she hissed.

Stephen didn't take offense one way or the other; he had no regard for what she thought of him. She was intelligent and well spoken, and she was undeniably beautiful. But the fact of the matter was that she was a stranger, and an enemy at that, now destined to be his wife. He was more displeased with the prospect than he had been when he had first entered the room.

There was no more point in conversation; they had said all that needed saying and anything more might see them start a physical battle. There was bitterness between them and a good deal of animosity, and with nothing more to do but wait, Stephen remained perched on the end of the table, watching the weak fire in the hearth and wondering what his future held for him with an enemy wife. He suspected he was going to have to be on his guard every hour of every day so she would not slit his throat while he slept. He suspected separate bowers would be in order, his with a big fat lock.

The night dragged on as the acrimonious mood settled. By his estimate, Stephen had been staring into the flames for almost an hour when there was a soft knock at the door. Rising, he went to the panel and unbolted it. De Lara was on the other side.

"The priest has arrived," he told him. "Are you ready?"

Stephen didn't say a word; he moved to grab his betrothed from her seat against the wall only to realize that she had fallen asleep sitting up. He paused, his hand on her arm, refraining from yanking her awake. For some reason, he didn't feel like being overly cruel to the woman in spite of the harsh words between them; he watched her as she slept, the gentle curve of her face and the way her perfect little nose twitched now and again. It was rather fascinating. The longer he watched her, the more entranced he became.

"Stephen," de Lara had come in to the room and was standing behind him. "Hurry up! There is no time to waste."

Snapping out of his trance, Stephen grasped her arm and shook it gently. "My lady?" he said quietly. "'Tis time to awaken. We have an appointment to make."

Startled, Joselyn awoke to two strange knights gazing down at her. Half asleep and forgetting where she was, she suddenly threw her fists up and caught Stephen in the mouth. His head snapped back but he maintained his grip on her as she screamed and fought. Tate came up beside him and, between the two of them, managed to get her on her feet. But she was still fighting.

"Lady Joselyn," Stephen wiped the trickle of blood from his split lip, understanding she was not fully awake yet. "Calm yourself. You are not in danger and you will not come to harm. You are at Berwick Castle, remember?"

Hair askew, Joselyn blinked unsteadily at the two enormous knights as they tried to lead her out of the solar. She brushed the hair from her face as her wits returned, the familiar bailey of Berwick coming into view.

The moon had risen fully in the time that she and Stephen had been sequestered in the solar, giving the landscape an eerie white glow. Being that it was July, she could smell the night blossoms upon the air, mingling with the smoke and stench of death. It was an odd smell. Taking a couple of deep breaths to clear her sleepy mind, she removed herself indelicately from Stephen and Tate's grasp.

"I am quite capable of walking unassisted," she informed them.

They allowed her to yank herself free. Neither man said a word as they continued to escort her across the bailey and into the great hall. It was still a crowded place, filled with English knights and lords, and somewhere near the hearth her family still hovered. The moment she entered the hall with a massive English knight on either side, however, her mother began to wail.

It was a chaotic sound that the husband tried to quiet and Edward tried to ignore. The priest was a fat man in dirty robes that smelled strongly of alcohol. The mother's wailing grew louder as Stephen took Joselyn by the elbow and guided her in the direction of the priest. Edward barked at the priest to begin the wedding mass and Stephen firmly pushed Joselyn to her knees. He knelt beside her, seemingly unaffected by the entire thing. There was strength and dignity to his posture while Joselyn seemed dazed.

Lady Seton's wailing grew to titanic proportions and she began lamenting her daughter's future loudly, almost drowning out the droning of the priest. Edward kept shooting the woman baleful looks, hoping Sir Alexander would take the hint and shove a fist into the woman's mouth to shut her up. But Seton was actually paying attention to the wedding ceremony, murmuring prayers in response to the priest's intonations. Infuriated with a new round of cries from Lady Seton, Edward picked up the nearest cup and threw it at her.

The woman screamed as it sailed past her head and into the wall behind her. Jolted, Joselyn almost bolted to her feet but Stephen held her firm as the priest made the sign of the cross in holy oil on their foreheads. But the woman's screaming continued and the priest was forced to speak louder and louder until he was almost shouting to be heard above the wailing. Edward would have thrown more cups had he been able to find them, cursing and muttering even as the priest prayed. Through the chaos, de Lara was the only one, other than Stephen, who kept his composure. Truth be told, however, had he possessed any less control, Tate would have been laughing his head off.

The priest finished with the final blessing and Stephen abruptly pulled Joselyn to her feet. Before she could draw another breath, he grabbed her upper arms and kissed her chastely on the cheek. As she opened her mouth to speak, her mother suddenly broke free and, with a piercing scream, hurled herself into the massively blazing fire.

Hysteria erupted as Joselyn and the other Seton woman, a grand-mother, screamed in horror. Without hesitation, Stephen grabbed his new wife and swept her swiftly from the hall. She was hysterical, beating on him and crying for her mother. But Stephen was resolute that she be removed from the bedlam. There was nothing either of them could do for the crazed mother and he had little doubt that it would have done Joselyn more harm than good to watch her mother burn to death.

As they crossed the bailey, they could hear the screams and shouts coming from the hall. Stephen was focused on the keep in front of him, thinking of the night ahead and the duty he must perform. It would undoubtedly be made more difficult by the events of the night. But his instincts to remove her from the hall had been correct; what they did not see was Edward preventing Seton from pulling his wife from the blaze as de Lara took his broadsword and gored the burning woman through the chest to end her agony.

Death was almost instantaneous and only then did de Lara pull the body from the hearth and extinguish it. The woman was barely recognizable. As Seton threw himself across his wife's scorched corpse, de Lara and Edward fell away to regroup, watching the Seton clan deal with their catastrophic loss. It had been a harrowing end to a harrowing day. They hoped, just between the two of them, that Stephen fared better.

☙

STEPHEN HAD TAKEN Joselyn into the keep, kicking down doors until he came to a room on the third level that had a small bed in it. It was a dirty room with an odd smell, but it didn't matter. It was private for his needs. He entered the room, slamming the door and bolting it.

He put Joselyn on her feet, watching as she tried to push past him and open the door. He grasped her around the waist and easily pulled her away from the panel. She struggled against him, trying to smack his hands away. He directed her over towards the bed but she was strug-gling so much that he ended up tripping over his own feet just so he would not step on her. Together, they tumbled onto the stiff, dirty pile of straw that constituted the crude mattress.

Joselyn was buried underneath him, sobbing her heart out. Stephen shifted so he would not smash her but he didn't get up entirely; she was still quite volatile.

"Relax, lady," he murmured with his mouth against the back of her head.

She twisted and heaved underneath him. "Let me go," she wept. "I must see to my mother."

Stephen thought on his last vision of Joselyn's mother as they had left the hall. The woman had been completely engulfed in flames and he knew there was no point to try and save her. Being a healer, and a very good one at that, he should have gone back into the hall to see if something could be done. But he also knew that, in his experience, serious burns were almost always fatal. And the woman had been consumed by the blaze, leaving little doubt that if she was not dead already, she very soon would be. He sighed faintly.

"There is no need," he rumbled softly. "If she is not yet with God, she very shortly will be."

Joselyn's weeping came to an abrupt halt as if shocked by his words. When she resumed her tears a few moments later, it was with great anguish. Stephen pushed himself off of the bed, pulling her up with him. As he knelt beside the frame, he grasped her by the arms and forced her to look at him.

"You have my sympathies on what has happened to your mother," he said with more emotion than he had exhibited since they had met. "But I can tell you with certainty that the moment she entered the flame, there was nothing anyone could do for her. It is a tragic thing to have witnessed and for that, I am deeply sorry. But you and I have a duty to fulfill and we must move forward with it."

Joselyn stared at him, her tears rapidly fading and a look of complete disbelief on her face. "Are you truly so unfeeling?" she half-demanded, half-pleaded. "You speak of my mother, not some unknown, unloved woman."

His blue eyes were intense. "I realize that," he said. "But I also know that there is nothing to be done for her. You must not dwell on it."

She tried to yank free of his grasp. "You are the coldest, most heartless man I have ever had the misfortune to come across," she hissed, managing to pull an arm free. She began climbing across the bed, away from him, leaving her tartan in his grip. "How can you show such callousness? If you are a Hospitaller as you said you were, then surely there is some compassion buried deep within your warring soul."

He stood up, watching her cower against the wall. The tartan in his hand was tossed against the wall. It landed in the cobwebs.

"The compassion I have is carefully reserved, not to be given lightly," he told her. "It does not belong with the dead."

Joselyn remained pressed against the wall as he turned away from her and began unlatching his plate armor. His reaction to her mother's situation only reinforced that he was an aloof, heartless man. God had never been particularly kind to her throughout her life and now she was saddled with an unemotional block of ice. Though her mind was still in the chaotic hall, her attention was focused on the enormous knight who was now her husband. He pulled off his wrist protection and moved to his breastplate, pulling it free and neatly piling the protection near the door. The more he removed, the more her attention was drawn away from the hall and to the situation at hand.

Joselyn was not a skittish girl; she was practical and sensible. She knew very well that she was now a married woman but beyond that, she knew little else. Having spent eleven years in the cloister had only prepared her for life serving the church. She knew virtually nothing of married life, of what was expected between a husband and wife. But she knew enough to know that her husband would expect his husbandly rights this night. Her experience with such a thing had been violent and painful. She expected this encounter to be no different from the disposition her new husband was displaying.

But truth be told, she was still in shock; shock from the surrender, shock from an unanticipated marriage, and shock over her mother's horrific end. It was enough to deaden anyone, but Joselyn was not an average young woman. She was a fighter. As Stephen removed the last of his plate armor and turned to her, she knew she could not surrender to the situation, as much as she wanted to. It would be easier to submit. But she never did things the easy way.

"I need your help to remove my mail." He pulled off his hauberk, or mail hood, and tossed it to the ground. Then he moved to the bed and held out his arms to her. "Will you pull, please?"

She gazed at him with a baleful expression. "Are you truly so hardened to everything?"

He looked at her, his arms still extended. "My mail, please."

"Does nothing in this world affect you in the least?"

"My mail, *please*."

"Answer me. As your wife, I would ask to be given that courtesy."

The arms remained hanging in the air between them. "I have no answer to give. I am what you see."

He was the most difficult person she had ever met. Frustrated, she reached out and grabbed the mail, grunting with great release as she pulled. Stephen bent over, allowing the mail to slide over his enormous body.

"My name...," Joselyn grunted as one arm came free and almost sent her over backwards, "is the Lady Joselyn Julia de Velt Seton," the other arm came free and she fell back onto the mattress with the weight of it, "and I am the eldest child of Sir Alexander and the Lady Julia de Velt Seton. My mother is a Northumberland de Velt and my father a Scot although he has Saxon forebears. I have been living at Jedburgh Abbey for eleven years where I was taught the arts of sewing, cooking, gardening, flower cultivation, shearing sheep and wool dying. I was also taught to read and write Latin and French, and I can play the mandolin. I am not a mindless, cowering female so you should know the manner of woman you have married."

By this time, Stephen was standing over her with his hands on his hips, listening to her speech. She spit it out rather angrily and he realized he very much wanted to smile at her spunk. But he kept his smile hidden, his manner strictly professional. He didn't want to let his guard down, not even for a moment. He'd known too many women in his lifetime that would use that sort of thing against him. Until he knew Joselyn better, it was best to keep up appearances.

"Thank you for the education," he said, bordering on sarcasm. "Since you are not a mindless, cowering female, I am assuming you realize that I am not undressing for my own comfort."

"What do you mean?"

"We must consummate this marriage."

She blanched but admirably kept her composure. "And if I refuse?"

"I would advise against it."

The pale blue eyes flashed. "Why? Will you rape me, too, if I do not submit to your husbandly attention?"

"I will do what is necessary to accomplish the task."

The man was as cold as stone and she believed him completely. Joselyn felt the sting of tears as she gazed up at him, quickly averting her eyes so he would not see. But it was too much; the strain of recent events took their toll and tears came as she started to unfasten the leather girdle around her slender waist. She stood up from the mattress and let the girdle fall to the ground. By this time, the tears were rolling and she sobbed as she began to unfasten her surcoat. The surcoat hit the floor and she went to work on her heavy hose, reaching underneath her shift to unfasten the ties and unrolling each one from her shapely legs. She was weeping deeply by the time she yanked the linen shift over her head, exposing her naked torso to the cold room. With a final yank of frustration and futility, she pulled her undergarments free and tossed them onto the floor.

"There," she wept, covering her naked chest with her arms and wiping her face at the same time. "Do what you must. I have made it simple for you to take what you want."

Stephen had stood still as stone throughout the entire exchange;

even now, as she stood before him in all of her naked glory, his cornflower blue eyes were fixed on her face. There had been a brief moment when he had visually inspected his new bride and what he saw did not displease him. She was magnificent. He also knew that it took an abundance of courage to do what she had just done and he was impressed. A small seed of respect sprouted for the woman as she stood a few feet away, sobbing pitifully yet prepared to do as she must. He knew it hadn't been easy for her and in that instant, the compassion he kept so carefully guarded began to find release.

Stephen was not a cruel man by nature. He was, in fact, inordinately kindhearted, which is why he kept himself so closely guarded. He stood there for a moment, listening to her weep. Then, very slowly, he reached down and picked up the tartan that he had flung on the ground. Moving to her, he gently wrapped it around her naked body.

"Come," his voice was a raspy whisper. "Lay down on the bed."

She was weeping so heavily that she couldn't speak. "But... but...."

He shushed her softly, picking her up bodily and laying her upon the old, scratchy mattress when she seemed unable to do it herself. Pulling off his soiled tunic, he turned her towards the wall and lay down beside her. Gathering her up in his arms, he wedged her soft body into a comfortable position against him.

"Sleep now," he murmured into the top of her head.

"But... but...," she tried to twist around to look him in the face. "You said... you said we must con... consumm...."

"Consummate the marriage," he finished for her when she couldn't seem to spit the word out. "We will. But not right now."

She broke out in fresh tears. "I do not know anything about the marriage bed," she lamented. "The only thing I know is from that warm summer day those years ago when that soldier... he did unspeakable things ...."

She couldn't finish and Stephen lay there in the darkness, thinking that perhaps he had been wrong in not believing her tale. There truly hadn't been any reason for her to lie to him unless she had been else compromised and did not want him to know it. Perhaps she was promiscuous and that was why her father sent her to Jedburgh. He simply didn't know her well enough to believe what she told him. He was reluctant to admit that he was afraid to believe her.

"Hush, my lady," he repeated, tightening his grip around her. "Go to sleep. Things will seem better in the morning."

Her sobs remained strong, as they do when all defenses are down and exhaustion causes a lack of self-control. Stephen's surprising show of kindness undid her. She was not used to anyone being particularly kind to her. Joselyn was running amuck at the mouth and there was no way to stop it.

"But that was not the worst part," she wept. "There was the baby...."

Stephen felt as if he had been hit in the chest. Her words had that effect on him and he lifted his head to look at her.

"What baby?" he demanded.

Her hands were on her face as he rolled her onto her back. She was weeping incoherently and he pulled her hands away from her face. "What baby?" he demanded again, less harshly.

Joselyn gazed up at him with her pale blue eyes and wet, dark lashes. Her face was sopping with tears but her sobs died somewhat as she stared at him. She didn't know why she was telling him all of this, only that she couldn't seem to stop herself.

"My... my baby," she hiccupped. "I delivered a son three days after my twelfth birthday. I know you said that you did not believe me, but if you wanted proof of what the English soldier did to me, the physic told me that the birth tore me asunder. There are scars everywhere."

Stephen just stared at her, trying not to feel horrified on behalf of the woman. Still, it was an appalling tale. She told it with honesty. He could see it in her eyes as she spoke frankly of something no young maiden should have to speak of. The compassion seeping into his veins began to flow more strongly.

"Where is the child?" he asked, his voice exceptionally gentle.

She wiped at her eyes. "My father took both the child and me to Jedburgh," she said softly. "I named him Cade Alexander, after my father and his father. The nuns cared for him and I was only allowed limited contact. He is eleven years old now, a strapping lad with dark hair the last I saw."

Stephen sat back, staring at her with mounting disbelief. "He has been with you at Jedburgh all these years?"

"Until he was seven years of age. Then the nuns sent him to foster at Ettrick Castle."

"Does he know you are his mother?"

She shook her head. "He does not. He was told that he was orphaned." She sat up slowly, sitting next to the man who was staring so openly at her. He didn't seem disgusted, or judgmental, and that gave her courage. "From time to time, the nuns bring me news that he is well. When he has completed his training, my father has agreed to return him home. Perhaps... perhaps then I will tell him that I am his mother."

Stephen's eyes were dull with the tragedy of her tale. "And what if he asks of his father? What will you tell him?"

She looked as if she was going to start crying again but she fought it. "It was not his fault that he was the result of a violent, ugly act," she murmured. "I am not sure what I will tell him, but it will not be the truth."

"Do you know where his father is now?"

She shook her head. "After it happened, my father told me never to speak of it again. I have no knowledge of what became of the soldier or who he was."

Stephen regarded her carefully, thoughtfully. "Surely you caught a glimpse of something that might give a clue as to where he came from. Did he say anything?"

"Nothing that I choose to repeat in your presence," she told him, but realizing by the expression on his face that he was only attempting to help her. Her brow furrowed as she struggled to bring forth thoughts that she had tried very hard to forget. "I... I remember that he bore the colors of gray and red. I heard someone say that those were the standards of the Earl of Carlisle."

Stephen gazed steadily at her. Then, he snorted, an ironic gesture that Joselyn misread as a haughty one. Ashamed, she backed away from Stephen and pulled the tartan more tightly about her. She was in the process of pressing herself into the wall again when he stopped her.

"Nay, lady, you'll not move away from me," he had her by the arm. "I was not laughing at you. I was simply thinking that after all these years, you may be in luck. Justice may yet come."

She was not sure what he meant. "What do you mean?"

Stephen tugged on her until she moved away from the wall and back in his direction. "Because Tate de Lara happens to be the current Earl of Carlisle," he told her. "Perhaps this man is still in his ranks. When he assumed the title, Carlisle Castle was already staffed. It had been since Harclay was executed. Perhaps this soldier is still within the earl's ranks."

"Who is Tate de Lara?"

"The other man who escorted you to your marriage. He has been in the hall all night."

She looked dubious and hopeful at the same time. "Is it possible? The soldier is probably long dead."

Stephen shrugged. "It is indeed possible, but if he is alive, more than likely he is still at Carlisle. Men at arms, unlike knights, tend to settle in one place and stay if the conditions are good. Are you sure he was a soldier and not a knight?"

She blinked in thought, trying to recall that which she had blocked out for so many years. "I am not sure, to be truthful," she said timidly. "He wore mail and a tunic, and his helm came off at one point. I know he had red hair."

"Unlike the boy."

She shook her head. "His hair is dark, like mine," she replied, trying to read the expression on his face. He seemed to have warmed up from the cold and harsh man she had been introduced to. "Will you find him?"

Stephen lifted a dark eyebrow. "I will do better than that," he replied decisively. "I will find him and when I do, I will kill him."

Her eyes widened. "Why would you do this?"

His blue eyes grew intense. "Because you are my wife. This man stole your innocence which belonged to me and for that, he will pay the price."

She gazed steadily at him, torn between disbelief and hope. "I am indebted, my lord," she said quietly. "It does not seem enough to thank you."

An enormous hand came up and he took her chin between his thumb and forefinger. He tilted her head to get a better look at her exquisite face. She had the most amazing eyes of pale blue, a striking contrast against her dark hair. He took the moment to openly study her, the first time he had done so since they had been introduced. Much to his horror, he could feel his defenses softening but at the moment, he didn't much care.

"You will not address me so formally in private," he said quietly, still studying her face. "I will answer to Stephen. Or Husband."

Joselyn gazed at him, feeling strange warmth bubbling in her belly. The longer he looked at her, the more the warmth seemed to spread, making it difficult to breathe. Even as he inspected her, she inspected him in return. His eyes were so vibrantly blue that she swore there was lavender in them. He had a beautifully square jaw, set like stone, and a powerful brow. Physically, the man was as close to perfection as she had ever seen.

Suddenly, he dropped his hand and rose from the bed. Startled, she watched him walk to the door and unbolt it.

"Where are you going?" she asked.

He looked at her, his expression harboring a strange shadow of remorse. He cleared his throat softly.

"To see what has become of your mother," he replied. "You will not leave this room until I return."

So he was not as hard as she had originally thought. His expression said it all and somehow, in some way, she felt as if a weight had been lifted off of her. It was kindness from a stranger she had not expected.

"I will not leave this room," she promised softly.

With a short nod, he turned from her and lifted the latch. She called after him before he could get away.

"Sir Stephen?"

He paused. "Aye?"

"For your kindness towards my mother," she grasped for words. "I... thank you."

He looked rather surprised by her gratitude. And then he looked guilty. Without another word, he quit the room.

CHAPTER THREE

JOSELYN WOKE UP the next morning alone in the small, dirty bed. It was light outside but she had no way of knowing what time it was. Stirring, she propped herself up on her elbows only to realize that at some point during the night, someone had piled a mound of woolen blankets on the bed and a fire burned low in the hearth. The wood was crumbling, indicating the fire had been burning for some time. Just the least bit curious, not to mention touched, she realized that Stephen must have returned at some point.

Sitting up, she swiftly remembered that she hadn't a stitch of clothing on. Her rough surcoat and shift were still on the floor where she had dropped them. In spite of the fire, the room was chilly and she moved to the edge of the bed, aiming for her clothing on the floor, when more items caught her attention that hadn't been there the night before.

A bucket of water and a small cake of white soap sat on a small table just to the right of the bed. Standing up, she hooted when her feet hit the freezing floor as she hobbled over to the soap and water. A folded square of linen was placed behind the bucket, presumably to dry off with, and her lips twitched with a smile. She could hardly believe that the cold, hard man she had met yesterday would actually provide her with such luxuries and kindness that she could scarcely comprehend. Perhaps he was not so cold and hard, after all. It was too good to believe.

Just as she picked up the soap, the final surprise caught her eye; folded up quite neatly on a small three-legged stool next to the water and soap, were at least two layers of different colored material. Intrigued, she picked up the first bundle and watched it unfurl into a splendid surcoat the color of cranberries. She fingered the fabric, noting it was very soft wool that was long of sleeve and square of neck. It was also unhemmed and unfinished.

Underneath it lay at shift made out of a material so fine and soft that it was surely made of clouds. Awed, she picked it up, rubbed it against her cheek and was delighted to note that it did not scratch her at all as the wool did. In fact, she had spent the past ten years wearing rough woolen garments of all kinds and her skin was constantly red and scratchy from the material. It was miserable but it was all she knew. The introduction of the white shift made of angel's wings had her reeling with delight.

Quickly, she threw off the dirty tartan and washed liberally in the cold water. She hooted and gasped as she lathered the soap and bathed, unassisted, in the corner of the dingy room. It had been the first bath she had taken in ages, so it was something of a delicious treat. The soap smelled strongly of pine but she didn't care; it was a wonderful luxury in a world that had very few. After she had washed her slender white body thoroughly, she stuck her head into what remained of the water in the bucket and lathered her hair up with the pine-smelling soap.

Her hair was trickier to wash than her body but she managed to rinse it relatively clean. Anything was clean compared to what it had been. And with that, she dressed in the soft white shift and pulled the surcoat over her head. There were latticed-strings on the bodice of the garment, strategically placed the length of her torso under each arm, and it took some time for her to lace them up properly. She'd never owned anything even remotely fancy and was having a difficult time navigating the strings. But once they were properly tied, it gave her a wonderful curvy appearance as the bodice emphasized her slender waist and full breasts. She had never worn anything like it.

With that, she put on her worn hose and under garments, feeling better of body and spirit than she had in months. Taking the drying linen, which was now damp, she put the three-legged stool next to the hearth, sat down, and proceeded to dry her hair near the warmth of the dim fire. She was still sitting there a half hour later when there was a soft knock at the door.

She stopped running her fingers through her hair to dry it. "Come in," she called.

The door opened and Stephen appeared. Joselyn did a double-take as he walked into the room and softly shut the door; in the light of day, he was far more handsome than she had remembered. She'd only seen the man in the dark or by weak firelight, never with the glory of the sun shining upon him. It made her heart pound strangely simply to look at him.

Stephen, too, was swallowing his mild surprise; since meeting Joselyn last night, her beauty, for the most part, had been completely obscured by her worn clothes and dirty tartan. The darkness of the night had also done much to shroud her. But sitting before him, clean and shiny, dressed in the new surcoat and shift he had brought her, she literally took his breath away. He'd never seen anything so lovely.

"Good morn to you, Lady Pembury," he suddenly felt quite dirty and disheveled next to this glorious creature. "I hope you slept well."

She stood up, a petite little thing against his enormous height. "I did, thank you," she nodded. A briefly awkward silence followed as they continued to appraise each other in the daylight. When the pause because excessive, she fingered the surcoat as if suddenly remembering it. "I assume you brought this for me?"

He nodded, noting how the cut of the garment gave her a figure like no other woman he had ever laid eyes on. "I thought you could use something clean to wear," he indicated the cranberry colored wool. "While checking the sentries just before dawn, I came across a merchant who was cleaning out his partially burned store. He had some women's garments that he had brought over from Paris to sell, so I bought the whole lot of them. Most of them smell like smoke, so I turned them over to the serving women here at Berwick to wash. This was the only garment that didn't seem to suffer any damage."

She stared at him. "You... you bought me more clothes?"

He nodded, walking halfway around her to better inspect the sur-coat and the way it draped over her luscious backside. "Aye," he paused, gaining a good view of her rump. "I suspected you did not have much of a wardrobe given the fact that you were wearing peasant clothing and tartan. As my wife, I should like you to be well dressed."

Joselyn was stunned, unsure what to say to the man. He had gone well out of his way to bring her something fine and she was momentarily speechless. "Then…," she started again. "Then I thank you for your generosity. I do not own anything fine or glorious. This is the first lovely garment I have ever had."

He moved back around to the front of her and faced her with his hands on his slender hips. "And it will certainly not be the last," he replied decisively. "Your beauty already outshines every woman in England. Putting you in fine clothing and jewels is like adding stars to the moon and sky; it simply enhances what is already breathtaking."

By the time he was finished, she was blushing furiously. When their eyes met, she grinned modestly and lowered her gaze. He laughed softly.

"You have never heard such things before, have you?" he asked.

She shook her head, still averting her eyes. "From the nuns of Jed-burgh? I doubt it."

He laughed again and she dared to look at him. He had a magnificent smile with big white teeth and a huge dimple in his left cheek. In fact, his entire face lit up when he smiled, changing his features dramatically. She was mesmerized.

"Well," he rubbed his cheeks as his smile faded. "You had better become used to flattery. I have a feeling it will not be the last time you hear it from my lips."

She continued to grin modestly, feeling his heated gaze upon her. Somewhat giddy, she went over to the bed and tossed aside the tartan in the quest to find her shoes.

"Have you broken your fast yet, my lord?" she was trying to slip her shoes on with quivering hands. The man had completely unnerved her with his glorious smile and sweet words. "I shall find the kitchen and procure some food."

He shook his head. "Unnecessary," he told her. "I have come to take you to the hall. There is food aplenty there."

Shoes on her feet, she faced him. As he watched, the smile faded from her face. She suddenly looked quite upset as if the entire world had just come crashing down on her. His brow furrowed, wondering about the sudden change of mood, when she spoke. The first words out of her mouth explained everything.

"The hall...," she swallowed and groped for words. "Would... would you please tell me where my mother is? How is she?"

His smile faded as well. He knew the question would come but he wished it hadn't. He was enjoying the first pleasant conversation they had ever had and didn't want to spoil the mood. Still, there was no use in avoiding the inevitable. She had to know the truth.

He sighed faintly. "Your mother is with God," he murmured. "There was nothing I could do for her."

The tears welled as he watched. "She is dead?"

"She is. I am sorry."

"Was... was she dead when you returned to her?"

Stephen thought of the gored corpse and how her father had held it and wept. "She was," his voice was soft and low. "She is no longer in pain, my lady. She is at peace."

Joselyn turned away, struggling not to sob out loud, but it was beyond her control. Covering her face with a hand, she wept deeply.

Stephen watched her heaving shoulders, feeling badly that he had brought such terrible news. Truth be told, he had brought her the new garments and other luxuries before she awoke, hoping to soften the blow. He was not as heartless as she had accused him of being and he didn't want her to think he was made of stone. It was no way to start a marriage. Moreover, there was more bad news to come.

"Your father and the rest of your clan were removed from Berwick before dawn," he reasoned that he might as well tell her all of it so she could grieve for everything all at once. "They are being escorted to Alnwick Castle where they will be held for trial. Your mother's body remains here for burial."

She wept as if her heart was broken. "You sent my father away?"

Stephen drew in a long, deep breath. "He is the king's prisoner, my lady. There was nothing else to do with him."

"Please," she went to him, her hands folded in front of her in a pleading gesture. "Please bring him back and I swear he will not cause any trouble. My father is old and unwell. I am afraid... afraid that confinement in the vault will only lead to his death. It will surely kill him."

Stephen was not without sympathy. "I cannot grant your request, lady," he said softly. "Your father is a prisoner of the king and only the king can make that decision."

Tears dripped from her chin and onto the cranberry colored wool. "First my brothers, then my mother...," she was growing increasingly hysterical as she once again turned away from him. "And now my father is gone. My family is destroyed. I have no one left."

Stephen didn't know what to say to that. She had every right to be distraught. Not knowing what else to do, he gave her a few moments of crying before reaching out and grasping her elbow gently.

"Come along," he said softly. "You will feel better after you have eaten."

She pulled her elbow away from him, although it was not cruelly done. "Nay," she breathed. "I... I am not hungry. If you do not mind, I simply wish to be left in peace."

Stephen watched as her small body was wracked with sobs. He was about to insist that she come to the hall and eat, but he thought better of it. The woman needed to deal with her grief in her own way.

He left her without a word, his heart heavy with sorrow for her. Somehow, between last night and this morning, he was coming to feel a great deal of compassion for the woman. It was apparent that life had dealt her a bitter blow at a young age, which didn't seem fair to him.

Certainly, most people had their share of hardships, but she seemed to have more than most.

As he crossed the bailey and headed into the great hall where Edward and Tate were sitting near the blazing hearth, he thought to take Joselyn some food so that she would have something to eat if she became hungry. Edward and Tate were discussing some future strategy, acknowledging Stephen when he began gathering hunks of cheese and a few apples.

"How is your wife?" Tate asked.

Stephen was picky with his apple selection; he inspected each one closely before deciding. "She is rested but understandably upset over the death of her mother and the departure of her family."

"Did you give her the garments you bought?"

"I did. She looks marvelous."

Edward elbowed Tate, grinning. "I told you she was a lovely girl, Stephen," the king said. "So now you agree with me?"

Stephen looked at the young king. "I never disagreed in the first place," he replied, tucking the cheese and apples into one hand and hunting for a nice piece of soft bread with the other. "Wait until you see her this morning. She looks like a goddess."

Tate just grinned and shook his head. "It sounds as if you are not entirely displeased with your marriage, then."

Stephen shrugged. "Time will tell once we've both had a chance to settle into it."

"Why did she not come down to join us for the meal?" Edward wanted to know. "Is she too worn out from your wedding night?"

Stephen fought off a grin at the crass question. "I never touched her," he said honestly. "When did I have time? From the moment we were married until this very second, I have been mostly away from her seeing to my duties as both husband and garrison commander. If this pace keeps up, we'll both be old and gray before I have enough time to properly consummate the marriage."

Tate wriggled his eyebrows and stroked his chin in a weary gesture.

"If I were you, I would make time. You cannot leave her untouched."

"I know," Stephen nodded patiently. "I will do my duty as soon as I am able and not a moment sooner. Besides, last night was not the right time. She was... well, understandably distraught."

Tate thought on the burning woman he had gored, his good humor fading. "Indeed," was all he could say. The trio fell silent a moment before Tate spoke again. "Speaking of wives, I must return soon to mine. I am anxious to see my children. The baby turned four months old yesterday and I have not seen him since he was born."

Edward shook his head. "How many does that make now? Six children?"

Tate nodded his head; his smile was returning. "Roman is due to be sent to foster at Kenilworth in September, something that my wife is not particularly thrilled with, but at seven years of age, I have told her that it is time for my oldest son to begin his training," he scratched his chin again, wearily. "Cate is almost six and beautiful like her mother, while the Alexander and Dylan are nearly five and have the entire castle living in fear of them."

Edward laughed. "They are hooligans. I can hardly wait to recruit them into my service."

Tate pursed his lips in agreement, thinking of his aggressive blond-haired twins that were almost as big as their eldest brother. "Arabella is three and chatters like a magpie, and now baby Dane rounds out the bunch. My wife is going to hunt me down if I do not return home soon to help out with the brood."

Stephen grinned at the thought of the Lady Elizabetha de Tobins Cartingdon de Lara, known to everyone as Toby, tracking her husband down like a bounty hunter to return him to Forestburn Castle. Fortunately for Tate, she was very busy with six children and hadn't the time to break away, but knowing Toby as they did, Stephen would not be surprised if she found a way. She was, if nothing else, a very determined woman.

"Enough of Lady de Lara," Edward waved his hands irritably, refocused on Stephen as the man found the right piece of bread. "I want to know about Lady Pembury. Is it really true that she has been living at Jedburgh since eleven years of age?"

Stephen picked up a piece of cloth used to cover the bread and carefully wrapped his wife's meal in it. "True enough, it would seem," he replied. "It also seems that the nuns have educated her well. She can even read and write both Latin and French."

"Truly?" Edward looked surprised. "A woman with an education. Shocking."

Tate lifted an eyebrow at him. "Elizabetha can read and write."

Edward made a face as if the entire idea horrified him, thinking of his own young wife who was well versed in most courtly things excluding the ability to read. He liked it better that way. Beside him, Tate rose on his big legs and stretched his muscular body wearily.

"Come along," he said to Stephen. "After you have fed your wife, I would have you show me the progress on the collapsed walls. I am uncomfortable with our vulnerability at the moment. The Scots may be defeated but they are not dead. I should not like to be caught unaware."

The two knights left Edward in the hall as they made their way out into the sunshine. Being July, and near the river, gave the air a heated, sticky quality that made wearing armor increasingly uncomfortable. Tate rubbed at his neck where his mail grated against his sweaty skin. To the east, they could hear the buzz of the insects as they lay fat and lazy in the moist river grass.

"So I take it that you did not tell Edward everything I told you last night about Lady Joselyn and her reasons for being at Jedburgh," Stephen muttered as they crossed the mud.

Tate continued to scratch his neck. "I did not," he replied. "If you want him to know, then you will tell him. That kind of information will not come from me."

"Do you plan to interrogate her about the soldier who raped her?" Stephen asked. "You know your men better than I. Perhaps you will recognize someone based on her description."

Tate nodded. "I will ask her when the time is right," he said, eyeing Stephen as they neared the keep. "Did you tell her what you did for her mother?"

Stephen cleared his throat softly. "There was nothing I could do for the woman."

"That's not what I meant. Did you tell her that you personally built the coffin she lies in, which is why you did not return to her last night? That is the reason you did not return to consummate the marriage and for no other reason than that. Moreover, you prayed over the woman for hours. Did you not tell her that, either?"

"I did not."

"Why?"

He shrugged. "I did not do those things so she would admire or revere me. I did not do them for glory. I did them because they needed to be done and because it was right that I should do them."

Tate sighed faintly, slapping Stephen on a big shoulder. "I know," he said in a low voice. "But she might like to know that her new husband is capable of such compassion. You are an accomplished man with an amazing spirit, Stephen. She might like to know that as well."

They entered the cold, dark keep. "She will know as time allows," Stephen replied. "She knows that I brought her the clothing."

Tate snorted. "Good Lord, man, that's the least of your generosity," he fell in behind Stephen as they moved up the narrow stairs. "She should know the character of the man she has married."

They reached the landing. "She will," Stephen said, knocking softly on the chamber door. After several long seconds and no answer, he knocked again. Still no answer, he opened the door.

The room was empty.

છ

THE DAY WAS sultry and sticky. The moisture rising up from the river was as thick as a fog, cloaking everything around it. In spite of Stephen's previous order to stay to her chamber, Joselyn had found her way from the castle and down to the river, thinking of the family she had lost. She felt so very alone. She needed time to clear her head, far from castles and knights and visions of blood.

Reaching the damp, sticky grass that grew in tall clumps around the river's edge, she found a sandy bar near the water and plopped down on it, her mind a jumble of grief and fear. Clad in the lovely cranberry surcoat, she gathered her legs up against her chest, lowered her face onto her knees, and wept.

So much of her life had been out of her control. The day she went to Carlisle with her father was the worst day of her life; it had changed everything. Her father had been ashamed of what had happened but her mother, a sweet simpleton, had coddled and supported her. Even when they realized the soldier's seed had taken root, her mother continued to protect her fiercely. It was her father who had insisted on keeping her hidden as her stomach grew large and round, hidden from family and friends alike. Her father had told everyone that she was visiting relatives in Aberdeen when she was really locked up in her bower of Allanton Castle.

The shame that had been instilled in her during that time still clung to this day. Everyone but her mother was ashamed of her. Now the only person who had never harshly judged her was gone and she wept painfully for the woman whose mind left her years ago. Joselyn wept for that sweet woman of memories gone by, of brothers she had once loved, and for a life that she would never know again. All of the tragic events from the past few months had overwhelmed her and she felt like she was living another life, one she did not recognize or like. It was like hell.

Something shuffled off to her right and she looked up to see a doe and fawn, a few feet away, drinking from the river's edge. The doe seemed to be singed from a fire but otherwise seemed well. Joselyn's weeping faded as she watched the two of them drink. When the fawn looked in her direction, she slowly lifted her hand to it, clucking softly. The doe seemed startled but didn't bolt; the fawn was genuinely curious. Slowly, the little creature came up to her and sniffed her fingers. She was able to tickle its nose.

Enchanted, she forgot her tears for the moment as the little fawn nibbled on her fingers. She giggled at the baby with no teeth trying to nibble on her. The mother seemed more interested in eating the fat summer grass around the river while the fawn drew closer to Joselyn. It was enough of a distraction to cause her to forget her appalling grief. For the moment, she was thrilled with the fawn. It allowed her to scratch its neck as it came closer, interested in what she might have to eat. The little animal sniffed her surcoat and bit at the material, tugging at it and trying to eat it. Joselyn gently pulled the fabric out of the little mouth and tried to interest it in some soft, moist grass. It was a sweet, peaceful moment, one she desperately needed.

But it was not meant to last. Suddenly, the doe hit the water with a resounding splash. Startled, Joselyn looked up to see an arrow sticking out of its neck. With a scream, she grabbed the fawn and dove for the ground, terrified that more arrows would come flying out at them. She could hear men yelling and a great deal of rustling about as bodies jumped into the heavy grass. As she cautiously sat up with the fawn in her arms, she could see a dozen or so English soldiers bearing down on the doe they had just killed.

The fawn bleated and a few of the men looked over at her. Joselyn watched with mounting fear as two of them made their way over to her.

"What are you doing here, woman?" one man demanded.

She was both frightened and angered. "You killed that doe. She has a baby!"

The man lifted a callous eyebrow at her. "The baby will be tasty as well." He tried to take it from her but she screamed and finally kicked him. He slapped her soundly.

"Enough," he snarled, grabbing her by the arm and yanking her with him. "I shall eat both you and the fawn."

Joselyn was terrified. She fought and kicked as the fawn bleated in terror. They hadn't made it twenty feet when the soldier's commanding officer, having heard the commotion, came upon them.

"You, there," he shouted at the soldier as he strolled down from a berm overlooking the river. "What are you doing with that woman?"

The soldier smiled lasciviously. "I found her by the river," he announced. "After I eat the doe, I plan to have her for dessert."

The commanding officer looked closely at Joselyn and gradually, his features paled. Shoving the man in the chest to push him away, he grabbed Joselyn at the same time. The soldier lost his grip and stumbled back.

"What did you do that for?" he demanded.

The officer was focused on Joselyn. "My lady," he sounded strained. "Does your husband know you are out here?"

"Husband?" the soldier repeated loudly. "What husband?

The commanding officer looked at the man as if he were an idiot. "Pembury," he said, looking back at the lady. "May I escort you to your husband, Lady Pembury?"

Joselyn was clutching the fawn with a death grip. She eyed the soldier and his commanding officer. "Aye," she said hesitantly.

The commanding officer looked rather ill as he took her elbow and helped her up the slope. "Are you well, my lady?" he asked. "You are not injured in any way, are you?"

"Nay."

"Be careful of this hill. It is very slippery."

He couldn't seem to do enough to help her. The soldier who had slapped her was still standing where they had left him, his face deathly pale and knowing he was a dead man if he remained at Berwick. Pembury would undoubtedly take issue with the fact that he had slapped his wife. As the luscious little lady and his commanding officer crested the hill and headed for the castle, the soldier took off in the opposite direction.

The commanding officer kept a good grip on her as they made their way to the postern gate of Berwick. It was the same gate Joselyn had used when she had headed for the river. As soon as they entered the gate, they could see that the entire castle was in an uproar. Soldiers were mobilizing into blocks and sergeants were screaming at them. Knights on chargers were forming loose ranks and she could hear shouting from the walls. Frightened, she clutched the fawn more tightly against her.

"What is happening?" she asked the commander.

The man studied the activity. "I do not know, my lady," he replied. "It would seem that there is trouble somewhere."

She looked up at the man. He was a seasoned man, older, with bushy blond eyebrows. He seemed to have an even manner about him and she felt comfortable with him. In any case, she was thankful he had saved her from the lewd soldier.

"Are you a knight?"

He shook his head. "Nay, my lady," he replied. "I command a battalion of the Earl of Norfolk's soldiers."

"How did you know that my husband is Stephen of Pembury?"

"Because I was in the hall last night with my liege when your marriage was announced. I saw your marriage and I saw what happened afterwards. A true horror, my lady; you have my sympathies."

She was not sure what to say to that so she lowered her head and clutched the fawn to her breast. The commander, however, kept talking.

"De Lara was merciful in ending your mother's suffering," he went on. "Later in the night when my men had watch of the northern wall, I saw Pembury personally building what looked to be a crate. I was told it was your mother's coffin. 'Tis a good man that would take the trouble to build a coffin himself, but I am sure you already know that."

By the time he was finished, Joselyn was looking at him intently. "He built a coffin for my mother?"

The commander nodded, looking strangely at her and realizing that she probably did not know, in fact, what Pembury had done by the expression on her face. And with that knowledge, he shut his mouth lest he say something else she did not know about. But Joselyn was not finished with him.

"You said de Lara was merciful to end my mother's suffering," she said, coming to a halt and facing him. "What did he do?"

The commander sighed heavily and shook his head. "I… I am sorry, my lady. I did not know that you were unaware of…."

"What did he do?" she cut him off.

The commander prayed that Pembury would not take his head off. He knew there was no way to avoid her. Those pale blue eyes were boring into him and he braced himself for perhaps the stupidest thing he had ever done. He told her.

"Your mother was in flames, lady," he lowered his voice. "There was no hope. De Lara put a broadsword through her chest and ended her suffering immediately. It was the merciful thing do to."

Surprisingly, she didn't fall into fits. She simply stood there, staring at him with those piercing blue eyes as if absorbing every word individually. When she spoke, however, her lower lip trembled.

"What else did you see?" she asked in a whisper.

The commander's palms were beginning to sweat. He very much wanted to get away from her at the moment. "Not much else, my lady," he said in a quiet voice. "My liege and I left the hall shortly after that. The next I saw was your husband building the coffin. He and de Lara took it to the chapel before dawn."

The little fawn bleated again and Joselyn stroked the animal, comforting it. She seemed stunned by the entire conversation. Slowly, the commander resumed walking towards the keep, gently urging her along with him. She followed stiffly, lost in thought.

Just as they were approaching the keep, chargers roared around the corner from the stable block. Joselyn heard someone shouting her name and she paused, looking up to see a massive man astride a dapple gray charger heading towards her. She didn't even recognize her husband until he bailed off the charger and rushed towards her, flipping up his visor.

"Joselyn," Stephen's blue eyes were wide with surprise. "Where have you been? We were just leaving to search for you."

Joselyn was intimidated by all of the weapons and steel; as big a man as Stephen was, dressed to the hilt in weapons and armor made him larger than life. She clutched the fawn tightly, struggling to find the correct words, when the commander at her side spoke.

"I found her down by the river, my lord," he told Stephen. "She was at the water's edge with her little friend."

Stephen didn't even realize he had her by both arms. He didn't remember grabbing her. Gazing down, he saw the tiny fawn in her arms and his confusion grew.

"Where did you find this?" he asked her.

Joselyn found her tongue. "I was at the water's edge when a doe and her fawn came to drink. Some soldiers killed the mother and I took the baby. It is too young to be alone."

He sighed, more relieved than he cared to admit that she was well and whole. He had been terrified that she had run off in her grief. Or perhaps she had been abducted by bitter Englishmen; in truth, he hadn't known. To see her well and safe was a surprise and a tremendous relief. With a great sigh, he put his gloved hand on her chin, forcing her to look at him.

"Are you sure that you are alright?" he asked softly.

She nodded. "I am fine. Just… hungry."

The cornflower blue eyes twinkled. Then, they abruptly darkened. Removing one of his massive mail gauntlets, he touched her left cheek with big, warm fingers.

"What is this?" he demanded quietly.

She had completely forgotten about the slap and tried to lower her face, but he would not allow it. He held her chin firm.

"I… I do not know what you mean," she replied evasively.

"There is a perfect handprint on your face. Who struck you?"

He immediately looked at the sergeant, who visibly blanched. Joselyn could see where Stephen's thoughts were and she shook her head vigorously.

"Nay, not him," she insisted. "He has been extremely kind. It was not him."

"Not him?" Stephen turned back to her, his square jaw ticking. "Then you know exactly what I mean. Who did this? And no more lying."

"I was not lying," she insisted hotly. "I simply do not see the need for you to punish some man who was only reacting because I kicked him."

Stephen was very close to losing his temper, highly unusual for the collected knight. He took his wife by the arm and pulled her into the keep, away from the men cluttering the bailey. Once inside the cool, dark entry that smelled like must, he faced her.

"Where have you been and who struck you?" he demanded in a voice that invited no dispute. "If you do not give me the answer I seek, I will lock you in our chamber and keep you there day and night. Tell me now or my punishment will be swift."

She was angry, frightened, exhausted and hungry. She opened her mouth to argue with him but tears came instead. She was having a devil of a time fighting them off.

"I went to the river because I wanted to be alone to think," she told him, trying not to sob. "While I was there, a doe and her fawn came to drink. The mother was killed by men from the garrison and one of the soldier's saw me on the banks. He tried to take the fawn from me so I kicked him. He slapped me in response and that is when the sergeant found me. That is all there is to it. I was not attempting to run away if that is what you were thinking. I simply wanted to go someplace to collect my thoughts and I ended up at the river's edge."

Stephen stared at her a long moment before finally wiping a weary hand over his face. He had just spent the past half hour in total panic and was not quite over it yet. "Who was the soldier?"

"I do not know his name."

"The sergeant will. I will ask him."

He was heading out the door and she grabbed him. "Where are you going?"

"To get answers from the sergeant.

He pushed forward but she dug her heels in and held fast. "Wait a moment, please."

He came to a halt. "What is it?"

She still had a grip on him, blinking away the remnants of her tears. "I was told you built a coffin for my mother last night. Is this true?"

She could see his expression soften at the swift change of subject. He didn't seem entirely angered by it; if anything, he seemed to calm dramatically. "Who told you this?"

"It does not matter. Is it true?"

He paused for several moments before reluctantly nodding. "It is."

"Did you put her in it yourself?"

"I did."

"And de Lara. I was told he ended her suffering at the tip of a broadsword."

Again, Stephen nodded slowly. Joselyn stared at him, realizing that what she had been told was true and the mercy of the two English knights struck her deeply. Men who did not even know her mother, who was in fact, an enemy, had shown her such compassion as most men would not have. It was an unexpected element from the same men who had hanged her young brother, a paradox she could hardly comprehend.

Fighting off tears, Joselyn slowly moved towards Stephen. It seemed as if she wanted to say something more but the words would not come. She came closer and closer until she brushed against him, her sweet, warm body against his hard mail. Stephen watched her, electrified by her close proximity, wildly curious about her behavior, when she reached up and gently put a hand behind his mailed neck. Tears streamed down her cheeks as she pulled gently, bending him down until his face was almost level with her head. Stephen waited for a slap or a punch, unsure of her motives, when she suddenly leaned forward and kissed him tenderly on the cheek. The unforeseen gesture was enough to send his heart wildly racing.

"Thank you," she whispered, her lips against his rough flesh. "For the kindness you showed my mother, I thank you deeply."

With that, she let him go and he watched, his heart in his throat, as she silently ascended the stairs to the chamber above. He could hear the fawn bleating and eventually a door closed softly. Still, he continued to stand there, feeling her kiss upon his cheek as he had never felt anything in his entire life.

All thoughts of anger, retribution and punishment were sucked right out of his head with that one tender gesture. When he emerged from the keep, it was to disband the search party and thank Norfolk's sergeant for his escort.

"What is your name, sergeant?" he asked.

"Lane de Norville, my lord," the man replied. "I serve Norfolk."

Stephen nodded shortly. "Sergeant de Norville, you have my thanks for tending my wife. I will make sure Norfolk knows of your diligence."

The sergeant saluted smartly and was gone. Even as Stephen went about his business, thoughts of the blue eyed, dark haired lady filled his brain until he couldn't see or think of anything else.

CHAPTER FOUR

T HE SCOTS WEREN'T finished yet.
      Stephen had never doubted that and was therefore not surprised when he mobilized about two hundred men from the castle to attack a section of the city that was experiencing a weak resurgence of rebellion. He and de Lara rode to the northwest section of Berwick's walled city to quell a group of about one hundred Scots who were attempting to retake the city section by section. Although it was not a particularly brutal battle, it was long and frustrating and went on well into the night. By the time they were finished, they had killed about thirty Scots and lost eleven men.

Stephen assigned extra men to protect that area of the city at night, before returning to Berwick. It was well after sunset and the castle blazed with the ghostly glow from hundreds of torches. The great hall was lit up, light from inside the room streaming out through the lancet windows. Exhausted, Stephen and Tate dismounted their chargers, turned the beasts over to the grooms, and headed for the hall.

"I shall check that portion of the city again after dawn," Stephen told Tate. "From what those rebels told us, there are more of them than we know still in the city."

De Lara nodded wearily. "I would imagine it is nothing tremendously organized. There are die hard rebels in any conquered people."

"Aye, but it will only take one or two strong men to organize them and then we will have to worry about the Scots retaking the city," he shook his head. "At least we have brought the suspected leader back with us and I fully intend to bleed the man dry of any information he might have. But I am nonetheless thinking of asking the king for more reinforcements to flush the rebels from the city altogether."

"You already have almost one thousand men."

"Indeed I do, but we had over eight thousand just two days ago. Most of the English commanders have already left and headed for home."

"True enough," de Lara rubbed his eyes. "I can send for another five hundred from Carlisle. Henry of Lancaster can send another five hundred. Perhaps you should ask Norfolk to leave a detachment; he is leaving on the morrow, you know."

"I know. I have already asked him to leave me as many as he believes he can spare."

They had reached the hall. Stephen opened the door and was hit in the face by the warm, fragrant air inside. It smelled like rushes and roasted meat, and he felt his hunger immediately. Stepping inside, it was a bright and busy world.

The first sight that greeted him was Joselyn, heading towards him from the east side of the room. She was dressed in the cranberry wool, her luscious figure emphasized by the cut of the garment. Her dark hair was pulled away from her face and the pale blue eyes were brilliant. Stephen watched her with appreciation as she smiled and curtsied politely.

"Welcome home, my lord," she said, glancing to de Lara and bobbing another curtsy. "Lord de Lara."

Tate acknowledged the lovely woman, grinning at Stephen when the man turned to look at him as if to reaffirm the fact that he had married a truly beautiful lady. Removing his helm, de Lara scratched his head and, still grinning, moved off towards the dais where a huge table of food was spread out.

Stephen didn't notice that Tate had left; he was entirely focused on his wife. She looked absolutely radiant, a far cry from the cold and dirty creature he had met last night. Sleep, new clothing and an improving relationship with her new husband had worked wonders. He could hardly believe it was the same woman.

Joselyn gazed up at him, feeling the intensity of his stare as if he had reached out and grabbed her. Her cheeks flushed a delightful shade of pink.

"I hope the meal pleases you," she said, sweeping her arm in the direction of the table. "There were virtually no provisions left at the castle and we only had what your men brought in since yesterday."

Stephen knew that the city of Berwick, including the castle, had basically been starved out during the siege but he made no reference to it. He didn't want to dampen the mood and there was no point in reiterating what they both knew. So he took her gently by the elbow and escorted her to the heavily-laden table.

"The fare looks quite generous, my lady," he reassured her.

In fact, he was quite surprised to see all of the food. There were dishes everywhere, things he didn't even recognize. But he remembered that during that unpleasant encounter last night she had told him that the nuns of Jedburgh had taught her the art of cooking. He had no idea what she meant until this moment. He gestured at the table, somewhat in awe.

"Good Christ," he couldn't help the soft exclamation. "Did you do all of this?"

She nodded, somewhat modestly. "Your men brought flour, salt, bags of dried currants and apricots, wine, a few jars of honey, bags of nuts, and slabs of mutton and pork. I did what I could with it."

He looked at her, stunned. "Surely you had help."

She shrugged, reaching down for a wooden plate filled with something gooey and sweet-looking. "There were two women that aided me. Berwick has no cook, so the servants take turns." She lifted the plate. "These are sweet cakes with apricots, nuts and honey. Would you try one?"

He just stared at her. Then, he reached for one of the pastries, realized he had his mail gloves on and paused to rip them both off, tossing them to the bench. He then took one of the pastries and put the entire thing in his mouth. Joselyn watched with trepidation as he chewed a couple of times, stopped, and then resumed at a slower pace.

"Is… is it not to your liking?" she asked timidly.

Stephen chewed a few more times before swallowing. He licked his lips and looked at her. "Lady, that was by far the most marvelous thing I have ever eaten and if you let anyone else have one, I shall be sorely disappointed. I would have them all for myself."

She grinned brightly and he returned her smile, adding a bold wink with it. In truth, the little cake had been luscious. He gestured at the rest of the table. "What else do we have that is decadent and wonderful?"

Everything was. She had cooked the pork in honey, the mutton in rich gravy, and had a variety of completely fattening breads about the table. The only vegetable they had were carrots, which she had boiled in honey and cloves, the only manner of spice that they had. They were exquisite. Stephen sat down next to his wife and ate until he could hardly move. Even then, there was still more food on the table and he continued to try everything put before him. As the night wore on and de Lara joined them, Stephen was so gorged that he was sure he would become ill.

Tate was no better off. He, too, had eaten himself sick and he finally excused himself as the hour grew very late. As Stephen licked his fingers of the last of the apricot pastries, he watched de Lara wander away to sleep off his overindulgence. Joselyn sat next to her husband, her trencher licked clean of the pork she had stuffed herself with. When Stephen glanced at her, he caught her staring at him and he smiled.

"Lady, if I had not already married you, I would have married you this instant based on the skill of that meal alone," he said, watching her blush furiously. "Do you mean to tell me that the nuns at Jedburgh taught you to cook like this?"

She shrugged modestly. "My tasks were mostly kitchen-related. One of the nuns was from Paris and she was a wonderful cook. I learned a great deal from her."

"No doubt," he replied sincerely. "But tonight was a feast fit for a king and I did not, in fact, see Edward at all this eve."

"He was here earlier," she told him. "I heard him tell some of his men that he would be leaving on the morrow."

Stephen scratched his black head wearily. "I see," he muttered. "Then I must seek the man out before he leaves."

Joselyn watched him shove a last pastry into his mouth, hardly able to swallow it because he was so full. She laughed softly at him.

"This will not be the last opportunity for you to eat pastries, my lord," she told him. "I will make more, I promise."

He grinned at her, burped loudly, and then rose to his considerable height. "See that you do," he commanded, but it was lightly done. "My lady, your culinary skill is beyond compare. I have never in my life had such a fine meal and I thank you deeply. I cannot help wonder if this was meant for a special occasion."

She stood up next to him, so petite against his considerable height that she only came to his diaphragm area. Her smile faded as she groped for words.

"I suppose it is a special occasion," she ventured. "I wanted to show my gratitude for what you have done for me and for my mother." Her smile vanished as she looked up at him. "I said terrible things to you last night, my lord. I called you heartless and cold, and clearly that is not the case. What you did for my mother, and for me, goes beyond what I believed you capable of. I am very sorry that I said such horrid things. I hope that someday you will forgive the tongue of a scared, exhausted woman."

His blue eyes grew warm and a faint smile played on his lips. "There is no need to apologize," he murmured. "I know it was a difficult night and I further know that I did not make it easier for you. War dictates my behavior, lady. Last night, we were still at war. Today, we are not."

She smiled gratefully. "You are too forgiving," she said. "But I thank you just the same. I hope this meal was a worthy token of my gratitude for your kindness."

Stephen reached up and stroked her tender cheek; he couldn't help himself. "It is more than worthy," he said softly. "As are you."

Joselyn flushed brilliantly and he laughed softly. "You're still unused to sweet words, are you?" he flirted gently.

She shook her head vigorously and he continued to laugh, taking her by the hand and gently pulling her away from the table. Together, they made their way towards the great hall entry door.

"Well, you had better become used to it," he told her frankly. "I intend to speak a great many sweet words to you in the days and years to come. Would you like to hear more?"

She was beside herself with embarrassment, but it was of a good sort. She had never in her life known any manner of flirting or interaction with a man, so her experience with such things was nil. Her cheeks were hot and she put her free hand on her face, looking away from him.

"I do not think I can," she said, muffled by her hand. "If my face grows any warmer I will go up in flame."

He laughed loudly. "I have not seen a woman go up in flame yet, no matter how flattering the words," he gazed up into the summer night sky, brilliant with stars. "Let me think. I suppose I could tell you that you are the most beautiful woman I have ever seen, but I believe you already know that."

She shook her head, hand still against her face. "Nay, I do not."

He bent over, peering down at her and trying to look at her lowered face as they continued out into the darkened courtyard. The night outside was cool and clear in sharp contrast to the sultry day, bringing some relief from the cloying hall.

"You do not?" he repeated, straightening. "A pity. Then I shall tell you, quite honestly, that your beauty outshines that of any woman I have ever known."

She peered up at him now that he was not trying to look her in the eye. "How many women have you known?"

He looked down his nose at her. "Only two or three."

Now it was her turn to laugh at him. "I would not believe that in the least."

"You would not?"

"Nay," she said firmly. "Sir Stephen, I am not sure if you realize this, but you are an exceptionally handsome man. I cannot imagine that every woman you have ever come across has not realized that, which leads me to believe that you have known more than two or three woman in your life. You probably have armies of them that follow you around, begging for a lock of your hair or a glimpse of your smile. Am I wrong?"

He suddenly grabbed her and pulled her tight against him, looking around frantically as if he was deeply fearful.

"Dear God," he breathed. "Now that you know my secret, will you protect me from these ravenous females?"

She laughed. "Not a chance. You must fend them off for yourself." He looked down at her as if she had just grievously insulted him. She would have believed it, too, had she not seen the smile playing on his lips.

"You are my wife," he reminded her pointedly. "It is your duty to protect me."

She cocked an eyebrow at him. "Oh, very well, you coward," she pulled away from him, hands on her hips as she looked around the bailey. "Where are they? Well?"

He just stood there and grinned at her. "I seem to have escaped them for now, but have no doubt, they will be back," he reached out a hand to her. "Until then, shall we retire and hope for the best?"

She laughed softly, placing her small hand in his and allowing him to lead her into the keep. Inside, it was dark and cold as they made their way up the spiral stairs to the second floor. There were two rooms on this floor; a smaller servant's chamber and then a larger master's chamber. Joselyn opened the door to the larger chamber and Stephen was surprised as he stepped inside.

At some point while he had been away, she'd had the smaller bed removed and replaced by a larger bed with a rope frame. A mattress sat atop it and he pushed on it, feeling that it was firm with fresh straw. Several coverlets draped over the bed, clean from what he could see, and the room itself had been cleaned and swept free of all dirt and cobwebs. A warm fire burned in the hearth and he turned to look at her curiously.

"Is this the same room you slept in last night?" he asked a question with an obvious answer, simply because it had been so nicely transformed.

Joselyn nodded, smiling at his approval. "I had the smaller bed removed and replaced with a larger one that had been stored in another room," she told him. "The same women who helped me with the cooking also helped me repair and re-stuff this mattress, and the coverlets were from a chest we found on the fourth floor of the keep. There is a room up there stuffed with all manner of items, things that the last occupant must have left behind. I had some of it brought to this room."

Stephen looked around to the table she had brought down with two fat tapers burning on top of it. There was a small chest under the lancet window and a pile of thick, pale linen atop the chest. He went over and fingered the material.

"What is this?" he asked.

She motioned to the canopy frame around the bed. "Curtains for the bed," she replied. "They are old and need to be mended, but I believe they are serviceable."

He nodded, letting go of the material and inspecting the corner near the edge of the bed. There was a little pallet on the floor, surrounded by rushes. He pointed at it. "What is that?"

She wandered over to see what he was pointing at. "That is for the fawn," she said. "He was sleeping there this afternoon."

"Where is it now?"

"In the kitchen with the servants. It is very warm in the kitchen and he seemed to like it better in there."

"So am I to understand that you now have a pet?"

"If you do not mind."

He gave her a smirk as if it didn't matter whether or not he minded.

She was going to keep it anyway and he would let her.

"I do not," he replied, facing his wife with his hands on his hips. "You have done an exceptional job with both the meal and this room. I am impressed with your accomplishments and your foresight to duty."

She smiled happily. "Thank you, my lord."

"What did I tell you about addressing me in private?"

"I meant, thank you, husband."

He winked at her. "Good," he said with a heavy sigh as he made his way back to the door. "I have duties to attend to before I retire for the night, but I will be back. You will stay here and not leave this room. Is that understood?"

She nodded. "I will not leave."

He moved to the door and she scooted past him, opening it for him. He smiled down at her, the cornflower blue eyes glittering with warmth.

"Good eve, husband," she said softly.

His gaze was steady. "I shall return," he replied. Then a hand came up, gently grasping her face. "Perhaps you will still be awake when I do."

She knew it was a request no matter how he phrased it. Her belly quivered with excitement, the heat of his touch sending waves of delight rippling through her body. It suddenly didn't matter anymore that this man was an enemy, a stranger she had been forced to marry. He was proving himself to be an exceptional man regardless of his loyalties. She was coming to like him just the slightest. She smiled, her lips quivering because her body was quivering from the thrill of having him so near.

"I will be awake all night," she told him, "watching for the hordes of women who follow you around like a wolf pack. I told you I would fend them off, did I not?"

He laughed softly and his other hand came up, cupping her lovely face between his two enormous palms. His smile faded as he gazed intently into her pale blue eyes.

"You did indeed," he murmured, somehow moving closer to her as he spoke. "I will hold you to that."

Not only was he moving closer to her, but she was moving closer to him as well. Joselyn didn't realize that she was fairly collapsing against the man, his enormous height and bulk filling every corner of her mind. She could see his full lips looming over her and feel the heat from his hands as if he meant to scorch every inch of her. She couldn't even think of a witty answer as he loomed closer still, his hot breath on her face.

Before she realized it, his lips were on her soft mouth, gently kissing her with the very first real kiss she had ever experienced. She had never been kissed on the mouth, not even by her father or mother, and she froze for a moment, evaluating the feel of his powerful lips upon hers. But her lack of reaction lasted only a fraction of a second. Without thinking, her natural instincts took hold and she returned his kiss, tasting his lips and suckling him gently as he carefully probed her soft mouth. It was apparently all of the encouragement that Stephen needed, because before Joselyn realized it, he had wrapped his enormous arms around her slender body and had backed her up against the wall.

She heard the door slam, unaware that Stephen had kicked it shut the moment his arms went around her. Her arms found their way around his neck and he lifted her up off the ground, bracing her against the wall as his tongue licked at her lips, demanding entry. Her mouth opened slightly and it was all the inducement he needed to invade her mouth, tasting her sweetness and gorging himself. Through it all, Joselyn held him tightly around the neck and mimicked his actions, passionate instincts she had never known taking hold. The more demanding he was with her, the more demanding she was in return.

While one massive arm held her against the wall, one hand moved freely down her back and across her torso, acquainting himself with the feel of her. She was petite yet curvy, healthy in the right places, and it aroused him enormously. He remembered her naked body from the night before when she had stripped in front of him and he was not at all pressured to admit that his lust had the better of him. He had told Edward and Tate that he would wait until the time was right to consummate his marriage. He knew that the time was now. In any case, he was going to take the opportunity.

But he was in battle armor, restricting him and no doubt biting into her although she'd not uttered a sound about it. Gently lowering her to the ground, he continued to kiss her as he used one hand to unlatch his armor. Joselyn, distracted from his probing mouth by the fact that he was no longer holding her close, pulled her swollen lips away from him to note what he was doing.

"Would you like me to help you with that?" she asked breathlessly.

Stephen could only nod. Quickly, silently, he unfastened the protection on his forearms, his breastplate, handing them over to Joselyn, who put them silently and efficiently into a neat pile against the wall. When it came to his mail, he held out his arms and she pulled it free. In little time, he was down to his tunic, heavy breeches and boots. He sat down on the bed and pulled his boots off, removed his tunic, and then looked up at his wife.

She was standing next to him, staring at his bare chest with the expression of someone who had never before seen such a thing. There was awe and fascination in her features. Stephen was powerfully built, with thick shoulders, neck and arms, a broad chest and slender waist. His chest was covered with a fine matting of dark hair and he sat patiently while she visually inspected him. He didn't want to rush her, not now when the experience was thus far such a gentle and passionate thing. As he sat and watched her, she moved toward him and reached out a hand, touching the hair on his chest.

Stephen closed his eyes at her delicate touch. Never in his life had he known anything so tender or erotic. Joselyn put two hands on him, running her fingers across his skin, experiencing the texture of his body for the very first time. Then her hands moved to his shoulders, inspecting the sheer size of them, before moving to his arms. They were toned and smooth. Her hands moved back to his chest and he reached out, pulling her against him.

Neither one of them said a word. They simply gazed at one another. Joselyn's hands came up from his chest, her fingers moving across his chin before lingering on his smooth lips. She was openly curious about him and he welcomed it. It was far better than the naked fear she had shown the night before. But Stephen couldn't stand it any longer and he leaned forward, capturing her lips with his own.

In a flash, he flipped her from his lap and onto her back, smothering her with his enormous body. His lips gently ravaged her as his hands went to work removing her from the cranberry colored surcoat. Joselyn was so focused on his lips that she was not paying much attention to what his hands were doing until he pulled off the surcoat. The shift followed shortly. When she was stripped down to her undergarments and hose, she began to grow apprehensive.

Stephen could feel her tense beneath him and he kissed her tenderly, pulling the hose off each leg gently while murmuring against her mouth.

"No worries, sweetheart," he whispered. "This is nothing to fear."

Joselyn's heart was pounding with both passion and fear. She gazed at the man's face even as he kissed her cheeks, her nose, and his touch as gentle as a butterfly's.

"I am not afraid," she breathed.

It was a lie and he knew it; he could feel her body tightening. So he stopped kissing her and looked her in the eye, his blue eyes soft with desire.

"You are very brave," he murmured. "But perhaps you did not consider that I might be afraid, too?"

Her brow furrowed as a smile played on her lips. "I do not believe that."

"You don't?" he lifted her hands, kissing the palms with great reverence. "I have never had a wife before. What if I do something wrong? You will be sorry that you married me."

Her grin broke through. "You are not doing anything wrong yet."

He nodded as if to concede the point, kissing her wrists and fore-arms. "I am not?" he kissed her left elbow and put her arms down, moving to her torso. He kissed her ribcage, just under her left breast. "What about that? Is that still good?"

She lifted her head slightly to watch him as her heart began to pound harder. "Aye."

He smiled seductively, lowering his head to kiss her across her ribcage, ending up just below her right breast.

"Is that still alright?"

"Aye," she could barely speak.

He lifted himself up slightly, kissing the skin immediately below her right breast. He was so close, in fact, that his nose brushed against her breast, causing the nipple to harden into a taut little pellet. His kisses moved nearly to her armpit before coming up again. This time, he was kissing the underswell of her breast, working his way up. When his lips closed over a peaked nipple, he suckled strongly.

Joselyn bit off a moan as his hot mouth worked her distended nip-ple. A big hand came up, gently fondling the breast as he continued to suck. Her arms, having lain inactive at her side, suddenly came up and her fingers intertwined in his black hair, pulling at the inky strands. He began to work both breasts, suckling her nipples with increasing strength until he was positively merciless with his attentions. Beneath him, Joselyn writhed and groaned with awakening desire. Then suddenly, he pulled himself up from her breasts and enclosed each one in a massive hand. His mouth found hers once more and he ravaged her with his lips as his hands massaged her warm breasts, damp with his saliva.

"Was that still good?" he breathed against her mouth.

She nodded incoherently and Stephen's hands left her breasts, re-moving her undergarments swiftly. His mouth blazed a heated trail down her neck, back to both breasts momentarily, before working its way down to the dark fluff of curls between her legs. His enormous hands moved to grasp her tender white buttocks, holding her pelvis to his mouth as he devoured the flesh of her lower belly. But when a hand touched the tender junction between her legs, she stiffened like a corpse.

His head snapped up, gazing into her fear-filled face. He stroked her cheek, her hair, gently.

"If I have not done anything wrong so far, will you still trust me?" he whispered.

She nodded although he could see tears in her eyes. His eyes grew intense.

"I know that the last time a man was this close to you, unspeakably horrible things happened," he murmured. "You did not deserve that and I will do all in my power to show you that the intimacy between a man and a woman is anything but horrific. It can be the strongest, most binding experience you will ever have. It will be pleasurable and it will be wonderful. Do you believe me?"

She nodded her head, breaking down into soft sobs. "Aye," she squeaked. "But… but you are not disgusted with me?"

His brow furrowed. "Good God, why would you ask that?"

"Because another man has touched me before you."

"It was not your fault," he said. "That soldier may have taken your innocence, but that is a very small part of what we are about to do. I am showing you what joy there is in intimacy between a man and a woman. No one on earth has ever shown you that, have they?"

"Nay."

"Then that, my dear lady, you have indeed saved for me, whether or not you knew it.

She began to weep more deeply and he lifted himself up, gathering her into his arms and pulling her close. His lips were on her forehead as he spoke.

"Hush, sweetheart," he murmured. "There is nothing to fear. I know you are terrified, but I promise you, there is nothing to fear. Please believe me."

She nodded and he held her face between his two enormous hands, kissing her forehead, her damp eyes, soothing her gently with his tender touch. When he moved back to the dark curls between her legs, he made sure to do it calmly and sweetly so she would not be overly startled. He began by gently caressing her inner thighs.

"What we are about to do is as old as man himself," he told her, kissing her breasts as he stroked her skin. "It is something every woman goes through, unless she is ugly and destined to be an old maid."

That brought giggles. But those giggles were quickly quelled as he began kissing the skin of her inner thigh. Joselyn realized quickly that she liked it very much. His mouth moved to the dark hair between her legs and he gently opened her legs wider, kissing the spongy curls and gently running his fingers over the thick lips. He felt her tense again and he lowered his head, gently suckling on the outer flesh of her Venus Mound.

From fear to utter delight and back again, Joselyn's head was spinning with a variety of sensations. Stephen's touch had her distracted and his bass voice had her lulled into contentment.

"A woman's center is quite lovely," he murmured. "'Tis pink and pretty, like a flower unfurling."

As he spoke, he gained a good look at her most private area. His fingers pulled her exterior lips apart and he was greeted with a scar that ran from her birth canal all the way to her anus. It was a thick, nasty scar and he could see immediately what she had been talking about; *the birth tore me asunder.* From the look of the scar he was surprised she hadn't bled to death. His stomach lurched at the thought of pain and anguish she undoubtedly went through. To think of such a lovely, sweet creature being subjected to such horror filled his chest with rage but he fought it. He calmed himself by knowing he would protect her from all things from now on. And more than ever, he was determined to seek justice for the crime against her.

He dipped his head and kissed the scar, nearly bringing her off the bed. But his hands stilled her, his gentle words soothed her, and his kisses resumed on the interior of her thigh. His fingers, so big yet so gently, stroked her intimately and he could feel her wetness the more he stroked. He moved to kiss her belly and focused on her delicious breasts again as he slipped a finger into her tight, scarred passage.

Joselyn did nothing more than moan as he thrust into her with his finger, more distracted by his mouth on her nipples. When Stephen finally lifted himself and placed his enormous manhood at her threshold, she hardly noticed. In fact, he thrust so gently into her that she didn't even realize he was inside her until he was about halfway seated.

Then she tensed again. But Stephen would have no part of it. He was so highly aroused that he would let nothing interfere with this moment and he gathered her close, kissing her deeply as he fully seated himself with firm, smooth pressure. Joselyn gasped and squirmed as he impaled her on his manroot, but to her credit she did not weep. She wrapped her arms around his neck and held fast, struggling to adjust her body to this invasive presence that was nothing as she had remembered from eleven years ago. Stephen's sensual invasion was warm, seductive, tender and passionate. He had done everything possible to ease her. And, not surprisingly, all she felt was ease.

And then he began to move in her, slowly at first, using his powerful buttocks to thrust gently into her small body. But his pace grew faster, his thrust more powerful, and Joselyn felt a wildly pleasurable jolt every time he would thrust his full length into her. It was as if his manhood was touching a special area deep within her body, something that, within just a few minutes of Stephen's measured thrusts, suddenly erupted in a burst of stars that rippled throughout her body.

A soft yelp escaped her lips and her body stiffened and pleasurable tremors raced through her. Stephen, feeling her release milking at his manroot, answered by spilling himself deep into her body. Even when they were both sated as their glorious tremors faded, he still continued to move within her, not wanting the experience to end. As he slowed his thrusts and caressed her silken skin, taking equal pleasure in the tactile as well as the emotional, words like Duty and Task popped into his mind. Into the dimness, he smiled; never in his life had he been given a duty that was less of a task and more of a pleasure. *She* was a pleasure.

They slept.

CHAPTER FIVE

D E LARA WAS up before dawn, walking the battlements of Berwick. The sun was threatening to rise and the eastern sky was turning shades of lavender and pink. Just as he passed through the gatehouse arch along the castle walls, he ran straight into Stephen. He looked startled to see the man.

"I did not know you were awake," Tate said. "I thought you would still be with your wife."

Stephen was clad in pieces of armor and mail, not his usual full battle regalia. He was shaved and even combed, looking extremely relaxed. Tate had a difficult time keeping the smile of his face as he watched Stephen's very contented expression.

"I have been up for a couple of hours," he replied. "I had to see Edward before he left. Moreover, I would be a poor garrison commander not to have my finger on the pulse of the outpost. I have been making my rounds."

"I did not mean to intimate that you were a poor commander and well you know it," Tate lifted an eyebrow. "I simply meant that you are occupied with a new wife who quite obviously has your attention. There is no shame in that."

Stephen cast him a long look, a knowing smile playing on his lips. "I would not be ashamed of her in any case," he replied, his blue eyes moving to the eastern horizon. "In fact, I was probably a fool to have resisted this marriage at the first. It is a great honor."

"Did you tell Edward that?"

"I did," he turned to look at Tate again. "And I asked for another five hundred men to reinforce the city."

Tate leaned against the parapet, his smoke-colored eyes watching the sunrise. "Did he tell you that I have already sent word to Henry of Lancaster for a contingent? I asked him last night when I could not find you anywhere. Assuming you were indisposed, I went ahead and made your request."

"He told me," Stephen replied. "It seems as if I will have a thousand men here in the next month to reinforce my ranks. Edward is leaving today, by the way. Are you leaving as well?"

Tate nodded. "I see no reason to stay since you have things well in hand," he replied. "Moreover, I am anxious to return home to see my wife and children."

"Give Toby my best."

Tate straightened up and slapped Stephen on a broad shoulder. "I will."

He began moving toward the tower stairs but Stephen called to him. "Would you please do me a favor before you leave?"

"Of course."

Stephen crossed his massive arms and moved toward him pensively. "Will you ask Lady Pembury about the man who raped her before you go? If this man is still in your ranks, I would have him sent to me immediately."

Tate nodded slowly. "I would be pleased if you would allow me to punish the man if, in fact, he is still in my ranks."

Stephen looked at him, the cornflower blue eyes hard. "I appreciate the offer, but I must dispense punishment. It is my right and my privilege."

Tate understood. He could also see that the husbandly right of punishment went beyond mere honor; there was a glimmer in Stephen's eyes that spoke of something deeper. If Tate didn't know better, he would suspect that Stephen was feeling something for his lovely new wife. It did not displease him.

"As you say," he replied. "Shall I seek her out now?"

Stephen shook his head. "She is not awake yet. Perhaps when she breaks her fast."

Tate was nearly at the tower stairs; the bailey was to his right, most of the expanse visible between the keep and the great hall. Movement down below caught his eye and he turned to see a small figure in a cranberry colored surcoat moving through the early dawn towards the great hall. Lady Pembury seemed to be in a hurry. Tate dipped his head in the direction of the bailey.

"Your wife is an early riser," he said, watching Stephen make his way over to the parapet in time to see Joselyn disappear into the rectangular great hall. "She must have a great deal to do today if she is up so early."

Stephen was heading for the stairs before Tate could get to them. They took the narrow spiral stairs quickly and emerged into the ward. Tate suppressed a smile at Stephen's apparent eagerness to get to his wife; the man was practically running.

"There is one more thing, something I was thinking on this morning," Stephen said as they crossed the dusty bailey. "Do you know of Ettrick Castle?"

"I do. It is held by the Earl of Buccleuch, Lord Alexander."

"Do you know the man personally?"

"I have met him twice but I would not say that we know one another. He is allied with John Balliol. Why?"

Stephen paused when they reached the door leading to the great hall. He scratched his head awkwardly, as if still thinking through what he was attempting to say.

"I did not tell you everything about my wife's rape at the hands of the English soldier," he said in a low voice. "The rape resulted in a child. That was why her father sent her to Jedburgh; to be rid of both her and the baby. When the baby came of age, he was sent to Ettrick Castle to foster."

Tate gazed steadily at him but not without some sympathy. He finally shook his head sadly. "Good Christ," he muttered. "She has known much sorrow, has she not?"

Stephen nodded faintly. "From what Joselyn tells me, the lad was never told that she was his mother. He was led to believe that he was an orphan. She intends to tell the boy someday about his parentage, minus the part about his father, but I thought perhaps that now that we are married, I would adopt the boy and bring him to live with us."

Tate considered that option. "A truly generous gesture, Stephen," he murmured. "Does your wife know about it?"

"I have not mentioned it."

"How do you think she will feel? That boy is the result of a brutal act. Perhaps she does not wish to be reminded of it on a daily basis."

"She is his mother. I believe that is a stronger instinct than the horror of her attack."

"Will you ask her at least?"

Stephen nodded. "I will," he muttered. "If she agrees, I would like for you to contact the Earl on my behalf and request that the boy be sent to Berwick."

Tate knew Stephen to be a deeply compassionate man but even he was surprised at the man's selflessness. It took a very good man to do what Stephen was suggesting, accepting his wife's child that was the result of a horrible crime years ago. Wanting to adopt the boy was a supreme gesture of benevolence. He clapped the man gently on the shoulder.

"Are you sure about this?" he asked.

"Very sure."

Tate shrugged his big shoulders. "Then if your wife agrees, I will ride to Ettrick myself and retrieve him."

Stephen seemed to be greatly relieved. With a weak smile, he led Tate into the great hall.

It smelled like smoke and old rushes. Joselyn was standing on the eastern end of the expansive room, speaking with an older serving woman who wore a severe wimple on her head. Her hair was pulled into a delightful braid, draping over one shoulder as curling tendrils of dark hair escaped it. Stephen and Tate approached her from behind and the serving woman, seeing the knights coming, fled.

"Lady Pembury," Stephen addressed his wife as she turned to greet him. "You are looking well this morning."

She smiled so radiantly at him that Tate felt as if he was intruding on a very private moment.

"Good morn to you, Husband," she said sweetly, looking to Tate and nodding her head. "And to you, Lord de Lara. It is a fine day today."

They were both so happy and cheerful that Tate fought off a grin. It was like watching two giddy children. "Indeed, my lady," he said, clearing his throat softly when a brief pause followed. "Lady Pembury, I was wondering if I might have a word with you."

"Of course," she said pleasantly and Stephen took her by the hand, directing her to sit on the bench near the dais. He continued to hold her hand as she sat and Tate deposited himself next to her.

"How may I serve you, my lord?" she asked Tate expectantly.

Tate looked her in the face as he spoke, knowing why Stephen was so smitten with the pale-eyed, dark-haired lady. She was truly exquisite. He could also see why Stephen wanted justice for the woman; what happened to her was truly an offense. As Tate looked at her, he realized that he wanted justice for her, too.

"Perhaps there is something I can do for you," he replied, eyeing Stephen as he carefully laid forth his words. "Your husband has confided in me of the brutal crime committed against you years ago by a man who presumably served the Earl of Carlisle. Both your husband and I are determined to seek justice for you and I would like to know what you remember of this man so that I may find him if he is still within my ranks."

Her pleasant expression faded and she looked up at Stephen when he gently squeezed her hand. It was difficult for her to speak unemotionally on the subject and she struggled not to tear up as she thought on his question. Stephen had told her he would speak with Lord de Lara about finding the man. She simply had difficulty believing that, with all of the other priorities going on at Berwick, they considered her issue important.

Her family had fought against these men for months, years, and she had lost three brothers and countless other relatives as a result. But she was having difficulty believing the hated English and these men before her were one and the same. She could not grasp the concept easily, made more difficult by Stephen's behavior over the past day. The man had gone from a stone-cold knight to a warm, compassionate husband and that, more than anything, had her believing that she was living a dream. Certainly things like this could not be real.

But real it was. She cleared her throat softly, struggling to answer de Lara's question. "It was a long time ago, my lord," she said faintly, hardly able to meet the man's eye for the subject at hand. "I... I have tried hard not to think of it for many years."

Tate nodded sympathetically. "I realize that, my lady. But if you can remember anything, anything at all, it might help us locate this man and bring him to justice."

Her brow furrowed and she clutched Stephen's hand tightly, as if the man had been her rock all her life. She realized that she felt tremendous comfort in his massive presence.

"He was a big man," she delved deep into the dark shadows of her mind. "I had never seen him before he grabbed me; not walking the streets nor in any of the stalls that my father and I were in. I do remember seeing several soldiers bearing the colors of Carlisle, which were crimson and yellow at that time. Perhaps he was in the group that I saw. I simply do not know."

"Go on."

She swallowed hard and felt Stephen give her another encouraging squeeze. She closed her eyes as if to see deeper into her mind's eye.

"He wore a tunic and mail and a helm with rivets across the brow," she said, her voice beginning to strain. "He smelled of ale. He had a red face and his teeth were green. I remember that because I had never seen anyone with such green teeth. At some point, his helm came off and I saw that he had auburn hair, wavy."

She was shaking by the time she finished. Stephen sat down on the bench behind her and put his arms around her, nearly swallowing her up with his muscular appendages. Joselyn was fortified by his presence, feeling safe and sheltered. It gave her strength.

"Did he say anything that might help us identify him?" Stephen asked her gently. "A name, a reference? Anything at all?"

She thought a moment. "Nay," she said slowly. Then, her eyes suddenly widened and she looked at Tate. "But he did have a scar on his forehead, an odd scar that was shaped like a half-moon. I remember seeing it when the helm came off, up at nearly the top of his forehead."

She was gesturing with her hand at the top of her forehead near the hair line. Tate's expression never changed as he thanked her for information that was undoubtedly difficult for her to speak of and excused himself. But at some point before he turned away, Stephen caught an odd flicker in his expression and he kissed his wife on the forehead and left her at the table to follow de Lara. Once outside in the bailey, he caught up to Tate.

"What is it?" he watched Tate come to a halt and turn to him. "What is the matter?"

Tate's expression was taut. "I had no idea who she was talking about until she mentioned the scar," he muttered. Then he put his hand on Stephen's big arm. "Get hold of yourself, man. I believe the soldier we are looking for came with me from Carlisle Castle."

Stephen's expression widened. "He is here?"

Tate's grip on Stephen tightened. "I am not positive, but I think so. I have a senior sergeant who has a scar just as she described, only his hair is gray. He was posted in the encampment to the west but I do not know where he is now. I do not assign individual soldiers their posts. I will ride out and see what I can discover."

Stephen was so tense that he was shaking. "Is it possible that he is here in the castle?"

Tate was reluctant to nod but he had no choice. "It is," he muttered. "My men are rotating their positions. It is entirely possible he has ended up in the castle in that rotation."

Stephen's heart was thumping against his ribs at the thought of the man who had raped Joselyn possibly being so near. When they had discussed the possibility of finding the man, having him right under their nose had not been a possibility.

"Find out where this man is and make all haste," he told Tate. "And if you discover that it is indeed the man we seek, then...."

"Then you and I shall decide what's to be done with him," Tate replied grimly. "Until then, however, I would not say anything to your wife. If she knows the man is here, it could do more harm than good. It may completely unnerve her and she has had more than enough upset over the past two days."

Stephen nodded, taking a deep breath to calm himself. "Of course," he said. "Not a word."

With a sharp nod, Tate headed to the stables to collect his charger. Stephen watched the man go, taking another breath for calm before heading back into the hall. He didn't want Joselyn to suspect anything out of the ordinary.

❧

THE MORNING MEAL was another heavenly affair from the genius of Joselyn's cooking talents. Stephen had eaten far too many of the little pastries she had made with the remaining apricots and nuts, complaining that she was going to fatten him up in swift time if she kept feeding him such marvelous food. Joselyn pointed out that he did not have to eat as much as he did, which prompted him to eat whatever remained on the plate simply to spite her. She had laughed and he had groaned.

The king's party had pulled out at mid-morning, heading to Bamburgh Castle where Edward's Queen was in residence, and Stephen had seen the man off. Edward was anxious to return to London, leaving five hundred royal troops at Berwick while taking the remaining thousand with him. Norfolk also pulled out, leaving three hundred men to reinforce Berwick. The remaining supporting forces were also mobilizing to leave and for the first time since being appointed Guardian Protector of Berwick, Stephen was fully in command. No more king or other nobles to interfere with his authority. Now, it was simply him and about twelve hundred men-at-arms and knights.

After the troops pulled out, it gave Stephen time to sit down and prioritize his tasks. He still had a prisoner from the previous night and he had not yet attended the man. It was to be his first duty as Guardian Protector so just after the nooning hour, he left the small solar on the ground floor of the keep and went in search of his wife. He found that he very much wanted to keep abreast of her location and activities, if for no other reason than to make sure she was safe. Odd how this wife he never wanted had very easily slipped into his way of thinking, as if she had always been there. It was an exhilarating and fulfilling feeling, something he had never before known.

He hunted through the great hall and out into the kitchen yard beyond. When he stuck his head into the kitchen as just a passing thought, he saw her seated on the floor. There were two other women in the kitchen, both busy with their tasks, but Joselyn was seated on the floor doing something he could not see. Curious, Stephen ducked through the doorway and into the kitchen.

She was feeding the fawn with a nipple made from a pig's bladder. As Stephen stood and watched, Joselyn giggled softly, stroking the little animal as it suckled furiously. More milk was spilling out of the bladder than actually getting into the hungry little mouth, but the fawn didn't seem to mind. He was so eager to eat that he was stepping all over Joselyn's lap as she tried to feed it. Stephen couldn't help but smile.

"So," he crossed his enormous arms. "I see you are trying to fatten him up, too."

The serving women started at the sight of the enormously tall knight but Joselyn merely smiled up at her husband.

"He keeps biting the bladder with his sharp little teeth," she told him. "There are little holes everywhere that are leaking milk."

Stephen laughed softly and made has way over to her as she continued to sit on the floor. He lowered his enormous bulk beside her, reaching out to pet the little fawn.

"He seems healthy enough," he said. "You make a fine mother deer."

She simply grinned and gazed up at him with sort of a dreamy expression. Stephen gazed back at her with an expression much like hers. It was sweet and adoring.

"I simply came to see what you were doing," he said. "I am preparing to make my rounds of the city and wanted to see you before I went."

Her smile faded. "Is there more trouble?"

He shook his head. "None that I am aware of, but I will have to make my presence constant during these days so that the rebels still within the city will know I can and will quickly quell whatever activities they may be considering. It is also important that they know I married Seton's daughter. They will think twice before resisting if they know I married a Scot."

Her smile faded and she looked back to the little fawn. "Then I will not keep you from your duties."

He could hear her change in tone and looked at her, wondering why she suddenly seemed so glum. He didn't know her well enough to be able to figure her moods out yet.

"What will you do while I am gone?" he asked.

She shrugged, tipping the bladder so the fawn could suckle the remaining milk. "Plan the evening's meal, I suppose. Do you know when you will return?"

He shook his head. "I do not. I would plan to serve it late, however."

She nodded, still not looking at him and he was puzzled by her manner. He realized that he did not like it at all. He wanted to see her smile, see the warmth in the pale blue eyes when she looked at him. He glanced up, noting that the serving women, although focused on their tasks, were undoubtedly close enough to hear their conversation. He also realized they were the same women he had given his wife's new surcoats to yesterday so they could clean away the smoke smell. He stood up and fixed on the woman closest to him, the one with the tight wimple.

"Were you able to satisfactorily clean my wife's clothes yesterday?" he asked.

The woman looked terrified that he was addressing her but managed to keep her wits. "I believe so, m'lord," she replied. "We soaked everything in vinegar. Even now, the clothes are drying near the kiln. They should be ready to iron soon."

"Very well," he said as he rubbed his eyes. He was tall enough that he was against the ceiling and the smoke from the cooking fire hovered against the roof, irritating his eyes. "How many garments are there?"

"Eight surcoats, three shifts and three pairs of undergarments, m'lord," the woman told him. "Jo-Jo will have a lovely wardrobe."

He looked down at his wife's dark head. "Jo-Jo, is it?" he muttered with a smirk.

She lifted her head to look at him. Although she smiled weakly, the pale blue eyes were still guarded. "These women served my parents," she told him. "They have known me since I was very small."

He smiled faintly and held out a hand to her. "Leave the fawn," he said softly. "Come walk with me."

Obediently, she handed the bladder to the other serving woman, a very old woman with a fat rump. Placing her hand in Stephen's open palm, she allowed him to pull her to her feet. Brushing off the cranberry wool, she held his hand as he took her out into the afternoon sunshine.

It was a bright day, sultry again, as they walked in silence through the kitchen yard. Dogs barked and scattered as Stephen took her into the main ward; around them, the day looked normal, just like any other day at any other peaceful castle. It was amazing how two days could change the feel of a place, from a blockaded, starving castle to one that was knowing prosperity at the hands of the English. Joselyn held Stephen's arm as they walked through the dust and flies.

"Although this was a forced marriage for us both, I would hope that at some point we will both find it pleasant," he finally spoke. "And for it to be pleasant, we must insist on total truth between us. Do you disagree?"

She paused and looked up at him. Her expression was one of disappointment. "Nay."

She abruptly averted her gaze and resuming their walk. Stephen pulled her to a stop and forced her to face him.

"Then tell me why you seem sad," he commanded quietly. "What is troubling you?"

She sighed heavily, shaking her head and keeping her eyes lowered. "It is nothing, my lord, truly…."

"My lord, is it?" he shook her gently. "I told you not to call me that. I am your husband. My name is Stephen. I would hear that from your lips always. Now, what is wrong?"

She tried to pull away, tried not to look at him, but he would have none of it. He suddenly pulled her tightly against him, trapping her arms and towering over her. When she finally looked up, it was into blazing blue eyes.

"Tell me," he whispered.

She sighed again, more slowly this time, thinking of how to phrase her thoughts. She knew of no other way than to simply come out with it. If he wanted to know, she would tell him. She could only pray he didn't think her foolish.

"You married me to form an alliance with the rebellion," she stated quietly.

He nodded. "Aye."

She cocked her head slightly. "Is that truly all you wish from this marriage? An alliance and a pleasant existence?"

His brow furrowed slightly as he studied her magnificent face. "It is as good a start as any. Why does this concern you?"

She lowered her eyes again, thinking that she was coming to sound idiotic. "It does not," she took a deep breath and tried to put her feelings into words. "I suppose it is as good as we can hope for considering neither of us wanted to marry and until two days ago, we were bitter enemies. But since yesterday, you have been so overwhelmingly kind to me that I thought… well, at least I had hoped that perhaps there would be more to our marriage than simple pleasantries. I know it seems silly, but I have heard of marriages where people are actually quite fond of one another and I was hoping…."

She trailed off, unable to continue, thinking that perhaps she sounded like a complete fool. But Stephen's blue eyes glimmered at her, a faint smile playing on his lips.

"You were hoping ours would be one of those?" he finished quietly for her.

She nodded, once. "I know it is silly," she said quickly. "I do not mean to place more expectation on this marriage than what goes beyond normal boundaries, so I apologize if I sound like a silly dreamer. I suppose I am. I never thought I would be married much less marry a man who is inordinately kind, so I suppose I am letting my silly feminine thoughts run away with me. You have brought out an unexpected romantic side of me that I never knew existed. Please forgive me."

He chuckled and his arms tightened around her slender body. "Sweetheart," he murmured, his lips against the top of her head as he pulled her closer. "If you have not already figured out that I am quite fond of you, then you are more naïve than I suspected. Already I think of you every moment when I should be focused on securing a very volatile city. Although it is true that the original purpose of this marriage was to secure an alliance, that factor has quickly become the very least purpose of this marriage. When I look at you, I see joy and purpose in life. I see a reason to get up every morning and a reason to fight for a peaceful world. I see a son not yet born with your sensibilities and my strength. I see a life I never imagined I would have. Can you not sense this?"

She was looking up at him by now, her eyes glimmering with un-shed tears. "Nay," she whispered. "I have only known you for two days. I have not yet developed my wifely mind-reading skills."

He laughed softly and kissed her on the forehead, embracing her sweetly in the middle of the busy bailey. For all they were aware, they were the only two people in the entire world. Nothing else mattered at the moment as new feelings and new sensations rained upon them. For the sequestered, humiliated woman and the closed-off knight, an unexpected world of joy had opened wide before them.

"There is something else that has been on my mind," Stephen murmured, his lips against her forehead. "Last night, you seemed the only one relaying apologies for your behavior when we were first introduced."

She pulled back to look at him. "I did. What makes you say such a thing?"

His expression was gentle, remorseful. "I should be apologizing, also. Although I was not attempting to be deliberately unkind, my behavior was rather harsh." He rubbed her upper arms gently, affectionately. "When you first told me of the attack against you, I told you that I did not believe you. I must apologize for that statement. It was wrong of me."

She looked curiously at him. "But... you have told me that you will make all attempts to locate this man and punish him. I knew you believed me simply by your actions. There is no need to apologize."

He shrugged weakly. "Perhaps not, but I would just the same. Last night when I saw the proof of the birth, it made me realize without a doubt that you had not lied. I am truly sorry I was so cruel. I pray you can forgive me."

She smiled faintly. "No need, Stephen. Those first few hours of our acquaintance have faded into memory. I hardly remember them."

He snorted softly, his gaze drinking in the beauty of her face. Then he pulled her into his arms once more, crushing her with his power. "I am already quite fond of you," he repeated. "I do not expect that my feelings will end there."

She reached up and threw her arms around his neck, relishing the power of the man as he picked her up off her feet and held her close.

Although there was a coat of mail between them, she could still feel his warmth. She imagined she could feel his passion as well.

"As I am quite fond of you also," she whispered pressing her lips against his ear. "Now, put me down before we create a firestorm for the gossips."

He laughed softly and set her on her feet. "Let them talk," he insisted. "It would be one measure of gossip I would be proud to be a part of."

She grinned and he kissed her, so deeply that she had to pull away or suffocate. With a smile, he kissed her nose, both cheeks, and gently released her. Taking her hand, he began to walk with her towards the keep.

"Now, what was I telling you before you so righteously distracted me?" he winked at her when she scowled. "Oh yes, I was telling you that I needed to make my rounds of the city today. I will also be busy with other tasks so I would ask that you stay to either the great hall or our chamber. I would advise against wandering to the river as you did yesterday."

"But what of the fawn? He will need to run and play."

"Let him run and play in the kitchen yard. You do not need to take him beyond the walls."

She nodded, though not entirely pleased. "Very well."

They had reached the keep and he paused, turning to face her. For a moment, he simply gazed at her, surely the loveliest creature he had ever seen. And she belonged to him. It was a satisfying thought.

"Now," he put his hands on his hips. "I must go to the armory and then attend some business here on the grounds before riding out into the city. Do you require anything before I go?"

She shook her head. "Not really," she said. "But I do have a question before you leave."

"And that would be?"

She shielded her pale blue eyes from the sun overhead as she spoke. "Perhaps this is not the right time to ask, but I was wondering about my mother," she said softly. "I was wondering when we are going to send her to Allanton for burial."

"Allanton?" he repeated.

"My family's home to the north."

His expression softened. "She will have to be buried at Berwick, sweetheart," he said quietly. "I cannot spare the men or time to send her back home. I am sorry."

She nodded as if to accept his statement but he could tell that it distressed her. "My father would have liked her to be sent home, I am sure," she tried not to sound demanding. "Do you suppose that someday we can send her home? If not now, then some day?"

He gave her a crooked smile. "I shall take her myself if it pleases you. But for now, I will arrange to have her interred in Berwick's vaults. Fair enough?"

She nodded, forcing a weak smile. "Fair enough."

"Good." He bent down and kissed her sweetly on the forehead. "I shall see you tonight."

Her smile turned genuine as she watched him walk away, the biggest man she had ever seen. But even for all his incredible height, there was nothing out of proportion or strange about the man. He was perfectly formed in every way. Her heart fluttered as he walked out of sight and she found herself sighing faintly when he was no longer before her eyes but just a sweet, lingering memory.

He was quite a man, English or no.

❧

THE SURCOATS THAT Stephen had purchased for his new wife had nary a scent of smoke once they were washed and dried in the sun. The serving women pressed the garments to crisp perfection and Joselyn had the unexpected treat of trying each one on so the women could hem the bottom. Some of the garments were so long that the serving women cut several inches off the bottom, stitching up the extra material with colored thread and creating lovely ribbons for Joselyn's hair.

Having spent half her life in rough woolen garments, the thrill of new clothing was almost more than she could stand. These were well-made garments produced from the most wonderful fabric Joselyn had ever seen. White, dark blue, deep orange, two different shades of green, a soft yellow, a rose color and finally a brocade pattern that had crimson, gold and blue rounded out the expensive booty she had acquired. Joselyn was giddy with delight as she tried on each one, vowing with each successive garment that it was the most beautiful one she had ever seen. Nay, *this* was the most beautiful one she had ever seen. On and on it went until the deep orange silk was finally finished and she was able to exchange it for the cranberry wool. With a long-sleeved, silken shift beneath, the orange silk was cool and swishy and delightful to wear in the warm weather. The wimpled serving woman tied a white ribbon around her waist as a belt and Joselyn had never in her life felt more beautiful. The contrast of the dark orange against her striking coloring was stunning.

"Ye look lovely, Jo-Jo," the wimpled woman said with satisfaction. "I have never seen such beauty."

Joselyn spun in circles, watching the bottom of the surcoat bell. "Thank you, Tilda," she said. "I have never seen anything like it."

Tilda watched Joselyn fuss with the ribbon around her waist. She had known the eldest Seton since she had been born and she knew well the tragic life the young woman had led. There had been a long period of time when Joselyn was at Jedburgh, but she had returned early last year to tend her increasingly senile mother. She had known little happiness and to see her so radiant did the old woman's heart good.

"Yer new husband is generous," Tilda ventured. "I have heard the men talking. They say he is a good man."

Joselyn nodded, smoothing her hands over the orange material. "Sir Stephen has been very kind to me," she answered, casting the wimpled woman a sidelong glance. "He has tried to be a good husband and do what is right."

"He is very tall," the wimpled woman said helpfully.

"Tall and big," the other old woman cackled from her stool in the corner. "He's the biggest man I have ever seen, saints have mercy!"

Joselyn grinned. "He is gentle and kind, Mereld," she told the skittish old woman. "He is nothing to fear."

But the older woman turned on her. "How can ye say such things?" she demanded. "He killed yer brothers, Jo-Jo. Does that not mean anything to ye or are ye so blinded by his beauty that ye forget what he's done?"

"Bite your tongue, you old fool," Joselyn snapped, her happy mood vanished. "He did not kill Thomas or William. He had no part in that."

The old woman stood up from her mending stool, hands full of strips of material that she was turning into ribbon. "Did ye ask him?"

Joselyn scowled. "Nay, I did not. But we spoke of Thomas and he would have told me had he had a hand in his death. He has been honest with me from the start."

"How do ye know?"

Joselyn growled and turned away from the old woman. She tended to be a naysayer even in the best of times but Joselyn was in no mood for her dour views. Moreover, she realized that she felt very protective of Stephen.

"I will not hear you disparage him, do you hear?" she scolded. "He has been very good and generous to me. He has even told me that he will bring the English soldier who raped me to justice. Stephen says he will find him and I believe him."

Old Mereld could see that her young lady was upset and didn't push further. The subject of Lady Joselyn's rape was something that no one talked about. It was a dark family secret that went deeper than they would dare acknowledge. The old woman had been present when a very young Joselyn had delivered the large male child that had nearly killed her. It had been a horrific birth and the old woman remembered praying continuously as Joselyn, only twelve years old at the time, had moaned and cried through three days of labor. It had been terrible for all of them and something they never discussed.

The man who had caused such pain and suffering was long gone, lost in the chaos of the Earl of Carlisle's execution those years ago. At least, that was the rumor. There were darker rumors that he was not the man responsible, that something more horrific bore the truth. But no one would confirm these darker horrors so the soldier was the accepted father of Joselyn's child. To hear that her new husband had sworn to bring the lost soldier to justice after eleven years was a bit of a dream that none of them had the heart to discourage. Joselyn believed in her new husband; it was good to believe in something.

"I hope so, Jo-Jo," Mereld regained her stool wearily. "For all of the horror the English have caused, 'twould be good if one of them tried to right the wrongs."

Joselyn had had enough. Frustrated with the bitter old servant, she quit the chamber that she and Stephen shared and made her way down the narrow stairs and out into the bailey. The day was beginning to wane and she could tell by the sun that there was no more than two hours of daylight left.

Her thoughts drifted to Stephen, of where he might be at this time, before shifting to the meal ahead. He had told her he would be late so she was in no hurry to begin preparations in earnest. The mutton from the previous night was back on the cooking fire, having been slow-simmering in a mixture of honey and cloves since mid-afternoon. But there would be bread to bake and sweets to make, and she smiled when she thought of Stephen stuffing himself with more sweet cakes and then blaming her for his gluttony. He was quite humorous at times and she liked that. She liked *him*.

As she headed towards the kitchen to not only check on the mutton but on the fawn she had left sleeping in a warm corner, she caught sight of the chapel off to the left. It was actually the base of one of the towers, a small room with a vault that ran beneath it. Stephen had told her that her mother was in the vault and she wondered if she should go say a prayer for her mother before the supper hour. She'd not yet prayed over the woman and she felt some guilt in that, but she knew her mother would have understood. Joselyn had been quite overwhelmed with the new life she found herself a part of.

Just as she turned away from the sight of the chapel, several foot soldiers entered through the main gate built into the massive gatehouse. It was a group of men bearing the blue and silver dragon standard of de Lara but she thought nothing of them until her gaze happened to fix on the one that was closest to her. He was an older man, with a full head of gray hair and an oddly shaped scar on his forehead. He was close enough that she could see it and when he smiled, he was missing several teeth. The teeth that remained, however, were a dark shade of brownish-green.

An eerie feeling swept her, growing more powerful by the second. The man was speaking to his colleagues and she froze in her tracks, listening to the sound of his voice. Something about it sounded horrifically familiar and she suddenly felt dizzy, her heart pounding loudly in her chest and her breath coming in strangled gasps. She tracked the man as he moved, like a hunter tracking prey, watching as he and his fellow soldiers headed towards the armory located in the tower near the chapel. They were laughing about something and had not noticed her. But the moment she heard the man laugh, the world suddenly began to spin.

She knew that laugh. God help her, she knew it. It was a laugh from her most horrific nightmare. A scream escaped her lips but she slapped her hands over her mouth lest he hear her, more terror than she had ever known bolting through her slight body. She stumbled backwards, kicking up dust onto her new orange silk. She fell to her knees, hysterical, before scrambling to her feet and taking off at a dead run.

Panicked grunts were escaping from her lips as she ran. She tore off into the southeast section of the bailey where a narrow tower anchored the wall. There was no particular reason why she ran in that direction; she was running blindly, without thought. There were a few soldiers in this area of the bailey but she didn't notice. She was running for the tower entrance, a safe haven in which to hide, in her blind determination to put as much distance as she could between her nightmare and safety. Her mind was a jumble of horror that she could not control.

Just as she reached the tower, a soldier was emerging, having just finished his rotation on the wall. Joselyn was incoherent with fright. She didn't even recognize Lane de Norville when he stepped into the dirt of the bailey. She simply plowed headlong into the man and, overwhelmed with the shock, fainted dead away.

Lane caught her before she could hit the ground.

CHAPTER SIX

T HE VAULTS OF the gatehouse of Berwick were narrow, low and cramped. With Stephen's bulk, the constraints made it difficult for him to maneuver. But the rebel prisoner he had captured last night in the brief skirmish had been shoved into one of the narrow cells and Stephen was intent on interrogating the man. Joined by de Lara and a few lesser knights that were part of his garrison command team, Stephen let his subordinates take the lead in the interrogation while he stood back with Tate and watched.

The vault was a nasty, dank place that reeked of urine and rot. Most of the Scots captured at the surrender of Berwick had been moved out of the city or killed, while several of Seton's men who had surrendered the city were now prisoners at the castle. The vault was two levels and could hold about fifty prisoners at any given time. The last count Stephen was given, there were seventy-six. The dungeons of Berwick were a hellish place.

After Stephen had left his wife, he had not planned to spend an over amount of time in the vault interrogating the prisoner, but the man had proven to be something of a challenge. Tate had joined him at some point during the afternoon and they stood silently while two of Stephen's knights went to work on the big Scot. Sir Ian Malcolm and Sir Alan Grantham were young, strong and fiercely loyal to Edward; they made a brutal pair of interrogators. But the man was tough and he would not answer any of their questions. Several hours into the interrogation, Stephen finally called his men off and stepped into the cell himself.

He was so tall that he was nearly bent over in half. The cell had other men in it, other prisoners, and he couldn't avoid stepping on a few legs as he made his way to the rear of the cell where his rebel prisoner was chained to the wall and sitting in his own urine. When he neared the big Scot, he crouched down several feet away, studying him.

"I am Pembury," he told the man. "I am Guardian Protector of Berwick. Do you have a name?"

The big Scot was a little bruised but none the worse for wear. He was not young nor was he particularly old, with blond hair and intelligent brown eyes. He was also a burly man with enormous hands. He gazed steadily at Stephen.

"Yer knights were unable tae get me name," he rumbled. "What makes ye think I shall tell ye?"

"Because I have politely introduced myself. The mannerly response would be to introduce yourself to me."

The Scots lifted an eyebrow. "A mannered man, are ye? Then ye dunna belong in Berwick. This is a place for men who fight like animals."

"Have no doubt I can out-fight and out-think you any time I choose. I would not be here now if I could not. May I have your name, please?"

The Scot stared at him. Then, he snorted. It was the first smile, or semblance of one, that the man had displayed all night.

"Ye tried a tactic none of these other idiots have tried," he told him. "Yer askin' nicely."

"I believe in treating all men with respect to a certain degree."

"Yer men couldna beat me name out of me."

"I am not beating you. I am simply asking."

The Scots cocked his head as if pondering the statement. After a moment, he simply turned away. Stephen, sensing that the man had no interest in conversing civilly, turned to leave. But a low voice stopped him.

"Kynan," the Scot said quietly. "Kynan Lott MacKenzie. When ye killed young Tommy Seton, ye killed me kin."

Stephen slowly resumed his crouched position. "You are related to

Alexander Seton?"

Kynan looked at him. "Aye," he said, losing some of his smugness. "It was a dastardly thing ye did tae young Tommy. He was a good lad."

Stephen didn't have an answer for him; he simply stared at him for a moment. "How are you related to Seton?"

"Alexander married me father's sister."

"And you have been defending the city against Balliol and the English?"

"'Tis young David's city, it 'tis."

Stephen grunted. "That is a matter for debate. Now it belongs to Edward."

Kynan pursed his lips. "Like his grandfather, he is. Young Edward wants Scotland just as Longshanks did."

Stephen studied the man carefully, wondering just how much to tell him about familial relations. He opted for all of it, hoping it would put the man in a chatting mood. Scots were, if nothing else, very loyal to their kin. Family relations meant everything. Stephen intended to use it to his advantage.

"Let us return to Alexander Seton," he redirected the conversation. "You said that your father's sister was his wife."

"Aye."

"That would make you a cousin to all of the Seton offspring; Joselyn, Alexander, Thomas, William and Margaret."

Kynan nodded his head faintly. "What are ye gettin' at, English?"

"Joselyn is my wife," he didn't hold back. "That makes me your kin as well."

Kynan's eyes widened. "Ye married Jo-Jo?"

Stephen nodded firmly. "The night the city surrendered."

"I dunna believe ye!"

"Shall I send her in here to confirm it?"

Kynan was growing increasingly outraged. He couldn't be sure that the man was not bluffing because he knew that the Setons had been at Berwick Castle when the English confiscated it. It was quite possible that the Guardian Protector, as he called himself, had married her simply to make his mark upon the Setons. The English were intent to force them all into submission any way they could, including a marriage. It was not out of the realm of possibility. The mere thought drove him mad.

"She's not meant for the likes of ye, English," he spat. "She's known enough humiliation."

A peculiar gleam came to Stephen's eye. "What do you mean?"

Kynan's ruddy face was growing redder. He stumbled over his words, not at all wanting to say what he meant. "She... she's meant for the cloister."

"Not anymore," Stephen's blue eyes suddenly turned hard. "Kynan, you and I are kin no matter how much you would like to deny it. I married Joselyn two nights ago and I have fully claimed her as my wife. Therefore, you will hear me now; I am finished toying with you. I will ask you a question and if I do not like your answer, I will go to my wife and take your insolence out on her. With every question you refuse to answer, or with every answer that does not tell me exactly what I need to know, she will receive your punishment. Is this becoming clearer to you? Deny me again and I will take it out Joselyn."

Kynan looked at Stephen with more emotion than the man had exhibited throughout his entire interrogation. He was horror stricken.

"What manner of bastard are ye?" he hissed. "Would you truly beat an innocent woman?"

Stephen's jaw ticked, his blue eyes searing with intensity. "I hanged an innocent boy in full view of his father. Do not doubt that I am capable of far worse things than that."

Kynan gazed steadily at the big knight, feeling a surge of power from the man like nothing he had ever experienced. He knew he was cornered and all of the resistance he had put forth suddenly faltered. He could not take the chance that the massive English knight would do exactly as he said. The man was easily three times Joselyn's size and would undoubtedly kill her. Joselyn had seen enough pain in her life.

What beatings and harassment could not achieve, a simple threat against his precious cousin would.

The English had won again.

"Ye're a lowly bastard for doin' this," Kynan's voice was barely a whisper.

"I know."

"Tell me what ye want and be done with it."

Stephen's expression bordered on triumph; not quite, but almost. He would not be so crass as to gloat. Rising, he made his way out of the cramped cell, stepping on a few more legs as he did. Once outside, he motioned to Ian and Alan.

"Ask him your questions again," he told them. "Make sure you understand everything he tells you."

The two young knights re-entered the cell. The prisoner's demeanor was quite a bit more cooperative, they quickly discovered. Tate stood with Stephen just outside the cell door watching what was, now, a rather subdued exchange. Tate nodded with satisfaction as Kynan Lott MacKenzie began to give forth the vital details they had sought all afternoon.

"Brilliant tactic, Stephen," he muttered.

Stephan, watching the activity in the cell with his massive arms folded across his chest, glanced at Tate.

"You heard me?" he asked.

Tate nodded. "Every word," he lifted an eyebrow at him. "Should I go tell your wife to run for her life?"

Stephen gave him a crooked smile. "Don't tell me that you believed what I said."

Tate shook his head, a twinkle in his eye. "I did not, but your prisoner certainly did. Most convincing."

"Perhaps we shall have something useful from him, after all."

The two of them fell silent, listening to the exchange in the cell. Stephen's thoughts were moving ahead to other tasks he needed to complete for the night, such as checking the guard posts, when a soldier descended the narrow stairs and moved straight for him.

It was one of Norfolk's men. After a few whispered words to Stephen, the big knight flew up the steps faster than Tate had ever seen him move.

CB

LANE DE NORVILLE greeted Stephen at the door to the chamber he shared with his wife. But Stephen blew past him so forcefully that Lane didn't have time to speak to him. He simply followed as Stephen entered the room, all but shoving anyone or anything from his path as he made his way to the bed. Tilda and Mereld were standing by the bed and fretting over Joselyn's state. They leapt out of the way when Stephen appeared.

Joselyn was unconscious on the bed with the fluffy white coverlet she had been so proud of. Stephen sat beside her, struggling to maintain his composure. As a healer, the man was legendary. He had been Edward's personal physic for years when the king was young. Stephen had spent so many years as a Hospitaller that he had acquired a massive knowledge in the healing arts. But he was foremost a knight and his knightly duties had overtaken those as healer as he grew older. Still, he was considered one of the best physics in the realm. At the moment, however, he was struggling to keep the emotion out of his evaluation as he looked at Joselyn's still, white form.

"What happened to her?" he asked as calmly as he could, opening one of her eyelids and then the other.

"To be honest, my lord, I am not sure," Lane replied. "I was just exiting the southeast tower when she ran right into me, and I do mean literally. I do not know if she even saw me. One moment, I was walking from the door and the next minute she is smashing into me. And then she collapsed."

Stephen checked her eyes and went for the pulse. It was strong and steady. He gently ran his fingers over her head, checking for any signs of bumps or fractures. He felt nothing. Puzzled, he checked her eyes again to note that her pupils were indeed equal and reactive. Then he ran his hands down her body, looking for any puncture wounds or scratches. He gently rolled her onto her side so he could check her backside, but it was without blemish. Rolling her onto her back again, he scratched his head and looked up at Lane.

"She collapsed?" he repeated. "Did she say anything before she collapsed?"

Lane shook his head. "Not a word, my lord."

Stephen looked back down at his wife, passed out cold on the bed. She didn't seem in distress other than the fact that she was unconscious and he put his hands on her face again to tilt her head up so he could look up each nostril, looking for blood. He checked her ears and her mouth as well. Nothing.

By this time, Tate entered the room. Having followed Stephen from the dungeons, he was understandably curious about Lady Pembury. He silently made his way to the bed, standing next to Lane as they watched Stephen examine his wife.

"What is wrong with her, Stephen?" Tate asked, concerned.

Stephen shook his head, genuinely baffled. "Nothing that I can see," he said. "No bumps, bruises or blood. Her heart is strong." He leaned forward, his hands on her face. "Joselyn, can you hear me? Wake up, sweetheart. Open your eyes."

She didn't move. Stephen tried again, this time gently rubbing her face, trying to stimulate her. "Jo-Jo, wake up. Open your eyes, sweetheart, and look at me." When she didn't respond, he looked back at Lane.

"You are certain that she said nothing?" he asked again, deeply concerned for his wife. "Did you hear her screaming at all? Any shouting or anything to indicate there was trouble?"

Lane shook his head. "Nay, my lord," he responded. "There was no indication at all."

Stephen sighed with confusion, looking back to his wife with increasing puzzlement. He picked up a limp hand and kissed it, pondering her state, before turning to Lane.

"My saddlebags and personal effects were moved into the armory when we arrived," he said. "I would ask you to retrieve them and bring them to me immediately."

"Will do, my lord," Lane spun on his heel and was gone.

After he fled, Tate moved up behind Stephen and together they gazed down at the still lady. Stephen was still holding her hand and began to rub it gently, stroking her arm and trying to elicit some response from her. But she remained safely tucked inside of unconsciousness.

"No fever?" Tate ventured.

Stephen shook his head. "None."

Tearing his gaze away from her face, he noticed she was wearing one of the new garments he bought for her, a lovely rich orange color with a deep neckline that showed off the delicious swell of her breasts. Stephen looked at his wife's flawless bosom a moment before taking the knuckle of his middle finger of his right hand and rubbing it briskly across her sternum, right in the valley between her breasts. For a person faking unconsciousness, the resulting pain from this action would cause them to startle. But Joselyn remained still.

Perplexed and increasingly concerned, Stephen simply sat and held her hand, kissing her fingers on occasion. He reasoned that as long as she was breathing and her heart remained strong, then she was not in any real distress. But something had happened, that was for certain. He wanted very much to know what it was.

Lane returned a short time later bearing big saddle bags plus two other satchels. He laid them all on the ground at Stephen's feet and the big knight dug through the bags until he came across what he was looking for. Drawing forth a good-sized black leather satchel, he set it on the bed at Joselyn's feet and began to rummage through it. Lane and Tate watched as he pulled forth strange phials, envelopes with exotic powders, and other implements that a healer would carry. There was a good deal of mysterious stuff in his bag. He finally found what he was looking for; a small glass phial with a cork stopper. He uncorked it and ran it under Joselyn's nose a few times.

With the second pass of the glass phial, she stirred. With the fourth, she jerked violently and her eyes opened. Stephen barely had time to pull the phial out of the way as she emitted a primitive, raw scream and bolted into a sitting position. She ended up in Stephen's massive embrace, her breathing coming in great, harsh gasps.

"There, there," Stephen had her tightly, soothing her. "'Tis alright, you are safe."

Her breathing was crazy, evolving into shattering sobs. Stephen pulled her closer and rocked her gently.

"All is well, sweetheart," he murmured. "I am here. Nothing can harm you."

Joselyn had awoken disoriented and terrified. But Stephen's voice had soothed her, gently bringing her back to reality. She understood that she was safe in his arms but it did not completely erase the mind-bending terror she felt. Her last memory was of that face from her deepest nightmare, suddenly alive and well before her. It had been too much for her mind to absorb and after realizing who the man was, she remembered nothing.

"I... I saw him," she wept hysterically. "*I saw him.*"

Stephen attempted to pull her face from the crook of his neck. "What do you mean? Who did you see?"

She was a sniffling, weeping mess. She fought Stephen as he tried to separate her from his powerful embrace. She continued to cling to him even as he tried to pull her back to get a look at her.

"Him," she gasped. "The... the soldier from Carlisle...."

Stephen's head snapped to Tate, *the soldier from Carlisle.* A thousand words were spilling out from Stephen's expression, words of shock and accusation and confirmation. Although he and Tate had acknowledged the fact that the man might be present in the castle, Stephen hadn't truly believed it. And he truly hadn't believed his wife would run into the man. No wonder she had collapsed.

"Are you certain, Lady Pembury?" Tate tried to be as gentle as possible. "Are you sure it was him?"

She nodded, bursting into tears again from the safe haven of Stephen's neck. Stephen stopped trying to peel her away from him. He simply sat there and held her.

"Did he try to hurt you?" Stephen's jaw was ticking as he asked. "Did he recognize you and come after you?"

She shook her head. "He did not see me," she sobbed. "But I saw him entering the armory. I ran as fast as I could to get away from him but... but I do not remember anything else. How did I get here?"

Stephen glanced over at Lane, standing near the chamber door. "Sergeant de Norville brought you," he told her. "He says that you were running wildly and crashed into him. Do you not remember?"

Her tears were fading, being replaced by a staggering exhaustion. "Nay," she wiped at her nose, her head still against Stephen's shoulder. "Did I hurt him?"

Stephen grinned, looking over to the sergeant. "She wants to know if she injured you when she ran into you," he told the sergeant. "Shall I tell her that you will recover?"

De Norville smiled, meeting Joselyn's gaze. "Hardly a scratch, my lady. I was more concerned that you had been injured in the collision."

Joselyn was looking at him with her pale blue eyes, still burrowed against Stephen's massive form. She was tucked into him, his enormous arms enfolding her like a cocoon. Gingerly, she lifted her head, studying the man closely.

"Once again you have come to my aid, sergeant," she said. "You have my thanks."

"None is necessary, my lady," Lane replied. "I was glad to be of service. Are you sure you are not injured?"

"I do not believe I have any injuries," she looked at Stephen. "But my head hurts tremendously."

Stephen asked for wine from one of the serving women. With one arm still around his shaken wife, he rummaged around in his black bag and drew forth a pouch. Opening it with one hand was tricky but he managed, dispensing the white powder into the wine and swirling it around until it dissolved. He handed the cup to Joselyn, who drank it timidly and made a face when she was finished.

"That was awful," she smacked her lips with dissatisfaction. "What was it?"

"Something to help your headache," he told her. "I need to speak with Lord de Lara. Will you be alright if I step outside for a moment?"

A look of panic swept her but she stilled herself, nodding once. He kissed her before rising, finding that he still had to peel her hands from his tunic. He kissed her hands and gently encouraged her to lie back down, which she did. With a flick of his finger to the serving women, silently indicating that they watch his wife, he moved from the room with de Lara and de Norville.

Closing the door softly, he faced de Norville first.

"It would seem that twice you have aided my wife and for that, I am deeply grateful," he said. "Because of your diligence to duty, I am putting you in charge of Berwick's House and Hold. That means that you will be in charge of security for the keep, kitchens and hall, and always be mindful of my wife's presence. It also means that you answer to me and me alone as Guardian of the Hold. Is this in any way unclear?"

It was a distinct promotion from a mere sergeant in Norfolk's ranks and Lane was visibly humbled. "It is clear, my lord," he replied. "I am greatly honored."

"It is I who am honored," Stephen replied. "I will notify Norfolk and request your service. I am sure he will agree when I explain the circumstances to him."

"Very good, my lord," de Norville responded sharply. "What is your first command for me?"

At this point, Stephen looked at Tate. "That depends," he said. "We have a bit of a situation involving my wife and I will defer to Lord de Lara at this point since it involves one of his men. My lord?"

Tate stood with his arms crossed and his legs braced, listening to the exchange between Stephen and Lane. When the attention focused on him, he lifted his eyebrows thoughtfully.

"You are not going to like what I have to say," he said to Stephen.

"Why not?"

"Your wife will have to personally identify the man who attacked her," he said. "The only way she can do that is to face him to confirm that he is indeed the man."

Stephen lifted an eyebrow. "She's terrified of the man. You saw what a mere glimpse of him did to her."

Tate shook his head. "Unless we want to condemn the wrong man, I do not see where we have a choice. Think with your mind and not your heart, Stephen. She must closely identify the man to ensure there is no mistake."

Stephen knew he spoke the truth. Sighing heavily, he averted his gaze a moment, shifting on his big legs thoughtfully. "You are correct, of course," he sighed again, thinking of Joselyn's reaction when she came face to face with the soldier who changed the course of her young life. "Give her time to recover and I will take her personally to find and identify this man. Lane, you will accompany us."

Lane nodded briskly. "Of course, my lord."

De Lara headed for the stairs. "I will send a few more men to you to take the man into custody once he is identified," he said. "For now, I will begin to gather my troops for the return to Forestburn Castle. I am anxious to go home."

Stephen gave Lane a few more orders, watching the man follow de Lara down the narrow stairs. Returning to his chamber, he found his wife standing in the middle of the room with Tilda and Mereld inspecting the skirt of the orange surcoat. He paused at the door, his eyebrows lifted.

"What's this?" he demanded without force. "Why are you out of bed? I told you to rest."

She looked up at him, great distress on her face. "Oh, Stephen," she breathed. "I am so sorry. I tore my new surcoat somehow and we are attempting to determine how to fix it."

He was not the least bit concerned as he put his hands on his hips and walked over to her, watching as the two old women discussed the best way to mend the dress.

"I would not worry overly," he told her. "You have eight more that are serviceable."

She looked miserable. "I must have torn it when I collided with the sergeant," she lamented. "I am terribly sorry. I did not mean to damage one of your lovely gifts."

He put his hand on her head, pulling it to his lips for a kiss. "As I said, not to worry. It was an accident."

He went over to the bed and sat down while the two servant women finished inspecting the skirt. When they were finished, they fled the chamber with plans for retrieving needle and thread. Stephen rose from the bed, shut the door behind them, and bolted it. He turned to his wife.

"Now," he lifted his eyebrows at her. "Are you sure you are well? Does your head still hurt?"

She smiled weakly at him. "It does, but I believe your potion is making it feel a little better," she replied. "What was that powder, anyway?"

He wriggled his eyebrows and went to her. "Mysterious stuff. Magic."

She cast him a dubious expression, knowing he was teasing her. "It is *not* magic," she said flatly. "What is it?"

He put his arms around her and pulled her close. "It is made from willow bark. It cures all manner of aches and pains. Do you not trust me?"

She snuggled against him. "Of course I trust you," she toyed with his tunic. "I just wanted to know what it was, 'tis all."

"You are a nosey woman."

"I know."

He bent over and kissed her. It was a gentle kiss that very quickly turned into something very powerful. It seemed that with each successive touch, each new moment of discovery, the flames of passion between them roared hotter and hotter. There was clearly something very special between them, something that Stephen was increasingly eager to explore. Joselyn's arms snaked up around his neck and she clung to him as his mouth ravaged her. When he straightened, he pulled her with him and her feet dangled almost two feet off the floor.

"A pity your head aches," he murmured against her cheek.

"Why?" she asked breathlessly.

"Because I cannot have my way with you. Certainly your aching head would prevent an over amount of enjoyment for you."

"I would not be so sure."

He looked at her, grinning. "Are you positive? You just had a tremendous fright. I would feel like a cad for taking advantage of a weakened woman."

She lifted an eyebrow at him. "Being in your arms gives me the strength of Samson. You are the best cure for my weakness."

His smile broadened, his gaze moving to her full lips as if contemplating their sweetness. "You are learning the art of sweet words quickly."

"I have a good teacher."

His mouth captured hers fiercely, suckling her sweet lips before plunging his tongue deep into her mouth. He was such a big man, so strong, and she was no match for his strength physically and could not match the power of his onslaught. She had one weapon over him, however, that she was not yet aware of; her sweet little hands to his head, his face, somehow undid him. He could feel them in his hair, on the sides of his face, and he realized there was not anything he would not do for her touch. It was such a small gesture yet a tremendously fulfilling one. He kissed the palms of her hands as they came near his mouth, returning to her lips once more and suckling her breathless.

Laying her on the bed, he stretched his big body over her, his hand moving down her neck to her arm and then to her breast. He kissed the swell of her bosom as he gently fondled her, thinking very seriously of removing her from her surcoat. But a loud bang on the chamber door stopped him.

It was loud enough to startle him right off the bed. Throwing open the door, he was fully prepared to ream whoever had interrupted his passion but bit the words off before they could come flying out of his mouth. Lane stood in the doorway, his fair face tense.

"Trouble, my lord," he said shortly. "You had better come."

Stephen didn't ask questions. He whirled to his wife. "Stay in this chamber and bolt the door. Do not open it for anyone but me or de Lara."

Joselyn didn't have a chance to reply before he slammed the door. She rushed to it, throwing the bolt, wondering what the trouble was and feeling fear in her heart. Oddly enough, though, the fear was not for her.

It was for her English-bred husband.

C3

THE SCOTS HAD returned.

About five hundred Scots had poured in through the main gate of the city of Berwick, killing several English soldiers as they launched their sneak attack. They plowed their way through the city straight to the castle and began to lay an unorganized, if not aggressive, siege.

De Lara had been caught outside of the city walls with the vast majority of his men and very shortly found himself in a bloody battle with a few hundred angry Scots. He had cursed himself for being stupid enough to be caught unaware. It was apparent that the Scots had waited until de Lara, the last of the great English earls still at Berwick, was separated from the garrison inside the castle. When the Earl of Carlisle went outside the city walls to muster his troops for the return home, the Scots had attacked. The old adage of divide and conquer was their war cry.

The Scots were indeed a furious bunch. Smoke rose from fires near the city walls as groups of Scots began to burn the city. They were raging like children, aimless, simply attempting to do as much damage as possible without thought to those they damaged. As Stephen stood atop the battlements of Berwick Castle and watched, he began to understand the pattern. Surrounded by Lane, Sir Ian and Sir Alan, they made a somber, calculating group.

"I would hazard to guess that they are planning on burning the city," he said to Lane, standing alongside him. "They would rather burn it than see it fall into English hands."

"It is already in English hands, my lord," Lane said frankly.

Stephen smiled ironically. "They are so blinded by their bitterness that they will cut off their nose to spite their face and call it victory."

Lane and the two young knights snorted in agreement, watching the smoke grow heavier near the main city gates. Dusk was approaching and a battle by night was not something Stephen relished. He wondered how de Lara was faring. They could hear sounds of battle in the distance but were too far away to catch sight of what was happening. Ian was reading his mind.

"Shall we take a contingent of soldiers to de Lara, my lord?" he asked. "There is no knowing how many Scots he is facing."

Stephen shook his head. "We cannot risk a breach of the castle. We must stay locked up tight. De Lara will have to fend for himself until such time as we can gain the upper hand and send help."

Ian nodded, the sunset reflecting in his dark eyes. He was a very tall, very slender man with large facial features. His counterpart, Sir Alan, was average in height but powerful. He had a rather wide-eyed appearance as he watched the city in smoke. Stephen passed a glance at him, suspecting the battles for Berwick were his first battles as a knight and he had not yet learned the art of viewing the blood and fear as part of the vocation. He was still young and anxious.

They began to see a flow of men moving towards them from the interior of the city. Hundreds of Scots were advancing towards them, howling like a barbarian tide and carrying several ladders they meant to put against the walls of Berwick to gain access. The castle itself sat upon a hill with a massive curtain wall that stretched down to the river. Stephen could see a group of Scots moving for the river, knowing they were going to immerse themselves in the water in an attempt to get around the wall in order to gain access. The siege was growing more critical.

Calmly, he turned to Ian and Alan.

"And so it comes," he said evenly. "Disburse your men along the walls and ensure that the postern gate is heavily guarded. We will have a contingent of men coming from the river side, so make sure you concentrate your men on that side of the castle. Ian, you have command of the river side of the fortress. Alan, you have the rest of the wall. Make sure it is properly covered. I will take the gatehouse.

The knights disbanded, going about their duties. Stephen remained on the wall of the gatehouse, watching the Scots as they charged the wall and began to put up their ladders. His helm, having been held in one hand, was placed atop his head and the chin strap secured. He was a knight in full battle armor, as deadly as any man who had ever walked the earth.

"Weapons!" he bellowed to the soldiers on the wall.

The troops sheathed broadswords and produced the smaller, shorter blades meant for close quarters combat. He had about five hundred men in the entire castle. Gazing at the group below, he hoped it would be enough.

CHAPTER SEVEN

T HE SIEGE OF Berwick waged well into the night and continued into the next morning. It was apparent that the attack on the city and castle had been planned since the defeat of the Scots at Halidon Hill, for the men from the north came well prepared with ladders and siege engines. Arrows, some of them Welsh in origin with their long, spiny shafts and serrated heads, had come flying over the wall and struck down several soldiers in a series of barrages. As daylight dawned, lovely and bright, Berwick Castle was in yet another horrific battle in a history that had been full of them.

Stephen and his men had spent all night upon the walls shoving back ladders of Scots attempting to breach the castle. Stephen had received a gash to his face when an enemy sword tip inadvertently struck him, barely missing his eye, but was otherwise unharmed. He had spent nearly all his time at the gatehouse fighting off ladders since the gatehouse was the flattest portion of land on which to brace a ladder. It was the Scots' rallying point.

The Scots were apparently calling in reinforcements because the swarm around the castle was becoming heavier. It made Stephen wonder what had happened to de Lara. He hoped the man had somehow survived. The alternative distressed him tremendously but he could not dwell on it. He was in the midst of his own mortal fight. He would fight off men from one ladder, shove it away from the wall only to see that two more had been put against the old stone walls of Berwick Castle. It was becoming apparent that they would have to do something drastic or the castle would eventually be breached and his mind began to work furiously for a solution.

Near him, a few of his soldiers were having trouble fighting off a group of Scots who were beginning to climb off their ladder and onto the wall. Stephen went to their aid, striking down two of the men and throwing one of them back over the wall. He didn't see the second ladder that came up behind him nor an angry Scot heading for him with a sword drawn. Someone yelled at him to beware and he turned in time to see a Scotsman upon him. He didn't have time to raise his sword; all he could do was try to duck the blow. But as he rolled to the deck, positive he was about to receive a nasty wound, an English soldier was suddenly behind the Scot and gored the man through the back. The enemy did nothing more than fall harmlessly on Stephen, who swiped the man off him and tossed him to the bailey below.

Stephen leapt to his feet, nodding his head at the English soldier to acknowledge his help.

"My thanks," he said. "I thought my living days were over."

The English soldier was older, with a worn and leathery face. But he smiled with the few green teeth he had and tipped his helm back, wiping at his sweaty brow. When his hand came away, Stephen noticed the thick, faded half-moon scar near his scalp line.

"A pleasure, m'lord," the man replied.

Stephen's blood ran cold as he envisioned the scar. Like a half-moon, it was an obvious feature like a nose or an eye. A wave of nausea swept Stephen as he held the man in his steady gaze, studying him, flashes of the horror that Joselyn had described rolling through his brain. The rape of a young girl, the pain and terror she felt, the subsequent child that resulted. All of it flashed before his eyes until all he could feel was fury.

"What is your name?" his voice sounded oddly strangled.

"Bowen, m'lord," the soldier replied.

"Whom do you serve?"

"Carlisle, m'lord," he said, his dark gaze moving in the direction of de Lara's distant troops. "There are about fifty of us in the castle. We were separated from Lord de Lara when the siege began. Do you suppose we will have a chance to aid the earl?"

Stephen didn't reply. He couldn't. When he should have been focused on a nasty battle, he found that all he could do was stare at the man before him. The nausea grew.

"You will answer a question, Bowen," he realized he was quivering. "Did you serve Andrew Harclay?"

"Aye, m'lord, I did."

"And eleven years ago in the city of Carlisle, did you rape a young girl?"

Bowen looked struck. When he didn't answer, Stephen produced the broadsword and put it at the man's throat.

"Answer me," he growled.

Bowen suddenly looked terrified. He tried to back away from Stephen but had nowhere to go. The parapet was behind him and a thirty foot drop to the bailey.

"I... I don't...," he stammered.

Stephen cut him off. "Tell me or I kill you where you stand."

Bowen's terror was turning into panic. "I don't remember!"

"You are lying. I will give you one more opportunity to answer me or I drive this sword through your neck."

Bowen was backed up against the parapet. The only place to go was down and he put up his hands in a pleading gesture. "I didn't rape her!" he warbled. "Her father owed me!"

Stephen paused, an expression of supreme confusion on his face. "What do you mean by that?"

Bowen was breathing rapidly with fear; his chest heaved laboriously. "The man had a gambling debt to me," he told him, his voice shaking. "He came into Carlisle often, to the barracks, and would engage in gambling with the soldiers. We all knew him. But he lost to me one time too many and when I tried to collect the debt, he couldn't pay. So I took his daughter instead."

"What do you mean you took her? You raped her?"

"I took what he had of value. It was my right to collect the debt any way I saw fit."

Stephen's nausea intensified. He just stared at the man, unable to fathom that manner of human being. It was the vilest thing he had ever heard. "She was eleven years old," his voice was a sickened rumble. "You stole the innocence of an eleven year old in payment for a gambling debt?"

The sword had backed off somewhat and Bowen regained a measure of his courage. He feared Pembury; they all did. But that fear did not prevent him from speaking his mind. Like most of the foot soldiers, he did not know that Pembury had taken a Scots wife. Had Bowen known that, he might have shown more restraint. Instead, his ignorance would cost him.

"I did not take her innocence," he grumbled. "It was not the first time her father had sold her off. She was a whore."

The sword went through his neck before he could draw another breath.

⚃

JOSELYN HAD SPENT an entire night listening to the sounds of battle all around her. Closed up in her bower with Mereld, Tilda and the fawn, they had huddled in fear as the sounds of hell filled the air. She felt as she had not a week earlier while she sat with her mother and father in the great hall of Berwick as the English closed in; they knew they were facing their demise. Little did she know at the time that it did not signify her death but her rebirth.

She hadn't slept the entire night, worrying about Stephen. She knew that if the Scots managed to take the castle, they would not hurt her. But she was terribly concerned for her husband. Not knowing if he was safe or dead ate at her like a cancer, odd since only the day before the man had been her enemy. But no longer.

As dawn broke, the smell of smoke was heavy in the chamber. A breeze was blowing to the east, carrying upon it smoke from the fires in the city. She dared to peer from the lancet window facing the bailey and part of the great hall and could see the wounded being carried into the great hall. It occurred to her that, as Lady Pembury, she should tend the wounded. Although life at Jedburgh had not prepared her for that, she knew her duty all the same. Stephen had told her not to leave the chamber but she could not shirk her duties. The wounded needed help and she was intent to provide it.

Moving away from the window, she roused Mereld and Tilda.

"We must go and help the wounded," she told them, pointing to Stephen's bags against the wall. "Gather my husband's things. He had all manner of medicine in his bags and we will take it down to the great hall where the wounded are."

The old women moved to do her bidding, struggling under the heavy bags. "Do ye know what to do, Jo-Jo?" Old Mereld asked. "Ye have never tended a wounded man before."

Joselyn shrugged. "If he is bleeding, we stop it. If he has a hole, we sew it up." She lifted her hands. "What more is there to know?"

The old woman scowled. "There is more to it than that. What if his bones are sticking out? What then?"

Joselyn opened her mouth to reply but a sharp bang on the door cut her off. Startled, she rushed to the bolted door.

"Who comes?" she demanded fearfully.

"Open the door." It was Stephen's muffled voice.

Thrilled, she threw open the panel and prepared to throw her arms around him. But Stephen charged in, grabbing her by both arms and lifting her off the ground. He continued to charge until he was clear across the chamber and had her cornered against the wall, trapped by his massive presence. She went from thrilled to terrified in the wink of an eye.

"Stephen," she gasped. He was not hurting her but the pressure from his grip was intense. "What is…?"

"Enough," he snapped, his blue eyes blazing into her. "No more half-truths or lies, Joselyn, else you will not like my reaction. You will tell me the absolute truth."

She was shaken. "Truth? What truth?"

"Your father," he demanded before she finished her sentence. "Did he use you to pay off his gambling debts? Is that why the soldier raped you?"

Joselyn's face turned white. They could all see it. Her trembling worsened. "Who told you such things?"

Stephen was so enraged, so sickened, that it was all he could focus on. He was in battle mode but now confronting perhaps the most important thing he had ever faced. In battle, he at least had the ability to protect himself with armor and shield. But with Joselyn, his heart was naked, his soul vulnerable, and he was having a difficult time. There was no defense. After what Bowen had told him, he could think of nothing else.

"It does not matter," he growled. "Is it true?"

Joselyn opened her mouth. But she could not speak and the tears came. "Let me go."

He shook her, hard. "Not until you tell me the truth," he seethed. "The rape by the soldier in Carlisle was not the first time a man had touched you, was it?" his voice was a growl. "There had been other times before that one, weren't there? *Weren't there?*"

She broke down, weeping. Before Stephen could force her to reply, old Mereld rushed forward with the fire poker in her hand. She slapped at Stephen's armored arm, trying to force the man to release Joselyn. When he didn't budge, she whacked him again.

"'Tis not her fault!" the old woman smacked his shoulder. "She had no choice! Her father forced her to!"

Stephen looked at the old woman, unable to speak for the revelations that were coming forth. Tilda rushed up, hovering nervously, also prepared to defend Joselyn against her enraged husband. Two old women against a massive knight was hardly a fight but they were prepared to defend their young lady to the death. There were truths to be known that, being servants, should not have come from their lips. But it was clear that Joselyn's life was at stake and they could remain silent no longer. The young woman had been through enough and now, when she had finally found happiness, old horrors were intent to ruin it.

"Alexander Seton knew her value at a young age," Tilda was almost weeping as she spoke. "He had a gambling sickness and when he could not pay his debts, he would use Jo-Jo as security. Some men would use her to work off the debt with labor while others would simply keep her as a guest for a time. But there were a few who... they would...."

By this time, Stephen had let Joselyn go. He faced the old women with more emotion than he had ever displayed in life. It was unrestrained, unbridled and spilling out all over the place.

"What would they do?" he demanded hoarsely.

Tilda twisted her hands anxiously. "She was young and beautiful, m'lord," the woman's tears broke through. "She developed a womanly body at a young age. They would take her to sport."

Because Tilda was crying, Mereld began to weep also. "She had no choice," the old woman wept. "Jo-Jo would run away and her mother would hide her, but Alexander would always find her and return her to the men to whom he owed the debts. Sometimes he would beat her for her insolence. It was finally Lady Julia who sent Jo-Jo to Jedburgh so she could be free of her father. Then she married off Lady Margaret by the time she was nine years of age so her father could not use her in the same way he used Lady Joselyn. Why do you think Lady Julia went mad? She had a husband who was a soulless devil."

Stephen just stared at them. His blue eyes were filled with shock. An eternity of silence followed, punctuated by the distant sounds of battle. But Stephen remained frozen as if unable to move, unable to accept what he had been told. When he finally closed his eyes to ward off the horror of Joselyn's life, tears rolled down his cheeks.

Slowly, he turned to his wife. She had collapsed on the floor, huddled against the wall and wept as if her heart were broken. He went to her, woodenly, his posture indicative of his exhaustion and emotional level. He crouched wearily next to her, gazing at her lowered head.

"Joselyn," he murmured hoarsely. "Look at me."

She sobbed harder, pressing her face into the wall. "Nay," she cried, holding out a hand as if to ward him off. "Go away and leave me."

He grabbed the hand, yanking her off the floor and into his arms. She fought him for a half second before succumbing to his powerful embrace. He held her tightly, his face in her hair. Her sobs undid him and tears fell from his eyes faster than he imagined possible.

"I will never leave you, ever," he whispered. "Why did you not tell me the truth?"

She sobbed her anguish. "How would you have accepted it?" she asked, almost angrily. "The night we met was bitter enough. How would you have accepted the truth? That you were forced into a marriage with a woman whose father abused her and used her to pay his gambling debts? But I had to tell you something. You would have found out quickly enough that I was not virgin, so I told you of the rape. It was not a lie."

He rocked her gently, knowing she was correct to a certain extent. He would not have accepted the truth well the night they met. He was dazed with the revelations but it did not change what he felt for her. If anything, it deepened his sense of compassion and connection with the woman. He could not believe how horribly she had been mistreated yet had still managed to maintain her fight, her sense of humor and her dignity. She was, in every sense, an amazing woman. At the moment, he felt extremely fortunate to have her.

He sighed faintly, wiping his tears from his face. "Then the soldier from Carlisle truly raped you."

She nodded. "He did," she whispered. "I did not know until afterwards that he had my father's permission."

"And the child?"

"He was a result of the rape. My mother committed me to Jedburgh so my father could no longer use me. She did it out of desperation."

"How... how many other times were you taken advantage of before Carlisle's soldier?"

"My father used me twice. The first time, I was nine years old."

Stephen grunted with the horror of it, closing his eyes tightly at the thought. The thought of his sweet, vulnerable wife being abused by faceless, nameless men made him physically ill. The nausea had returned full force. Joselyn abruptly pulled her face from the crook of his neck and looked at him, her pale blue eyes wide with grief and horror.

"I do not blame you for your disgust," she murmured. "It disgusts me also, more than you can imagine. I wept the night you consummated the marriage because all I have ever known is the brutality and pain of coupling. I did not know it was meant to be a sweet and intimate act, and even if you walk from this room and never touch me again, I will always revere you for showing me that such tenderness existed. You have been the one ray of sunshine in a life that has known little and for that, I thank you."

He held her face in his two hands, gazing into her lovely features. There was no disgust in his heart, only adoration. He rubbed her cheeks with his thumbs.

"Then the man to punish is not the soldier from Carlisle but your father," he murmured. "You have always defended him most staunchly."

She was not sure how to respond. "Good or bad, he is my father," she offered with a shrug. "He always felt great remorse for what he did, but his sickness was stronger than his loyalty to me."

"What he did to you was evil."

"I know," she whispered. "But it was finished eleven years ago. I try not to think of it. With time, the fear and resentment for my father has faded. I had not seen him for almost eleven years until he recalled me from Jedburgh last year. And then when I saw him again, it was as if he were a different man. He was changed."

"How?"

She shook her head. "I do not know, exactly. It was as if he had grown beyond his sicknesses. He had been kind and respectful since I have returned home. For the first time in my life, I felt safe with him."

Stephen drew in a long, steadying breath as his anger began to shift from Bowen to Alexander Seton. "Be that as it may, it is well and good that the man is away from Berwick," he said, "for surely he would be in mortal danger right now. The man will pay for what he did to you, mark my words."

Joselyn was calming as she listened to his words and watched his expression. She timidly touched his chin, his square jaw. "I am sorry I did not tell you all of it," she murmured. "I was afraid to at first but increasingly afraid as we grew to know each other. You are like no man I have ever known, Stephen. I did not want to lose whatever warmth was growing between us. It means everything to me."

"And to me," he responded softly, relishing the feel of her gentle hands on his face. "But I will ask you now and let this be the end of it; is there any other humiliation I should know of? Anything else you have been afraid to tell me?"

She looked rather sad. "Isn't what you've been told quite enough?"

He smiled weakly, leaning forward to kiss her gently. "More than enough."

Her eyes began welling again. "Do you forgive me, then?"

"There is nothing to forgive. I understand why you did not tell me at the first. But let that be the end of any secrets between us."

"I promise." She suddenly threw her arms around his neck, holding him fast. It was a powerful, impulsive gesture. "Oh, Stephen, I do love you."

He heard her words like an arrow into his heart. They embedded themselves, held fast, never to be let go. He had only known the woman two days but within that time, he felt closer to her than he had ever felt to anyone in his life. Gone was the sense of self-protection. His emotions were flowing freely for her and he could not stop them. He squeezed her so tightly that he heard her grunt as all of the air was forced from her lungs.

"And I love you also," he whispered so only she could hear him. "I will love you until I die."

She broke into soft tears at his declaration and he kissed the side of her head, her cheek, and finally her lips. It was an unbridled display of emotion between them, feelings and emotions that had grown into something neither of them could have anticipated or expected.

All the while, Tilda and Mereld stood back, watching the exchange, more relieved and joyful than they could express. Thinking they should perhaps leave the couple alone, they moved to the door but Stephen caught a glimpse of their movement from the corner of his eye and stopped them.

"Nay," he told them, standing up with his wife still wrapped in his arms. "You will stay here with Joselyn. The battle is still waging and I would have everyone safe."

Joselyn wiped the last of the tears from her eyes, gazing up into his handsome face. "But I saw many wounded being moved into the hall," she said. "We must tend them."

He shook his head. "You will remain here. It is not safe for you outside of the keep."

"Who will tend the wounded?"

He wriggled his eyebrows, moving to collect his saddlebags with her still wrapped against him. "Most fighting men have experience tending wounds," he told her. "There are plenty of men to tend the injured."

"Where are you going?" she asked as he moved for the door.

He set her gently on her feet. "The battle still rages," he told her, slinging the enormous packs over his shoulders. "I must return and end it."

She looked perplexed. "You left a battle to speak with me?"

His intense blue eyes bore into her. "There is nothing more important than you."

He seemed like he wanted to say more but refrained. Kissing her again, a lingering gesture, he slammed the door shut behind him.

⊘

HAVING BEEN A Hospitaller for many years, and spending a good deal of time in the Holy Land, Stephen was well versed on more than the knighthood or the art of healing. He had also picked up strange and wonderful information in his travels, one being the secret weapon called Greek Fire. He'd seen it used, many times, and had been given the secrets of its composition by an alchemist he had befriended in Tyre. Stephen had the ingredients for Greek Fire with him although he doubted he had enough to accomplish his intentions. Still, he had to try. The Scots quest to mount the walls was stronger than before.

He found Lane near the gatehouse and sent soldiers running for Ian and Alan. When he was finally joined by the two knights, he pulled his men into the armory for a swift and private conference.

"I have an idea that will turn the tides against the Scots should it be successful," he said quickly. "There is not much time and I need your help. We need as much quicklime as we can get our hands on. Does anyone know where we can find some?"

Lane and Alan looked perplexed while Ian suddenly appeared very excited.

"There is a good deal of it in the kitchen," Ian said eagerly. "There are bags of it. The Scots were using it during the siege of Berwick before their defeat at Halidon to aid in the burial of their dead."

Stephen's eyes fixed on him. "Get it," he commanded. "Get all of it. And take as many men as you need to accomplish this. Bring it back to the armory."

Ian and Alan fled, leaving Stephen with Lane. Stephen knelt over one of his saddlebags and began removing leather pouches.

"Here," he tossed one to Lane. "Set this against the wall and go and find the biggest cauldron you can. And hurry."

Lane quit the small room, leaving Stephen to organize his ingredients. After several long minutes, during which Stephen was called to the wall to help fend off more invaders, Ian and Alan returned with several men-at-arms bearing sacks of quicklime. There were a total of seven bags of the ingredient mined from the limestone quarries in Yorkshire. It was a very common ingredient with, as Stephen had learned, a variety of uses. It had been at Berwick to use liberally over the dead to prevent the spread of disease. Lane returned shortly with another soldier, bearing an enormous iron pot between them.

Stephen was working with a building sense of urgency. The Scots seemed to be increasing their onslaught and he knew it was only a matter of time before a significant number managed to mount the walls and make their way down to the gate, which they would then open to admit their comrades. Then the castle would be compromised and their duty to hold the city would be made more difficult. Stephen knew that time was not on their side.

He ordered the quicklime dumped into the pot. White dust billowed up, coating them and causing a chorus of coughs. Into the quicklime, Stephen dumped his mysterious ingredients of yellow sulfur powder and saltpeter. He stirred it with Ian's broadsword, the only thing he could find at the moment, watching the ingredients integrate. The screams and shouts from the attack were growing louder and he finished stirring quickly.

"Now," he said. "Refill these quicklime sacks, cut a hole in one end, and dispense this powder along the top of the parapet. We will need a thick, heavy line from one end of the castle to the other, all along the top of the wall. Make sure there is no break in the line. Go!"

The men-at-arms used their helms to scoop white powder into the sacks. Taking a sack for each man, they dashed from the armory to the walls and began laying a thick, white line along the top of the wall. When all of the men were gone, including Lane, Ian and Alan, Stephen took the leather pouches that had contained the saltpeter and filled them with the remaining mixture. There were five in all.

He had to kill three Scots in order to move to the center of the gatehouse to start the chain reaction that would literally set fire to the wall of Berwick. He was counting on the hot, rapid fire caused by the quicklime mixture to chase off the invaders. The fighting was worse than before and he knew there was no time to waste. Taking all five pouches, he lit them one after the other with a flint and stone.

The pouches flared into a wild, brilliantly blinding white light. Stephen threw the pouches on the Scots at the gate below, watching them explode and spread fire over several men at once. Soon, there were a few dozen men below that were on fire and their screams of pain filled the night air. What was worse, however, was when their friends tried to put the fire out with water. It would make the fire burn hotter and brighter. It was a horrifying predicament as the smell of burnt flesh began to drift upon the night breeze.

But Stephen wasted no time in viewing his handiwork. He sparked the flint and stone and lit the nearest streak of white powder, watching it flare brilliantly and burn swiftly down the length of the wall. On and on it would go, lighting the next trail of white powder, until it reached the wall facing the river. There was a huge flare as it picked up another row of white powder and then continued along the wall, to the south side of the castle, and continued onward. Stephen and most of his men watched with bated breath as the fire eventually encircled the entire castle.

The Scots on ladders were repelled by the flame. It lit their tartans on fire, a blaze that only grew worse when water was doused upon it. Men began jumping from the ladders and the ladders themselves went up in flame. It quickly became a retreat of chaos. Stephen stood by, watching the complete change in the tides, as Lane, Ian and Alan finally rejoined him.

"Brilliant, my lord," Ian said with satisfaction. "Your fire has worked magic."

Stephen grunted. "Perhaps it will give them pause should they think to charge the castle again," he tore his eyes away from the intense white blaze and looked at his men. "Mount as many men as we can spare and prepare to ride to de Lara's aid. And there is enough powder left that you can take some pouches filled with the stuff to throw at any Scots foolish enough to get in your way."

The knights were gone, leaving Stephen standing with Lane and watching the Scots fall away from the walls. It was soon readily apparent that no more Scots were willing to try and mount the walls so long as the fire burned. Stephen had a few men take whatever remained in the cauldron to sprinkle on the fire and refresh the flames. Then he had the men gather whatever peat and wood they could, stoking the blaze atop the walls so that the Scots would forget about trying to attack the walls again. So long as there was flame, Stephen figured, it would discourage both the Scots and their ladders.

Stephen rode out into the burning city to aid de Lara who, by that time, had managed to chase off most of his attackers. He was weary but in one piece. Tate and his men helped Stephen clear the city of the remaining rebels, who fled north. But they did not flee before inflicting as much damage as possible on the citizens of the city of Berwick. As dawn broke, Stephen and Tate returned to Berwick Castle and walls that were still flaming a brilliant white light that could be seen for miles. It looked like the entire castle was on fire, creating an eerie glow against the pink and purple sky.

Stephen headed straight for the vault and Kynan Lott MacKenzie.

CHAPTER EIGHT

J OSELYN HAD NO idea what time it was when she was awakened by soft noises in her chamber. It was bright in the room, indicating the late hour. Lying curled up on her side, she opened her eyes to see that Stephen was very carefully attempting to remove his boots. She lay there, not moving a muscle, as she watched him pull off first one boot and then the other, very carefully setting them down against the wall. He was trying desperately not to make any noise but in his weary state, he was not doing a very good job. She could hear him grunting and groaning softly as the boots and tunic came off. Finally, she took pity on him.

"You grunt like an old bear," she said softly.

He pulled the tunic over his head, grinning down at her. "Is that so?" he tossed the tunic into the corner. "And you snore like one"

Her head came up, a frown on her lips. "I do not snore."

He laughed softly, going to open the door and issuing orders to a soldier that was near the landing. He called for hot water and food before shutting the door and bolting it.

"Aye, you do," he made his way over to the bed somewhat stiffly. "You make a very sweet whistling sound. I find it very charming."

He sat down beside her and she lay her head back down again, studying the fatigue on his handsome face. Though the cornflower blue eyes were glimmering, she could tell that he was exhausted, perhaps spiritually as well as physically. It had been a very long night for them both and she was hesitant to ask him too many questions about the siege, fearful that she would not like his answers.

"Is the battle over?" she finally asked.

He nodded, raking his hand through his black hair. "For now," he replied. "Hopefully we've given the Scots pause to think next time they try to attack the city. I would hope that peace will hold out for a time so that the citizens can at least recover."

She thought a moment on that. "Between the English attacking the city and the Scots counter-attacking, I would imagine that everyone has had their fill of war."

"Everyone but the Scots," he grunted. "The city is in shambles."

She propped herself up on an elbow. "I would like to help those put out by the constant warring," she put her hand on his enormous thigh. "There must be something I can do for the citizens of Berwick."

He put his massive hand over her small one. "'Tis a noble thought, but you have plenty to do at the castle," he said. "Moreover, the city is still a dangerous place. I do not want you exposed to the hazards of a rebellion. There is no knowing when the Scots will attack again."

She cocked her head thoughtfully. "But I am Scots. They would not harm me," she squeezed his hand. "These are my people, Stephen. They are in distress and I feel very strongly that I must help. The constant battles have surely left them in great need."

He opened his mouth but a knock on the door interrupted them. He went to the door, opening it to admit two soldiers with a big iron pot of steaming water and Tilda bringing up the rear with a wooden tray of food. Stephen took the food and chased everyone from the room. Bolting the door, he set the tray down and collected a large piece of bread from it; taking a huge bite, he faced his wife.

"How would you help?" he asked, chewing.

She sat up and swung her legs over the side of the bed. "Attend those who are injured, perhaps provide food to those who have none," she ventured with a shrug. "I would help however I can. I simply cannot stay locked in this keep, well away from those who are fighting for young David's cause."

He swallowed the bite in his mouth, his cornflower blue eyes taking on a peculiar gleam. "When you married me, your loyalty became to England."

She fixed him in the eye. "When I married you, my loyalty became to you and only you. But that does not mean I do not feel concern or pity for my people."

He regarded her a moment before the warmth returned to the blue eyes. "Well put," he said. "But can I at least have a few hours of peace myself before I have to delve into this subject?"

She grinned and rose from the bed, moving to the wardrobe that was against the wall, the one that she and the servants had moved down from the upper floor. "Of course," she said. "Sit and eat your food and I shall help you bathe when you are finished."

He grunted yet again as he sat on the bed, feeling his fatigue in every fiber of his body. Plus, he was old for a fighting man at thirty years and seven. His body had taken a lot of abuse over the years and he was beginning to pay the price. He devoured most of the bread, the cheese and all of the wine as Joselyn removed some items from the wardrobe. He watched her as she set out a few squares of drying linen and the bar of white soap that smelled like pine. It was his soap. He had provided it to her to wash with because he had nothing else to offer. He made a mental note to purchase sweet-smelling soap for his wife that she would like better than his manly pine.

Joselyn was very busy as Stephen ate his meal. She was clad in a heavy shift, one of the newer garments he had bought her, and she quickly donned the old broadcloth surcoat over it to work in. It was still dusty and dirty, having been one of the only garments she owned up until two days ago, but she did not want to get any of her new clothing wet as she helped her husband bathe. Due to her chores at Jedburgh, she was well versed in things like washing or bathing, although she'd never personally washed a man. But she did not experience a flicker of apprehension as she prepared to help Stephen wash. She was, in fact, eager to do something for him. The man had so far done all of the giving since she'd known him and she was eager to give back something in return, as small a gesture as it was.

In fact, since their conversation the night before when all horrors had been revealed, she was extremely eager to make a life with this man who seemed so capable of forgiveness and understanding. With every moment that passed she was learning the character of this man whom she had married and her sense of gratitude grew. She never imagined herself to be so fortunate and she was determined never to take one moment of her new life, or new husband, for granted.

The pot with warm water was big enough for Stephen to sit in if she put a three legged stool in it. She looked over at her husband as he finished the last of his bread.

"Do you have a razor?" she asked.

He nodded, dipping his head in the direction of his bags against the wall. "In there."

"May I retrieve it?"

He nodded and she went to his bags, carefully pulling items out and setting them on the floor until she came to a long steel razor wrapped in heavy linen. She removed it, and a horsehair brush, and went back to prepare his bath.

"I am ready when you are, my lord," she told him, putting a little water on the pine soap and working it into a heavy lather with the horsehair brush.

Stephen brushed off his hands, stood up, and removed his breeches. He went straight to the pot and climbed in, seating his bulk on the stool. It was a tight fit in the pot but manageable. Joselyn turned to him with an empty bowl in her hand, smiled, and went to work.

Stephen sat with his eyes closed as the warm water coursed over him. It was the most relaxing, wonderful sensation he could imagine. He let his mind clear of all thoughts except for those of Joselyn as she hovered next to him, carefully pouring water over his head and body. She doused him several times before picking up the lathered brush, the soap, and going to work.

Stephen grunted as she began to soap him within an inch of his life. She vigorously soaped his back, his chest and his arms. She used the brush to scrub the gore and dirt from his hands, under his nails, before softly commanding him to lift his arms, which he did, fearful that his docile wife had suddenly turned militant on him. She soaped his armpits, ribs and belly before he was allowed to put his arms down again. He had tried, once, and she had growled at him. So the arms went back up and he grinned broadly.

It was difficult to keep from laughing as she ordered him to stand up so she could wash the rest of him. He had a fairly significant arousal by this time and had to bite off his guffaws as she tried to work, red-faced, around it. By the time she commanded him to sit back down again, her cheeks weren't quite so red. She rinsed him off thoroughly over and over before picking up the brush again and lathering up his beard.

Stephen sat stock-still as she carefully shaved him. He was able to watch her at close range as she worked, the gentle curve of her face and the sweet bow of her lips. He found himself studying every pore on her skin and counting how many dark eyelashes she had. She had the most beautiful eyes. Finally, when he was clean-shaven, she wiped off his face and set the towel aside. Stephen thought she was finished until he felt her lathering his shoulders again. He was about to ask her what she was doing when she set the soap down, put her small hands on his shoulders, and began to rub.

He groaned and dropped his chin to his chest, wallowing in the pure pleasure of the massage. Her little hands applied gentle pressure as she rubbed away the knots that the burden of his command had created. It was heavenly.

"Good Christ," he muttered. "Who taught you to do this?"

Standing behind him, Joselyn smiled modestly. "My mother used to do this for me when I was pregnant," she said softly. "I was so miserable the entire time that she would do this for me to help me feel better. Do you feel better?"

He could barely nod, succumbing to extreme relaxation. "You have no idea how much better," he mumbled. "Your hands are magic."

"Thank you, husband."

He reached up when her hand came close to his neck and grasped the hand gently, pulling it to his lips for a gentle kiss. But that was not enough for him and he pulled more insistently, pulling her from behind him so that she was standing next to him. His big hands cupped her face and he kissed her tenderly. Suddenly, his arms went around her and he was pulling her inside the tub.

Joselyn's arms went around his neck, giving in to his tremendous strength, as he pulled her into the tepid water with him. Her broadcloth surcoat was wet but she didn't care. Her focus was on her husband, his sweet kisses and his clean, pine-smelling body. It was all so new and exciting, this relationship they were beginning to share; where she once feared a man's touch, now she craved Stephen's. When he began removing her clothing, she didn't protest. Soon enough, the broadcloth came off and the shift went over her head. Both ended up tossed into a corner.

Naked in his arms, she ended up straddling his lap, facing him, as his mouth and hands ravaged her. Stephen had managed to stoke a raging fire within her, one that caused her breathing to come in heavy gasps and her body to tremble. His great hands were on her breasts, followed by his mouth, and she gasped softly as he suckled first one nipple and then the other. His enormous arousal was between them, hard and throbbing, and he fingered her woman's center gently, ensuring that she was wet enough for his entry. She was hot and slick, and it drove him mad. Taking her by the waist, he lifted her up and impaled her upon his demanding arousal.

The first thrust had him seated almost completely. Joselyn gasped at the swift, insistent entry and wrapped her arms around his neck, holding fast as he grasped her buttocks and held her firm as he thrust again. Holding her against his pelvis, he thrust into her repeatedly as her tight walls pulled at him, enjoying every withdrawal and every thrust with the greatest of pleasure. As delightful as it was, however, they were in a moderately awkward position on the stool and, still embedded in her, he rose and stepped out of the pot.

He had no idea how he made it over to the bed The next thing he realized, she was on her back on the mattress and he was driving into her hard enough to rattle her teeth. He thrust so hard that he ended up scooting her to the head of the bed and she put her hands up against the wall to prevent her skull from smacking into it. Stephen held her tightly, driving deep into her womb, feeling more power and sensation than he had ever known when she suddenly stiffened and he could feel her sugared walls spasm. She bit off a cry on her hand, biting down so hard that she left deep red welts. When Stephen felt his pleasure approach, he resumed kissing her, tasting her mouth as his seed spilled deep into her body.

He was still kissing her when his thrusts died completely, but his kisses were far gentler, more adoring, as if to convey the depth of emotion he was coming to feel for her. His hands moved over her body tenderly, inspecting the texture of her skin and memorizing the feel of her hard nipple in his fingers. He glanced up at her, seeing that she lay with her eyes closed and an arm over her eyes. He kissed her chin, fondling a breast, and she groaned with pleasure and wriggled her hips. He was still embedded in her body and the action from her hips stirred his lust again. In little time, he was hard again and he made love to her a second time, far more slowly and luxuriously, feeling her multiple releases before he joined her.

When it was over, Stephen fell into an exhausted sleep with his great head on Joselyn's chest. He started snoring heavily almost immediately and she smiled faintly, knowing how fatigued the man was. Very carefully, she shifted so that she could grasp the coverlet and pull it up over them both without waking him. She jostled him slightly but he didn't rouse. Pulling the coverlet up over them both and wedging a pillow under her head so she would be more comfortable, Joselyn wrapped her arms around Stephen's head and neck and languished away the hours as he slept on her.

She couldn't think of anything on earth she would rather do.

CⳄ

STEPHEN AWOKE JUST as the sun was setting and made love to his wife twice more before allowing her out of the bed. Even then, it was only because she begged to use the chamber pot. With a grin, he rolled onto his back, an enormous arm behind his head as he gazed out of the lancet window while Joselyn discreetly went about her necessities. When she finally emerged into his line of sight, she had pulled a shift on and a rich yellow surcoat that was marvelous with her dark hair. She looked like an angel. He gazed at her, sighing with appreciation. She smiled at him, running his horsehair brush, now dry, through her dark hair.

"It is approaching the evening meal," she said. "Will you not rise and attend?"

"Will you be there?" he flirted gently.

She returned his flirt coyly as she brushed the ends of her hair. "I will be wherever you are, my lord."

He grinned, lifting his right hand a crooking a finger at her. "Come here."

She fought off a grin, gliding across the floor until she came within an arm's length of the bed. "Aye, my lord?" He reached out and snatched her, causing her to fall across his chest. Her dark hair splayed across them both as his smoldering cornflower blue eyes bore into her.

"I must confess something," he murmured.

"What is that?"

"I do not want to share you with anyone tonight."

She blushed furiously. "But you must eat."

He ran his hand through her hair, studying her lovely face pensively. "Perhaps," he sighed, grasping her hair and bringing it to his nose. "But more than that, I am reluctant to admit that I do have duties that I must attend. I do not want to leave you."

"What duties?"

He wriggled his eyebrows. "It has been a few hours since the end of a particularly nasty assault against the city and castle. I must see how things have settled."

She cocked her head. "Settled?"

"To see if anything has changed. To assess the state of the city and castle."

"Oh," she nodded in understanding, watching him smell her hair. "May I come with you as you go about your duties?"

He went from smelling her hair to touching her face. "I am sure they would not interest you."

"Please?"

He opened his mouth to refuse her but gazing into her lovely, eager face, he found that he could not. He wanted to be with her as much as she wanted to be with him. The more time he spent with her, the more he never wanted to be separated from her.

"Very well," he nodded with resignation. "Finish dressing and get your shoes on."

With a grin of triumph, she leapt off the bed and furiously finished brushing her hair. Stephen watched her a moment before tossing the coverlet off his naked body and digging into his bags for a clean pair of breeches. As Joselyn braided her hair in a single braid that draped elegantly over one shoulder, Stephen pulled on his breeches, and unfurled a clean tunic. He pulled it over his head, adjusting the sleeves on his big arms, all the while watching Joselyn as she tied off the end of her braid and went on the hunt for her slippers. She was an enrapturing creature to watch.

Stephen sat down to pull on his massive knee-high boots. He didn't even realize his eyes never left Joselyn as she moved quickly about their chamber. He found himself memorizing the way she moved, every fluid shift of her body. It was magic.

Her shoes were finally on and she planted herself in front of him, the pale blue eyes glittering expectantly.

"Well?" she said in the same tone she had used when she had ordered him to lift his arms in the bath. "Where is our first destination?"

He suppressed a smile and rose from the bed, towering over her.

"The walls."

"Then let us waste no more time."

"Aye, General."

She grinned at him, watching his smile break through and then laughing at him. He took her hand and led her from the bower, from that magical chamber that had provided them with hours upon hours of discovery. It was a safe haven for them, a retreat, and a place of worship. Stephen shut the door behind them, looking forward to their return to the chamber.

The sky was splashed with shades of blue and purple as they entered the bailey. It had been a warm day and the ward was dusty, dogs running about and soldiers going about their duties. Clouds of dust billowed up from their feet as they moved across the bailey. The hall was lit and inviting, and they could see people inside as Stephen took her to the wall. From the vantage point high above the city, the views at sunset were spectacular but for the devastation below.

Mounting the top of the stairs and stepping onto the wall, Joselyn paused at her first clear vision of Berwick since the many battles over the past month had ravaged it. From her position, she could see that certain sections of the city were fairly untouched and smoke rose from cooking fires in those areas. But a vast area of the city was burnt and destroyed. Life, as far as she could determine, did not exist there. It was a sobering reality, one she hadn't truly grasped until this moment.

Stephen had started across the wall walk but paused when he realized she was not following. He turned to see her gazing out over the dying city with tears in her eyes. He retraced his steps, putting his big arm around her shoulders in a comforting gesture.

"Come along, sweetheart," he murmured.

She blinked and the tears spattered. Quickly, she wiped them away. "There is so much destruction."

"I told you there was."

"I suppose I did not realize how bad it was."

Stephen's gaze moved out over the city. He was accustomed to the sight. "War tends to devastate all it touches. The city was not too terribly off after Halidon but the counter attack the past couple of days saw that particular aspect changed. The Scots did a good deal of damage."

She turned to him. "But why?"

He studied her expression, wondering if she already knew the answer and was simply asking to see what his reaction would be. The truth was, no matter how wildly in love he was, he had only known the woman a few days. Before that, she had been his enemy. Stephen was not naturally trusting, not even with his wife. With him, trust was something to be earned.

"Because they would rather ravage the city than see it ruled by the English," he explained carefully. "Surely you know that."

She sniffled delicately. "But it makes no sense. Many of our kinsmen live here."

"Kinsmen and rebels," he muttered, his gaze moving out over the city again as he thought of Kynan Lott MacKenzie deep in the vault of Berwick. "I would not worry about it if I were you. Berwick will know peace again someday."

She allowed him to pull her along the wall walk, lifting her skirts so she would not step on them as they mounted steps leading to a higher portion of the parapet. "What is the difference between rebels and Scots who simply fight for their king?" she asked.

He shrugged faintly. "Rebels are generally subversive and uncaring about who they devastate. They are so determined to destroy the enemy that they will even kill Scots who get in their way. That makes them particularly dangerous."

She thought on that a moment. "My father was not a rebel. He cared very much for Berwick and her people."

Stephen paused at the entrance to a corner tower. He still found it difficult to believe that after all her father had put her through, she still spoke kindly of him. "As I said, I would not worry about it if I were you," he touched her face gently. "I have the situation well in hand."

"What do you mean?"

He wriggled his eyebrows and took her hand, leading her into the dark and gloomy tower. "I have a rebel leader in my vault. Once he tells me what I need to know, I will do what needs to be done in order to quell these insurgents once and for all."

They emerged from the tower onto another section of the wall walk. "Scots are a stubborn bunch," she said dubiously. "I would not be surprised if he would die before telling you a thing."

"It is possible."

"Who is this rebel leader?"

He paused with something that sounded like a grunt; in fact, it was a pensive release. He was not surprised that she had asked the man's name but he hadn't decided whether or not he had planned to tell her should she ask. Drawing a long, deep breath, his blue-eyed gaze moved over the smoking landscape of the north side of the castle.

"A man of some influence."

She waited for more of an answer and lifted her eyebrows expectantly when none was forthcoming. "Who is he?"

Stephen looked at her then, cocking his head as he did so. He released her hand, folding his massive arms across his broad chest.

"Does it matter?"

She shrugged, shaking her head. "I suppose not," she said. "I was just curious, 'tis all."

"You are also venturing into information that does not concern you."

Her mouth popped open in surprise at the rebuke but she quickly shut it and averted her gaze. "I am sorry," she moved around him, continuing their walk. "I was simply making conversation. I was not attempting to extract vital information out of you. And I thought that if perhaps I know this man, I could help you."

He reached out and grasped her arm before she could get away. It was not a harsh gesture and she came to a halt, still keeping her gaze averted.

"Help me?" he was looking at her even though she was not looking at him. "How on earth would you do that?"

She shook her head, gently but firmly pulling her arm free of his grasp and continuing along their walk. "It does not matter," she said. "Let us speak no more of it."

He watched her take a few steps away from him before calling to her. "Jo-Jo," he commanded softly, firmly.

His tone made her come to a halt and face him. "Aye, husband?"

His blue eyes were glittering, reflecting the magnificent colors of the sunset. Slowly, he closed the distance between them. His eyes remained fixed on her.

"I did not believe you were attempting to extract vital information from me," he said quietly. "But there are certain things, especially pertaining to my command of Berwick, that do not concern you. It is better that you do not know."

She gazed up at him openly. "Why? Because I am the daughter of your enemy?"

He almost looked amused. "Nay," he took her hand and brought it to his lips. "Because you are a lovely, delicate woman and things involving war should not trouble you. I would have you worry over things like the evening meal or the latest fashion, not rebels or a burning city. I do not want you to worry over anything serious and deadly."

"So you would rather have me live in ignorance?"

He gave her a lopsided grin. "I would rather protect you. You should not be burdened with the realities of war."

She watched him kiss her hand gently. She could see that he was being sincere. "Although I appreciate your desire to protect me, the truth is that war is our reality," she told him softly. "It is what brought us together. It is what constitutes our life. You must not worry about protecting me. I have seen much in life. I understand the realities of it."

His smile faded. "But that was before you married me. As your husband, I should like to shield you from unsavory things. I do not want you to have a care in this world other than me and our life together. Does that make any sense?"

She put her hand up, touching his freshly shaved cheek. "Of course it does," she agreed. "But you cannot put me in a glass house for the rest of my life. It is my nature to want to help, to do what I can for you and those I care about. I would feel useless and bored if my only cares were what to prepare for supper or what dress I will wear tomorrow. Will you not let me be a true partner to you and not simply a wife in name and body only?"

He gazed into her pale blue eyes, feeling her sincerity, seeing a stronger, deeper side to this woman he had married. There was a good deal of strength in the petite little body. It made him love her all the more.

"I never thought to have a wife at all much less one who wants to do more than simply carry my name," he said, kissing her fingers again. "Where should we begin?"

She smiled, rubbing her hand against his smooth cheek. "You can tell me who you have in the vault. If I know him, perhaps I can tell you what I know of him. Perhaps it will help you."

"You would betray one of your kinsmen?"

"I would help my husband. I told you, my loyalty became yours when we married."

Time will tell, Stephen thought. But he would give her the benefit of the doubt until she proved otherwise. His heart told him to trust her even if his head was still reluctant.

"Kynan Lott MacKenzie," he finally said.

Joselyn's pale blue eyes widened and her mouth popped open again. "Ky?"

"He is your cousin, I believe."

"How did you know that?" she demanded softly.

"He told me."

Her mouth was still hanging agape. She was struggling with her surprise. Stephen watched her carefully, analyzing her reaction. An unbridled response would tell him a good deal about the loyalties in her heart; Scots or her English husband. He prayed it was the latter, anything less would devastate him.

Joselyn closed her mouth and blinked away her surprised expression. "Aye, he is my cousin," she concurred. "His mother and my mother were sisters. I saw much of him as I was growing up."

She spoke without hesitation or reserve which made him feel better. He did not get the sense she was hiding anything so he moved forward.

"Tell me what you know of him," he asked.

She tucked her hand into his enormous elbow and, pensively, they resumed their walk. "He is older than me," she said. "He was my aunt's only child and a brother of sorts to me."

He shook his head. "That is not what I meant. I meant tell me what you know of him as a fighting man."

She shrugged. "All I know is what I heard from my father," she told him. "Ky commanded about five hundred MacKenzie and McCulloch men who my father used to attack the English on a regular basis. If you know anything about the Clan McCulloch, then you know they are aggressive and without fear. They will attack with rabid fury and were the most aggressive of my father's men. If I remember correctly, they were at the battle of Halidon."

His brow furrowed. "How would you know that?"

"I heard my father talking about them."

Stephen fell silent, digesting what she had told him. *Five hundred men*. Since the rebels had been quite aggressive since Berwick surrendered to the English, it was possible that Kynan's men were involved. But MacKenzie had not confessed to that, not even when Stephen had threatened to take his insubordination out on Joselyn. In fact, Kynan hadn't been particularly helpful with anything. Either the man was particularly clever or he truly didn't know anything, which Stephen found difficult to believe.

"Do you think he has been leading the rebel attacks?" Joselyn's soft voice interrupted his thoughts.

He looked down at her. "It is possible that he has some responsibility for them. But he was bottled up in the vault during the siege yesterday and therefore had no direct involvement in that particular incident."

Joselyn's brow furrowed as they made their way to the northeast turret. Stephen could see Ian in the distance, standing tall and lanky near the dark tower, and he was distracted. But Joselyn's thoughts were still on her cousin, down in the depths of Berwick's vault. Kynan was no fool. He was a seasoned soldier. Her father had told her that the man was quite cunning.

"Have you asked him what he knows?" she asked.

Stephen's focus shifted off of Ian and back to Kynan as he thought of the two days of interrogation and the sparse information it had brought forth in spite of their best tactics.

"Aye."

"Has he told you anything useful?"

"I would not worry about that if I were you."

It was his way of telling her that it was none of her affair. She had figured that out quickly. But she persisted.

"Would you like me to find out if he knows anything more?" she asked, so soft he barely heard her.

He came to a halt and peered at her as if she had lost her mind. "What?" It was all he could think to say.

She faced him with waning confidence. The look in his eye was not one of agreement. "I asked if you would like for me to find out," she offered again. "He might tell me things he would not tell you."

Stephen stared at her a moment before his brow furrowed in disbelief. "Jo-Jo, although I appreciate your offer, my answer is a resounding nay," he told her, almost sternly. "I would not be so unscrupulous as to use my own wife for subversive means."

Her mouth twisted with the rejection, thinking on how to explain what it was she was suggesting. "I know you would not," she said quickly. "You are a wise and moral man. But if there is a chance my cousin will confide in me what he knows about the rebel activities, then will you not at least consider it?"

"No," he said flatly, noticing that Ian had seen him in the distance and lifted an arm to him. "Come along, I still have rounds to make."

"Stephen, wait," she grabbed hold of his arm and dug her heels in. "I am not trying to anger you, truly, but please consider what I am saying. If there is a chance I can get information for you that will save lives, I am willing to do that. Berwick cannot take another siege. She is already shattered."

He came to a halt but his jaw was ticking faintly as he looked at her. "Sweetheart, I appreciate your offer. I sincerely do. But I will not involve you in things that do not concern you."

"Do not *concern* me?" she repeated, incensed. "Of course they concern me. Every time you lift your sword for a battle, it concerns me. Every time an innocent person dies as the result of men who do not know when they are defeated, it concerns me. Many men died as a result of this latest siege. If I can help you prevent another occurrence, you should at least let me try."

"Is this what you meant by offering to help?"

Her lovely brow scrunched up and she half shrugged, half nodded. "Aye, I suppose it was. I have been offering to help you since practically the hour we were married. This is something I believe I can truly help you with. I know Kynan will talk to me."

He grunted and turned away from her, unwilling to agree with her. But Joselyn remained fixed in place as he walked away, feeling her anguish rise, unable to fathom why he was being so stubborn.

"Do you not understand, husband?" she called after him. "It is your life I am trying to save."

Her words were nearly shouted. Stephen came to an unsteady halt, sighed heavily, and turned around to face her. She was about twenty feet away, standing there with tears in her eyes. He could see them. With another sigh, this one of regret, he retraced his steps, watching her wipe away the errant tears before he came too close. He was staunchly, absolutely against what she was suggesting. He did not want her involved in the dirty dealings of war and politics. But her offer was both noble and brave. It impressed him. By the time he reached her, he couldn't think of anything else to do but reach out and pull her against him. She threw her arms around his waist and squeezed him tightly.

"Jo-Jo," he muttered into the top of her head, kissing it. "Sweetheart, you are very courageous and selfless to make such an offer. I understand you are trying to help. But I would keep you as far away from war and politics as I can. I do not want you involved in such things. Do you not understand that I am trying to protect you?"

She looked up at him, her pale blue eyes watery. "And do you not understand that I am fearful that the next raid might bring about your death? You are the Guardian Protector of Berwick, Stephen. It would be a great victory for the Scots to kill you and I simply cannot stomach the thought."

He smiled gently at her. "They are not going to kill me."

She shook her head and shoved her face into his chest. "You cannot know that. You cannot know the errant arrow or hidden dagger that would claim your life."

He held her close. "That is true," he agreed softly. "But I have managed to stay alive for thirty-seven years and have become quite good at it."

She didn't like his attempt at humor. "All my life," she murmured against his tunic. "All my life I have been haunted with sorrow and bad fortune. I never even imagined I would ever marry much less marry a man who has accepted me as I am. I know happiness now that I never dreamed possible." She lifted her head to look at him. "If I lost you there would be nothing left to live for. I would throw myself from the battlements and never doubt for a moment that it was the right thing to do. I could not live without you by my side."

The smile had faded from his face as he gazed deep into her pure blue eyes. He gently cupped her face in his enormous hands, studying her, feeling her passion and sincerity that touched him deeply.

"You would do me a greater honor by continuing to live your life in dignity and wisdom," he replied. "For everyone to see that Pembury's wife was a lady of strength and honor would do me the greatest glory. I could ask for no better legacy."

As he watched, her eyes filled with tears and her lower lip trembled. "I would not want to live without you."

He kissed her nose. "But you would. I would ask this of you as a fitting tribute to our love."

"Will you please let me help you?"

"I am deeply appreciative of your offer but again I must decline."

She began to cry softly and he rocked her gently, cradling her against him. The sun was almost completely down and the city below was alive with cooking fires. He let his gaze settle on the city a moment as he held his wife, immersing himself in her warmth and softness. She was such a sweet, delightful creature and he was very sorry she was upset. But he would not, under any circumstances, grant her request, as difficult as it had been for him to deny her.

Soft footsteps came from behind him and he turned slightly to see Ian standing there, uncertain. The young knight cleared his throat softly.

"My lord," he said timidly, eyeing Lady Pembury buried in her husband's arms. "The posts have reported in. Will you hear the information?"

Stephen nodded, preparing to gently release his wife when she suddenly pulled free, turning her back on the men so she could compose herself.

"Go ahead," she said. "I shall wait here for you and enjoy the views of the city."

Stephen's gaze lingered on her. "I will be a brief moment."

She nodded, wiping at her eyes. As she took a few deep breaths for calm and focused on the city below, Stephen and Ian moved several feet away, locked in quiet discussion. The more they inched away, the more Joselyn inched in the other direction. She kept turning around to glance at her husband to see if he had noticed. He was quite a distance away, listening seriously to Ian's report. When he turned his back on her completely, Joselyn silently made her way back towards the gatehouse. It did not matter if he had denied her or not. She knew she had to do as she must.

She knew where the vault was.

CHAPTER NINE

THE SOLDIERS WEREN'T sure what to do at first.

An aggressive woman identifying herself as Lady Pembury was demanding to see one of the prisoners and, not knowing the true identity of the woman with the slight Scottish burr, they grabbed her and threw her in the nearest cell because she would not leave when they told her to. But the cell they tossed her into also fortuitously contained Kynan Lott MacKenzie, who was beside himself with astonishment when his well-dressed and lovely cousin was thrown unceremoniously into the cramped vault with him and nine other men. His mouth flew open at the site of little Jo-Jo Seton.

Everyone in his cell was chained to varying degrees so no one could make a swipe for her. Her safety was not truly in jeopardy. Somewhat terrified but wildly happy she had ended up in Kynan's cell, Joselyn made her way over to her cousin against the far wall. She put her arms around his neck and hugged him tightly.

"Ky," she pulled back, looking into his dirty and bruised face. "Are you well? Have they injured you?"

Kynan shook his head, his still-astonished gaze moving over his cousin. "Jo-Jo," he breathed. "Are ye well, lass? What have they done tae ye?"

She shook her head as his rant gained volume. "They have not done anything to me. I am uninjured," she added for effect, "for the moment."

Kynan studied his beautiful young cousin, a look of extreme sorrow on his face. "Oh, Jo-Jo," he moaned softly. "The big English knight told me he'd married ye. Is it true?"

Joselyn's smile faded somewhat. Once Stephen noticed she was missing, she knew he would suspect where she had gone. Time was therefore limited and she was determined to find out what she could before Stephen found her and dragged her out by the feet. She was willing to risk his wrath in order to help him. And she was willing to betray her kin.

"'Tis true," she crouched next to Kynan, playing the part of the fearful Scot. She hoped the performance was good enough. "King Edward forced me to marry him to form an alliance between the English and the Scots. They sent my father to the dungeons of Alnwick Castle. You must help me, Ky. I must get away from here."

Kynan rattled his chains. "I canna help ye, lass. They have me caged like a beast."

Joselyn grabbed his arms desperately. "Then tell me where I can go, who will hide me. I must get away from my husband where he cannot find me."

Kynan looked as stricken as she sounded. "Jo-Jo, would that I could help ye, lass. I canna do anything tae help ye."

Joselyn was becoming caught up in her act. Tears popped into her eyes. "They killed my mother," she began to weep. "They will kill me next. Please tell me where to go. I must flee!"

Kynan's expression slackened. "Julia," he repeated, shocked. "The English bastards killed her?"

Joselyn nodded, her hand against her mouth in a dramatic attempt to hold back the sobs. "Aye," she whispered. "Please help me, Ky."

He stared at her, feeling helpless and furious at the same time. "I dunna know what I can do," he muttered. "There was a battle last night. I dunna know where me men are now."

"What do you mean?"

"I dunna know where they were holed up. I canna send ye out into the world if I dunna know where they are, tae take ye in tae a safe haven."

"But I must escape to them. Please help me, Ky. You must tell me where to go."

Kynan was torn. His young cousin was truly distraught and it never occurred to him not to believe her. He was simply afraid that her husband, the big English hound, would track her and by doing so, find his men. She would lead him right to them. But he could not refuse to help his cousin, not when she had suffered from such a terrible life now made worse by a forced marriage. Aye, he knew about the life that Uncle Alexander had put her through. It was a deep family shame. He found he was desperate to aid her, to help her break free.

"Go south on the main road towards the cemetery," he hissed at her. "There's a church. Find the priest. He'll tell ye where tae hide."

Joselyn squeezed his arms gratefully. "Thank you," she murmured with great relief. "To know that I can escape to safety means the world to me."

They could suddenly hear banging and voices coming from the entry to the gatehouse. Men were calling to each other and voices were being raised. Someone was calling someone else an idiot. The man sounded angry. Eyes wide, Joselyn remained crouched next to Kynan, still clutching the man's arm. It did not take long before Ian appeared at the cell door. His dark eyes fixed on her, at the far end of the cell.

"Lady Pembury," he motioned angrily to the jailer to open the door. "What are you doing in here? Your husband is searching for you, my lady."

"I was visiting my cousin," she told him.

Ian was beckoning to her. "This is no place for you, my lady. Please come with me immediately."

With a heavy sigh that sounded to Kynan like a sob, Joselyn rose and went to the cell door that was now opening. Kynan watched her pass through it, into the possessive grip of the same English knight who had beat him.

God help her, he thought grimly.

❦

JOSELYN AND IAN ran into Stephen just as they were exiting the vault.

Stephen's eyes fixed on his wife with great relief and a shadow of irritation. Ian had her by the arm, leading her towards her husband.

"She was in the vault, my lord," Ian handed her over to her husband. "She said that she was visiting her cousin."

The relief in Stephen's eyes cooled as he gazed down at her. "I see," he rumbled, focusing on his wife. "I went to our chamber to see if you had returned there. I sent Ian to the vault on the chance that you might have disobeyed me. I see that you have."

Joselyn made the only tactical move she could make, considering he was correct to be angry with her. She didn't like the look in his eye. She threw her arms around his waist and buried her face in his tunic.

"Forgive me," she begged softly. "I had to try. I felt strongly that I had to try. I cannot see you fight another battle that might result in your death. Please do not be angry with me."

She was prattling and Stephen's annoyance faded. He was simply glad she was safe, whether or not she had disobeyed him. If he was honest with himself, he knew she had gone there all along. She had, if nothing else, great determination. With a sigh, he put his big hand on her head, buried against his chest, and turned her for the keep.

"Alright, sweetheart, alright," he shushed her gently. "I am not angry. But I am disappointed that you would not respect my wishes."

"I am sorry," she repeated, genuinely contrite. "But I was sure he would tell me things that he would not tell you and if I can prevent another battle, Stephen, I feel very strongly that I must do so. Would you let me die if you could prevent such a thing?"

They were approaching the dark, towering keep. "I already do," he said quietly as they entered the door. "Everything I do, I do to keep you safe. Yet you seem intent on fighting me at times."

He helped her up the steep spiral stairs. "It is not my intention to fight you," she said as they reached the landing. "But if I can help you create peace for Berwick, why do you not let me?"

They reached the chamber and Stephen opened the door. "Must I go through this with you again?" he sighed.

Joselyn entered the room, realizing that Mereld or Tilda must have come in because the fire was stoked and there was food on the small table. She went over and sat on the bed. She suddenly didn't feel like arguing with him any longer.

"Nay," she said with defeat, averting her eyes. "You do not."

He watched her dark head, his blue eyes glimmering at her. He removed his big leather gloves and set them on the table.

"Shall we eat?" he asked. "Someone has gone to the trouble to bring us food."

She shook her head, still looking away from him. "I am not hungry."

He went over to the bed, took her by the hand, and pulled her to stand. Leading her over to the little table, he sat in the oak chair and pulled her onto his lap. He began ripping the bread apart, handing her the soft white middle.

"Was disobeying me worth the effort?" Stephen asked softly as he shoved a piece of bread into his mouth.

Joselyn looked at him. "What do you mean?"

"Did he tell you what you wanted to know?"

She pondered his question with a sinking heart. If she told him the truth, then Stephen would take a battalion of men to the church that Kynan had described. All he would succeed in doing would be scattering the rebels and possibly getting himself killed in the process. The thought sickened her. It sickened her more that she was about to lie to him, convinced she could do what he could not. Kynan's men would trust her. Perhaps she could convince them to surrender. It was a foolish thought but the idea of Stephen lying dead with an arrow through his heart made her think foolish, desperate thoughts.

"He told me that he was caged like a beast," she said, forcing the soft white bread to her mouth and chewing slowly. "He wanted to know how I was. You told him that we were married?"

Stephen moved for the hunk of warmed-over mutton with just a hint of his wife's marvelous sauce from the day before. "I did," he took a big bite. "I wanted him to know that I was now his kin."

"Why?"

He looked at her. "Because it will give him pause, knowing he is related to me, before trying something foolish against me."

She lifted a dark eyebrow at him. "Scots fight whomever they choose, whenever they choose. It matters not if they battle kin or strangers."

His blue eyes twinkled. "Perhaps," he agreed, chewing the mutton. "But I wanted to give the man something new to consider next time he orders his rebels to attack."

Joselyn lifted her shoulders, chewing her bread as if it were made of sawdust. Stephen watched her as she forced herself to eat, fighting off a grin. They finished eating in silence. Joselyn had, in fact, finished long before he had, unable to stomach more to eat. Her thoughts were dark, lingering on what Kynan had told her, formulating a plan that would save her husband. She could think of little else.

When Stephen finally finished eating, it was well into evening but he was not tired, having slept all day. He had duties to return to but was reluctant to leave his wife. Not simply because of their conversation of the past several minutes but because, quite simply, he did not want to be without her. In spite of what happened up on the wall, he rather enjoyed having her with him. But she could not go with him where he needed to go and he stood up with his wife still on his lap, scooping her up as he rose. Without a word, he carried her over to their bed and set her gently upon it.

"I must return to the walls for now," he told her. "I will return in a few hours."

She stood up from the bed, her eyes big as she gazed up at him. "Do you fear more trouble this night?"

He lifted his shoulders, moving for the armor he had propped up against the wall earlier in the day. He began to methodically don it.

"Not in particular," he replied, watching her as she moved forward to help him with his leather buckles. "But we must be vigilant."

She focused on fastening his greaves to his shins as he held the armor in place. There was hesitance in her voice as she spoke, as if she did not want to rehash everything they had so recently discussed. He knew her fears on the subject well enough. It would do no good to repeat them. Moreover, she did not want to make him suspicious that Kynan had told her more than she had let on.

"I would have you be careful, then," she said softly. "As I said, you are the Guardian Protector of Berwick. It would be a great prize for a Scots to plant an arrow in your chest."

Stephen felt her mood, the sorrow she was radiating, and he began to feel some remorse for having so strongly resisted her attempts to help him. When he should have been glad that she was not arguing with him about it, he began to feel some regret. Truth be told, he was deeply touched that she was so concerned for him. He'd never had someone so deeply concerned for his welfare.

"Have no fear, wife," he said softly, watching the top of her dark head. "I have a reason to survive the night."

She looked up at him with questioning eyes. "What is that?"

He smiled warmly, pulling her to her feet and into his arms. "I have you," he brushed his lips across her nose. "You give me reason enough to live."

Her mood relented somewhat and she put her hands on his cheeks as he kissed her face. "I am sorry I disobeyed you," she whispered. "I never wish to upset you. But if my disobedience can save your life, I will gladly make that choice every time."

He stopped kissing her long enough to fix her in the eye. He sighed heavily. "We are never going to agree on this subject."

"I fear not."

"You are a stubborn wench."

She lifted her shoulders with a proud flair. "I am Scots."

He pursed his lips as he shook his head. "Scots has nothing to do with it. You are a woman, that is reason enough."

A twinkle of mirth came to her eye and the hands on his cheeks pinched them gently. "I am a woman in love who would do anything to keep you safe," the mirth from her eyes fading as she gazed into his cornflower blue orbs. "Please remember that, Stephen. Everything I do, I do because I love you and would do anything to ensure we have a long and happy life together."

He nodded in resignation, kissing the tip of her nose again as he gently released her. "I know," he reached over for the breast plate propped against the wall. "Let us not delve into that subject again. Help me finish with this. The sooner I take the wall, he sooner I will return to you."

She watched him as he donned the remainder of his armor, not at all sure that he truly understood her position. More and more, she knew what she needed to do. She needed to help end this conflict because every time her husband took the wall or went on patrol, the chance of his death was magnified. Every time he returned to her whole, she considered it a stroke of good luck. She feared that the luck would not hold out indefinitely. With every second that passed, she felt more and more strongly that she must protect him. She had to do something.

Stephen noticed that she would not look him in the eye as she finished helping him with his armor. He attributed it to the fact that she was upset with the events of the evening. When she finally finished securing the last strap on his torso armor, he put a finger on her sternum. When she looked down to see what he was doing, his finger came up and bopped her gently on the nose. Rubbing her nose, she looked up at him only to see that he was grinning at her. Reluctantly, she grinned back.

"You will stay here where I know you are safe," he put his big hands on her upper arms. "Lock the door after I leave. Is that clear?"

"Aye," she nodded as she stopped rubbing her nose. "But I was hoping to check on the fawn."

He shook his head. "I am sure the fawn is safe and fed in the kitchens where you last left him," he told her. "If it will make you feel better,

I shall go and check on him myself."

She agreed. "Thank you."

He winked at her, bending down to kiss her sweetly on the lips. Joselyn threw her arms around his neck and met his kiss passionately, to which Stephen quickly succumbed. Hungrily, they licked and suckled at each other until he finally groaned and pulled away.

"Any more of that and I shall never make it to my post," he growled, although he stole one last kiss. "I shall return."

She nodded, gazing up at him with her pale blue eyes and kiss-swollen lips. She looked quite demure and obedient as he picked up his helm and winked at her again as he quit the chamber. Dutifully, she bolted it after he left. She purposely bolted it loudly so he would hear it and then she leaned against the door, her ear pressed to the wood as she listened to his footfalls fade.

Moving to the lancet window, she peered outside to the portion of the bailey she could see from her vantage point and was rewarded by the sight of her massive husband as he crossed the bailey towards the kitchens. Just watching him walk made her feel warm and giddy. The man's stride was confident and powerful. Every moment that passed saw her love him that much more. And she had to protect that love at any cost. She only hoped he could forgive her for her necessary deception.

Quickly, she went to work. Stripping off her surcoat, she dressed in one of her newer surcoats, the dark blue with the long, belled sleeves. The dark color would blend well into the night. She dressed warmly, finally wrapping herself in the dusty Seton tartan. All the while, she planned in her mind over and over what she was to do, where she was to go. Kynan had told her to head south on the main road towards the cemetery. She knew the area. She was to seek the priest at the church near the cemetery.

Joselyn was smart enough to wait until the changing of the guards to make her move and slip through the postern gate leading to the river. Wrapped in the dark tartan, the guards never saw her in the shadows under the silver moon. Like a night wraith, she slipped along the wall and into the river, making her way down the river in shoulder-deep water until coming ashore about a half mile downriver.

Wet and cold, she persevered on towards the main road leading out of town.

⁂

THE FAWN WAS fat, warm and happy in the corner of the kitchen where Mereld and Tilda had been feeding the little thing. It bleated at him and attempted to suckle his fingers when he tried to pet it. Leaving his wife's very spoiled pet to its happy corner, Stephen made his way across the darkened bailey towards the gatehouse, the massive structure lit by torches against the night sky. As Stephen drew close, he came across de Lara emerging from the warm and stuffy great hall. Stephen came to a halt as Tate caught up to him.

"So," Stephen said with a twinkle in his eye. "Have you recovered from your brush with death?"

Tate grinned wearily. "Damnable Scots," he grumbled. "It simply underscores my need to return home."

Stephen grunted. "When are you leaving?"

"At dawn," Tate replied. "But I am not heading straight home. I intend to take a detour to Earl of Buccleuch."

Stephen sobered. "Thank you," he said softly. "Will you escort the lad back to Berwick?"

"I thought I would."

"Will your wife wait that much longer for you to return home?"

Tate made a pensive and apprehensive face, as men do who fear the reaction of a woman. "She will have to. A few more days will not make much difference in the end."

"Perhaps," Stephen lifted an eyebrow. "But if she turns her anger on me since this is an errand on my behalf, know that I intend to point all necessary fingers back at you. I do not want to suffer the wrath of Lady de Lara."

Tate shook his head. "Coward," he muttered, scratching his chin as he sobered. "About the boy, how much do you want me to tell him?"

Stephen shrugged faintly. "I am not entirely sure," he said. "You have four young boys. I would solicit your advice on the subject."

Tate exhaled wearily, gazing up at the stars. "I can tell him the purpose of returning to Berwick to soften the blow," he looked at Stephen. "Or I can simply wait and let you tell him. You will be the boy's father, after all. It might be best coming from you."

"But he will have more time to understand and accept the situation if you tell him," Stephen countered thoughtfully, crossing his big arms and kicking at the dirt beneath is feet. "Perhaps Joselyn should tell him. She is his mother, after all."

"That is more than likely the best option."

"Agreed."

Before Tate could continue the conversation, Lane appeared out of the darkness. Stephen did not like the look on the man's face as he approached.

"What is it?" he asked before Lane could speak.

Lane didn't look particularly eager to tell him but knew there was little choice. "I was seeing to the changing of the guard about the hall, keep and bailey," he explained quickly. "With the guard changing in the keep, I happened to see one of your wife's women as she was leaving your chamber. When I asked if her mistress was settled for the night, the woman faltered. There was something in her expression, my lord, that made me suspect all was not as it should be. So I...."

Stephen's jaw flexed dangerously and he was already moving towards the keep. "To the point, de Norville."

Lane and Tate began to run after him. "Your wife is not in her room, my lord," Lane almost shouted at him and Stephen came to an abrupt halt. His blue eyes blazed at the sergeant, who continued rapidly and succinctly. "I have already sent men to get horses. We sighted your wife from the postern gate about a quarter of a mile downriver."

"What?" Stephen exploded, incredulous. "Are you sure?"

"Aye, my lord," Lane replied, feeling as if he had grossly failed in his newly appointed post. "The old serving woman confirmed as much."

"Damnation," Stephen spat in an uncharacteristic display of emotion as he whirled for the stables. "Did you ask the woman where my wife was going?"

"Nay," Lane replied quickly as they rounded the corner of the hall and headed to the stables that smelled strongly of hay and dung. "I thought it more important to find you and tell you that your wife has left the castle. There will be time enough for interrogation when we recover her."

By the time they reached the stables, several soldiers were already emerging with their mounts. Two grooms were saddling the chargers and in little time, Stephen was mounted and with a contingent of a dozen armed men, they roared from the open gates of Berwick and out into the deepening night.

Stephen couldn't even imagine where Joselyn was going. He struggled to stay on an even keel because something deep inside him couldn't fathom the worst. He felt sick to his stomach as her last words to him suddenly made some sense. *Everything I do, I do because I love you and would do anything to ensure we have a long and happy life together.* He couldn't imagine what the foolish woman was up to.

He had to find her.

CHAPTER TEN

IN HER RIVER-WET garments, Joselyn was extremely cold. The night was not particularly chilly but the wet wool was clinging to her skin, rendering her shaky and cold. However, walking briskly was heating her up, creating an odd body temperature. In the recesses of her mind she knew she would become ill from all of this, but it didn't matter. She had to find the old churchyard on the edge of town. It was her own personal mission.

So she trudged down the road, trying to stay to the edge where hedgerows grew so that she could stay out of sight. She only hoped she could make it back to the castle before Stephen discovered her missing, but somehow, she knew that he would find out. The man was as sharp as a knife, his mind and intellect were keen, and as she half-ran and half-walked down the road, she began to wonder if this undertaking had been at all wise. If Stephen discovered her missing, she would have to come up with a plausible explanation as to why she had left. She could not tell him the truth because it would only bring about her fear of him rousting the rebels himself and possibly getting himself killed in the process. So she had to think of another explanation, a lie that would save her husband's life.

The road was empty due to the many battles that had rattled the area for the past several weeks. Joselyn walked past several homes and businesses that were ruined. The sight of the burned-out structures distressed her but she pushed onward, her focus on the church that was not too far off. The darkness around her buzzed with night birds and foraging creatures as she picked up the pace; she had no time to lose.

Eventually, the hedgerow of heavy bushes disappeared and she could see the church off to her right in the distance, outlined against the dark sky. There were no lights apparent. The structure appeared dark and ghostly. She slowed her pace as she drew closer, keeping out of sight as much as she could. Her sight was fixed on the stone building in the distance. She paused completely, watching the church to see if there were any signs of life. There was none. After several long minutes of waiting and watching, she carefully moved on.

As she stepped out of the shadow of the edge of the hedgerow and began to cross the dark field that separated her from the church, the thunder of hooves sudden approached from behind. Startled, she could see several soldiers heading towards her from the road and she bolted in the opposite direction, racing towards the church. But another group of horses abruptly came at her from the other side of the hedgerow, cutting off her flight. Very shortly, she was trapped.

Terrified, Joselyn clutched the tartan around her as big men on horseback surrounded her. It was a dark night and it was difficult to tell immediately if the men were Scots or English. It was chaotic, dark, and the horses were snapping. She instinctively recoiled. But one of the men dismounted and even in the darkness, she realized that she knew the man. There was no mistaking the size of her husband and her heart sank at the sight. Somehow, someway, he had found her. Her mission to save him was over before it began.

"Oh, Stephen," she breathed, with sorrow. "How did you find me?"

Stephen's eyes were appraising as he gazed down at her from his lifted visor. He just stood there a moment, looking at her, before shaking his head in bafflement.

"What are you doing?" he asked simply.

"Are you going to beat me?"

He just shook his head again, this time with disgust. "Do you honestly feel the need to ask that?"

She blinked, knowing she had been righteously caught. She had taken a chance and it had failed. Every time she tried to help the man, to take matters into her own hands by trying to do something to aid the peace of Berwick, she managed to fail. Perhaps she should simply give up and trust that Stephen would not get himself killed. He'd been keeping himself alive for many years before she met him. Perhaps she simply needed to have faith in him. Gazing into his suspicious eyes, she realized that she needed to tell him everything and tell him quickly. No lies, no evasiveness. As it was, he thought she was about to betray him. She could read it in his face.

"Nay," she swallowed, pulling the tartan off her head and letting it fall to the ground. It was a gesture of defeat, not unnoticed by Stephen. Her shoulders slumped as she forced herself to look him in the eye. "I do not need to ask that question for I already know the answer. But you may change your mind. I lied to you. I lied to you because I felt I could do what you could not."

He maintained his even expression, though there was wariness to it. "And what is that?"

"Find the rebels. Find them and discover what their plans were."

He just looked at her. "For what purpose?"

Her pale blue eyes glimmered in the weak moonlight. "So I could tell you. Then the next time they attacked, you would be ready. Perhaps you could defeat them once and for all and stop this madness that continues to perpetuate itself. So much fighting and dying, Stephen. I told you that I did not want you to be a casualty. If I can prevent your death, I will. I would do it a thousand times over. I would die if it meant you would live. Do you still not understand that, husband?" Tears began to fill her eyes. "Everything I do, I do because I love you and would do anything to ensure we have a long and happy life together."

He began to understand what was going on and his shock at her escape, his disappointment at finding her far from the castle, began to fade. Perhaps he was a fool to believe her, but he did. He simply couldn't believe anything else.

"So your cousin did indeed give you information," he ventured quietly.

"Aye."

"What did he tell you?"

She looked extremely guilty. "He told me to go south on the main road towards the cemetery," she looked over her shoulder at the darkened church in the distance. "He said that the priest would tell me where the rebels were."

Stephen looked at the church also, as did a few other men who happened to hear what she said. "The priest is part of the rebellion?" he glanced up at Lane and Tate, who were gazing down from their mounts as the situation unfolded. Noting their uneasy expressions, he refocused on Joselyn. "If that is true, then we are exposed here. God only knows who could be lingering about, watching us even now. We must return to the castle immediately."

He grasped Joselyn by the arm and led her over to his charger. "But now that you know, are you not going to confront them?" she asked.

"Not with only a few men," he grasped her around her slender waist and lifted her up into the saddle, noticing her clothes as he did so. "You are all wet. You will be lucky if you do not catch your death of chill."

He was scolding her, much more mildly than she deserved and she knew it. "I am sorry," she said softly, painfully. "I thought I could help. I truly did."

"We will discuss it later. Right now, we must return to Berwick."

"Are you angry with me?"

"Furious."

"Do you hate me, then?"

He didn't reply and she shut her mouth, tears spilling over. He had every right to be angry and hateful, and she was beginning to feel like the most worthless fool in the world. But those thoughts were cut short when something cold, powerful and painful suddenly plowed into her back.

Stephen heard the high-pitched whine of the arrow a split second before it hit Joselyn, sitting high and exposed on the saddle. Horrified, he caught her before she could topple, somehow managing to mount with her in his arms as Tate began to bellow orders to the men. Soon, they were scattering back to the road, thundering at top speed back towards the castle. Stephen could only feel complete terror as Joselyn lay limp in his arms, a nasty arrow protruding from her back. He honestly didn't even know if she was alive. Never in his life had he known panic, not for himself but for Joselyn. He was clearly experiencing it now and it was more than he could comprehend. It was a nightmare.

More arrows sailed overhead as they retreated down the road but there was no rebel army to follow. There was not even any shouting or screaming as the Scots liked to do; simply an odd, dead silence with the ambush of arrows. The retreating English reached Berwick in little time, de Lara rousing the fortress on high alert as they passed through the massive gatehouse. Tate was off his horse as Stephen raced through the gate, extending his arms for the unconscious Lady Pembury as Stephen reined his charger to a halt. The woman slid off into his embrace as Stephen, in his haste, nearly fell off his mount behind her.

"Watch the arrow," Stephen's deep voice was quivering as he took a moment to examine his wife. "Do not jostle it. Hold her still."

Tate had Joselyn in a bear hug, her arms and head over one shoulder as he held her carefully around her torso. She was completely lifeless as Stephen examined her with shaking hands. The first thing he did was feel her neck for a pulse. It was weak and rapid. The sigh of relief that came out of his mouth was nothing Tate had ever heard out of the man. It was like the exhale of a dying man, venting emotion never before experienced.

"Get her up to our chamber," Stephen commanded hoarsely. "I need to remove this arrow."

"Stephen," Tate was extremely concerned with the man's pale face and shaking hands. "Perhaps I need to send for a physic. I have a very fine surgeon within my ranks and...."

"No," Stephen snapped, his jaw ticking furiously. "I will not trust the life of my wife to anyone but me."

"I did not mean to suggest otherwise," Tate could see how disturbed the man was, completely out of character for the normally in-control knight. "I simply meant as an extra pair of trained hands."

Stephen didn't reply. Tate was not even sure he really understood what he was suggesting but he let it go. Lane and a couple of soldiers had already raced ahead to the keep, throwing open doors so there would be no delay in getting Lady Pembury to her bed. Stephen had Tate by the arm as the two of them moved as quickly as they could to the great keep of Berwick, maneuvering the narrow stairs to the chamber on the third floor.

Entering the chamber, Stephen began to rip off pieces of armor, tossing the protection into the corner with a great ruckus. He tore his gloves off, reaching out to carefully take his wife from Tate. Between the two of them, they managed to turn her around and lay her on her stomach. Stephen fell to his knees beside the bed, demanding his medicament bag, which someone put next to him. His hands went to the arrow that was embedded just beneath his wife's right shoulder blade.

It was in a bad spot. Stephen knew just by looking at it and his heart sank. Many vital veins ran through the area and his concerns multiplied. He struggled to compose himself, to maintain his control, as he carefully began to peel away the material around the wound to gain a better look. After several long moments of close examination, he finally let out a heavy sigh and raked his fingers through his dark hair in a frustrated gesture.

"What is it?" Tate was standing next to him. "What do you need, Stephen?"

Stephen had to shake his head to clear his vision, his mind. He rubbed at his eyes, struggling to think clearly. "The wound is not bleeding much, which concerns me," his voice was raspy. "This is a very vital area with a good deal of blood flow, so I suspect the arrow is acting like a barrier and preventing her from bleeding to death. Removing the head will be like undamming a river; everything will flow."

Tate crouched down next to him, watching the man's big fingers dance gently over Joselyn's slender back. He could feel the man's grief as it radiated out of every pore of his body. "What will you do?" he asked.

Stephen inhaled deeply, clearing the last of the panic from his mind. He had to think clearly if Joselyn had any hope of surviving. He knew what had to be done, as he had done this kind of thing before, many times. But never on someone he loved.

"Send for your surgeon," he said. "I will need an experienced assistant. And find the serving women and tell them I need boiled linen, all they can manage, and hot water."

Tate relayed the orders to Lane, standing just inside the door, and the man went on the run. Meanwhile, Stephen continued peeling back the torn and bloodied material away from the wound, trying to think professionally about the injury and not from the position of the emotional husband. It was extremely difficult. When the material was pulled away sufficiently and he touched the arrow shaft again just to see how deeply it was buried, Joselyn suddenly let out a groan.

Stephen was down beside her in an instant, his face looming next to hers. "Jo-Jo?" he asked gently. "Can you hear me, sweetheart?"

Her pale blue eyes remained shut but her lower lip began to tremble. Tears began flowing from her eyes.

"It hurts," she whispered.

Stephen thought he could very well cry himself at her declaration. "I know," he kissed her wet face gently. "I'm so sorry. I know it hurts."

"What happened?" she breathed.

He wiped the tears from her face. "An arrow," he murmured. "We were ambushed."

"Are you all right?"

"I am."

She sighed faintly. "Then I am content," she whispered. "But I am sorry. I... brought this about. I should not have... I should have told you...."

She faded off and he kissed her cheek again, her limp hand. "Not to worry," he said softly. "It was not your fault. I will heal you as good as new."

She twitched, crying out softly when excruciating pain radiated throughout her body. The tears fell faster. "Please," she breathed. "It hurts so much. Please... remove it."

Stephen kissed her hand, her face. "I will, love, I promise."

He began to rummage about in his bag, blinking back tears as he looked for one of the mysterious powders he used from his days as a Hospitaller. It was a powder derived from a flower that was grown far to the east, expensive and rare, but with astounding medicinal qualities. He kept it in a bladder envelope, tightly sealed. He found it carefully wedged at the bottom of his bag and he drew it forth, asking for a cup of wine. Someone handed him a wooden cup, half-full, and he poured some of it out on the floor before dispensing a careful measure of the white powder. He stirred it with his finger and tasted it.

"Tate," he looked over his shoulder. "Pull her up so that she can drink this. Gently, please."

Tate's capable hands reached down and, at Stephen's direction, grasped her carefully by the torso. Joselyn wept in pain as he lifted her with extreme care, struggling to drink the liquid that Stephen was tenderly attempting to administer to her. She was in so much pain that she could hardly think, but Stephen's gentle coaxing helped her drink the contents of the cup. Once the bitter brew was down, Tate lowered her carefully back to the mattress.

"There," Stephen set the cup down and stroked her dark head. "Soon the pain will fade and you will sleep."

Eyes closed, she licked her lips, tasting the last of the brew. "Thank you," she whispered. "Stephen?"

"Aye, love?"

"Please tell me that you do not hate me for not telling you the truth."

He couldn't stop the tears then. He put his lips on her cheek, eyes closed as his tears gently fell on her dark hair. His head against hers, he spoke.

"I love you more than my own life," he admitted against her flesh. "I know you were not being deliberately malicious. I know you thought you were trying to help."

She began to cry again, pitiful sobs as he gently shushed her. His big hand stroked her dark hair as he kissed her temple, whispering words of comfort that only she could hear. Eventually, the tears faded and she drifted into a heavy sleep. Stephen continued to stroke her hair until he heard her heavy, steady breathing.

Silently, he began to assemble what he would need to remove the arrow. Tate pulled up a stool next to the bed and sat, watching Stephen as the man focused on what he must do. He could only imagine the turmoil he must be feeling.

"What more do you want me to do?" he asked quietly.

Stephen glanced at his sleeping wife. "You have tended battle wounds before."

"I have."

"I am going to need you to hold her still while I operate."

"Operate?"

Stephen nodded, removing a tiny razor-sharp dagger from a leather sheath. "I need to work very quickly so I need for her to stay very still. You must hold her down by the shoulders so she cannot move her upper body. I am fearful that if I do not sew quickly enough, she will bleed to death. And I cannot sew if she is thrashing about."

Tate watched him carefully lay out his instruments. Tate had known the man for almost twenty years and knew him to be perpetually stoic and confidently in control. He'd never seen him otherwise until the past few days. The introduction of a wife had rattled Stephen to the core and Tate felt a good deal of pity for him. He knew, from experience, how a woman could unbalance a man's normally calm character.

"I am sorry, Stephen," he said after a moment. "Sorry that your post as Guardian Protector has been nothing as you expected."

Stephen looked up at him, the blue eyes bright. "Nothing as I expected but better than I could have dreamed," he forced a smile. "Make no mistake; Joselyn is the biggest prize of all. Had I known I was to marry her, I would have insisted we make much shorter work of the siege of Berwick."

Tate smiled faintly. "I am pleased to hear that. You and I have been through much together, have we not? I am pleased that you found a woman that you are fond of."

Stephen scowled gently. "Fond of? I love her."

Tate laughed softly, scratching his chin as the heady mood lightened, if only for a moment. "Then you understand how I feel about my wife. Love is a whole new world to experience."

Stephen's eyes twinkled dully as his gaze moved to the sleeping form on the bed. "Do you remember that before you married Elizabetha, I tried to woo her from you?"

"I do."

Stephen looked at him, then. "I am glad I did not."

"So am I."

They laughed softly, remembering those days of love and war and competition. But it was a fond memory, one that made their friendship stronger. Tate and Stephen, and Kenneth who was off on the Welsh border, had a stronger bond than even most brothers. As they shared a quiet moment before the storm to come, Lane reappeared with a small, gray-haired man. Kelvin of Gloucester had been a physic for many years but not long in the service of the Earl of Carlisle. Still, he had a strong reputation, almost as strong as Stephen's. One look at the woman on the bed with the arrow protruding out of her back and he went straight to Stephen.

"How can I assist, my lord?" he set his ratty satchel down next to Stephen's neat and organized bag.

As Stephen and the old physic conferred, Lane made a few attempts to quietly get Tate's attention. The fourth attempt worked and Tate left his stool to go to Lane.

"What is it?" he asked.

Lane cast Stephen a glance before answering. "Rebels are in the town once again," he said quietly. "They are beginning to burn to the south. The castle is sealed and the battlements are preparing. Sir Alan and Sir Ian have seen to it."

Tate hissed, knowing why Lane was keeping his voice down. Stephen had enough to worry over. If he knew the rebels were on the move again, he would be extremely torn between aiding his wife and doing his duty as Guardian Protector. Before Tate could reply, however, Stephen turned to them both from his crouched position on the floor.

"Probably the same rebels who ambushed us," he said. "If they are burning to the south, then they are more than likely moving north from the church where we were attacked."

Tate lifted an eyebrow. "You must have the hearing of God to have heard the sergeant's report."

Stephen nodded faintly although there was no room in his expression for humor. His gaze moved to Joselyn, sleeping deeply on the bed, before looking down to his instruments carefully laid out on the floor.

"It should take me a few minutes to remove this arrow and stitch the wound," he sounded firm, decisive. "Have my charger readied. Mount one hundred men and wait for me in the bailey."

"I shall go," Tate countered. "You must stay here with your wife. She needs you more than Berwick does."

"And I shall do my duty to both," Stephen still would not look at him, more focused on what he was about to do with Joselyn. "De Norville, get my soldiers mounted. Have Ian join the party and wait for me in the bailey. Those are your orders."

Lane looked at de Lara, who nodded faintly. When the sergeant left to carry out Stephen's orders, Tate moved towards the bed where Stephen and the physic were preparing to begin their operation.

"Do you still want me to hold her?" Tate asked quietly.

Stephen nodded. "Aye," he finally looked up at Tate and the turmoil in the man's eyes was unfathomable. "Hold her tightly. She'll not like this in the least."

Old Mereld arrived with steaming water and hot, boiled linen just as they were preparing to cut into Joselyn. The old woman whimpered at the sight of an arrow protruding out of her mistress' back but kept her head. She'd heard the rumors of Lady Joselyn's injury but the reality was sickening. She busied herself with the linens and hearth as the operation began. The mood grew serious, critical, as Stephen went to work.

He had been right. At the first jostling of the arrow, Joselyn awoke with a howl. She screamed into the mattress as Tate held her down and Stephen's skilled hands worked quickly and steadily. Stephen blocked the screaming from his mind, focusing on what he needed to do in order to save her life. He had to push it all aside and detach himself. But it was the hardest thing he ever had to do. Had he let himself feel her screams, it would have cut him to shreds.

As the war party gathered below in the bailey, they could hear the screaming from the Guardian Protector's third story window. It went on for what seemed like hours, abruptly stopping as if whoever were doing the screaming had been suddenly silenced. The men looked at each other uneasily, knowing the sound had been coming from Lady Pembury. Lane and Ian exchanged apprehensive glances, especially when the sound abruptly stopped. In uncomfortable silence, they waited.

When Stephen made his appearance in full battle armor minutes later, no one dared say a word. De Lara was right behind him and the two of them mounted their chargers, very business-like, and led the war party out to meet the rebels as if nothing else in the world mattered.

Some wondered if Lady Pembury's agony had affected her professional-knight husband. He seemed completely unmoved. But in truth, the lowered visor prevented anyone from seeing the tears covering Stephen's face.

He was devastated.

CB

THE CELL DOOR slammed open with enough force that dust and flotsam rained down from the ceiling. Shaken from an exhausted sleep, Kynan looked up to see Stephen bearing down on him. The big knight reached down and yanked Kynan into a seated position.

"Enough of this," Stephen snarled. "I have had enough of you and your reckless rabble. If you do not help me put an end to these constant raids, I shall hang you from the battlements as we hanged your cousins. I shall leave you for the ravens to pick the eyeballs from your rotted skull so listen to me and listen well: there is much I can stand in warfare and very little I cannot. What I cannot stomach are reckless idiots who have no true direction or conviction as they wreak havoc. Your rebels from the church at the southern end of town launched an ambush that seriously wounded my wife. Then they proceeded to burn a large section of the southern end of Berwick and murdered one of my knights. This has to end, MacKenzie. It has to end now."

By this time, Kynan was wide awake and staring balefully at Stephen. "What do ye mean about Jo-Jo? How did they hurt her?"

Stephen slammed the man back against the stone wall, speaking through clenched teeth in an uncharacteristic fit of anger. "She took the information you gave her about seeking the priest at the church at the southern end of town and went there. Your rebel brethren were waiting and launched an ambush. They struck her with an arrow. Even now she fights for her life and I swear by all that is holy, if she dies, every Scot within a fifty mile radius of Berwick will die. Man, woman, child, I care not. I shall slaughter them all unless you help me end this rebellion. Is that in any way unclear?"

Kynan was pale with fury, with distress over Joselyn's injury. "She is dying?"

Stephen was a wreck. Not only had he seen Joselyn injured this night, but he'd watched Ian fall to a morning star that nearly tore his head from his shoulders. That same morning star ripped through de Lara's left arm. Now Stephen's fury was unleashed and he was focused on Kynan as the source of his anger. He had little control over it at the moment.

"She is very sick," he said honestly, calming for the first time since entering the cell. He was so unused to fits of fury that he was sweating profusely with it. "I do not know if she is dying. Only time will tell."

Kynan sighed heavily, scratching his dirty head. His defiance was leaving him now that those he was allied with had injured his cousin. Somehow the situation was not clear cut any longer. Joselyn was hurt by men who Kynan had said would help her. *His* men. He was beginning to feel some guilt for that and with that guilt came defiance.

"Ye only married her ta cement an alliance," he growled. "She's a Scot. She's a symbol of submission ta ye. Dunna pretend as if her sickness tears at yer heart."

It was the wrong thing to say. With a roar, Stephen grabbed the man by his tartan and lifted him off the floor, tossing him to the opposite side of the cell. He would have killed him had de Lara not been there to stop his rage, the man's left arm heavily bandaged. Trying to hold Stephen back was like trying to tackle a raging bull. Doing it with a bad arm was nearly impossible.

"No, Stephen," Tate hissed at him. "You'll not kill him. We shall never get to the bottom of this if you do. Think man, *think*. He is your only link to the rebels."

Stephen stopped pushing against de Lara long enough to pause, his blue eyes blazing with unbridled rage. His gaze was fixed on Kynan even as Tate tried to calm him.

"No killing," Tate's voice was firm, steady. "You need him if you are to end this."

Stephen was visibly shaken, struggling to calm himself. He'd nearly killed the man with his bare hands purely out of anger. He'd never snapped like that before, not ever, and it was an awesome realization. He took a deep breath, puffed out his cheeks, and seemed to cool. His characteristic calm began to take hold again. But it was difficult. Eyes still on Kynan in the corner, he rubbed wearily at his neck.

"I need Ken," he muttered. "I need the man here. I need his wisdom and his sword."

Tate nodded faintly "I agree," he said. "I shall send for him to-night."

"Do you think Mortimer will spare him?"

"He will have to."

Tate tried to tug him from the cell, but Stephen was still fixed on Kynan. After several long moments during which Stephen further calmed, he eventually dislodged Tate's grip from his arm and took a couple of steps in Kynan's direction. He faced the prisoner much more like his old self and not a raging lunatic.

"You and I will be very clear from this moment forward," he said, his voice hoarse but steady. "I married your cousin to form an alliance; that is true. But she loves me and I love her, and there is nothing in this world that I would not do for her. I would pull the stars from the heavens or walk through fire if she wished it. Now she lies gravely wounded and my heart is in pieces in spite of what you think. It aches as no man's heart has ever ached. If you have any loyalty to your cousin, then you will help me end these raids. The Scots are defeated. The English are in charge of Berwick. The sooner your people come to terms with this, the better for all of us. I need your help. Joselyn needs your help. Do right by all of us."

Kynan's glare was dull, bottomless as he gazed up at Stephen. "I can find out who did this to Jo-Jo but I canna do it from inside this coffin."

"'Tis more than that and you know it. You will rot here unless you tell me what I want to know."

"I shall not help ye crush my people more than ye already have."

"If that is all you can see in this situation, then you are a fool."

With that, he turned and quit the cell with Tate and Lane on his heels. The guard locked the grate and the cold clang of the bolt being thrown echoed through the vault. Kynan sat against the stone where Stephen had tossed him, smarting and disoriented with the turn of events. The conversation with the English knight had him reeling in spite of everything.

The situation was not so clear after all.

ℭ

THE FIRST THING she was cognizant of was that her eyelids felt as if they weighed one hundred pounds apiece. They were so heavy that she couldn't open them. And her head pounded painfully. Joselyn tried to lick her lips but there was no moisture in her mouth, not a drop. She must have sighed or made a noise, because Stephen was suddenly beside her.

"Jo-Jo?" he whispered. "Are you awake, sweetheart?"

She tried to speak but all she could manage to utter was a pathetic groan. A cool cloth touched her cheek and brow.

"Sleep, love," Stephen whispered, kissing her on the cheek. "Just sleep."

She did. Fading off, she spent an indeterminable amount of time in blissful darkness. But then the dreams came, crazy things, in which she could see her parents again. Her father, her mother, her grandmother. All making themselves busy in her dreams. They rushed past her, around her, and she could not keep track of them. Then she was back at Allanton, her family's home, and she could even smell the violets that grew in great bunches against the manor wall. She was in the kitchens, watching her grandmother cook barley loaves and her mother was boiling down apples to make the wonderful apple butter she used to put up every fall.

She wanted some of that apple butter.

But she couldn't seem to make it over to the hearth where her mother was cooking. She was rooted to the chair, sitting, watching everyone else go by her. Her grandmother picked up the barley loaves and they suddenly burst into flame, ashes falling to the floor. The kitchen seemed to be heating up and the apple butter boiled over, spilling into a fire that was now shooting flames into the room. She tried to get away from the flames but she couldn't move. Everything was hot and frightening around her. She began to think that she might be in hell. It felt like it. And it was growing hotter.

Stephen had been awake all night, watching Joselyn sleep heavily.

She awoke once, he thought, but she promptly fell back asleep. Just after dawn, sleep claimed Stephen as well as he sat next to the bed, his great head on the mattress near Joselyn's still form. He had been asleep for a few hours when the mattress began to twitch, rousing him from his exhaustion.

His head came up, alert, as he fixed on Joselyn. She was quivering and he immediately put his hand on her head, feeling a fairly significant fever. Though he had expected it, still, he had hoped the heat of the wound would pass her by. It was disheartening but he was not overly panicked about it. It could be controlled. He removed his hand from her head and sent Tilda, sitting quietly in the corner, for plenty of cool water. As he moved for his medicament bag, Joselyn spoke.

"Apple butter," she mumbled.

Stephen froze at the sound of her voice, his brow furrowing as he attempted to figure out if she was lucid or not.

"Apple butter?" he repeated, amusement in his voice. "Do you want apple butter?"

Surprisingly, her eyes lolled open and she tried to push herself up using her left arm. The right arm, bandaged against her body by Stephen to keep it immobile, was useless.

"Apple butter," she said again, then slammed back onto the mattress.

Stephen tried to steady her so she would not rip out his stitches. "Lay still, sweetheart," he said soothingly. "All will be well."

She didn't seem particularly eased by his words. "Apple *butter*," she said insistently, rolling about.

Stephen held her still as she tried to squirm. "I will get you apple butter if you stop moving," he told her. "Jo-Jo, can you understand me? You must be still."

She stopped fidgeting and the pale blue eyes opened, staring into space. Stephen waved a hand in front of her eyes but she didn't track his movements, nor did she blink. She just stared. Had he not been concerned about the fever, he would have found her behavior rather humorous. But he realized she was mildly delirious. With one eye on her, he went back to his medicament case to find something for her fever.

Suddenly, she bolted upright, nearly pitching herself off the bed. Stephen grabbed her before she could fall and gently laid her back on the bed, trying to position her so it would not put any strain on her wound. She reached up her good arm and began scratching at his face and neck, as one would scratch an itch. It was not violent in the least but he dodged her wriggling fingers as he tried to hold her still.

"Jo-Jo, sweetheart, you must be still," he insisted gently. "Be still, love."

She scratched at his stubble, his mouth, and began to giggle. Then her arm fell back to the mattress and she tried to claw her way off the bed. Stephen corralled her.

"Apple butter," she sighed.

He sat on the bed beside her, his massive arms braced on either side of her slender body, and watched her eyes slowly close. With a faint smirk, because her behavior was truly funny, he shook his head and dared to move back to his bag once more.

Rummaging through his bag, he extracted a leather envelope of another whitish powder. He dared to move away from the bed and collect a cup with a small amount of wine in it, left over from a meal he'd had the night before.

Dissolving some of the whitish powder in the wine, he went back over to the bed and gently gathered Joselyn into one massive arm while carefully coaxing her to drink the contents. She was semi-lucid and able to follow his instructions somewhat but didn't like the taste of the dissolved powder. Stephen still held her in one arm as he set the cup aside and was surprised, when he looked back down at her, to realize she was awake and focused on him. He smiled faintly.

"Are you truly awake?" he whispered. "Or am I to receive more demands for apple butter?"

She blinked at him. "Apple butter?" she repeated slowly. "I... I had a dream that my mother was making apple butter. Did I ask for some?"

He was more relieved than he could express that she was lucid and able to respond. It was the first such occurrence since the arrow had plowed into her back and he took her left hand, kissing it tenderly.

"You did not ask, madam, you commanded," he grinned at her. "Unfortunately, you are the cook in this family. I cannot make it."

She sighed faintly. "I was having unsettling dreams," she murmured. "My grandmother was there, too. And my father. We were at Allanton and then everything burst into flame."

"Dreams can be strange sometimes, especially with illness." His hand toyed with her fingers as he held her. "How do you feel?"

"Very sore," she whispered, closing her eyes for a brief moment. "How badly am I wounded?"

His smile faded somewhat. "Bad enough," he replied. "The arrow did some damage but it was not as bad as I had feared."

"Did you fix it?"

"I did. Do you not remember?"

"Nay."

He said a silent prayer of thanks that she did not remember the agony and the screaming from the previous day. It was, however, something he would carry with him for the rest of his life. He would never be able to forget her howls as he held her down and dug into her beautiful back. He leaned over and kissed her hot forehead once, twice, before pulling away and fixing her in the eye.

"You will heal," he assured her softly. "But you and I will come to an understanding, madam. No more withholding truths from me. No more running off to try and save the entire town of Berwick."

She looked away from him. "I was not trying to save Berwick. I was trying to save *you.*"

"I understand, but I do not need saving. As it was, I had to save *you* and that put us all in danger. Do you understand?"

She nodded, once, and closed her eyes. Not having the heart to scold her any further, he kissed her cheek and hugged her as tightly as he could without causing her pain.

"I will say, however, that I admire your bravery, Lady Pembury," he whispered. "But I have never been so terrified in all my life as I was when I realized you were gone. I never want to go through that horror again. Will you promise me?"

She began to cry softly and he rocked her gently, holding her close and feeling her heated body against him. The fever was mild but she was still very ill, so he laid her gently on the bed and pulled the coverlet over her. He thought she had drifted off to sleep as he rose from the bed to put his medicaments away, but she whispered softly to him.

"Stephen?" she breathed.

He paused. "What is it, love?"

"Lay here with me, please," she murmured. "I am afraid."

"Afraid of what?"

Her eyes opened, like pale blue stones within her pasty face. "I am afraid I am going to die."

"You are not going to die."

Her eyes welled again and her lip began to tremble. "God is punishing me," she wept softly. "I lied to you and God is punishing me. He guided that arrow into my back."

He shook his head. "That is not true. God would not punish you so."

She wept pitifully. "Aye, 'tis true. I will never lie to you again, I swear it. I do not want to die. I do not want to leave you."

She was off on a crying jag. Stephen set down the things in his hand and sat back down on the mattress. Very carefully, he stretched out beside her, pulling her against him as best he could without jostling her shoulder. She groaned once or twice before he found a better position and they were finally settled. She calmed as his arms went around her, snuggling against him as far as she could go without causing herself pain.

"Thank you," she whispered.

His head was against hers, his mouth on her hair. "My pleasure."

"I love you, Stephen."

He kissed her dark head reverently. "I love you, too, sweetheart."

Tate came to the chamber sometime around noon to see how Lady Pembury was faring. He quietly opened the door only to find both Joselyn and Stephen sleeping the sleep of the dead as the world around them went on. The day was sunny, the bailey busy with life, but in their chamber, Stephen and Joselyn were completely unaware. Their world was quiet and protected. With a faint smile, Tate shut the door, posted a guard, and left with the instructions that they were not to be disturbed. Even Tilda was turned away when she returned with the water.

Everything was going to be alright.

CHAPTER ELEVEN

HIS NAME WAS Sir Kenneth St. Héver. He had served with Tate de Lara and Stephen of Pembury as the third in the trio of knights that was the most reputable and powerful in all of England at this time. The three of them had been bodyguards to young Edward the Third when the youth had fled his mother and Roger Mortimer.

Together, the trio had kept young Edward alive and ensured the fall of Mortimer and Isabella so that Edward could assume his rightful place on the throne of England. Even before that, their association had been a long and honored one. Kenneth, being the oldest of the trio, had even served in his very young years under Edward the First. At thirty-eight years, he was seasoned, wise, terrifying and gifted.

He was also the most feared of the three. Tate was brilliant and powerful while Stephen was the strongest merely by his sheer size, but Kenneth went beyond size and intelligence. He was not as tall as Stephen and perhaps slightly taller than Tate, but he was broader than even the broadest man. And it was pure, unadulterated muscle. He had an enormous neck, square jaw, and eyes that were so blue they were nearly silver. His close-cropped hair was so blond that it was nearly white and thick blond lashes surrounded his shocking blue eyes. He had a reputation for being exceptionally unfriendly though never unfair, and called no one friend except for de Lara and Pembury. Sir Kenneth St. Héver was a knight's knight. He was the man that most knights could only hope to be.

At the fall of Roger Mortimer, the young king had gifted Sir Kenneth to Garson Mortimer, a cousin to Roger who had sided with young Edward. That had sent Kenneth to the Welsh Marches, the first time in fifteen years that he had been separated from Tate and Kenneth. But it had been a very honorable post he had assumed at Kirk Castle keeping the Welsh at bay. Still, he was eager to see his friends again, men he'd not seen in almost a year.

It was this man who had ridden hard for five days after he had received the missive from Pembury asking him to come to Berwick Castle. Knowing that Stephen would not have asked for him unless he had a very good reason, Kenneth had ridden day and night to reach Berwick. It had been an exhausting journey but he was not particularly concerned with that. He was more concerned with why Stephen had called for him.

Fortunately, July was a good month to travel. No rain, no inclement weather, and he made good time. As he reached the outskirts of Berwick, he could immediately see that the town was in shambles. Great sections of it were burned and as he rode deeper into the town, he could see how destitute the people were. It was just after the nooning hour and the peasants eyed him suspiciously as he rode into town. Another English knight was not a welcome sight. He passed children who were sitting in the gutter weeping with hunger. It was a sobering sight.

Berwick Castle was on a hill by the river, surrounded with massive walls. As he neared the castle, he could see the activity up on the battlements. He could also see that the castle was buttoned up tightly. There was no moat, only sheer walls that towered overhead. He came to a halt at the main gate, an opening with a massive iron gate in front of a pair of massive wooden doors, and called up to the sentries. After he announced himself, the massive wooden doors, and the iron gate, were eventually cranked open.

He guided his foaming charger into the gatehouse, emerging into the dusty bailey. It was an enormous area, penned in by several towers, a hall off to the left and a keep to the right. He pulled his charger to a halt somewhere between the keep and the hall, looking about his surroundings. There were soldiers everywhere and a few servants. A young stable servant timidly approached to take the charger, who snorted and snapped at the lad. Kenneth dismounted stiffly, stretching his muscular body as he reached into a saddle bag and pulled forth a muzzle. Muzzling the horse, he removed his bags and headed into the hall.

The great hall was empty, surprising at the nooning hour. Sitting at the massive, scrubbed table, he tossed his bags onto the table surface and grumbled orders to the nearest servant. The man was to bring him food and send for Pembury, in that order. A serving wench eventually brought him bread, cheese and wine and he tore into it with gusto. He hadn't eaten in over a day. As he was downing the wine, a familiar voice came from behind him.

"God's Blood," Stephen hissed. "It is about time you got here."

Kenneth turned around, the very rare event of a smile on his lips. He stood up, taking Stephen's outstretched hand and shaking it longer than necessary. For a man who kept his emotions buried deeper than most, it was a strong display of sentiment.

"You are looking well, Stephen," Kenneth said. "Perhaps older and fatter, but well."

Stephen laughed. "Fatter, indeed. When you discover what a fantastic cook my wife is, you'll go to fat and do it gladly."

Kenneth displayed emotion for the second time in as many seconds. "Wife?" he repeated, stunned. "What wife?"

Stephen sobered and let go of the man's hand, motioning for him to sit back down. "The Lady Joselyn de Velt Seton Pembury," he said. "She is the daughter of Alexander Seton, the Commander of Berwick Castle until it fell to Edward. At our king's insistence, I married her to cement England's stake at Berwick."

Kenneth nodded faintly in understanding. "I see," he was still rather shocked, studying Stephen's expression for any signs of distress. "You do not seem troubled by this."

Stephen shook his head. "Not at all," he realized he was somewhat embarrassed to tell his friend the truth, simply because they had always considered romantic love a fool's emotion. At least, they had once.

"You may as well know that I adore the woman. She is my heart."

Kenneth's white eyebrows lifted. "Is that so?"

"It is."

Kenneth stared at him a moment, still shocked, before finally shaking his head. "Then all I can say is congratulations," he said, shifting the subject because he was not sure what else to say on the event of Stephen having taken a wife. "So why am I here?"

Stephen lowered himself onto the bench beside him. "Much has happened since you and I last saw one another, but the majority of it has happened within the last month," he paused before he started his story. "The siege of Berwick was brutal. Many died and the politics of the story is something that will be told for hundreds of years to come. It was savage, even by our standards. My wife was wounded in an ambush ten days ago. A fever still lingers within her and her health suffers. Her cousin, one of the leaders of the rebellion, is in the vault right now. We have been plagued by raids and I believe this man holds the key towards ending them. I have sent for you because my attention has been on my wife, as foolish as it sounds. I have never been this close to a woman, Ken, much less love her, and my attention is not on my post as Guardian Protector of Berwick. I need your wisdom, man. I need your sword and your good sense to help me discover the source of these raids once and for all, for I find that my focus is not where it should be. As long as Joselyn remains ill, I cannot think on anything else. She consumes my being."

Kenneth was gazing steadily at him with no judgment in his expression. In fact, the usually ice-cold silver eyes were oddly warm.

"Then you did right to send for me," he said after a moment. "I was bored at Kirk, anyway. The Welsh are behaving themselves for the moment and I was thinking on taking up sewing to pass the time until I received your missive. Thank you for this opportunity to reaffirm my manhood."

It was the kindest possible way to express what they both knew. Stephen was, for the first time in his life, having a weak moment and

Kenneth put a spin on the situation that allowed the man to retain his dignity. Their friendship was that deep. Stephen understood this clearly, smiling weakly and clapping him on an enormous shoulder.

"I am indebted to you," he said quietly.

"Aye, you are, but someday I will call you to help me quell the Welsh and you will rip them apart with your bare hands," Kenneth could see that Stephen needed reassurance that he was still the most powerful knight in the realm. "There is no one fiercer in battle that you, Pembury. Even I am afraid of you."

Stephen broke down into soft laughter, prompting a grin from Kenneth. Kenneth downed the last of his wine as Stephen sobered and rose from the bench.

"You need to meet my wife," he said. "She knows you are here and if I do not bring you to her, she will come down here herself."

Kenneth rose. "Is she bedridden?"

Stephen shrugged as they made their way out of the hall. "Not really," he said. "At least, I cannot keep her there. She gets up and walks around when I am not with her, so I have taken to being with her nearly every moment. She was struck by an arrow in the ambush and poison still flows through her veins. I cannot seem to cure her of it."

Kenneth squinted as they emerged into the sunny weather of the bailey. "Does she weaken?"

Stephen shook his head. "Strangely, not much. She eats well and behaves rather normally, but the fever is still there. Faint, but still there. I am afraid it will flare at some point and overtake her if I cannot rid her of it."

Kenneth could see how the mere idea greatly distressed him. "If anyone can cure her, you can," he said confidently. "I have seen you raise the dead, Stephen. Your skill is second only to God himself."

Stephen smiled faintly. "Let us hope so."

They crossed the keep in relative silence as Kenneth looked around, acquainting himself with the place. It was big and functional. The enormous keep loomed ahead and he gazed upward, sizing up the structure.

"This is an impressive castle," he said. "And a most impressive title as Guardian Protector of Berwick. Where is de Lara, by the way? I thought he was fighting with you."

Stephen nodded as they entered thc dark, cool keep. "He left several days ago to run an errand to the Earl of Buccleuch. He shall return shortly."

"What errand?"

"Bringing my wife's son back to Berwick."

Kenneth peered oddly at him. "Your wife's son? She was married before?"

Stephen paused on the second floor landing. "No," he said quietly. "She was raped by an English soldier as a very young girl. Her father sent the child away, naturally. Tate has gone to bring the child back. It is a long story for another time, Ken, but trust me when I say my wife has had a horrendous life. Yet she is the sweetest, most beautiful woman you have ever seen. I am anxious for you to know her."

Kenneth nodded faintly, neutrally. "As I am anxious as well. If she is so important to you, then I shall treat her with all due respect."

Stephen grinned at him as they took the stairs to the third floor. Reaching the door, he knocked softly.

"Jo-Jo?" he called. "May we come in?"

The door quickly opened and Kenneth was in for a shock. Other than being oddly pale, an astoundingly beautiful woman was standing in the doorway. Clad in a stunning surcoat of pale blue, she was a tiny little thing with pale blue eyes and luscious dark hair. She smiled at Stephen with her straight white teeth and dimpled cheeks and Kenneth could see immediately why the man was so smitten with her. She was spectacular.

Stephen took her hand and pulled her against him, facing Kenneth as he did so. "My lady," he said. "This is my closest friend, Sir Kenneth St. Héver. Ken, this is my wife, the Lady Joselyn Pembury."

Kenneth bowed graciously. "My lady," he greeted. "Stephen did not exaggerate about your beauty. You are indeed the most beautiful woman in all of England."

Joselyn chuckled softly. "You are too kind, my lord," she said in her deliciously sweet voice. "I am very pleased to meet you. Welcome to Berwick Castle."

"Thank you."

She eyed her husband with disapproval as she spoke. "I apologize that I did not meet you in the great hall and provide you with a satisfactory meal, but my husband is rather stingy about that. He will only allow me out of this room once a day and I had to choose – greeting you when you came or sharing the evening meal. I chose the evening meal."

Kenneth wriggled his eyebrows, his gaze moving between Joselyn and Stephen. "I would have chosen the evening meal as well, my lady."

She smiled at him. "Will you at least come in and sit? Let us become better acquainted."

Stephen squeezed her gently. "He did not come to stave off your boredom," he scolded lightly. "He is here to help me, remember? I must show him the castle. We have much to discuss and you will see him tonight."

She made a face at Stephen, one that Kenneth found very charming and very funny. "Can I at least come and walk with you?" she asked.

"No."

"Why not?"

With a growl, Stephen picked her up and carried her back into the room, depositing her on the bed. "You will stay here and rest," he instructed firmly. "I will see you later."

She scrambled off the bed. "Stephen, I have been lying in bed all day. I feel fine. Can I please come and walk with you and Sir Kenneth?"

Stephen's jaw ticked as he looked at Kenneth, pointing a finger at his wife. "Do you see what I must deal with? She is as difficult as a spoiled child."

Kenneth fought off a grin. "Leave me out of this. You will not like my response."

Stephen pursed his lips at him. "I already do not like your response, you traitor," he turned back to Joselyn. "Please, sweetheart. Stay here and we will return later. You must rest."

Joselyn grabbed on to his arm and refused to let go. "Please," she begged softly. "Just five minutes. Let me walk with you just five minutes. I promise I will not allow myself to become too tired."

He gazed down into her lovely face, knowing he was going to relent no matter how much longer they debated the subject. He had realized one thing very quickly in the early days of this marriage; he would cave to her every desire with hardly a measure of resistance. He had been a slave to her for the past ten days, since she had been injured, catering to her every request, small or large. But in truth, he didn't mind. He loved every minute of it.

"Very well," he sighed with exasperation. "But only five minutes. And if you argue, I shall not let you come outside for a week. Are we clear?"

She smiled brightly at him and patted his cheek. "Very clear, my angel."

Stephen just rolled his eyes, took her by the hand, and led her out of the chamber. Kenneth preceded them down the stairs and they ended up in the bailey. Joselyn found herself between the two enormous knights as she held on to Stephen with two hands, as if afraid he was going to get away from her.

"Tell me, Sir Kenneth," she began. "Do you have a wife also?"

Kenneth shook his head. "I do not, my lady."

"Oh?" Joselyn looked up at him. He was a brutally handsome man with his pale blond hair and white lashes. He had a square jaw and a very manly face in general. "I cannot believe some deserving young woman has not snapped you up. What is your background?"

Kenneth didn't like to talk about himself, especially to someone he didn't know, but he responded out of respect for Stephen. "My father was a knight for Henry Percy," he told her. "My mother was a daughter of Princess Blanche, eleventh child of Henry the Third."

Joselyn looked at him, surprised. "Your grandfather was King Henry?"

"Aye."

"Tate and Kenneth share the same grandfather," Stephen put in. "They are distant cousins."

She looked up at Stephen. "The Earl of Carlisle?"

Stephen nodded. "Tate is the first born of Edward the First. His mother was a Welsh princess, a daughter of Dafydd ap Gruffydd. Had Edward been married to Princess Dera, Tate would be the king of England."

Joselyn came to a halt, her mouth open wide with shock. "You have allowed me to become so familiar with this man who should be king?" she was appalled. "Why did you not tell me of Tate's lineage?"

Stephen was amused. "It was not your concern. Moreover, he is not king. It is not improper for you to befriend him, especially as my wife."

She lifted a well-shaped eyebrow at him. "And what about you? Is there anything you have not told me about your lineage? Are you related to Christ perhaps and I do not know it?"

Stephen laughed at her and gave a gentle tug to resume their walk. "We are all brothers of Christ, Lady Pembury," he said. "But in answer to your question, I have told you everything about me. I do not have such grand relatives as Kenneth or Tate."

"Peasant," Kenneth muttered with mock disdain.

As Stephen grinned, Joselyn recommenced walking beside her husband. "I do not have such grand relatives, either," she turned to Kenneth once more. "Now more than ever, I am curious as to why you are not married. With your heritage and handsome looks, you could command a fine bride."

Stephen laughed as Kenneth tried not to look too uncomfortable. "All in time, Lady Pembury," he said. "I would not worry overly about it if I were you."

"But she is right," Stephen insisted, goading the man. Kenneth was such a serious character that these opportunities were rare. "With both Tate and me married, you are the last one. We must find you a bride."

"I will find my own bride. I do not require your help. In fact, I fear it."

"Why?"

"Because you would saddle me with the most petulant woman you could find."

Stephen laughed uproariously. "I have several in mind, in fact."

Joselyn grinned as her husband and Kenneth bantered back and forth. She was simply enjoying being out and about, under the bright sunshine and embraced by Stephen. In the days since her injury, she'd felt better quickly enough after he removed the arrow but the wound was still oozing and she had been running a slight fever for almost nine days. It was enough to cause her to exhaust easily, which is why Stephen kept her in bed most of the time. He couldn't seem to figure out why the fever was still active and made her take a variety of medicaments from his magical bag. She accused him of experimenting on her, which he was not. He was simply attempting to find the right medicine that would cure her.

More importantly, however, was something she had kept from him simply because she couldn't be positive and she didn't want to spook him. Her menses had been due on the days following their marriage but still had not yet come. She attributed it to the stress of the marriage and her wound, but she could not be sure. Perhaps the fever was somehow preventing her cycle. The thought of bearing Stephen a son thrilled her but she well remembered her last pregnancy and how she was sick the entire time. She could hardly even hold water down. That part, in fact, did not thrill her. So she kept it to herself, knowing the next few weeks would tell for sure.

That was, of course, in the event that God had forgiven her for both disobeying and lying to her husband. Ten days after the ambush, she was still convinced that God had punished her for being wicked. Every time she thought of leaving her room when Stephen was not around, she reminded herself what her disobedience had gotten her. She could no longer rationalize that she was trying to help her husband by contacting the rebels. The plain truth was that she had lied to him. She tried not to hate herself for it.

So she relished the time they spent together, especially in moments like this. Walking next to Stephen's enormous form, she felt proud and happy, and extremely lucky to be alive. He was sweet and attentive with her, no mention of her disobedience and lying since she had apologized for it. For the past ten days, life between them had been unimaginably wonderful.

Stephen and Kenneth were still bantering back and forth by the time they reached the kitchens. Stephen came to abrupt halt and looked at her.

"Your five minutes are up," he said. "Back to bed now."

She shook her head vigorously and let go of him, standing just far enough away that his long arms couldn't grab her.

"Just five more," she pleaded. "I am not tired in the least. It feels wonderful to walk about. Please, Stephen?"

He put his big hands on his hips and cocked an eyebrow at her. "What did I tell you? If you argue with me, I shall not let you out for a week."

Gazing up at him with her pale blue eyes, her lower lip stuck out in a pout and he folded like an idiot. Reaching out, he took her hand with gentle irritability and they resumed their walk.

"Oh, very well," he snapped softly. "Five more minutes."

But she dug her heels in as he tried to pull her forward. "Can we collect the fawn? He hasn't been outside in some time and needs to walk about, too."

"Nay."

"Please, husband?" she smiled prettily and folded her hands in front of her as if praying to him. "Please?"

Stephen looked as if he were about to burst a vein but he kept his irritation in check. He simply pointed at the kitchens and she dashed inside, emerging a short time later with the fawn in her arms. Putting the little thing down, it stood unsteadily for a moment before bounding off. Before Stephen could stop her, Joselyn was bounding after it. He called to her a couple of times as she chased the animal around but gave up when she ignored him. With a heavy sigh, he and Kenneth resumed their walk.

"I saw as I arrived that the town is fairly destroyed," Kenneth wisely changed the subject away from Lady Pembury based on Stephen's frustrated expression. "Have the raids been constant?"

"They were very violent in the first few days following the surrender," Stephen was watching Joselyn run around. "But they have died down considerably in the past seven days. Perhaps two or three very small skirmishes, but for the most part, it has been relatively quiet. However, I know they are not over. I have a very bad feeling that the rebels are building up to something big."

"What do your scouts say?"

"That there is very little activity anywhere in the city. The outskirts seem deserted. I fear the Scots have gone somewhere to regroup and attack in larger numbers."

Kenneth grunted in agreement. "They simply would not have faded away voluntarily."

"Nay, they would not have."

They had circled around the yard and had reached the postern gate that led to the river. Joselyn had cornered the frolicking fawn a few feet away and they watched her as she knelt down to pet the little animal. Stephen looked particularly pensive as he watched his beautiful wife tend the little creature. His frustrated expression had softened into one of adoration.

"Joselyn's cousin is one of the rebel leaders," he said quietly. "The man has been in my vault since the city surrendered. We have tried repeatedly to wrest information from him and what information we were able to obtain ended in Joselyn being wounded. I am concerned that he is our only link to the Scots who are unwilling to accept English rule of Berwick."

Kenneth grunted. "Let me talk to him. Perhaps I can… persuade him to tell us what he knows."

Stephen wriggled his eyebrows. "Be my guest."

As Kenneth split for the gatehouse and the vault within, Stephen made his way over to his wife as she knelt down next to the fawn. He stood over the pair for a moment, watching her scratch the spotted little head.

"'Tis time to return to your room," he told her. "Your five minutes has long been expired."

She gazed up at him. "Can I bring the fawn?"

He shrugged and she stood up, holding the little animal to her chest. Stephen put an arm around her shoulders and led her back to the keep. He took the animal from her as they mounted the narrow stairs to their chamber, but Joselyn took the animal back from him once they reached the room.

"Now," Stephen put his hands on his hips, watching her as she set the little creature down near the warm hearth. "I am returning to Kenneth and I want you to stay here and rest. You are not to play with the fawn or jump about. You are to get in bed and lie still. Is that clear?"

She turned to him, properly obedient. "Aye, my angel."

He looked at her strangely. "Angel? Why do you call me that?"

She went to him, stood on her tip toes to kiss him. But she was not tall enough so he bent down to allow her to kiss him sweetly on the cheek.

"You are an angel to me," she smiled when their eyes met. "My guardian angel."

"I am the Guardian Protector, not a guardian angel."

She shook her head. "You are an angel. You are *my* angel."

He pursed his lips to let her know how ridiculous he thought she was, but in truth, he was rather touched. "If you think sweet words will cause me to allow you to run amuck as you please, then think again. I shall not fall victim to your flattery." He pointed insistently at the bed.

"You are going to lie down on that bed and rest even if I have to sit on you."

She giggled at him and his response was to kiss her deeply, his big hands in her hair, on her face. He was having a difficult time taking a firm stance when she was so sweet and charming. It made him love her all the more.

"I was not showering you with empty flattery," she insisted as he smothered her with kisses. "I was thanking you for taking such good care of me."

He pulled back, his cornflower blue eyes warm. "You are welcome."

She grinned, rubbing at his cheeks affectionately. "My sweet, handsome angel."

He wrinkled his face and tried to pull away. He sensed coercion coming. "I am leaving now."

She held on to him dramatically. "My sweet, sweet husband," she made loud kissing noises at him. "You are the most powerful, handsome and adorable man in all the land. You are so kind and generous. You are so…."

He was trying to pull away but he was not doing a very good job. He covered his face with his hands when she threw her arms around his neck and began peppering him with insincere kisses. The ploy was now in full force but he couldn't seem to get away from her. In truth, he was not trying very hard. He was enjoying it.

"Cease!" he roared weakly. "You will not change my mind. You cannot leave this room until the evening meal and nothing you say will change the fact."

She laughed loudly when he tripped and fell backwards over the bed. She pounced, straddling his belly and kissing the hands that covered his face as Stephen feebly tried to defend himself.

"Stop!" he commanded.

"Never!" she responded devilishly, wrapping her arms tightly around his neck. "Look at me, Stephen."

"No," he mumbled fearfully behind the hands over his face.

"Do it," she shook him. "Remove your hands and look at me."

He shook his head. "I am afraid to."

"I promise I will not hurt you."

His snort reverberated off his hands. "I am not afraid of that. I am afraid you will bewitch me into doing your will."

She smiled, kissing his hands gently. "I promise I will not bewitch you," she said, laying her cheek against the back of his enormous hands. "Now look at me."

He splayed his fingers, the blue eyes glimmering with humor. "I am looking at you. Now what?"

She sat up, still perched on his belly, and began to peel his fingers away, one at a time. She kissed each finger as it came away. Then she pulled both hands off, rough and calloused things. She put them against her cheeks.

"I will rest for the afternoon if that is your wish," she said softly. "But I would like permission to see to the evening meal when the time comes. This is a special occasion, after all. It is not every day that Kenneth St. Héver visits. I want to make sure everything is perfect so he will be impressed with the kind of woman you married."

He stroked her cheeks with his thumbs before pulling her down onto the bed and taking the dominate position over her. He lowered himself, gently feasting on her neck and collarbone, tasting her sweetness. The playfulness was over and the gentle passion was beginning.

"He knows what kind of woman I married," he breathed. "The most wonderful woman in England."

She wrapped her arms around him, holding him tightly as he progressed from kissing to fondling her. He hadn't made love to her since before her injury and she suddenly very much wanted to feel him against her, inside of her. In the past ten days, the man had become her entire world. Her lips found his earlobe.

"Take me," she whispered.

He shook his head. "Nay, sweetheart, as much as I would love to, I have duties to attend to right now."

"Duties can wait. 'Tis been too long, Stephen. Take me now."

He shook his head again and lifted his lips from the swell of her bosom. The cornflower blue eyes were glazed with passion as he gazed at her.

"You are still ill," he insisted gently, cupping her face. "I do not want to tax you. You must get well before we can…."

She put her hands on his head, pulling him down to her. "I am fine," she teased as her lips brushed his. "Please, Stephen. Do not deny me."

He knew he should not but his willpower was not strong enough. When she plunged her little pink tongue into his mouth, he was lost. Her surcoat came off beneath his gentle, eager hands and his mouth latched on to a tender nipple. Joselyn groaned softly as his lips moved over her breasts, her torso, his touch gentler and more reverent than she had ever known it to be. When he finally impaled her on his great phallus, she wrapped her body around him and moved with him, feeling his great strength around her and in her. His touch said a million words his lips couldn't seem to and she whispered in his ear as he thrust into her, telling him of her love for him. Her softly purring voice only heightened his fervor.

He released himself deep into her body, feeling her slick walls pull at him. Well after their passion climaxed, Stephen continued to hold her tightly, embedded in her sweet body, his chin on the top of her head. He didn't think it was possible to love something as much as he loved her. He couldn't remember when his life did not revolve around the woman.

"Now," he shifted slightly so he could look at her, burrowed warm and deep in his arms. "After all this, you must promise me no more argument. You will stay here and rest while I attend Kenneth."

She lifted her face up to his, kissing him. "I promise, I will stay here."

He pecked her on the nose, the lips, before reluctantly releasing her and going in search of his clothing. Joselyn sat up, the coverlet clutched to her naked breast as she watched Stephen dress. She was sorry when he pulled his breeches over his tight buttocks; she rather liked watching his naked behind. In fact, there was much about Stephen's naked body that she liked, unusual for a woman who had viewed men with such fear and loathing before her marriage. Stephen had changed a great many things about her. He had changed *her*.

She was still daydreaming about him when he finished dressing and turned to her. He fiddled with the mail around his upper arm, watching his wife as she smiled up at him. He finished with the mail and returned her smile.

"You may see to the evening meal if you feel up to it," he told her. "But that is the extent of it. No walking around, no over-exerting yourself. Swear it."

She nodded obediently. "I swear."

"Good." He winked at her. "I will see you later."

"I love you, husband."

He paused, his hand on the door latch, his cornflower blue eyes lingering on her. "I love you, too."

He winked again and was gone. When the door was shut, she got out of bed to lock it. She thought briefly about dressing and going to the kitchens, but the evening meal was hours away and she did not want to be viewed as disobeying Stephen's command. But there was something more on her mind with the appearance of Kenneth. She knew he was here to help Stephen in dealing with the rebellious Scots. She had tried and failed. Now Kenneth was here and, at some point, would undoubt-edly visit Kynan. Joselyn wondered if a word from her to her cousin would convince the man to tell Kenneth and Stephen what they wanted to know. Perhaps Kynan would feel sorry that Joselyn had been injured by the very people he was trying so hard to protect. She wondered if she should not make one last attempt to aid her husband. She simply couldn't let it go entirely.

She had to try one more time.

CHAPTER TWELVE

KYNAN WAS SHOCKED to see Joselyn gazing at him in the dim light. He almost hadn't seen her in the darkness, through the big iron grates that kept him caged like an animal. The last he had heard, she was gravely injured. Perhaps even dying. But the woman standing on the other side of the iron bars appeared beautiful and healthy. For a moment, he thought he might be dreaming.

But Joselyn smiled at him and he knew it was no dream. Kynan was chained on the leg by a big, heavy, rusty cuff that had cut into his leg and caused a raging infection. He struggled to his feet, making his way towards the bars as far as he could before the chain stopped him. He reached out just as she did, their fingertips brushing.

"Jo-Jo," he breathed. "Are ye well, lass? The big *Sassenach* told me ye had been wounded."

Joselyn was on borrowed time. She had tried to bribe the guards to let her in, promising them sweet cakes in exchange for a few moments with her cousin. But that hadn't worked so she became angry with them and told them that she would tell her husband that they had tried to molest her if they didn't let her in, which had drawn the desired reaction. The threat of Pembury's wrath held weight. So they had followed her into the vault to make sure that she did not come to any harm in addition to ensuring that she would not somehow try to free the prisoners. They lingered back, keeping track of the time and watching every move she made, so she kept her voice lowered.

"I am much better," she whispered. "It is true, I was injured. But my husband healed me."

Kynan drank in the sight of her, angered at the helplessness he was feeling. "What happened?" he demanded softly. "How did ye end up in the line of fire?"

She didn't want to tell him the truth, that she had used the infor-mation she had coerced from him to help her husband. She didn't want him to know she had betrayed his confidence.

"It does not matter," she replied softly. "All that matters is that I am well and Stephen healed me. Ky, you must help me, please."

"How?" he raised his voice and she shushed him. "I'm trapped. I canna do anything for ye, lass, and ye know it."

As he grew agitated, she grew desperate. Her expression was be-seeching. "Ky, listen to me," she whispered. "I do not have much time, so you must know this; my husband is a good man. I lied to you when I told you that the English killed my mother. You know she had been mad for some time. She had thrown herself into the fire and they mercifully ended her life before she burned to death. I could tell you so many wonderful things they have done for me but I do not have the time. All I can tell you is that I lied to you. My husband has not been terrible to me. In fact, he is the most wonderful man I have ever met."

Kynan stared at her as if she had gone mad. "The big brute?"

"Aye."

His eyes narrowed. "Have ye lost yer mind, lass?"

Joselyn smiled as she shook her head. "Not at all," she replied. "With everything that has happened to me… my husband has over-looked all of it and he loves me deeply. He is kind, compassionate and brave and I love him with all my heart. I want to help him and protect him. Will you please help me do that?"

Kynan's brow furrowed as if he did not understand her words. "Help ye?" he rattled his chains. "I am the one who needs help, Jo-Jo."

Joselyn was frustrated that he was not getting her message. "If you help me, I will convince my husband to release you," she made a promise she was not sure she could keep, but she had to gain his cooperation. "I need your help. I need you to tell me what you know about the Scots. What are they planning, Ky? Are they preparing to attack Berwick again?"

He studied her a moment, eventually backing off the grate as his manner cooled. He could see that somehow, someway, her English husband had bewitched her. She was more loyal to him than she was to her own people, or at least she believed she was. Her young mind was confused.

"I wouldna know what me men are planning," he said after a moment. "I have been locked away in the bowels of this place. If me men are planning an attack, I'm not a part of it."

Whatever warmth they had experienced when she came into the cell was evaporating. Joselyn could feel it. Mistrust hung over him like cloud.

"Ky, please," she gripped the iron bars, her pale blue eyes boring into him. "He is the only man who has ever been kind to me and I love him. Can you not understand? I do not care about Scots or English loyalties. This is not about politics or kings or war. I only care about my husband and I will do anything to keep him safe."

"Including betray yer kin?"

"My kin tried to kill me," she fired back. "I have the scar on my back to prove it. Why would you protect these people?"

Kynan backed away from the grate, his eyes riveted to her. He was unsure, confused, exhausted by his tribulations and baffled by his cousin's love for her English captor. The knight had professed the same feelings, so with Joselyn's confirmation, he was coming to understand that they shared something very special. Still, her shift of loyalties was unsettling. He couldn't be glad for her new-found happiness just yet.

Joselyn watched him move away from her, back to the shadows that had become his home. She watched him with eyes of sadness, of agony, wishing he could understand what she was attempting to accomplish. But he did not understand. All he knew was that Stephen was the enemy. He probably thought she was the enemy, too. The thought infuriated her.

"If you will not help my husband, then I will say this and speak of it no more," she hissed, fighting off tears. "If something happens to

Stephen because of you and your foolish rebels, I swear to God that I will never forgive you. And I will hate you for the rest of my life."

Kynan simply hung his head. Joselyn walked from the vault in tears.

 CȜ

THE EVENING MEAL at Berwick Castle that evening was an extravaganza of culinary delight. After her encounter with Kynan, Joselyn had retreated to the kitchens to prepare her masterpieces. The stores had been somewhat replenished and she had a variety of ingredients to work with, and work with it she did. She had fowl prepared a variety of ways and with sauces such as plum and currant. There were also several egg dishes; eggs beaten and mixed with milk, cheese and herbs, then baked. There were tons of nuts and cheeses, with great loaves of bread baked with a variety of herbs and other ingredients incorporated into them. But most of all, there were pickled lemons shipped all the way from London, a most impressive and expensive addition. Every time Joselyn ate one, her lips puckered up and her eyes watered terribly so she was not too fond of them. And, of course, she made sweet cakes for her husband with loads of honey and walnuts.

Stephen and Kenneth arrived late to the meal and looking some-what subdued. But Stephen had a smile and a kiss for his wife as he took a seat on the bench, delving into the roast chicken in front of him. Kenneth followed suit and between the two of them, they ate almost half of what was on the table. Stephen would not share the sweet cakes with Kenneth until the man threatened to fight him. Begrudgingly, he shared his treats.

The hall was warm and fragrant with smells of food and the sounds of soft laughter. In addition to Stephen, Kenneth and Joselyn, several senior soldiers and knights were also in attendance, including Lane de Norville and Sir Alan. They were all most complimentary of the meal and Joselyn blushed prettily as the perfect hostess. Stuffed and ill with too many sweets, Stephen could not have been prouder. She was sweet, polite and good at conversation but when she brought about the subject of helping Kenneth find a wife again, Kenneth indelicately changed the subject by asking if there were more sweet cakes in the kitchens. No, there weren't, but she had something just as wonderful. Joselyn leapt up and disappeared from the hall.

Wine in hand, Stephen watched her go, returning his attention to Kenneth only when Joselyn left his sight. He noticed that ice-blue eyes were appraising him. Stephen lifted his eyebrows at the man.

"Why do you look at me so?" he demanded.

Kenneth stared at him a moment before grunting and lifting his wine to his lips. "You know why."

Stephen's good humor faded. "You are not going to start that again, are you?"

Kenneth licked the wine from his lips. "You know it is for the best. I told you earlier. My discussions with your Scots prisoner were not particularly fruitful." He had no idea that he had missed Joselyn's visit to Kynan by minutes, resulting in a very defensive and agitated prisoner. "Nonetheless, I do not like the gist of the small conversation we did have. I think it would be best if you sent your wife away from here, someplace safe. You must get her out of Berwick for I fear the lack of Scot activity these past several days are leading to a bigger, more organized build-up."

Stephen looked frustrated. "She is safer here than she would be traveling on the open road. Anywhere I would send her is days away and I cannot go with her. I do not want her exposed if I cannot be there to protect her."

Kenneth grunted. "Now you are being ridiculous. Send her with a contingent of soldiers and a couple of knights. Send her to de Lara's holding."

"Forestburn Castle?" Stephen shot back, bordering on shouting.

"Aye, Forestburn," Kenneth lifted his white eyebrows at him. "It is the safest place for her. Toby will take good care of her until this madness is over."

Stephen pursed his lips at him and looked away. Kenneth watched him a moment before finally draining his wine. He set the cup down and leaned forward on his elbows.

"Why did you bring me here, Stephen?" he asked.

Stephen would not look at him. "That is a stupid question."

"Nay, 'tis not. Tell me."

Stephen was fidgeting angrily. "To assist me."

"I am trying to do that yet you resist. I see this situation more clearly than you do, my friend. Why do you refuse?" Even though Kenneth already knew the answer, he still wanted to hear it from Stephen's lips. But Stephen refused to answer him, so Kenneth supplied the words. "I know you do not want to be separated from her. But would not you rather have her far away and safe than have to worry about her in an overrun fortress?"

Stephen looked at him, then, the blue eyes dull with both anguish and reluctance. He looked as if he were preparing to retort but suddenly shut his mouth and looked away again.

"Must we speak of this now?" he mumbled.

"There is no more time, Stephen. You must send your wife to Forestburn and do it now."

Stephen was silent a moment, contemplating. He finally sighed heavily, as if he had just given up a mighty battle. He raked a hand through his dark hair, fidgeting, apparently settling the situation in his own mind.

"Very well," he murmured, bringing his gaze up to meet Kenneth's. "I must trust that you are seeing the situation more clearly than I am. If you say that I must send my wife away, then I will trust you. But I will ask a favor of you."

Kenneth was relieved that Stephen was finally coming to his senses. "You do not have to ask," he said. "Just tell me what you would have me do."

"Escort Jo-Jo to Forestburn. If I cannot be with her, then I would trust her life only to you."

Kenneth nodded slowly. "If that is your wish, then I shall do it."

Stephen looked rather defeated, returning his attention to his chalice. "She is the most important thing in the world to me, Ken. More than castles and kings, Joselyn matters above all."

"I understand."

Stephen didn't say anything more but it was obvious that his depression was growing. Joselyn emerged back into the hall at that moment, carrying a tray covered with a white cloth. She was smiling as she approached the table and set the tray down between the two men. Standing so close to Stephen that she was butted up against him, she faced Kenneth.

"Our stores have been replenished in the past few days and we were fortunate enough to have a small supply of sweet salt," she told him. "I was able to make cakes from it. I do hope you enjoy them."

She pulled the cloth off the tray and both Stephen and Kenneth peered at the contents with interest. They were small, round cakes with a white substance smeared on the top of them. Stephen, never one to be shy when it came to his wife's cooking, ran his finger across the white, creamy substance and tasted it. Deciding it was well worth eating, he picked up the little cake and bit into it. Custard oozed out from the other side and he had to move fast to slurp it all up. Kenneth, seeing that Stephen was well into a feast of sweet custard, popped a whole cake into his mouth and chewed with relish.

"These are marvelous," Stephen licked his fingers. "What is in them?'

Joselyn beamed. "I made the cakes from white flour and sweet salt," she told him. "Then I made custard from eggs, milk and sweet salt. When the cakes were done, I cut them in half and put the custard in the middle. The white cream on the top is made from sweet salt and milk."

"Dear God," Kenneth popped another in his mouth. "These are the most amazing cakes I have ever had. What is this sweet salt you speak of?"

Stephen had another whole one in his mouth. "I first had it in the Levant," he told him. "It looks like salt but is extremely sweet, hence the name sweet salt. There is a supplier in London that I get it from and he ships his supplies from the Far East. It is not cheap nor is it plentiful, but I have been spoiled by it, more so now with my wife's skillful cooking."

Kenneth grabbed two before Stephen could get to them, shoving them both into his mouth. "I believe I have had it before," he said, mouth full. "It is sweeter than honey."

Stephen nodded, taking the last cake before Kenneth could snatch it. "It is an utter indulgence," he sucked the custard off his fingers, pulling his wife against him with his left arm. He kissed her on the cheek. "Remarkable as always, Lady Pembury. Kenneth will now return to the Marches with tales of your legendary culinary skills and make me the envy of every man on the border."

Joselyn grinned shyly, accepting a hug from her husband and a wink from Kenneth. Stephen then burped loudly as Kenneth fought down the urge to vomit, both of them so full they could barely move. As Joselyn grinned and wiped the sweat from her brow, Stephen suddenly noticed how rosy her cheeks were and put a hand to her forehead.

"Christ," he hissed, immediately standing. "Your fever is flaring."

Joselyn's smile vanished as she put her hand to her forehead as if to reaffirm his diagnosis. "I do not believe so," she insisted, fearful that he was going to take her to bed and tie her down. "I just came from the kitchens and they were quite warm. I feel fine, truly."

He would not even respond. He put his arm around her shoulders and turned her for the door. But they hadn't taken three steps when the entry door suddenly squeaked back on its hinges. Into the warm and fragrant hall emerged the battle hardened figure of Tate de Lara.

In full armor minus his helm, the man looked weary and stubbled as he pulled off his massive leather gloves. His gaze fixed on Stephen and Joselyn.

"Lady Pembury, you are looking well," he greeted Joselyn before looking to Stephen. "Can I safely assume that the only reason you are leaving the great hall is because there is nothing more to eat? I have ridden twenty miles since early this morning and was hoping to make sup before you inhaled everything not nailed to the table."

Stephen grinned. "There is still plenty of food left, although Kenneth and I have managed to eat all of the sweets. You should have arrived earlier."

Tate heard Kenneth's name, suddenly noticing the man as he rose from the table several feet away. A weary grin creased Tate's mouth as he and Kenneth came together in a powerful handshake, reaffirming bonds that had been present since they were youths. Although Tate had a brother, Kenneth was like one and it was a satisfying moment as he gazed into the familiar features. Even perpetually stone-faced Kenneth's expression warmed at the sight of his friend and liege.

"Ken," Tate greeted. "Good to see you, man. You are looking fat and old.

Kenneth lifted a blond eyebrow as Stephen piped in. "That is exactly what he said to me," he said. "We must find better insults, or at least more original ones. We are getting too predictable in our old age."

Tate laughed softly, letting go of Kenneth's hand as he studied his friend. He was very glad to see him. "Are the Marches treating you well?"

Kenneth nodded. "Well but boring," he replied. "I was infinitely thankful for your summons to join Stephen. It feels strange not to see both of you every day, fighting side by side as we did for all of those years."

Tate slapped the man on the shoulder. "It goes against the natural order of things for the three of us to not serve together," he said, eyeing Stephen as he did so. "And speaking of serving, may I have a word with you, Stephen?"

"Of course," Stephen took Joselyn's hand and passed her off to Kenneth. "Can you please see Lady Pembury back to our chamber?"

Kenneth took her hand in his big warm palm. "It will be my pleasure."

"Take her directly to the chamber, Ken. No walking around and absolutely no returning to the kitchens no matter how much she begs."

Kenneth lifted an eyebrow at Stephen as he tucked Joselyn's hand into the crook of his elbow. He began to lead her away. "Is he always so overbearing?" he asked her.

Stephen pursed his lips at the question as Joselyn cast him an impish glance over her shoulder. "Most always," she turned back to Kenneth. "But he means well."

"Do not be so tolerant, Lady Pembury. You do not really want to return to bed, do you?"

Joselyn fought off a grin, speaking loudly enough so that Stephen could hear her. "Perhaps there is something extremely devilish and strenuous that I should be doing instead."

Kenneth nodded as if he knew exactly what she meant. "We'll find something."

Stephen grunted to catch their attention, reminding them that he was indeed hearing every word as they meant he should. "If she is not in the bed when I return to our chamber in five minutes, I will hold you personally responsible, St. Héver. And I promise you will not like my reaction."

Kenneth cast him a disinterested glance before looking back to Joselyn. "What shall we do?"

Joselyn lifted her shoulders. "He is rather big. Perhaps we should listen to him."

"I am not afraid of him. Well, not much."

"Should we do as he says?"

They were at the door by that point. As they passed through the threshold and out into the mild night air, Kenneth cast a pointed look at Stephen.

"Let him wonder if we have."

They were gone through the door. Stephen's expression was still molded into a disapproving frown as he returned his attention to Tate, who was grinning quite openly at him. He shook his head at the sight of Stephen's face.

"Since when are you without humor?" he wanted to know. "Kenneth is usually the serious one and you are usually the one I cannot keep straight. What has happened to you?"

Stephen grinned reluctantly. "My humor is intact but not when it comes to my wife's health."

"Health?" he repeated. "What is wrong with her? She looks well enough."

Stephen shook his head. "She has been running a slight fever since she was wounded. I cannot seem to rid her of it."

Tate nodded in understanding. "Whatever is causing it, I am sure you will cure her," he said, eyeing him as he moved on to a more important subject. "Perhaps seeing her son might improve her health."

Stephen's dark eyebrows rose with realization, surprise. "So you have the boy?"

Tate nodded. "Cade Alexander is in the gatehouse warming himself by the fire," he said. "He is a well behaved, thoughtful boy and Buccleuch was reluctant to let him go. But after I explained the circumstances, of which he was unaware, he released him."

"Have you spoken to the lad at all?"

"A little. Enough to know that he likes dogs, enjoys war playing, and has your wife's blue eyes. He is a handsome boy."

"Did you tell him why he is coming to Berwick?"

Tate shook his head. "I am going to leave that up to you."

Stephen nodded, digesting the information. In truth, now that the boy had arrived, he was not quite sure how he was going to feel towards the child given the fact that he was a product of an extremely harrowing act against the woman he loved. On the other hand, the boy was a part of Joselyn. For that fact alone, he would treat him as a son. But there were a few things unsaid between him and de Lara. He cleared his throat softly, crossing his enormous arms and looking rather uncomfortable.

"Just so you are aware," he said quietly, "because of Jo-Jo's injury and subsequent illness, I never told her that you went to retrieve the boy."

It was Tate's turn to raise his eyebrows. "She does not *know*?"

"Nay."

"And you let me leave to retrieve the child without telling me?" There was disapproval in Tate's voice. "I told you that she should be the one to make the final decision. Perhaps she does not want the boy here, reminding her of a most heinous and violent crime against her."

Stephen put up his hands in supplication. "I told you that she has been too ill to discuss it. I will tell her tonight, this moment, in fact. But I told you before, I strongly believe that her maternal instincts will erase any fear or horror she might feel. He is her son, Tate. She will want him with her."

Tate just growled and shook his head. He made a move towards the food-laden table, but not before he jabbed a finger at Stephen. "Tell her now," he rumbled. "And when I am finished eating, I am returning to Forestburn and my own wife who, by the way, is probably already on her way here to drag me home by the ear. And if she is, I will expect you to defend me since the only reason I am still here is because you sent me on a fool's errand."

He was speaking angrily, although it was without force. He was exhausted more than anything else and Stephen knew it. But he had a point. He followed Tate to the table, watching the man grab a massive hunk of herbed bread and tear into it.

"I need to speak to you about your return to Forestburn, in fact," he said quietly.

Tate just rolled his eyes. "Leave me in peace, Pembury. For a few bloody minutes, just leave me in peace and let me eat."

Stephen fought off a grin, watching Tate try to ignore him. "I have another favor to ask of you."

"I am going to take my sword and drive it into your gut if you do not leave me alone."

"Wait until you hear me out before drawing your sword, please."

"Good God," Tate snarled. "What is it, then, and be quick about it."

Stephen didn't say anything for a moment. He stood there, trying to force the words out, but it was an extremely difficult struggle. He didn't want to say them. But he knew he had to.

"I want you to take Joselyn with you when you leave," he said quietly. "I want her out of Berwick."

Tate stopped chewing and looked at him. "Why?"

Stephen inhaled slowly, wearily. "Because Ken seems to think that the Scots are building up to a major attack. He interrogated Joselyn's cousin earlier today and based on the man's information, Ken feels that the lack of recent activity means the Scots are preparing for something big. If that is true, then I do not want Joselyn within these walls. I want her safe."

Tate swallowed the bite in his mouth. "And what do you feel, as the Guardian Protector?"

Stephen lifted an eyebrow, slowly. "I cannot say that I am in complete agreement, but the lack of activity, any at all, is troubling."

"Ken has never been an alarmist."

"I know. That is why I am taking his advice regardless of how I feel. Perhaps he is sensing something I am not."

Tate took another bite of bread. "If that is true, then I should not leave. I should remain here with you."

Stephen shook his head. "We are expecting reinforcements from Henry of Lancaster any day now," he countered. "It is not necessary for you to stay."

Tate fell silent as he swallowed his bread and delved into a big beef knuckle. "You know," he said casually, "it has been a long time since you and Ken and I have fought side by side. I am not sure I want to miss that."

"If you do not take Joselyn to Forestburn, then Ken has already said that he will. I have a feeling Toby would rather see you than Ken."

"Toby will eat Ken alive if he shows his face instead of me."

"So you will take her when you go?"

Tate sighed faintly, some of the fight gone out of him. He resumed chewing, more slowly. "What will you do about the boy?"

"Send him with her. They can take the time to get acquainted."

De Lara scratched his head with exhaustion, digesting both his meal and the information the night had brought. "Will you tell him of his parentage before I leave?"

"When will you leave?"

He shrugged and wiped at his mouth. "More than likely on the morrow. If you are comfortable with what troops you have here, there is no reason for me to stay any longer."

"Good," Stephen agreed. "The sooner you remove Joselyn from this place, the better I will feel."

With nothing more to say, Stephen left Tate devouring half a cow while he left the warm, stale great hall for the cool evening outside. Dogs barked in the distance and sentries with torches lit up the battlements. Stephen surveyed the bailey as he passed through en route to the keep, half-expecting to see his wife somewhere in the confines. He would not have been surprised to see that she had convinced St. Héver to disobey a command. But there was no wife lurking in the shadows of the bailey so he entered the keep, mounting the stairs just as Kenneth was descending. They nearly crashed into each other and Stephen had to back down to the bottom to allow Kenneth to descend. The big blond knight was moving faster than usual.

"What is wrong with you?" Stephen demanded. "You move as if the Devil is on your heels."

"The devil is," he lifted a white eyebrow, moving for the entry. "Your wife was attempting to coerce me into taking her fawn out for a night stroll. She said if I did not do it, she would be forced to take it. I had to run away lest she snare me for the task."

Stephen snorted. "Coward."

Kenneth was out the door, walking backwards as he jabbed a finger at Stephen. "The woman is bewitching, Pembury. She looks at you with her pale blue eyes and it is impossible to deny her."

Stephen shook his head with a grin on his face. "You are telling me something I already know." He lifted his voice as Kenneth moved further away. "De Lara leaves on the morrow for Forestburn. He is taking Joselyn with him."

"Good!" Kenneth shouted from mid-way across the bailey.

Stephen's grin was still on his lips when he reached his chamber and opened the door. Joselyn was sitting on the bed, removing her shoes, her head snapping up when Stephen entered. She smiled, mostly because she was glad to see him but also because he was still grinning. She cocked her head.

"Why are you smiling?" she asked.

He rubbed his chin wearily, yawning with the sudden heat of the room. "Because you have scared Kenneth away," he told her, putting out a hand to stop her as she went to set her shoe on the bed. "Wait a moment. I have a need to speak with you before you undress for bed."

She was interested and curious. "Of course. What about?"

Stephen's smile faded as he gazed down at her, wondering for the first time how she was going to receive the news of her son being within the walls of Berwick. He had meant well when he had sent Tate to retrieve the boy, but now he wondered if he had done the right thing. He was suddenly uncertain. He moved to one of the two large chairs that flanked the table in the room and lowered himself down.

Stephen sat forward with a deep sigh, leaning his elbows against his knees and letting his hands hang. It was clear that he was pensive as he focused on Joselyn, meeting her inquisitive expression.

"Jo-Jo, you know that I love you and there is nothing on this earth that I would not do for you," he began quietly. "I have done something... questionable. I hope you will forgive me."

She shook her head faintly, having no idea what he was talking about. "I would forgive you anything, my angel. What is it?"

He smiled faintly in response before his smile faded away. "I have a confession that must not leave these walls."

She grew very serious. "I would never betray you."

"I know that. But you must understand that what I did, I did for you."

"What did you do?"

He inhaled deeply again as if gathering courage. "The soldier that raped you," he began quietly, so quietly that it was nearly a whisper. "I killed him."

Joselyn's eyes widened. "You... you *killed* him?"

He nodded slowly. "During the siege those weeks ago when I came to you demanding the truth of what your father had done to you. Do you recall that day?"

She nodded, suddenly looking as if she was about to cry. "I do."

Stephen could sense the mood of the conversation turning grave. "The soldier with the scar on his forehead saved my life upon the battlements that day," he tried to sound as if he was not struggling with the conversation, which he was. "I thanked him before I realized who it was. When I confronted him about your rape, he said that you were not virgin when he had taken you. He called you a whore so I killed him."

Joselyn burst into quiet tears and hung her head. Stephen went to her, drawing her into his massive embrace and holding her tightly. He lay back on the bed, taking her with him, holding her while she wept. His lips were on her forehead as he spoke.

"He can no longer hurt you," he murmured. "I had to tell you what I had done so that you would not live in fear of seeing this man for the rest of your life. But know this, I would kill a thousand men just as easily in order to keep you safe and happy. You are the most important thing in the world to me."

Her weeping increased and she lifted her head, throwing her arms around his neck and squeezing him tightly.

"I love you," she murmured, tears on her lips as she kissed his face. "You are my angel and I love you more than life."

He didn't say anything for a moment, holding her close and burying his face in her hair. His attention was momentarily diverted as he realized that she didn't feel as warm as she had earlier. He felt a good deal of relief that her fever was apparently abating. With that comfort, he moved on to the next piece of news he needed to deliver.

"There is something else you must know," he said softly, pulling his face from her hair and focusing on her red-rimmed eyes. "You told me once that the child that was the result of the rape was fostering at Ettrick Castle. Do you recall?"

She nodded, sniffling. "His name is Cade."

"I asked de Lara to fetch the boy. He is here at Berwick."

Her eyes abruptly widening to titanic proportions as his words sank in. Her mouth popped open and in an instant, the tears were vanished. "He is here?" she breathed with shock.

"Aye," Stephen replied steadily. "That is why I asked for your forgiveness. I should have asked you how you felt about a reunion with him but I did not. I had Tate go to Ettrick and bring the boy back to Berwick. He is your son, Joselyn, and because he is part of you, he is a part of me as well. With your approval, I should like to adopt the boy."

She stared at him, the pale blue eyes wide with astonishment. "You would become his father?"

"If you will allow it."

She continued to stare at him, overwhelmed. There was so much amazement and delight in her heart that she could hardly contain or express it. Her hands were on his cheeks, her pale blue eyes boring into him, as words of gratitude, amazement and blessing tumbled over and over in her mind. It went beyond what she ever believed the man capable of. His graciousness was without measure.

"You honor me, Stephen," she finally whispered, the emotion apparent in her eyes. "There are no words to express my love for you or the joy that is in my heart at the moment. To thank you seems wholly inadequate."

He smiled faintly, touched by her reaction. "Then you approve?"

She nodded so strongly that her hair ended up in her eyes, throwing her arms around his neck again and holding him fast against her. Then she abruptly bolted off the bed.

"Where is he?" she demanded.

Stephen grabbed her by the wrist so she would not run wild. "Sweetheart, listen to me," he tried to force her to focus so he could finish telling her what he must. "Cade has no knowledge that you are his mother. He does not even know why he is here. It would be well for you both if we treat this very carefully. You must be gentle when you explain the circumstances of his parentage."

Joselyn was in a haze of delirium, but she understood what Stephen was trying to tell her. Or, at least she thought she did. She nodded her head eagerly, struggling to control her excitement.

"I will tell him that I am his mother and he should be happy, don't you think?" she said enthusiastically. She suddenly threw her arms around his neck again, knocking him off balance. "Oh, Stephen, thank you for bringing him back to me. Thank you from the bottom of my heart."

He coughed as she knocked him in the throat, torn between his caution and her joy. "Sweetheart," he unwrapped her arms and held her still, fixing her in the eye. "You cannot go charging up to the boy and announce you are his mother. Do you understand that?"

She nodded eagerly but began jumping up and down. "Where is he?"

He sighed heavily. Her reaction was not what he had expected but he was pleased nonetheless. There was also some satisfaction to it. He had told de Lara that he believed her maternal instincts to be stronger than those of the horrible memory the boy embodied. He had known her well. Still, he knew she needed to calm down before he took her to see the boy. He didn't think it would bode well for either of them if she affectionately attacked the lad and scared him off. He grasped her face gently and kissed her.

"Come along," he said softly.

It was a struggle to get down the spiral stairs. Joselyn was behind him, moving faster than he was, and he swore she would have run him down in her haste had he not had a good hold of her. When they reached the entry level, he took her into the small solar where he had taken her the first time they had met. This was the room where they had become acquainted with dark and short words to one another. He forced her to sit on a stool near the hearth as he took a flint stone and sparked some life into a bit of dry kindling. In little time, a warm fire was growing. When he was certain the blaze would not flare out, he turned to his wife.

She was perched on the stool, gazing at him expectantly. He put a massive palm over her hands folded in her lap.

"I will bring the boy to you," he said. "I want you to stay here and think calmly on what you are going to say to him."

She nodded, trying to think on his words but realizing she was too excited to adequately do so. She didn't want to say the wrong thing. As he stood up to leave, she grabbed his fingers. "I do not think I can be calm or emotionless when I speak with him," she said, her gaze suddenly imploring. "Do you think... that is, would you tell him for me? I think you would do a better job of it than I can at the moment."

His cornflower blue eyes twinkled. "I will tell him if that is your wish."

"It is."

He simply nodded, squeezed her hand, and quit the room. Joselyn heard his footsteps fade away, taking a deep breath and struggling to compose herself. As the fire snapped in the hearth and the room warmed, all she could do was wait for the moment she had dreamed of for eleven years. But she had never dreamed it would come about under these circumstances, not in her wildest fantasies. Closing her eyes, she bowed her head and thanked God yet again for Stephen of Pembury.

In the dark dustiness of the bailey, Stephen made his way across the dirt towards the great gatehouse of Berwick. He glanced upwards, noting the sentries on the battlements and the faint light from the torches illuminating their way. All was quiet for the most part as he entered a small room on the ground floor of the gatehouse where the sentries usually congregated on cold nights. There was a hearth, a small table and little else. As soon as he entered the room which, with his bulk was no easy feat, he came face to face with a young boy seated at the table.

He would have known his wife's eyes anywhere, for the boy most definitely had them. Big, pale blue eyes gazed up at him anxiously and Stephen had to swallow his momentary shock. The boy also possessed his wife's fine features and he actually stared at the lad a moment, dumbfounded by the sight. He was the spitting image of Joselyn. The child had dark auburn hair, long around his ears, and as he stood up, Stephen noticed that he was already taller than his mother. He was a big, healthy lad. Stephen took a deep breath before speaking.

"You are Cade?" he asked.

The boy nodded. "I am, my lord," he replied.

"I am Stephen. You will come with me."

"Aye, my lord." The boy's handsome features twisted somewhat. "May I ask a question, my lord?"

"What is it?"

"Am I in trouble?"

Stephen suddenly realized how it must look to the child. A big man came to take him from virtually the only home he had ever known, without explanation, and brought him to an unfamiliar castle with strangers all around. Now another big stranger was making demands. If the boy was frightened, he didn't show it, which pleased Stephen immensely.

"Nay, lad," he motioned for the boy to follow. "Gather your belongings and come with me."

Cade scooped up his measly satchel and did as he was told. He scampered after Stephen, walking very quickly to match Stephen's big strides. As Stephen strolled back to the keep, Cade was fascinated by his surroundings. Ettrick Castle was not nearly as big as Berwick. He was distracted by the dogs upon the battlements for a moment and had to run to catch up with Stephen as the man drew near the keep.

Once inside the cool, dark keep, Stephen opened the first door they came to and ushered Cade inside. It was dark but for a small fire in the hearth. As his eyes adjusted to the darkness, Cade realized there was a young woman in the room, gazing back at him with eyes as wide as the heavens. One look at Cade and she suddenly burst into tears. While Cade was afraid he had done something to warrant such a thing, the massive knight closed the door to the solar and went to kneel beside the weeping woman.

Cade watched curiously, with some trepidation, as Stephen put his enormous arm around the woman's shoulders and kissed her on the temple. Then the knight looked at him.

"As I said, my name is Stephen," he said quietly. "I am Baron Lamberton, Guardian Protector of Berwick. This is my wife, the Lady Joselyn."

Cade was not sure how to react, so he simply bowed because he didn't know what else to do. But his gesture caused the lady to weep harder and he watched, wide-eyed, as Stephen comforted her.

"Cade," Stephen began as gently as he could. "What do you remember about your childhood?"

Cade cocked his head. "Childhood, my lord?"

"When you were very small. What is your earliest memory?"

Cade blinked his big blue eyes thoughtfully. "I... I remember being with the nuns," he said, having no idea why the knight was asking such questions. "I remember being in the gardens and eating carrots out of the ground. Is that what you mean?"

Stephen smiled faintly. "Aye," he replied. "And your parents? Do you know anything about them?"

Cade shook his head, his deep auburn hair glistening in the flame. "Nay, my lord. I never knew my parents. I was told they died. That is why I went to live with the nuns. Why do you ask?"

By this time, Joselyn had stopped crying and she was gazing back at the boy with warmth and gentleness. He was very well spoken. Stephen glanced at her before continuing the conversation, noting the expression on her face. She was in love with the boy already. He continued carefully.

"I ask because the nuns were mistaken, Cade," he said softly. "Your parents are not dead."

Cade's expression washed with disbelief and then confusion. "They are not dead?"

Stephen shook his head. "Nay," he replied. "Does this displease you?"

The boy had to think about it. He scratched his head, his brow wrinkling up into a frown. "I...I do not know," he said honestly. "You say they are not dead?"

"Nay."

"But how do you know?"

"Because Lady Joselyn is your mother."

Cade's focus was riveted to Joselyn, who struggled not to burst into tears again. She smiled timidly for lack of a better reaction as the boy stared at her, she thought, with some horror. After an eternity of silence and uncertain staring, Cade finally lowered his gaze and seemed to shrink away.

"I do not have a mother, my lord," he turned for the door, unable to look at them, terrified by these confusing strangers. "Can I please go home? I want to go back to Ettrick."

Joselyn looked at Stephen with horror but Stephen was fixed on the frightened, disoriented young man. He moved away from Joselyn and went to stand next to Cade, who was by now struggling not to cry. The boy's head was lowered, his hair hanging over his eyes. Stephen cleared his throat softly.

"I realize this is a surprise, Cade," he said softly. "You have been alone your entire life and suddenly a stranger says she is your mother. But you must not judge so harshly. It is not that your mother wished to be separated from you. What happened was out of her control. She loves you now and has always loved you."

Big, fat tears rolled down Cade's cheeks and splattered onto the dusty floor. Stephen knelt down beside the boy, feeling genuine sorrow for him.

"I am sorry that you are upset by this," he said with concern. "It was not our intention to upset you but I am not sure there was any simple way to tell you this news."

The boy just stood there as big tears rolled off his face. He was struggling so hard to be brave, wiping furiously at his cheeks as if angry at the tears for falling. He clutched his satchel to his chest, holding silent for quite some time as the news sank deep.

"I want to go home," he whispered tightly.

"I would like for you to stay and hear me out. Will you do this?"

Cade shook his head, struggling not to sob. "I do not want to hear anymore. Please let me go."

Stephen sighed faintly, not daring to look at his wife. He was afraid to see the anguish in her eyes. "Please, Cade," he said gently. "Please let me finish. This is important."

Cade just stood there, holding his satchel against him as if it were a shield to protect him. He was disoriented and frightened. But there was also a small part of him that was very, very curious and, more than that, desperately hurt. He didn't even know why, but he was hurt.

"W-why?" he finally whispered.

"What do you mean?" Stephen asked softly.

Cade continued to silently weep, silently wipe at his wet eyes. "If she is my mother, why did I go live with the nuns?"

Stephen looked at Joselyn then; surprisingly, she was composed. She sat with her hands folded in her lap, looking imploringly at Stephen in response to Cade's question. Stephen sighed faintly as he turned back to the boy.

"Because your father is dead and your mother was too young and too ill to tend you." It was a sweet and noble lie. "She never stopped loving you, Cade. But she knew that the nuns could take much better care of you than she could. She loved you so much that she had to make a very hard decision that was best for you."

Cade tried not to sob, fighting so hard to be strong. Watching the young man struggle just about broke Stephen's heart. He was not beyond such compassion. Cade kept wiping at his damp face, trying hard to compose himself as he finally turned and looked at Joselyn. She returned his gaze with a surprising show of strength and composure.

"You should have kept me," the boy suddenly hissed, though it was without force. "I am strong. I could have worked when I was old enough. You did not have to send me away where no one would love me."

Stephen watched his wife's reaction very carefully, hoping she would not crack, but the most she did was nod as if to agree.

"I was very ill when you were born," she told the child. "I was also only twelve years old, just a year older than you are. I was very young, Cade. I did what I thought was best so that you would always have food in your mouth and a roof over your head. Please understand... understand that I loved you so much that I would do anything to ensure you had a comfortable life. To have kept you would have been selfish because there was no way I could have provided for you on my own. I loved you so much that I had to give you to someone who could take care of you."

It was not exactly the truth but Joselyn was following Stephen's lead. She was not sure Cade would understand how he really ended up at the abbey. Perhaps it was best to spare him some things. By this time, Cade's tears were fading as he stared at the woman who looked a good deal like him. The pale blue eyes studied her carefully as he struggled to accept what he was being told.

"You were only twelve years old when I was born?" he asked, almost suspiciously.

Joselyn nodded. "Aye."

"I will be twelve years old in two months."

Joselyn couldn't hold back the smile. "I know, on the fifth day of the month."

Cade's eyes widened briefly. "You know my day of birth."

She laughed softly. "Of course I do."

Oddly, that small gesture seemed to convince him. This whirlwind of a day that had brought stunning news still had his head spinning, but he wanted to believe. He truly did. His tears vanished as his gaze lingered on Joselyn a moment longer before turning to Stephen. By now, the knight had risen from his crouched position and Cade had to crane his neck back to look the man in the face. He was positively enormous.

"You told me that my parents were not dead," he said," yet you also told me that my father died. I do not understand."

Stephen could see that Cade was an intelligent, thoughtful boy. He liked him already. "It was the truth," he told him. "Your real father is dead, but since I am the lady's husband, I am now your father. Both of your parents are living and would like it very much if you would consider living with them for a time. We would like to be your family, Cade, if you will allow. I know it is a lot to ask after all these years, but perhaps you will consider it."

Cade scratched his head. He had a lot to absorb in his eleven year old brain but, the more he thought on it, the less distress he felt. In fact, he was feeling somewhat pleased and overwhelmed at the moment. He could hardly believe any of it but there was something deep inside of him, afraid yet excited, resistant yet not. He had always wondered what it would be like to have a mother and father. He was shocked that he was actually going to find out.

"You are a baron, my lord?" he asked.

Stephen nodded. "I am," he replied. "At such time as you return to Ettrick Castle to foster, it will be as the son of Baron Lamberton. Does this displease you?"

Cade shook his head. "Nay, my lord."

"Will you stay with your mother for a time and come to know her before you return?"

Cade turned to look at Joselyn again, who was smiling faintly at him. He stared at her, nodding after a moment, before turning back to Stephen.

"Who was the knight that retrieved me from Ettrick?" he wanted to know.

Stephen lifted an eyebrow, putting a massive hand on the lad's shoulder. "That," he said, "was the Earl of Carlisle and uncle to King Edward."

Cade's mouth popped open. As a boy, he was understandably impressed by men with titles and weapons. "You are his vassal?"

"And his friend."

Cade's young face suddenly lit up. "You are so rich and powerful, my lord?"

Stephen laughed softly, turning the boy in Joselyn's direction. "No more than anyone else, lad," he said. "I have duties to attend to. Will you watch over your mother while I am gone? It would be a good time to come to know her."

Cade nodded, setting his satchel to the ground and hunting for a place to sit. Joselyn watched the boy, memorizing every line of his face and every lock of his hair. She was still dazed by his appearance, as if she was living a dream, but it was a dream well worth living. She wanted desperately to know her son and watching him interact with Stephen, and the way Stephen had handled the boy, had touched her deeply.

"Are you hungry, Cade?" she asked. "There is much food in the great hall."

Cade nodded. "Aye, my lady. I could eat."

She stood up. "Come along, then. I will also take you to the kitchens were my fawn is. Would you like to see him?"

"You have a fawn?"

"I do."

"But how did you catch him?"

Stephen stood out of the way as she opened the door, leading the young man from the room. "His mother was killed so I took him," she said, passing by her husband as she spoke to her son. "Do you like sweet cakes?"

The boy nodded eagerly. "I do, my lady."

"If my husband has left any untouched, I shall be happy to feed them to you."

Stephen grinned, watching the two of them walk from the keep, wondering how long it was going to be before Cade grew a round belly with all of the sweet cakes Joselyn would undoubtedly feed him. Still, he was relieved and pleased to see that they were at least getting along after their uncertain beginning. He could not have hoped for better.

As he walked out of the keep behind them, he didn't miss when Joselyn turned around and blew him a kiss. He winked in response. He stood there a moment, watching them walk towards the hall, touched when Joselyn slipped her hand into the crook of Cade's arm and the boy didn't back away. He looked a little surprised, but didn't pull away. When they disappeared into the warmly lit great hall, Stephen gazed up into the starry night, silently thanking God for the appearance of Cade Alexander Pembury.

CHAPTER THIRTEEN

K ENNETH WAS A man with a plan.

He had been in the hall with Tate when Lady Pembury had returned with a young man who was about her size and looked a great deal like her. Kenneth and Tate had vacated the table when the boy arrived so that Joselyn could have some private time with him. But they left for another reason as well. They wanted to continue their conversation in private.

The night was mild, a blanket of stars blazing across the dark sky. Kenneth and Tate crossed the bailey towards the gatehouse, noting the enormous form of Stephen on the parapet next to the gatehouse. He was in conference with several soldiers. Tate's dark eyes lingered on Stephen, silhouetted against the night sky.

"Are you sure that you do not want to tell him?" he asked.

Kenneth shook his head. "He is too emotionally involved in his personal life right now," he replied. "He is not thinking clearly."

Tate grunted in disagreement. "His decisions have been flawless since assuming this post, Ken."

Kenneth came to a halt, crossing his massive arms and casting a distracted eye out over the bailey. It was clear that he was somewhat edgy, with much on his mind. "I am suggesting we release MacKenzie so the man can lead us back to the rebels," he said in a low voice. "The man is useless in the vault. Something has to be done because as it is, Berwick is a target waiting for an attack. It is my sense that the rebels are building but Stephen does not seem to think this is so."

Tate watched Kenneth's body language. He was tense, highly unusual for the man who was consummately cool even in the heat of battle.

"He trusts you," Tate replied evenly. "He has already told me that he is sending Joselyn back to Forestburn with me come the morrow. I would say that is a strong indication that he is listening to you. So why not tell him what you wish to do with his prisoner?"

Kenneth looked at him, then. He fell silent a moment as he contemplated his answer, a cautious answer that could be construed as disloyal. He wanted to be very careful in his words.

"Stephen's wife is Scots," he said carefully. "Until two weeks ago, she was the daughter of the enemy. Then she became Stephen's forced bride."

Tate's brow furrowed. "True," he replied. "But they are deeply in love with each other, Ken. What are you driving at?"

Kenneth lifted his big shoulders. "I am saying that one does not change lifelong loyalties in a matter of days," he replied quietly. "But I cannot tell Stephen that. He loves and undoubtedly trusts the woman. But I do not know her and what's more, I do not by nature trust her. She is Scots. It is an unfortunate fact that what Stephen knows, his wife probably knows. If Stephen knows that we are releasing Kynan, then his wife will know it."

Tate could understand his concern but he did not agree. "Are you saying that she is somehow feeding information to the rebels?"

"It is a distinct possibility."

Tate shook his head. "I have come to know the woman as well, Ken. She is not a traitor. When she married Stephen, she became loyal to her husband."

Kenneth's ice-blue eyes glimmered weakly in the moonlight as he regarded his liege and friend. "I understand she attempted to escape more than a week ago."

Tate saw where he was leading and he sighed faintly, conceding the point. "She did make an attempt."

"What did she tell Stephen of her reasons for attempting to escape?"

Tate licked his lips as he turned away, unable to look Kenneth in the eye. "She told him that she was seeking the rebels so that she could discover their plan and tell Stephen."

Kenneth lifted an eyebrow. "And he believed her?"

Tate nodded slowly, looking at his boots. "He did."

"Do you know her well enough to know that she was telling the truth?"

Tate just looked at him. After a moment, he simply shook his head and looked back at his feet. He couldn't answer. Kenneth sighed heavily.

"You know that Stephen is closer than a brother to me," he lowered his voice. "I would lay down my life for the man. But as he is deeply in love with his new wife who happens to be the daughter of the man who led Berwick's defenses against Edward, I fear that he is not thinking clearly. As strong as Stephen is, as powerful a warrior, it appears that there is one weak link in the defense of Berwick and it happens to be Stephen of Pembury."

"Because of his unabashed love for his wife."

"It blinds him to the fact that she is the enemy. She could be closer to the rebels than Kynan is for all we know. The night she escaped Berwick, who is to say that she was not going to tell the Scots all she knew from the mouth of Pembury himself?"

Tate knew he made complete, utter sense but it was difficult for him to fully agree with him. Joselyn Seton did not seem the treacherous type. But, then again, sometimes devils were disguised as angels. He didn't know what to think.

"You told Stephen that he must remove his wife because you believed there was an imminent attack," he finally said. "Is this true? Or are you simply trying to remove Joselyn out of Berwick to separate her from the rebellion?"

"Both," Kenneth said honestly. "And I am also hoping that if she is removed, Stephen will stop seeing the situation through the eyes of a besotted lover."

They didn't say anything to each other for quite some time, each man lost to his thoughts. The night above was still and dark as night birds sang in the distance and sentries went about their rounds on the parapets above. Finally, Tate spoke.

"You will tell Stephen of your reasons for wanting to release Mac-Kenzie but make no mention of your suspicions of Joselyn," he said in a tone that suggested it was a command. "I suspect if you do, it will ruin your friendship with the man."

Kenneth nodded, understanding the delicate nature of the situation. "I would never tell him my suspicions. What I have said is between you and me alone. Moreover, I would not hurt Stephen in such a manner. I would as soon cut out my tongue. But I have the advantage of seeing the situation without emotional bias."

Tate knew that. They were all treading on thin ice. "I will take Joselyn with me to Forestburn on the morrow and we shall see if the situation at Berwick takes a turn for the worse."

"I sincerely hope not. I hope I am wrong, on all accounts, but I cannot help my natural suspicion."

"I know." Tate glanced up, seeing Stephen above. The man spotted them both and was heading in their direction. "Stephen is coming. Prepare carefully what you will tell him."

Kenneth nodded, watching Tate turn on his heel and head off into the darkness. With a deep breath, he turned to face Stephen as the man emerged from the gatehouse stairwell. Gazing into the familiar face of the man he loved like a brother, he prayed he was wrong.

About everything.

03

JOSELYN HAD BEEN weeping most of the night and when she was not weeping, she was sleeping fitfully. She didn't want to leave Berwick, or Stephen, and was very vocal about it. When dawn began to approach and the eastern sky took on purple hues, Stephen had her up and into a bath while Tilda and Mereld packed three large trunks with her new garments and possessions.

But the bath was not soothing her in the least. Joselyn had worked herself up into such a state that she felt faint and dizzy, and ended up back in bed wrapped in a soft linen shift with long belled sleeves and a hemline that dragged the floor when she walked. Stephen tried to coax some food into her but she couldn't eat. She would not even drink. She simply lay there with her arm over her eyes as Stephen sat on the bed next to her and held her hand.

Down in the bailey, sounds of de Lara's party as they prepared for the return to Forestburn echoed against the stone. Stephen could hear them. As the day began to deepen, he finally sent for soldiers to take Joselyn's trunks down to the bailey and sent the two old maids to pack their own possessions. He would send them with his wife so she had people of comfort around her. But Joselyn was still feeling horrible, eventually curled up on her side and dozing heavily. Stephen was torn about sending her on to Forestburn in this condition but he suspected most of it was in her mind. She had worked herself up a great deal.

"Jo-Jo," he stroked her dark hair. "Sweetheart, you must finish dressing. You have a long journey before you and you cannot hold up de Lara's return more than you are doing."

Joselyn's eyes rolled open, the pale blue orbs fixing on her husband. "Must I go?" she whispered.

He leaned down and kissed her forehead. "Aye, you must," he told her, trying to sound firm. "I gave you my reasons last night. It will only be for a short time and then I will come for you. But you will be safe at Forestburn, away from the war that surrounds this place."

She began to tear up again. "But I want to stay," she whispered tightly. "If I go and the Scots attack, what will happen? What if... what if you are injured?"

He scooped her up into his arms. "That will not happen," he told her, trying to force her to sit up so he could help her with her surcoat. "But I do not want the added worry of having you here in a fortress under attack. I want you safe."

Tears popped from her eyes and streamed down her face but Stephen tried to ignore them as he picked up the surcoat that Mereld and Tilda had left out. It was a dark blue *Perse* fabric, very fine and soft, and light for the more mild temperatures of summer. Stephen stood Joselyn on her feet and forced her to put her arms up, pulling the thing over her head and then fastening the ties. There were two at her waist and one big one that laced up the front of the bodice from her naval to her sternum. He grumbled the entire time about playing serving maid, but the truth was that he was enjoying it. The garment accentuated her glorious figure to a fault and Stephen was aroused as he tightened the ties. He kept running his hands over her torso, smoothing the dress, feeling her warm body beneath his palms.

Joselyn had wept silently through most of it, finally quieting enough to put her hose on herself. She tied them off with dark blue ribbons, so focused on her task that she didn't see the lust in her husband's eyes until it was too late. Suddenly, he dropped to his knees and threw up her skirts, his mouth on her legs as he shoved her back onto the bed. Joselyn gasped with surprise as he began to gently kiss her pelvic region, the insides of her thighs. All she could see was the skirt of her surcoat over his head as he went to work.

"Stephen," she gasped. "Please... not now...."

His head popped up and he pulled the skirts off his head, mussing his dark hair. He could see her pale face gazing back at him breathlessly and he pulled her skirts down contritely.

"Sorry," he reached out and pulled her up to sit. "The thought of not seeing you for some time... well, it eats at me as it eats as you. If I were any weaker, I would be joining you in your tears. But I know that our separation is only temporary and I comfort myself with that thought. You should as well. You should also comfort yourself with the idea that this will give you and Cade a chance to spend time together and to get to know one another. Forestburn is a lovely place and you will enjoy the hospitality of Tate and his wife a great deal. They are like family to me."

She gazed at him, her expression so sad that he could feel his composure waver. "But when will you come for me?"

He touched her chin affectionately and stood up. "As soon as I can,

I swear it. When the threat passes, I will come."

"But that could take years."

He shook his head. "It will not be years, Jo-Jo, more like a few weeks at the very most. Be a good girl and no more complaining, please? It will not change the way of things."

She lowered her gaze and silently went to fetch her shoes. She sat back down on the bed and pulled her slippers on, all the while remaining silent and submissive. Stephen opened the door and bellowed for a soldier, who came on the run. He shoved the last trunk at the man, who took it downstairs. Finally, he turned to Joselyn as she ran the horsehair brush through her hair, watching her as she braided it into a thick braid that hung over one shoulder. The more he watched her, the more his heart began to long for her. He had grown so attached to her that it was difficult for him to think of Berwick, and him, without her. But he had to stay strong, for her sake.

As Joselyn finished with her hair, she turned and looked at him. Their eyes met and he smiled sweetly at her. Joselyn returned his smile, but in her case, it was weak and resigned. More than that, she suddenly had an odd gleam to her eye that peaked Stephen's curiosity.

"If I tell you a secret, will you promise that I can stay here with you?" she propositioned him.

Stephen shook his head. "I will make no such promise but you may tell me your secret."

She shook her head and turned her nose up at him. "I will not tell you a thing. You will simply have to wait to find out."

He lifted an eyebrow. "Find out what?"

"I am not going to tell you."

He suddenly swooped on her, wrapping her up in a big bear hug and growling as he nibbled her tender earlobe. Joselyn squealed.

"Stop it!" she commanded, although there was little force behind it. "I am not going to tell you unless you promise that I can stay here with you."

"I am not going to promise."

She made a face as he kissed her loudly on the side of the head and released her, going to retrieve the lightweight cloak that was hanging by the door. It was a dark color so as not to show dirt, which made it excellent for travel. He swung it around her shoulders, adjusting it in a fatherly gesture. When their eyes met as he was fastening the ties, she stuck her tongue out at him.

He laughed heartily as he led her from the chamber and down the stairs. He held her hand tightly, memorizing the feel of her flesh against his. When they reached the bailey, de Lara's contingent was ready to leave. It was clear that they were waiting for her. Stephen led her towards the first provision wagon that held all of her possessions. Mereld and Cade were in the back of the wagon, but Tilda was missing. Joselyn's perusal around the bailey showed the plump woman hustling towards them from the direction of the kitchens with the fawn wrapped in her arms. She reached the wagon, out of breath.

"I did not think you would want to leave the fawn, my lady," she said, gasping for air.

Joselyn smiled as she petted the animal, practically the only smile she had shown all morning. "Of course not," she took the little beast, hugged it, and then extended it to Cade. "Would you like to tend him for me?"

Cade nodded eagerly and took the fawn from her, very pleased to take charge of the pet. As Stephen and Joselyn smiled at the lad, Tate walked up.

He was clad in full battle armor, well used and expensive stuff. His dark eyes moved between Stephen and Joselyn, and Stephen could see the veiled impatience in the depths.

"If there are no more delays, I should like to depart," he told Stephen pointedly.

Stephen nodded, sweeping his wife into his big arms and planting her on the wagon bench next to the driver. He helped her smooth her cloak and placed the oil cloth over her lap that the driver handed him, a cover designed to keep the dust and elements off her. As Tate made his way back to the head of the column and the men began to move out, Stephen held Joselyn's hand and gazed deeply into her pale blue eyes.

"Take care of yourself and enjoy your trip," he said softly. "I will send word to Forestburn to let you know how the situation at Berwick fares."

Joselyn nodded, struggling not to burst into tears again. She didn't want to go but knew that begging would only leave a bitter taste in both their mouths when he refused. She didn't want that lingering between them at her departure. So she kept silent on the matter.

"Please take great care, Stephen," she murmured. "I will miss you with every breath I take."

"And I, you."

"I love you very much."

He kissed her hand sweetly. "I love you, too, sweetheart," he replied. "I will come for you as soon as I can."

The wagon began to move and he was forced to drop her hand. Her pale blue eyes were riveted to him as the wagon pulled away. "You had better make it sooner rather than later," she told him.

He was halfway following the wagon as it lurched forward. "Why is that?"

"Because I do not think you want your son to be born at Forestburn."

After that, de Lara's trip back to Forestburn was delayed another four hours while Stephen, Tate and Kenneth celebrated. Stephen was bloody drunk by noon.

CHAPTER FOURTEEN

THE LADY ELIZABETHA de Tobins Cartingdon de Lara was a beautiful woman with golden brown hair and almond-shaped hazel eyes. She was truly stunning to behold. As her husband's army passed through the massive gate of Forestburn Castle, she was waiting.

Tate was the first one through the gate, spying his wife and their six children as they clustered near the entry. He was off his charger before the animal came to halt, running at the brood and nearly being attacked by three young boys. He tried to hug them all but he didn't have enough arms, so he knelt on the dirt while five of his children clustered around him. When all of the little faces were properly kissed, he stood up and pulled his wife into his arms. He gazed at her a long moment, reacquainting himself with her beautiful face, before kissing her sweetly.

Joselyn watched the touching reunion from her perch on the wagon, smiling when two of Tate's young sons suddenly started fighting. Tate released his wife, pulled the boys apart, and then tried to focus on the infant in his wife's arms. It was apparent he wanted to be everywhere at once, to kiss everyone all at the same time. He did his best, obviously in love with his family as a father should be.

Joselyn sat patiently as Tate got reacquainted with his wife and children. She was enamored with the way Tate responded to his offspring. The eldest was a boy around seven or eight, a very handsome and stoic lad, while his two blond-haired brothers, about five years of age, slugged it out like men. Then there were two girls, one about six and one about three or so, with long, curly dark hair and doll-like features. They clamored around their father and he took the time to give each child his undivided attention, even the twin combatants. And when he was done with the children, he hugged and nuzzled his wife the way Stephen hugged and nuzzled her. It made her heart ache for Stephen as she watched the exchange.

But her sorrow was set aside as Tate grasped his wife and began to walk towards the wagon. Joselyn sat straight as they approached.

"Sweetheart, I would like to introduce you to someone," he was speaking to his wife as he gestured to Joselyn. "You will be thrilled to meet Stephen's wife, the Lady Joselyn. Lady Pembury, this is my wife, Elizabetha. She answers to Toby."

Toby's eyes widened briefly at the introduction before a huge smile spread over her face. She handed Tate the infant in her arms and approached the wagon, gazing up at Joselyn with her beautiful almond-shaped eyes. The first thing she did was grasp Joselyn's hand.

"Lady Pembury," she said. "I cannot tell you how happy I am to hear the news. I had no idea Stephen had taken a wife."

Joselyn liked her already. She smiled. "It was a rather sudden marriage, my lady. I fear it was a surprise to us both."

Toby laughed softly and squeezed her hand. "I would like to hear all of it," she said. "Please come inside and allow me to show Stephen's wife such hospitality."

Joselyn was comforted by Toby's manner. There was something nurturing and loving about it. Joselyn warmed to her right away and she began to wonder if all English were so nice. She'd grown up being told quite the opposite. Tate turned the baby back over to his wife before reaching up and lifting Joselyn off the wagon, setting her down gently.

"Take great care of her," he instructed his wife. "Stephen is probably only now overcoming the great aching head that surely resulted from celebrating the impending birth of his first son. We do not want to ruin his happiness."

Toby couldn't stop smiling as she reached out and took Joselyn by the hand. "I will treat her as if she is made of glass and feed her great and fattening things," she said, winking at Joselyn. "I know something of bearing children. I will tell you everything you need to know."

Joselyn's smile faded somewhat as she glanced at the wagon, watching Cade climb down from the back of the bed. "I have had some experience," she admitted reluctantly. "That young man is my son."

Toby looked at Cade. The boy was eleven or twelve, taller than his mother. A wave of both confusion and shock spread over her as she realized that Lady Pembury must have been incredibly young when she had given birth. She tried not to let her confusion show as she glanced at her husband before looking back to Joselyn.

"I am looking forward to coming to know you and your son, Lady Pembury," she said the only thing she could say in light of the puzzling situation. "Please come inside and let us come to know each other."

Joselyn let Lady de Lara take her by the hand and lead her towards the massive four story keep, a big block-shaped structure that stretched skyward. Tate stayed in the bailey, playing with the children he hadn't seen in weeks. Toby, infant in her arms, took Joselyn into the dark, cool keep.

The long flight of retractable wooden steps deposited them into the second floor entry. Toby took Joselyn into a small room directly ahead, one that had the luxury of furs on the floor and three very well made chairs of oak and fabric. It was a small but lavish room. Toby indicated for Joselyn to sit in one of the chairs as she took another. Joselyn, on her best and most formal behavior, couldn't help but smile at the green-eyed, downy-haired infant in Lady de Lara's arms.

"How old is the baby, my lady?" she asked politely.

Toby looked down at the child. "Dane is four months old. My husband has not seen him since he was newly born."

Joselyn smiled as the baby stared at her, wide-eyed. "He is beautiful."

Toby smiled her thanks. "As your son will be when he is born," she said confidently. "Stephen is such a brutally handsome man that surely all of your children will be comely. You cannot be too advanced in the pregnancy. How are you feeling?"

Joselyn shrugged faintly. "Weak and ill at times, but not too terrible."

"That is good." Toby's gaze lingered over the beautiful dark-haired lass that had married Stephen of Pembury. Not knowing the woman, she was careful how she started the conversation. "I am so happy that Stephen has found a wife. Please tell me how you met."

Joselyn had a quirky expression on her face. "He captured Berwick and we met," she said simply, then offered more of an explanation. "My father led Berwick's defenses against the English. When King Edward captured the city, he ordered Stephen to marry me as the daughter of the defeated enemy."

Toby's smile faded. "I see," she said, unsure how to respond. She cleared her throat softly. "I have known Stephen for many years and you would not find a better man if you searched the entire world for him. He is...."

Joselyn held up a hand to stop her. She could see that Toby was concerned about the situation, not knowing what had transpired since the event of the forced marriage. "Do not be troubled, my lady," she said, a twinkle in the pale blue eyes. "I quickly grew to love him and he grew to love me as well. We deeply adore one another and I am thankful that things happened the way they did. Stephen is a remarkable man."

Toby sighed with relief and her smile returned. "He is indeed," she said. Then, her hazel eyes glimmered impishly. "Shall I tell you of the Stephen I know? The prankster, the one so willing to play a joke on...."

"You will not tell her any of that," Tate entered the room with children either in his arms or trailing after him. "I shall not be blamed if the woman runs off in horror. If that happens, I shall tell Stephen it was all your doing."

Toby laughed, as did Joselyn. "He is a prankster?" Joselyn repeated. "I have not yet seen that side of him."

Tate just shook his head as Toby jumped in. "The man is vicious with his tricks," she said. "Why, I recall being told that when King

Edward was younger, he had a habit of falling asleep by the fire. Stephen would move the lad's boots to the edge of the fire so they would start smoking. Once, the boots caught fire and Edward was forced to jump into a lake to quench the flames."

Joselyn was laughing at the mental picture. Tate shook his head reprovingly at their basis for humor.

"Edward burned a toe," he told them, although he was fighting off his own smile. It *had* been rather humorous at the time. "He never forgave Stephen for that."

"Did he pay him back for it, my lord?" Joselyn asked.

Tate was grinning, trying not to, as he shrugged. "He thought he was when he forced Stephen to marry you," he winked at her. "But the joke continues to be on Edward."

Joselyn could only smile in return, her gaze moving bashfully between Tate and his wife. But the baby began to fuss and Toby eventually rose to her feet.

"Dane needs to be fed," she said, looking to Joselyn. "I shall show you to your chamber, my lady, and then you and I will continue this conversation later if that is agreeable."

Joselyn rose. "Most agreeable, my lady," she replied. "Thank you for your hospitality."

Toby eyes glimmered warmly. "You are part of our family now," she said. "And it is my wish for you to call me Toby."

Joselyn felt very humbled, very welcomed. "You will please call me Joselyn as well."

"Jo-Jo," Tate said, watching his wife lift an eyebrow at him. "That is what Stephen calls her,'" he told her.

Joselyn laughed softly. "It is a pet name I was given long ago. I will answer to that as well."

Toby shifted the baby to the other arm as Tate put his arm around her to escort her from the room. "Come along, Jo-Jo," she said. "I am sure you wish to rest. You have had a long journey."

Joselyn followed the pair from the room. Just as she hit the landing,

Cade entered the keep, his young face flushed with wonder and some confusion. He'd had much traveling and upheaval in the past few days and was still trying to process it. Here he was in another unfamiliar keep with people he barely knew, his satchel clutched against his chest as he looked to his mother. She smiled reassuringly at him.

"I shall put your son in your room with you," Toby said, looking to the boy before Joselyn could reply to that somewhat shocking statement. "What is your name, lad?"

"Cade, my lady."

Toby smiled at him. "Cade, I am glad you have come," she said frankly. "My son, Roman, is in desperate need of companionship from a boy such as yourself. He spends his days being set upon by his younger brothers. Perhaps you and Roman can become friends and entertain one another."

Cade's blue eyes were wide but he nodded, looking to the boy that Lady de Lara was indicating. Roman de Lara was a few years younger than Cade, a handsome boy with his father's good looks. The two lads sized each other up but Toby did not give them a chance to form any opinions. She grasped her son by the arm and pulled him in Cade's direction.

"Roman, take Cade outside and acquaint him with Forestburn," she instructed. "Then you may take him to the kitchens and find something to eat."

Roman nodded his head, knowing it would be futile to resist or negotiate orders from his headstrong mother. He motioned for Cade to follow him.

"Come on," he said rather gruffly.

Cade eyed him. "Where are we going?"

"You heard my mother. I have to show you Forestburn."

He sounded displeased. Cade studied him, trying to determine early on if he was friend or foe. He decided he had nothing to lose by trying to make a friend. "I have a fawn," he said. "Would you like to see it?"

Roman's unhappy expression change in an instant and he nodded his head. Together, the boys quit the keep and took the stairs to the bailey below. Toby, Tate and Joselyn watched them as they moved back towards the wagons before Toby finally turned to Joselyn.

"Your room is up the stairs, first door on the left," she said. "I will have your trunks brought up and will join you when I am finished feeding the baby."

Joselyn smiled her thanks, moving to the stairs and gathering her skirts when she suddenly found herself flanked by the twins. Dylan and Alex de Lara looked up at her with the wide-eyed, open stare that children often have when studying someone new. She gazed back at the boys, unsure what to say, when Dylan reached out and took her by the hand.

"Come 'long, lady," he said in his surprisingly deep baby-voice. "I will show you."

"You will?" Joselyn allowed the child to take her hand. "Why, thank you very much, good sir. I am honored."

Her other hand was suddenly grabbed by Alex, who began tugging her towards the steps. "Come," he demanded. "I will show you too."

"Ah, I have two escorts?" she said. "I am indeed humbled, gentlemen."

"Don't fall," Dylan told her as they took the first step.

Joselyn passed a somewhat humored glance at their parents as she allowed the bold twins to pull her up the stairs. They were very gentlemanly about it but it seemed to be something of a competition between them. Tate and Toby watched them escort Lady Pembury up the stairs before turning to each other.

"Do you think we can trust those two with her?" Tate quipped. "We might never see her again."

Toby cast him a disapproving glance. "They are learning to be gentlemen. They will take good care of her."

"If they do not tie her up and try to burn her at the stake first."

Toby hissed at him. "They do not do that any longer. Well, for the most part. They usually only do it to the men-at-arms who are foolish enough to agree to play with them."

Tate laughed softly, thinking of the aggressive, domineering twins that the king loved so well. "Speaking of men-at-arms, I must go and settle the men," he said, taking the two remaining children, Arabella and Cate, by the hand. "But there is something I must tell you about Lady Pembury first."

Toby cocked her head. "What about her? She seems delightful."

"She is," he agreed. "And Stephen is madly in love with the woman. Her departure from Berwick was not a pleasant thing for either of them."

"Then why is she here?"

He sighed faintly, picking up little Arabella when she tugged on him. "Because it is felt that Berwick is under threat of an imminent attack and Stephen did not want his wife there should this occur," he replied, his voice low. "She is very worried for Stephen. She wept almost the entire trip here."

Toby pursed her lips sadly. "Poor thing," she murmured. "I know how she feels."

Tate kissed her gently once, twice, relishing the taste of the love of his life. He had missed her desperately. "One more thing," he whispered, his lips against her soft mouth. "Her son, Cade, was the result of a rape when she was eleven years old. Stephen is adopting the boy as his own, but it could be a rather sore subject if you ask Lady Pembury who Cade's father is. I would not bring it up if I were you."

Toby stopped kissing him, her eyes flying open wide with horror. "My God," she breathed. "What a horrible happening. The poor woman."

"Indeed," Tate kissed her once more and moved for the door with his daughters in each hand. "Just be aware in case the conversation, however innocently, takes a turn in that direction."

Toby nodded firmly. "I will make sure it does not."

He winked at her as he quit the keep. "Good girl," he said. "I will see you later."

Toby stood there, holding on to the fussy baby, thinking of Stephen's lovely wife being raped as a child. It was enough to make her feel ill. But the woman seemed delightful, balanced, and she liked her already. Still, there were apparently mysteries with the woman and if anyone could handle the mysteries, it was Stephen of Pembury. The man was a greater man than most. With a sigh of sorrow, she retreated to her chamber to feed her very fussy son.

☙

KYNAN HAD BEEN released the same day Joselyn had left for Forestburn, only they allowed Kynan to believe it was an escape. A foolish guard with his attention diverted and Kynan was a free man. But Stephen and Kenneth had been prepared, hiding out as they watched the man steal a horse and tear off into the city. With a sharp whistle, Stephen had flicked his wrist at the four soldiers who were waiting in the shadows and the men rode off after the escaped prisoner. And with that, they would wait for word of Kynan's activities.

But word didn't come soon enough. At dawn, exactly two weeks after releasing Kynan, the first wave of Scots hit Berwick like water crashing upon rocks. Whatever had been rebuilt in the brief peace had been quickly shattered, and the citizens of Berwick began to run for their lives. Waves upon waves of Scots infiltrated the city in a calculated bunch, looting and killing as they went. Fires were started and huts began to burn as the smoke drifted over the city on a strong southern breeze.

Stephen was already on the battlements with Kenneth when the invasion began. Calm and collected, the knights went about donning their heavy battle armor, knowing they would be in for something ugly and long. This is what they trained for, what they had participated in, for the majority of their adult lives. Stephen was glad to have Kenneth with him. It gave him both comfort and confidence. They had fought many wars together. And he was very glad that Joselyn was well away from what was sure to be traumatic and bloody.

It was bad from the start. An overwhelming tide of Scots made their way straight to the castle, but this time, it was in a much more organized fashion. It was clear that this attack was much better planned. Stephen watched, flanked by Kenneth, Alan and Lane, as enormous siege towers began to roll through the city streets, heading for the castle. He could see them from his post high on the gatehouse and counted a total of four. It made sense to him now what the Scots had been doing during the lull that followed the last skirmish. They had been building siege towers and preparing. This time, they intended to take back the castle and, consequently, the city.

The Scots also had archers, not particularly well trained, but in a concentrated mass that fired barrage after barrage into the castle. It kept the Englishmen's heads down. Stephen ordered his archers to focus on the siege engines as they came in range, raining fire arrows onto the wood. But the Scots had been clever. They had soaked the wood in water for days, causing it to swell up and become very moist, and flame could not gain hold. When Stephen saw what was happening, he had to think quickly. The stakes of the battle were growing higher.

"The damn siege engines are wet," Kenneth came up beside him, having watched several barrages of flaming arrows fall away ineffectively. "If we cannot light them on fire, we are in for a cozy dance when they come upon us."

Stephen nodded. "I know," he replied. "We need something that will stick on them and burn at the same time."

"Oil?"

Stephen nodded. "If we had enough of it, which I do not believe we do." He caught Alan and Lane's attention as the men stood several feet away, watching the engines approach. "Start boiling water and oil, as much as you can find. We are going to pour it through the murder holes in the gatehouse if they breach the entry. Alan, do you remember what we did the last time the Scots attacked?"

Alan nodded swiftly with a gleam in his eye. "Quicklime and sulfur fire."

Stephen nodded firmly. "Bring it, all we have left. And I want you to bring all of the rags, pitchers and jars you can find."

Kenneth watched the men flee in their quest to do Pembury's bidding. He watched the first siege engine pull to within a quarter mile of the castle.

"What are you planning?"

Stephen's blue eyes were riveted to the sight of siege engines and more Scots on the horizon. "I have an idea," he replied vaguely.

Kenneth had to admit, it was a very good idea. They produced the oil incendiary devices first. Carefully pouring oil into a gourd, they would stick a rag in the end, light the rag, and throw it at the siege engines, two of which were upon them and ready to open up. The gourds would shatter against the damp wood, spilling burning oil all over the place. Stephen and his men began hurling the oil bombs at the men on the towers, lighting them on fire and generally creating havoc. When the men on the siege towers would panic and run from the burning oil, archers on the walls would cut them down.

Stephen and Kenneth, with their muscled arms and power, threw the hardest. They would sail the bombs from the gatehouse into the siege towers, splashing burning oil everywhere. As the oil began to run low, Alan and Lane began to assemble the bombs with the quicklime, sulfur and saltpeter, filling the remaining pitchers they had, and even earthenware jars from the kitchens, before securing them with a strip of linen at the opening and using it as a wick.

The first quicklime bomb that Stephen threw exploded like a starburst against a group of men below who were heading to the main gate with a battering ram. It scared the men more than it hurt anyone and most of them dropped the ram and ran off with their tartans smoking. Stephen and Kenneth threw a few more of the bombs before Kenneth took an armful and turned for the tower stairs.

"I am heading to the postern gate," he said. "I do not trust these fools that all of this activity at the gatehouse is not a ruse."

Stephen gave him a grin. "What makes you think this is a ruse?

There are thousands of Scots all over the bloody place. They are everywhere."

Kenneth's lips twitched. "I think all of Scotland has come down around us. What did you do to make them so angry?"

Stephen shrugged in an exaggerated gesture as if he had no idea. "I make them furious simply by living."

"You have the same effect on me."

They snorted as Stephen gestured to the bombs that Kenneth was carrying. "The postern gate is heavily protected but I agree with you," he said. "Take what you must in case you need to defend it."

Kenneth descended the stairs and emerged into the bailey, dodging a flurry of arrows that came sailing over the walls. The castle was completely surrounded by Scots, more than he had ever seen, and he was concerned as to how long Berwick could hold out against such an onslaught. It was worse than he had originally imagined it would be. He wondered what happened to the spies they sent out after Kynan, presuming that the men must have been discovered and killed. But that was his last calm thought before he came into view of the postern gate, seeing immediately that it had been torn off its hinges in a massive breach. There were dozens of English fighting off a flood of Scots who were struggling to pour in through the man-sized gate. It would only allow one man at a time but the Scots were attempting to dispute that. Limbs, heads and bloody bodies littered the area near the gate.

Kenneth dropped the bombs and unsheathed his broadsword. Before he rushed on the group, he turned in the direction of the gatehouse and bellowed one harrowing word.

"Breach!"

Stephen heard Kenneth from his post on the gatehouse. It was a booming, stressful cry. He would have known it anywhere. He ran to the east side of the gatehouse, able to see the postern gate from his vantage point. He could see a flood of men pouring through the opening.

"Seal up the gatehouse," he snapped to the soldiers on the parapets, jabbing a finger at the two closest to him. "Get to the keep and seal it. Same for the great hall. *Move!*"

The men ran to do his bidding as both portcullises dropped and the soldiers began sealing up the gatehouse and towers, compartmentalizing their fighting areas so that if one portion was breached, another one would not automatically be compromised. The English were calm and decisive as they sealed up the castle and Stephen watched with satisfaction as one area after another was sealed off. But he also noted with some concern that the Scots seemed to be multiplying. They were literally everywhere and he divided his attention between watching them breach the bailey and the siege engines that were preparing to breach the walls.

Two of the siege engines were burning thanks to the oil bombs. Apparently, not all of the wood was wet and the dry wood had caught fire and was burning heavy smoke into the noon sky. The Scots struggled to dismantle and move aside the burning siege engines and pull the non-compromised towers up to the wall. It was a long process that had slowed them down considerably. However, the fight in the bailey was in full force and Stephen watched from the walls as Kenneth and about two hundred English soldiers fended off what must have been hundreds and hundreds of Scots. Stephen could see Kenneth near the gate itself, his massive broadsword cutting down man after man. He had to grin at the man's enthusiasm.

On the north side of the castle, ladders were being pushed up against the walls. Stephen could hear the call for assistance go up from the northern wall and he moved to help along with several other soldiers. By the time he got to the north wall walk, several ladders were already alongside the walls and the enemy was beginning to mount the parapets.

Stephen unsheathed his broadsword, smelling blood.

CHAPTER FIFTEEN

I T HAD BEEN over two weeks since Joselyn left Berwick. She was counting the days since she last saw her husband because he had told her that their separation would not be a long one. No more than a few weeks, he had told her. Well, a little over two weeks was a few weeks as far as she was concerned and she was growing increasingly anxious. She had mentioned it to Lady de Lara, who in turn told her husband to send a soldier to Berwick to see how the situation was faring.

The soldier also carried a missive from Lady Pembury to her husband, something sweet and short. Joselyn was coming to see that Lady de Lara was most definitely the route to go in order to have her wishes known to Tate. The words were not even out of Toby's mouth before Tate was moving to fulfill her requests. But, then again, Stephen was the same way with her.

Not that the past two weeks had been terrible. On the contrary, she was having a marvelous time. Toby was sweet and hospitable, and she liked her very much. She and Cade had also come to know each other better during this time and she could see that he was a generally sad boy but eager to please. She wanted to make him happy, to see him smile more, so she spent as much time as she could with him when he was not playing with Roman and the twins. But as time passed and Cade began to realize that a life he had never expected was opening up to him, he began to show more joy in things.

Joselyn had played a child's game of cards with him the night before, along with Roman, Cate, Dylan and Alex, and she was coming to see the happy boy beneath the sad façade. Roman and Cade had conspired to cheat against Dylan and Alex, causing the twins to start fighting each other, and Joselyn had sat back and watched while Roman and Cade nearly busted a gut laughing about it. It had been truly hilarious to watch and in that small gesture, she found herself falling more deeply in love with her son. He would make Stephen proud.

It was near the nooning meal on this warm day as Joselyn sat with Toby in Toby's well-appointed solar. Toby was without the baby as the child napped in the room above her head, and her other children were outside with a big, burly man who had been introduced to Joselyn as Wallace. Joselyn was not entirely sure about the gruff old man when she had first met him but she had come to see that he was something of a grandfather to the de Lara children. They clearly adored him. She was not sure if he was a servant or a soldier, but mostly, he was a playmate and mentor. When the children weren't with Tate or Toby, they were with Wallace.

Cade was with him, too. She could hear the children playing some sort of game from the bailey as she worked on a piece of needlepoint in a frame. She had never had much time for lady-like pursuits so this was fairly unfamiliar territory. She had jabbed her finger with the needle several times as Toby sat across from her and wrote on parchment. Joselyn had discovered that Toby managed all of Tate's books and estates, and she greatly admired the woman for her learned ways.

"Ouch!" Joselyn jabbed herself for the tenth time in as many minutes, sucking the finger with the blood prick. She looked at Toby. "I am not getting any better at this. I would do better chopping wood."

Toby snorted, looking up from her quill. "You have not given yourself enough time to become familiar with the techniques," she said encouragingly. "I think your bird looks very good."

"It is a butterfly."

Toby stared at her a moment before breaking down into laughter. "Your butterfly looks terrible."

Joselyn burst into snickers. "You do not have to be so cruel about it," she teased.

Toby lifted an eyebrow. "Did you not know that about me? I am a cruel woman."

Joselyn watched her return to her books, her smile fading. "Nay, you are not," she said softly. "You are one of the kindest people I have ever met. Growing up, I never truly had a friend. Then, when I went to Jedburgh, emotional attachments with others were discouraged. The nuns believed the only attachment should be to God. I suppose this is the first time I have ever had someone to really talk to."

Over the weeks, Toby had heard more of Joselyn's harrowing life and she looked at the woman, her expression soft with sympathy. "You and I had the same kind of life," she replied quietly. "Before I met my husband, I managed my father's affairs because he was too drunk to do it, tended my bedridden mother, and raised my little sister. My entire life revolved around ensuring that our family survived. I never had a friend, either."

Joselyn smiled timidly. "Do you suppose we are friends now?"

Toby nodded her head emphatically. "Of course we are. We will be the greatest of friends forever."

Joselyn's smile grew. "I hope so," she said sincerely. She watched Toby as the woman winked at her and returned to her parchment. "Would you tell me how you and your husband met?" she asked as she returned to her sewing.

Toby paused, looking at Joselyn with twinkling eyes. "Good Heavens," she exclaimed softly. "Where to begin? Tate came to my father's town seeking donations for young Edward, not yet the king at that time. Tate was Edward's protector, uncle, father all rolled into one. Stephen and Kenneth were the king's bodyguards. I met all three of them at the same time."

Joselyn forgot about the ugly needlework before her, much more interested in Lady de Lara's story.

"Was it love at first sight?" she asked.

Toby looked at her as if she were mad. "Absolutely not," she said firmly. "Tate and I had a very rough start. He did not like a woman who spoke her mind. But he warmed to me, eventually."

Joselyn thought back to when she and Stephen had first met. "Odd you should say that you and Tate had a rough start," she said faintly, thinking back to that turbulent day. "Stephen and I had no less a rough beginning. We were forced to wed on the eve of surrender, neither one of us wanting to wed the other, and during the ceremony my mother went mad and threw herself into the hearth. Stephen took me from the hall before I could watch her burn to death."

Toby's eyes opened wide with horror, with sorrow. "Oh, Jo-Jo," she murmured. "I am so sorry to hear that. Truly."

Joselyn shook her head, thinking it odd that the memory didn't pain her like it once did. "It was terrible, that is true," she replied. "But in a strange way, it was also how I came to discover what kind of man I had married. Stephen built a coffin for my mother and prayed over her for hours from what I was told. And he did this without even knowing me. He did it because it needed to be done."

Toby watched the way Joselyn's face softened when she spoke of Stephen. Knowing the man as she had for years, she was thrilled beyond measure to see such adoration in the woman's eyes.

"Stephen is a wonderful man," she agreed softly. "So is Kenneth. You and I are extremely fortunate to be admitted into their exclusive club. Surely no finer men walk the earth."

Joselyn smiled, thinking on her enormous and handsome husband. "I have offered to find Sir Kenneth a wife," she said. "He does not seem too keen on the idea."

Toby laughed. "He will be when he meets the right woman. Stephen was never too keen on the idea, either, but that has changed."

"Only because he was forced to marry me."

"Then perhaps we need to force Kenneth into marriage."

Joselyn pretended to agree. "What enemy daughter can we saddle him with?"

Toby laughed heartily, returning to her parchment and still snorting. Knowing Kenneth as she did, it was a humorous suggestion indeed.

Joselyn pushed aside thoughts of Stephen before they dampened her mood, returning to her own project to keep her mind occupied. As they resumed focus on their individual tasks, the soldiers on the walls began taking up a cry. From where they sat in the solar, both women could hear it and Joselyn looked at Toby with both fear and curiosity. Toby cocked an ear, listening.

"It sounds as if they are opening the gates," she said after several moments.

Joselyn struggled not to get too excited. "Perhaps the soldier has returned from Berwick."

Toby could see that the woman was ready to jump from her seat. "If it is, we will know soon enough," she said steadily. "Relax and resume your sewing."

Joselyn forced herself to calm and resume her needlepoint. But her hands were shaking, something that didn't go unnoticed by Toby. She knew very well what it was to wait for a husband who was away at war. But time passed as they continued with their tasks, sitting in comfortable yet expectant silence, until bootfalls echoed against the retractable wooden stairs.

Joselyn heard them first, her hand frozen above the fabric, still clutching the needle, as Tate entered the solar. He glanced at his wife but his focus was mostly on Joselyn. He opened his mouth to speak but he was not fast enough.

"Well?" Joselyn stood up, gazing at him expectantly. "We heard the sentries. Did the messenger return from Berwick?"

Tate was trying to think of a calm way to relay the information, not only for Joselyn but for Toby. He didn't want to upset either of them but knew he had little choice. Before he could get the words out of his mouth, a massive body suddenly walked up behind him, wedging itself in between Tate and the door jamb. Joselyn's eyes widened at the sight.

"Kenneth!" she gasped, dropping the needle in her hand and almost tripping over the fabric loom when she tried to stand up. She made her way unsteadily towards a very dirty, bloody Kenneth, appalled by what she was seeing. The longer she stared at him, the more horrified she became. "Why are you here? Where is Stephen?"

Kenneth gazed at her. He had been in battle mode for days and it was difficult to calm himself enough so that he didn't sound like has barking orders or hollering at the enemy. As Joselyn drew close, quivering, he reached out and grasped her slender arm with his dirty, bloody glove.

"Berwick fell," he told her softly.

Joselyn stared at him, hearing his words but not truly comprehending them. She didn't reply for the longest time, struggling in that dark world between hysteria and reason. She almost couldn't bring herself to ask the question but knew she had to.

"Where is my husband?" her voice sounded small.

Kenneth took a deep breath, struggling not to be emotional, struggling to deal with the delicate lady. All he could see when he looked at her was Stephen's face and it pained him like nothing he had ever known.

"I managed to escape but Stephen did not."

"You have not told me where he is."

"The Scots have him."

Joselyn's eyes rolled back in her head and Kenneth caught her before she could fall to the ground. He scooped her up into his arms as Toby leapt to her feet and pointed up the stairs.

"Take her to her chamber," she commanded. "Up the stairs, first door to the left."

Kenneth swept Joselyn up the stairs, followed by Tate and Toby. He moved swiftly to Joselyn's room, kicking open the door so hard that he broke one of the hinges. He took Joselyn to the well-made bed and laid her gently on the mattress.

Toby was at Joselyn's head, her soft hands on the pale face. "Tate, please send for water and salts," she demanded softly.

Her husband went to the door, bellowing to the serving wench that was always lingering somewhere about the keep. He went back into the room, peering critically at Lady Pembury. But she was out cold and he turned to Kenneth.

"I will mobilize my men and return with you," he said, suddenly hissing. "Damn Stephen. I told him that I should not leave if an attack was imminent but he insisted because Henry of Lancaster was on his way with reinforcements. Damn him!"

Kenneth shook his head wearily. "It would not have mattered if you had been there," he said, his voice heavy with exhaustion. "You would have been taken prisoner or worse. I was fortunate to have escaped. I have never seen so many Scots."

By this time, Toby turned to look at Kenneth, tears brimming in her eyes. "When did you last see Stephen?" she asked.

Kenneth sighed heavily, so very exhausted. He didn't even want to think about that day but forced himself.

"The postern gate had been breached," he said hoarsely. "Soon thereafter, the walls were compromised. Stephen was upon the walls but there were just too many Scots. It looked like the whole of Scotland had been unleashed. I last saw Stephen as the walls were swarmed and the castle breached. He was on the ground with several Scots pummeling him."

Toby's eyes spilled over. "But they did not kill him?"

Kenneth shook his head. "They seemed more intent to beat him. It was as if they knew who they were looking for and went right to him." He shook his head again and began to look around for a chair to sit down before he fell down. "They want him alive, Toby. God only knows what they are going to do with him."

None of them seemed to notice that Joselyn's eyes were open as she lay prone upon the bed. She had heard most of what Kenneth had said, her expression vacant and bordering on madness. She was so far beyond grief that she could not think coherently.

"He is Guardian Protector of Berwick," Joselyn whispered, causing the three of them to look at her. But she continued to stare into space, unfocused and muttering. "He is a fine prize."

Tate had become so fond of Joselyn that he had nearly forgotten she was the daughter of Alexander Seton, the man who had led Berwick's defenses against Edward. Her entire relationship with Stephen had been based on war and conquest. At least, it had been once. Now it was quite different but the fact remained that she had been the enemy, once. He knelt down beside her and took her chin in his hand, gently, forcing her to look at him.

"What are they going to do to him, Joselyn?" he whispered earnestly. "What do you know?"

She fixed her pale blue eyes on him and he swore he saw grief and madness such as he had never witnessed with in the depths. "Know?" she repeated. "I do not know anything for certain. But Edward hanged my brothers in full view of my father. Many Scots witnessed this. Who is to say that they will not do the same to my sweet Stephen?"

"Or something worse."

Joselyn's hands flew to her head as if to hold her brains in. "Dear God," she gasped in anguish. "My sweet angel. What have they done to you?"

Tate's eyes lingered on her a moment before rising to stand. He looked at Kenneth. "Did you send word to Edward when you fled Berwick?" he asked quietly.

Kenneth was sick to his stomach by Joselyn's reaction, by the emotion filling the room. "I sent six men south; two ride for Edward while the others ride for Derby and Chester," he said. "Hugh de Ferrets can mobilize an army to Berwick in a week and d'Avranches can ride from Chester in about the same amount of time. Each man carries thousands. I have told them to summon their allies and make with all due haste for Berwick Castle."

Tate nodded. Kenneth was efficient as always. But he wondered deep down if it would be too late. It had already been a few days since Berwick's capture. Time, for Stephen, was surely running out. All of the armies in the world could not prevent the man from hanging if the Scots wished to make an example of him. Tate needed to do something and he needed to do it now. He couldn't wait for armies to mobilize. He needed someone inside. Stephen needed the help of a Scot.

Slowly, he turned to Joselyn. She was lying on the bed as Toby stroked her long, dark hair. The woman was weeping deep, excruciating sobs, her agony finding release through her tears. It was painful to hear. He muttered to Kenneth.

"I have an idea," he said.

Kenneth studied him with exhausted eyes. "What?"

Tate jerked his chin in Joselyn's direction. "Her father led Berwick's defenses against Edward," he whispered. "Perhaps she would be willing to use that status."

"And do what?"

"Infiltrate Berwick." When he saw Kenneth's dubious expression, he hardened. "Ken, this is a job for ten thousand men or just a few. An army is not enough yet too many. If the Scots have Stephen, he is in the vault while they decide what to do with him. He is indeed a prize and they will use that to their advantage. But if his wife can enter Berwick and negotiate for his release, as one of their own, it might work."

Kenneth was trying hard to see his logic. "If anything happens to her, Stephen will kill us both. If he is dead, he will rise from the grave but if he is alive, he will tear Berwick apart just to get at us."

"Do you have a better idea?"

"She is not a soldier."

The last two lines were choppy, overlapping, as each man stressed his point. Tate stared at Kenneth a moment before shaking his head. "If I had another choice, I would not use her. But if we want to see Stephen alive again, then I do not believe we have any other option. This is for her as much as it is for him."

Kenneth looked at the woman, weeping on the bed, before emitting a heartfelt sigh. He shook his head. "I do not like any of this."

"Nor do I. If I felt there was another way, then believe that I would take it."

Kenneth finally nodded, sighing heavily. "What if we discover that Stephen is dead? Worse yet, what if they execute him in front of her just to make a point?"

Tate didn't have an answer to that so he said the first thing that came to mind. "Then you will marry his widow."

Kenneth stared at him for a long moment before rubbing his eyes wearily. He simply turned away, lacking the strength to argue. Tate, meanwhile, went to Joselyn, kneeling down beside her once again.

"Jo-Jo," he said softly but urgently. "I am going to Stephen's aid but I need your help. Will you help me?"

She opened her watery eyes, sniffling. "Of course I will," she choked. "But what can I do?"

Tate didn't look at his wife, afraid he would see her reaction to his next question and it would weaken his resolve. "Those are your people who hold him," he said. "You must go and secure his release. Thousands of English could not accomplish what one Scotswoman can. You are Stephen's best hope."

Joselyn's pale blue eyes widened and she sat bolt upright, looking at him with a cross between shock and excitement. "Me?

Tate nodded. "You know these people and they know you. As Alexander Seton's daughter, your word would hold much weight."

Joselyn gazed at him steadily, understanding what he was saying. But to her, there was more to it. "I would not hold as much weight as my father," she said carefully, watching his expression shift. "If you release my father, I will convince him to plead for Stephen's release."

Tate's expression hardened again. "The same father who sold you to pay his gambling debt? Stephen would never allow it and neither will I."

Joselyn knew he spoke the truth. In fact, she was not sure she could convince her father to plead for the man's release so she let the subject go. "Then what do you want me to do, Tate?" she half-asked, half-begged. "Please tell me and I will do it."

Toby interjected; she couldn't help it. "Tate, you cannot think to send her into the heart of a battle," she was deeply distressed. "She is with child. The strain would be too much."

Tate looked at her. "I seem to remember my pregnant wife helping me escape from Roger Mortimer," he reminded her, smiling when she rolled her eyes in defeat. "Pregnancy has nothing to do with it. Heart has everything to do with it. And Lady Pembury has heart. She is stronger than we know."

"And love," Joselyn said softly, wiping the remaining tears from her face. "I would walk through fire and ice for Stephen in any case."

Toby looked sick as she faced Joselyn, putting her soft hand on the woman's arm. "I know," she muttered. "Unfortunately, I know all too well. I have been in your position and I did exactly that."

Tate was gazing warmly at his wife, memories of her sacrifice long ago filling him with respect and adoration. He kissed her cheek as he looked to Joselyn.

"You must be strong," he told her. "Stephen deserves nothing less."

Joselyn's tears were nearly vanished now that she knew she would be doing something, anything, to help gain his release. Things didn't seem so hopeless now. "I would die for him without reserve."

The warmth in Tate's eyes faded. "Let us hope it does not come to that."

03

IT WAS A good looking fortress if they did say so themselves.

Roman and Cade had built a fort of rocks in the northwest corner of Forestburn's bailey, something that Tate had helped them with when he was not busy with other things. It had been a time of bonding with his eldest son and with Cade, the boy who had never known the joy and comfort of a parent. But a burly old man by the name of Wallace had been the principal labor force and had also been given the duty of chasing away Alex and Dylan when they wanted to take it over.

In fact, once the fortress was built into what looked like nothing more than a three foot tall ring of stones, the twins made it their goal in life to kick Roman and Cade out of it and claim it. Tate and Wallace would watch the battle, giggling like fools at the antics. It made for great entertainment.

And this day was no different. Roman and Cade had risen at dawn and took bread and cheese out to their fortress. As they sat and ate, they discussed how to create a shelter inside of it. The little fawn had a bed of rushes and grass in the corner and they were proud of their only occupant. But as they played lord and masters, Alex and Dylan emerged from the keep with their father and headed directly for the fortress. Since they had been warned about charging into the fort and throwing punches, they came to within several feet of the stone circle and began throwing rocks over the side. Roman and Cade found themselves under siege and the battle of the day began.

They continued to play well into the morning. At one point, the twins charged in and roughed up their brother, who was saved by Cade when he grabbed both twins by the neck and shoved them back outside of the fort. The twins ran crying to their father, who told them that rather than try and steal Roman's fortress, perhaps they should build one of their own. Soon, a second fortress was under construction in the southwest section of the bailey. Old Wallace was confiscated as slave labor.

Roman and Cade watched the building with interest. They wanted to make sure that Dylan and Alex's fort was not bigger than theirs. If it was, it would be automatic grounds for an attempt at conquest. Tate was helping the twins somewhat but was distracted when the sentries on the walls sent out a cry. He left to go to the gatehouse as Roman and Cade watched.

"C'mon," Roman told Cade. "Let's go see who is coming."

The boys ran across the bailey just as the gates cranked open, admitting several men in armor. The boys scattered out of the way, staying clear of the chargers, but Cade recognized one of the men. He had seen him before, back at Berwick. As he and Roman ducked out of the way, he pointed him out.

"I have seen that knight," he said to Roman. "He was at Berwick."

Roman watched as the massive knight dismounted his charger and removed his helm. "That is Kenneth St. Héver," he informed him. "He used to serve the king but now he serves the Earl of Wrexham. He and my father are best friends."

As the boys watched, Tate made his was over to Kenneth. It was evident early on that the subject of their conversation was quite serious. The boys watched with growing concern as Tate put a hand on Kenneth's shoulder as he walked past him, heading towards the keep. After depositing his helm on his saddle, Kenneth followed.

The boys couldn't help but notice that Kenneth looked like he had been through a grinder. He was dirty, worn and bloody. They looked at each other at the same time, with the same thought.

"A battle!" Roman gasped. "Something must have happened!"

Cade's brow furrowed. "He was at Berwick when we left," his eyes suddenly opened wide. "Do you suppose Berwick was attacked?"

Roman's sharp young mind was working furiously. "Let's go and see!"

They raced across the bailey, dodging men and horses, climbing the stairs to the keep just as Kenneth disappeared inside. By the time they entered, Tate and Kenneth were standing in the doorway speaking to Toby and Joselyn beyond. But something happened and Joselyn was suddenly in Kenneth's arms. When the boys saw this, they hid underneath the stairs, listening as Kenneth carried Joselyn up to her chamber. They could hear the adults and their concern, voices fading as they entered the chamber above. Bravely, the boys followed.

They hid in the shadows of the second floor landing, listening to Kenneth and Tate speak of a besieged Berwick. Somewhere in that conversation, the realized that something had happened to Stephen. Lady Pembury was weeping and the boys could hear Tate devising a plan to return to the castle and save Stephen. Lady Pembury was somehow a big part of the plan. When they had heard enough, they scampered back down the stairs and returned to their fortress in the sunny, dusty bailey.

Neither boy spoke for quite some time. They sat against their stone walls, lost in thought as the bustling bailey went on around them.

Roman kept looking at Cade, noting how serious and disturbed he looked.

"You should not worry," he told him. "My father will save Stephen."

Cade looked at him, his young brow furrowed. "But they are sending Lady Pembury to save Sir Stephen," he said. "Your father said she was his best hope."

Roman shrugged, fidgeting with some of the rocks that the twins had thrown over the wall. "Nothing will happen to her. My father will protect her. He is the greatest knight in the land."

Cade was in turmoil, struggling with terrible thoughts. He had grown to love his mother and he did not want to see her in danger. More than that, he was very worried for Stephen, a man he admired a great deal.

"But…," he stammered, trying to voice his thoughts. "I only just got parents. I do not want to lose them, not when I just got them."

Roman knew the story. They had talked about it one night after eating a batch of sweet cakes that Lady Pembury had made. Too many sweets had loosened Cade's tongue and the story of his life, up until that very moment, had come spilling out. Although Cade was thrilled to have found his mother, he was deeply proud to become the son of a baron. It was a life he had never dreamed he could have, now being threatened by war and politics.

"So what do you want to do?" Roman demanded. "You cannot do anything my father hasn't already thought of, you know. He'll get Stephen back. You'll see."

It was not good enough. Cade shook his head. "I am going with them."

Roman snorted. "You cannot. My father will not let you."

"Then I shall sneak out," Cade shot back. "I shall sneak out and follow them and when my mother goes to get Sir Stephen, I will help her."

Roman was about to tell him how stupid he was but he couldn't bring himself to do it. He could see that Cade was serious, terrified he was about to lose parents he had only just met. Then he began to think of what a fine adventure it would be. Surely his father would not be angry with him when he helped save Sir Stephen from the Scots. He grew excited and scared at the same time.

"You should not go, you know," he said pointedly. "You might just get in the way."

Cade shook his head vigorously. "I will not," he insisted. "No one will pay attention to me. I'm just a boy. I cannot do any harm. But what they don't know is that I'm going to be the one to free Sir Stephen. Scots are fools!"

Roman nodded in agreement just because Cade was so enthusiastic about it. "Well," he said reluctantly. "If you are going, then I'm going with you. You may need help."

Cade was not so sure he needed a sidekick but he eventually nodded. "Very well," he said, eyeing his young friend. "But I give the orders."

Roman's mouth popped open. "But my father is the earl!"

"I'm older!"

Roman backed off, unhappy that Cade had pulled age rank on him. But he was not so unhappy that he didn't want to go. He didn't want to miss the chance to make his father proud of him. He finally pursed his lips in a gesture of defeat.

"So what do we do?" he asked.

Cade was not sure yet. But he was working on it.

CHAPTER SIXTEEN

S TEPHEN THOUGHT HE had been asleep but couldn't be sure. It could have been another bout with unconsciousness. He'd spent three days chained up to a makeshift stock with no shelter from the weather and hardly any water. He couldn't remember the last time he ate. He thought perhaps the morning before the battle began but he was not sure. Whatever damage they had done to him in the beating following the capture of Berwick had been complete and thorough. His mind and body were thrashed.

So another day began as dawn turned the horizons shades of pink and purple. The massive keep was to his left and he kept himself sane by remembering the days he spent there with Joselyn. He would close his eyes and go back to the day they had met and the subsequent days that saw him fall madly in love with the woman. He imagined what their son would look like, a boy with dark hair and cornflower blue eyes. Stephen's father possessed the same color eyes; they were a Pembury trait. He imagined the expression on his father's face when he saw his grandson for the first time. Stephen just hoped he was alive to see it.

The Scots were burning the last pile of English dead this morning, the scent of burning flesh lying heavy in the air. Stephen was not sure if Kenneth was part of those funeral pyres but he didn't think so. The last he saw the man, he was severing heads and limbs. He seriously doubted Kenneth had been killed in the battle. So the question remained what happened to him.

Alan had been killed when the wall had been breached and Stephen hadn't seen what had become of Lane. Too many Scots and not enough English had been an eventual recipe for disaster. The English soldiers were simply overwhelmed by the sheer number. Henry of Lancaster, delayed by weather further south, had arrived on the outskirts of Berwick on the eve of the first day of battle only to find it completely under siege. With one thousand men, Henry tried to fight his way to the castle but was repelled by the Earl of Moray and his allies. Under heavy casualties, Henry withdrew.

Stephen didn't blame him. The odds were too great. He was just thankful that he had listened to Kenneth and sent Joselyn to Forest-burn. He could deal with his captivity and uncertain future, but if Joselyn had been compromised, his anguish would have known no bounds.

He must have passed out again shortly after dawn because he re-gained consciousness just as he fell to the ground. Someone had cut him loose from the stocks. He was suffering from several broken ribs as well as a cracked right wrist and multiple cuts and bruises. He had suffered the broken ribs when he had first been captured and the fractured wrist had come courtesy of a bitter Scots who did it to show off to his friends. He was beaten and weakened from exposure and no food, unable to resist when several men picked him up off the dirt and hauled him across the compound. They ended up dragging him inside the keep, inside the solar where he had first formally met his wife. The room had a multitude of memories but he couldn't spare the energy to reflect. He could only lie on the floor in agony where they had dropped him.

He paid no attention to the sounds of people in and out of the solar, to the door opening and closing. It grew silent in the room as he lay there, exhausted and injured, his eyes closed to the pain that throbbed through his body. He had no idea that he was not alone.

"Well, *Sassenach*," came a low, somewhat weary voice. "They beat ye like a dog, did they? I confess, I expected worse."

Stephen's eyes opened. The only thing in his field of vision was a portion of the hearth. He could barely move.

"You have me at a disadvantage," he whispered. "It is difficult for me to address you from my position on the floor but you will forgive me that I cannot stand."

A body was suddenly beside him, on his knees, and Stephen found himself looking into Kynan's dark, intelligent eyes. The Scotsman shook his head as their gazes locked.

"Ye're mangled, man," he said. "I have sent for food. They've got no cause tae be treatin' ye like this."

Stephen closed his eyes. "I am the enemy," he replied quietly. "They can do with me as they please."

Kynan stayed on his knees next to him, studying the man. He could see how badly injured he was and something inside him, however reluctant, sought to give him some comfort. Maybe it was because of the last conversation he had with him. The words rang round and round in his head. They had ever since he had spoken them. *I married your cousin to form an alliance; that is true. But she loves me and I love her, and there is nothing in this world that I would not do for her.* It was something that had broken down Kynan's hatred of the man and even now, all he could see was Joselyn's husband on the ground, not an English enemy. If Joselyn loved him as he said she did, and he had no reason to believe otherwise, then Kynan was reluctant to destroy something that had undoubtedly brought joy into her life. And with the life she'd had, he just couldn't bring himself to cause her more pain. He sighed faintly.

"Where is Jo-Jo?" he asked softly.

Stephen grunted. "Well away from here."

"She was not here when the castle was besieged?"

"Nay," Stephen said faintly.

Kynan watched the man a moment before emitting another sigh and planting his buttocks on the ground beside him. His gaze drifted over the big man.

"So the situation has turned," he muttered. "It was ye looking at me through the iron grates. Now I am the one lookin' at ye. Ye're a sight, man."

Stephen's blue eyes were dull with pain. "I can imagine that I am," he whispered. "What do you plan to do with me?"

Kynan's jaw flexed. "I didna tell them tae do this to ye," he said in a low voice, avoiding the question. "I told me men tae take Berwick back but I dinna tell them tae beat ye tae death."

Stephen shifted on the ground, grunting with pain as his ribs screamed. "Your men knew exactly who I was," he said. "They came right for me with clubs, not to kill but to subdue. You must have told them who I was."

Kynan nodded faintly. "I told them tae take ye alive if they could."

Stephen thought of the four soldiers he had sent to follow Kynan in the hopes of gaining information on the rebellion. The men had never returned. He closed his eyes to the irony of it all, how things had turned out so badly. He thought he was a better soldier than that. Maybe he was not. Or maybe his thoughts had been too preoccupied with his new wife to pay close attention to the castle he was supposed to be commanding. Though Kenneth had never said anything to him directly, he knew the man's thoughts. He knew Kenneth too well to not know what he was thinking. Maybe Kenneth had been right.

"So our great plan turned the tables on us," he muttered, his lips against the floor, his breathing coming in heavy draws. "We let you escape, MacKenzie. I had men following you. But it seems that you outsmarted them and turned the tide against me."

Kynan lifted a dark brow. "I knew ye did," he replied. "It was too easy for me tae escape tae be convincing."

"What of the men who followed you?"

"Dead," he said without distress.

Stephen had suspected as much. "So you came to take back Berwick."

"Me men were already comin' back tae Berwick, gatherin' the clans while I was in yer vault."

"You knew this?"

His dark eyes glimmered. "There is much I know that I didn't tell ye."

"I figured that out."

The door to the solar opened and a soldier entered with a tray of food and a pitcher hanging from his hand. Kynan motioned for the man to set the goods down on the nearest table. He didn't speak until the man left the room and even then, his voice was very quiet.

"You will tell me the truth, Sassenach," his tone was odd, almost pleading. "Ye told me once that ye loved Jo-Jo. Is this true?"

Stephen's eyes opened at the mention of her name and he turned his head slightly, looking at Kynan. "Why do you ask?"

Kynan's jaw tightened, torn between stubbornness and deep compassion for his cousin. He finally lifted his shoulders. "Because I want tae know. Answer me."

"I told you that I did. That has not changed."

Kynan absorbed the statement, pondering his next move. "I pray tae God that ye're sincere. She feels the same way about ye."

"How would you know that?"

"She told me," Kynan replied, eyeing the man on the floor. "She… she's not had a good life."

"I know," Stephen answered softly. "I know all about her life and what her father did to her. There are no secrets between us. To elaborate on my answer, I love her more than life. I would die for her without question."

Kynan could only hold his gaze a moment longer before looking away. He finally sighed heavily. "I was afraid of that," he muttered. He fidgeted with his boot a moment as if pondering his thoughts. "Me mother and Julia Seton were sisters. I remember when Jo-Jo was born. I was just a lad but I remembered the most beautiful babe I'd ever seen. Julia was married tae a sick man. Alexander was a gambler and he gambled away most of her dowry, their fine things, and their money. He was also a drinker and would spend days drunk with wine. There was times when there wasna food on the table so Julia would bring Joselyn tae our home. My mother would feed and take care o'them.

And then Joselyn grew older and that's when the trouble started."

Stephen was staring at him fairly lucidly. "Kynan, I do not mean to be abrupt, but Joselyn has told me all of this and I do not want to hear it again. It feeds my anger like nothing else and makes me want to kill her father."

Kynan's expression was dark as he regarded the fallen knight. "What did she tell ye about the child?"

"That he was the result of a rape by an English soldier in repayment for a gambling debt."

Kynan stared at him, finally shaking his head and looking away. There was anguish in his features. "Still she protects him."

Stephen found himself forgetting all about his agony and injuries as he listened to Kynan's hissed words. He shifted his big body, ignoring the screaming pain as he struggled to sit up. Kynan saw what he was doing and grabbed hold to assist. But Stephen was so heavy that it was like trying to prop up a horse.

"Protects who?" Stephen demanded. "Who is she protecting?"

Kynan was inches from the man's face. In that instance, he could see that everything he had told him was true. He did love Joselyn with a deep and agonizing vengeance. Stephen was nearly beaten to death, but still, his only concern was for his wife. Kynan spilled the truth without regard to whether or not he should. He had a point to make and he would make it.

"Her father," he whispered.

Stephen just stared at him, the agony in the blue eyes unfathomable. "She told me that the soldier raped her and fathered the child."

Kynan had a good grip on him. "He did rape her," he murmured. "But she was already pregnant from her father."

Stephen suddenly couldn't breathe. He stared at Kynan, his words rolling over and over in his mind, struggling not to go mad at the mere suggestion. It was fantastic, horrific and sickening all rolled in to one.

"Who told you this?" he finally hissed.

Kynan was trying to be kind, he truly was. He could feel the man's pain radiating from his very pores, reaching out to infiltrate him and make him hurt, too. But Kynan's hurt on the subject had dulled a long time ago. What remained was disgust and sorrow.

"Julia," he muttered. "Alexander had confessed that he had taken his daughter's innocence in a drunken rage. He allowed the soldier tae rape Jo-Jo to cover up the resulting pregnancy."

"Then it was not in repayment for the gambling debt?"

"It was. But it was a sickenin' coincidence."

Stephen seemed frozen, unable to respond. The revelations were too overwhelming and he was struggling like a drowning man to keep his head above water, his mind sane in the face of madness. "She told me that she had her innocence taken when she was nine years old," he whispered in a strangled tone. "She said she had been used by her father twice before the soldier raped her and… oh, my dear God… she said her *father* used her twice. It never occurred to me that she meant literally."

"She did," Kynan replied. "Did ye not understand that?"

Stephen couldn't even think straight. He was filled with such anguish that it was spilling everywhere. "So Cade is her father's child?"

"Julia thought so, but I suppose we'll never know for sure."

Stephen closed his eyes and collapsed back onto the floor. He was such a big man that Kynan couldn't support his dead weight. But he leaned over Stephen as the man lay on the floor, half-conscious and reeling.

"Listen tae me, *Sassenach*," he lowered his voice, speaking urgently. "I dunna tell ye the ugly family secrets tae drive wedges between ye and Jo-Jo. I tell ye because the child has known no happiness in her life and if ye truly love one another as ye say ye do, then I canna be the cause of more pain tae her. Alexander Seton is a wicked devil who hurt a young girl and gave no thought tae what he did. I watched it. From the time I was a young lad, I watched it happen and could do nothing tae stop it."

It was a passionate speech, enough for Stephen to open his eyes and look at him. The blue eyes were dazed, but fire still burned within.

Nothing Kynan could say would destroy the love he had for Joselyn. If anything, it made him more in love with her, fiercely protective over this woman who had known such shame. He blamed himself for not completely understanding what she had told him. He should have been more intuitive, asking more questions to make it easier for her to tell him everything. She had tried. He knew that. But he hadn't understood clearly. His heart ached so badly for her that he could feel the physical impact deep in his chest.

"Nothing you have said changes how I feel about her," he muttered. "I love her more than I ever did. The child she carries is the result of a deep and abiding love that will never die."

Now it was Kynan's turn to look shocked. "Jo-Jo is pregnant?"

Stephen nodded weakly. "All the more reason to send her from Berwick. I want my wife and child safe."

Kynan puffed out his cheeks, digesting the news and realizing he was thrilled with it. Stephen watched him with half-lidded eyes, seeing a flicker of a smile cross the man's lips. That was the moment he began to think that he might have an ally in Kynan Lott MacKenzie.

"You told me once that I was not for the likes of Joselyn," he muttered. "What made you change your mind?"

Kynan sat back slightly, regarding the big English knight. After a moment's reflection on that conversation long ago, he lifted his shoulders and averted his gaze.

"The best thing that coulda happened tae her was marrying ye," he said. "She came tae me before Berwick was retaken, beggin' fer me help. She wanted me tae tell her what I knew and I wouldna do it. She told me that if anything happened tae ye that she would hate me forever."

Stephen watched the man's profile. "And this bothers you."

He shrugged again. "Jo-Jo is like me little sister and I canna stomach her hate." He finally looked to Stephen. "Ye offer her yer protection and love. I could see it in her face when she told me of her feelings fer ye. English or no, ye'll always have my respect fer making the lass happy."

"Your family means that much to you?"

"Doesna it mean that much tae ye, too?"

He had a point. "So what are you going to do?" Stephen wanted to know.

Kynan looked over at the tray of food on the table. He reached for it, setting it down on the floor next to them. Then he took the pitcher.

"I'm gonna try and lift ye up tae drink this," he indicated the pitcher. "After that, we'll discuss yer future."

C3

TATE KNEW THAT Kenneth was furious with him. Although Kenneth was, more than any other man alive, able to control his emotions in any given situation, Tate knew simply by the look in Kenneth's eye that he was beyond furious. He was livid. He further knew this because Kenneth stuck to Joselyn as closely as a mother hen, making sure she was comfortable, fed, not too hot or cold, and generally well taken care of. It got to the point where Joselyn actually had to chase him off. The man was as clinging as a shadow.

Tate knew that Kenneth was reluctant to use Joselyn as an envoy to gaining Stephen's release. But both men knew she was Stephen's only chance, even if Kenneth was not ready to openly admit it. He was more concerned with protecting her for Stephen's sake, while Tate, although protective, was willing to let her take the risk in order to save her husband. Both men were greatly torn. The closer they drew to the outskirts of Berwick, the more Kenneth's fury turned to resignation. He was coming to accept the fact that Joselyn was, indeed, Stephen's only hope.

The party to Berwick consisted of Tate, Kenneth, Joselyn and about fifty men-at-arms. As they drew to within a mile of the city, Tate cut to the northwest and made his way to the River Tweed about a mile to the west of the castle. Whiteadder Bridge lay before them, an expanse of wood across the gently flowing river. They could see the castle from where they stood, a massive bastion poised at river's edge. Joselyn in particular gazed longingly at the castle, a place where she had known some of her worst and best memories. She must have stood there for quite some time because it took her a moment to realize that Tate was trying to get her attention.

He stood behind her, clearing his throat softly. Kenneth stood slightly behind Tate, still looking rather unhappy about the entire thing. The men-at-arms were gathering the horses and moving back through the summer grass to the trees that bordered the river, where they would hide until the venture was over. As the morning grew warmer and the insects from the river danced about, Joselyn faced Tate and Kenneth.

"Do not worry so," she said, more for Kenneth than for Tate. "I shall ride to Berwick and demand to be given my husband. It should not take long."

Tate hoped she was not truly so naïve. "We have discussed a course of action," he reminded her. "It would be better if you do not show emotion where it pertains to Stephen. It could be used against you if they feel your loyalty is to him and not your kinsmen. You need to claim him as one would a possession."

She thought on that a moment, her long-lashed eyes turning to behold the castle once more. She was quivering with anticipation, the desire to discover what had become of her husband causing her heart to thump painfully against her ribs. It was a struggle not to become emotional but she knew that Tate was right. She had to show as little emotion as possible. She had to be strong and firm if this plan was going to work.

"I would like to know where Kynan is," she said as she turned back around, looking at Kenneth. "You said that you released him."

Kenneth cocked a blond eyebrow. "We released him so that we could follow him and hopefully discover the rebel plans. It was a gamble that did not pay off, one that I will take full responsibility for."

"Do you think he was part of the force that captured Berwick?"

"I would stake my life on it."

Joselyn digested the information, increasingly eager to be on her way. She refused to believe that Stephen had been killed. She was convinced he was somewhere in the walls of Berwick and she would find him no matter what.

"Very well," she said, moving for her small gray palfrey. Tate took her arm and lifted her up into the saddle as Kenneth fussed with the stirrups. "I will return as soon as I can and I swear to you that Stephen will be with me."

Tate gazed at her, nodding his head after a moment. There was so much more to it than just her simple statement. *I swear to you that Stephen will be with me.* Since her initial breakdown at the news of her husband's capture, he had seen a growth in courage fill the lady. She was not aggressive and bold like his wife, who was the bravest and strongest woman he knew, but she had a steely strength in her that he was coming to see. He had a feeling that, if cornered, the lady would come out swinging.

"Ride to the castle and demand entry as the daughter of Alexander Seton," he went over their plan one last time. "Once inside, you will ask to be shown your husband. You will further insist to whoever is in charge that you demand the release of your husband, which is well within your rights."

"But if they do not release him, what should...?"

He cut her off. They had been over this several times. "You will tell them that the king has agreed to release your father from captivity at Alnwick in exchange for Pembury. It is a fair trade, one that I doubt they will refuse. Your father is very important to young David Bruce, heir of Robert. If they have a chance to bargain for his release, they will do it."

Joselyn listened seriously to his instructions. But when he was finished, she fixed him with an intense gaze. "You realize, of course, that if they refuse to release him, I will not leave him. I will stay in captivity with him."

Tate nodded slowly. "I understand completely."

Joselyn gave him a brave little smile, her gaze moving to Kenneth.

"I will bring him back, Kenneth," she said sincerely "You need not worry. All will be well."

Kenneth didn't like it when the focus was on him. He made his way over to her, unable to voice the fears roiling in his chest. For lack of anything comforting or confident to say, he cupped her head in his two massive hands, kissed her cheek, and walked away. There was resignation, sorrow and helplessness in the gesture, something that touched Joselyn deeply. She knew how worried he was. She and Tate watched him go before looking to each other.

"Go, now," Tate encouraged her. "Stay calm and follow the plan we discussed. I am sure I will be seeing Stephen by supper."

Joselyn forced a smile at him as she kicked the little palfrey, urging the animal to the road and across the bridge beyond. Tate watched her cross the bridge and continue along the road, heading for the massive fortress in the distance. The closer she drew to the structure, the more his anxiety grew. Behind him, Kenneth had turned around to watch as well.

Watch Joselyn ride straight into the jaws of the lion.

CHAPTER SEVENTEEN

K YNAN HAD STEPHEN on a makeshift bed in the solar of the keep. He was too injured to make his way up the steps, so after feeding Stephen a loaf of bread, old mutton and stale wine, he piled some old rushes against the wall and lay Stephen upon it. In less agony than he had been in days, Stephen fell into a heavy sleep.

Kynan sat in a chair and watched the man sleep, eventually rubbing his eyes wearily as he wondered what in the hell he was going to do. The rebel force that had reclaimed Berwick consisted of many clans under the command of the Earl of Moray, John Randolph. Although Randolph was not at Berwick, several of his burly generals were. It was those men that Kynan worried about. The same men had been at the siege of Berwick and had seen the atrocities perpetrated by the English, particularly with the young Seton boys. Pembury had been involved in that travesty. Kynan had been hearing rumblings for a few days that Moray's generals wanted to hang Pembury in vengeance.

Kynan was not sure how he was going to prevent such a thing but he knew that he would do his best. Watching Pembury sleep, he thought on Joselyn's words of how the man had overlooked all of the shameful things that had been heaped upon her. His love had been unconditional. Kynan wondered what kind of man could hang young boys but love a woman who had been seriously compromised. It was an odd paradox that he pondered, finally rising from his chair and hunting about for something to light the fire with. Even though it was mid-day outside and sunny, the room was cool. Finding no peat or charcoal, he opened the door with the intention of hunting for burning material when a faint female voice caught his attention.

It was coming from the bailey. He could hear it through the lancet window just to the left of the entry door. Curious, he opened the door, assaulted by the bright light and shielding his eyes from the sun. His heart leapt into his throat as he spied the source of the sound.

Joselyn stood in the bailey, clad in a pale traveling cloak, her luscious dark hair braided and draped over one shoulder. Holding the reins to a small gray palfrey, she was speaking to several large, dirty Scots, Moray's men, and Kynan bolted from the keep, practically flying across the dusty bailey until he reached her. He had no idea why she was here or what she was saying to the guard, but it didn't matter. Kynan didn't want her around men such as this and he was terrified and angry as well as confused. As he came upon her, he reached out and grabbed her.

Joselyn screamed at the swiftness of the action, terrified until she saw who it was. Then her face lit up. "Kynan!" she exclaimed softly. "I am so glad to…."

Kynan didn't let her speak further. He was yanking her away from Moray's guard, pulling her with him towards the keep. His actions were indicative of an extremely angry man and Moray's men looked both surprised and disappointed at her sudden removal.

"*Hoot*, mon!" one of the guards spoke to Kynan. "We saw her first!"

Kynan's rage was boundless. "She's me sister and if ye move against her, I shall kill ye!"

That seemed to calm the amorous guard. They knew Kynan Mac-Kenzie and the man's reputation. He fought alongside the McCulloch and everyone knew that anyone involved with the McCulloch was crazy and blood-thirsty. Moreover, he was Seton's kin. That reason alone was enough to garner some respect, so they let him yank the lovely woman away without another word. When Kynan was sure they weren't going to challenge him, he looked at Joselyn.

"You foolish wench," he hissed. "What are ye doin'?"

Joselyn fright returned as she stumbled after him. "I have come to get my husband."

"How did ye get in here?"

Joselyn tripped on her own feet and almost fell to her knees. "I rode here from Forestburn," she replied, annoyance mingling with her fright. "I came to the gates and told the guards that I was Alexander Seton's daughter. They let me in. Stop pulling!"

Kynan ignored her demand although his grip eased somewhat. "I cannot believe ye would chance yer life so foolishly," he snarled.

Joselyn was trying to pull away from him angrily. "I came for my husband," she insisted. "Where is he?"

Kynan came to an abrupt halt at the door to the keep, speaking through clenched teeth. "Ye were well away from here," he growled. "Ye should have stayed away. It 'twas stupid of ye tae come back."

She scowled, bordering on tears. "Where is Stephen?" she was starting to break down. "I am not leaving without him and I will kill you if you stand in my way. Do you hear me?"

She was yelling by the time she finished the sentence, so much for remaining unemotional. Kynan could see, in her expression as well as her words, that she was absolutely serious. With another growl, he yanked her inside the keep.

Once inside the cool, dank entry, he slammed the heavy oak door and turned to her, grasping her by the arms.

"Jo-Jo," he was far less angry, far more concerned. "Ye shouldna have come back, lass. 'Tis far too dangerous fer ye tae be here."

Joselyn was struggling against her tears. "Where is my husband?" she demanded again. "He belongs to me and I want him back."

Kynan shook his head sadly. "Jo-Jo…."

"I will tear this place apart looking for him," she snapped. "Tell me where he is or I will…."

Kynan shushed her before she could finish, turning her for the solar door. "He is going tae be angry with ye," he stated the obvious.

Joselyn was unsettled and confused by Kynan's rough appearance, upset by her own emotions, so much so that when Kynan thrust her into the small solar, she didn't notice anything about it except that it was the room where she and Stephen had first met, the room where she had first spoken to Cade. It was dark in the room so she didn't see her husband lying against the wall, partially blocked by the only table in the room. She turned to Kynan as the man followed her into the chamber, shut the door and bolted it.

"What in the world are you doing?" she demanded. "Let me out of here this instant and take me to Stephen."

Kynan put up his hands. "Jo-Jo, ye must stop…."

Joselyn suddenly balled a fist and thrust it into his face. "Deny me again and I will beat you within an inch of your life!"

Kynan's eyebrows lifted. "So ye threaten me, ye little chicken? 'Tis about time ye showed yer backbone."

She took a swing at him and he dodged it, laughing. Then he grabbed her fists and stilled her, turning her around to the wall. But Joselyn was still struggling, determined to punch him in the nose, when she suddenly caught sight of something massive on the floor. She would not have paid attention to it has she not noticed a boot. It took her a moment to realize she was looking at Stephen and all struggling came to a halt.

With a whimper, she raced around the table, knocking it over in her haste, and falling to her knees beside her husband. Stephen was sleeping heavily and it didn't take her long to see that he had been badly beaten. His handsome face was cut and bruised, and his lower lip was swollen. Tears of horror, of relief, of joy popped from her eyes as she gently put her hands on his face. He was warm in her hands, alive, but most definitely injured. Then the sobs came.

They were deep and pitiful. Kynan knelt beside her, his hand on her back as he tried to give her some comfort.

"I'm sorry I couldna prevent this, Jo-Jo," he muttered. "They had him tied tae the stocks fer three days, leaving him without food or water. I brought him in here but I have not tended his wounds. I dunna know how badly he's been hurt."

Joselyn had never been so distraught. Other than his death, it was her worst nightmare come to life. She leaned down, kissing Stephen's face, tasting her tears on his cheeks. But even as she wept at the sight of him, she realized that the man needed help. Tears and sorrow would not heal him. He had tended her before with his vast medical knowledge and although she didn't know a tremendous amount about healing, it was time for her to return the favor. Stephen needed her help and she was determined to give it. She tried very hard to stop her tears, wiping her face with her hand.

"Our chamber is on the third floor," she told her cousin. "Stephen's possessions should still be there including his medicine bag. 'Tis a big, black leather satchel with all sorts of mysterious things in it. You must bring it to me immediately."

Kynan nodded, rising to his feet. "What else do ye need?"

In truth, she really didn't know. She rattled off a few things in a panic. "Water and wine, I suppose. And bring me any bed linens you can find, if your men have not stolen them already. He needs to be made more comfortable."

Kynan was already moving. "Bolt the door when I have left. Dunna answer it fer anyone but me."

Joselyn jumped up and did as she was told, throwing the bolt when he left and then swiftly returning to Stephen. She struggled not to cry as she ripped off her gloves and pulled off her cloak. The gloves went onto the floor and her cloak went over Stephen to cover him. She put her hands on his face, kissing his cheeks.

"Stephen?" she whispered, struggling not to crack. "Can you hear me, my angel?"

He drew in a deep, long breath and she tried again. "Stephen, 'tis me. Open your eyes, my angel. Open them and look at me."

He did. But he stared at her for almost a full minute without reacting. Joselyn peered with concern at the cornflower blue eyes. He didn't appear to see anything at all. His eyes were simply open, staring into space and unmoving. She was growing scared.

"Stephen?" she whispered. "Can you see me?"

He suddenly blinked and the eyes came into focus, staring at her as if absolutely horrified. His pale face tightened.

"Joselyn?" he repeated, raspy. "Is… is it really you?"

She smiled, the tears returning full-force. "Aye," she leaned down, kissing his parched lips. "'Tis me, my angel. I am here."

Since his right wrist was broken, he could only grip her with his left hand. His eyes were wide with astonishment.

"I thought I was dreaming," he rasped. "I saw you but thought it was my mind playing tricks."

She shook her head, falling against him and trying to hold him. But he grunted as she came down on him and she startled, recoiling at the sound.

"I am so sorry," she gasped, her expression creased with pain. "I did not mean to hurt you."

He grunted again, shifting slightly and reaching out to grasp her with his left arm. "You did not, sweetheart," he lied for her benefit. "But I would like to know what you are doing here. You are supposed to be at Forestburn."

He sounded much calmer than he felt about it, rather proud that his horror and shock hadn't come blasting out at her. Dazed, muddled and in utter anguish, he could only think of his wife and her unwelcome, yet welcome, appearance. He was thrilled, confused and terrified at the same time.

"I was," she pressed against him as much as she dared so she would not hurt him. "But Kenneth escaped Berwick and came to tell us what had happened."

There was some relief for him in her statement. "Ken is unharmed?"

She nodded. "He is fine," she replied. "Tate sent me to take you away from here."

He lifted a dark eyebrow at her. "*Tate* sent you?" he repeated, extraordinarily unhappy at the news. "He and I are going to have words about this and not pleasant ones. I cannot begin to describe how displeased I am at the moment."

Her warm expression faded and she wiped the remaining tears from her cheeks. "You will not be angry with him," she told him. "He would not have asked it of me if there had been another way. You must trust that we have a plan for this."

"That is nonsense," he hissed. "I cannot believe he would play with your life in such a way."

Joselyn put her hand on his cheek. "He is not playing with my life," she insisted. "Moreover, I would have come with or without him. I could not sit back while my kin holds you prisoner. I had to come. Do you not understand, husband? I love you and would do anything to help you. Surely you know that about me by now."

He did, but he was still agitated. "I have always trusted Tate with my life and, consequently, your life as well. That is why I sent you to Forestburn. I feel as if I have been betrayed."

Joselyn sighed. "It was not easy for him to make the decision," she said, defending de Lara. "Kenneth was deeply opposed to it. In fact, I saw him arguing with Tate quite strongly. Even Toby was opposed. She threatened to hide me from her husband. But Tate said something that caused them both to reconsider their stance. He said that Toby saved him from Roger Mortimer once and that women are stronger than we know. He believes I can do this and I am strong with his confidence. Do not weaken me with your anger."

Stephen's building rage abruptly cooled. He touched his wife's head, feeling her soft hair beneath his hand. It was the most wonderful sensation in the world and he thanked God that he was given another chance to touch her regardless of the circumstances.

"Your strength is not in question," he murmured. "Simply de Lara's sanity."

She pursed her lips at him in irritation. "Stephen, I do not want our first words in weeks to be cross ones. I am doing exactly what you would do if the situation were reversed. I am going to do all I can to get you out of this place."

Stephen felt himself folding, resigned because he knew there was nothing he could do about it. "I do not want our first words in weeks to be cross, either," he agreed. "But you should not have come back. You were safe at Forestburn and that thought has kept me alive. Now that you are here, my worries for you are overwhelming."

She leaned down and kissed him gently. "I know," she whispered. "But as the daughter of Alexander Seton, the last man to hold command over Scots at Berwick, my word carries weight. I am going to demand you be released to my custody."

Stephen stared at her a moment before sighing faintly. "They will not do it," he breathed. "I am the Guardian Protector of Berwick. They mean to make an example out of me."

She knew what he meant but refused to accept it, shaking her head so hard that her hair came loose. "Nay," she insisted strongly. "They are not going to do anything to you. They will release you and I am going to take you out of this place."

Stephen looked at her, unable to refute her. It would do no good. He knew the truth of it and she did not. When he saw tears in her eyes again, he reached up with both arms and pulled her down to him, holding her against his battered torso. Joselyn clung to him and wept, holding him tightly. But she quickly composed herself, knowing her tears would not help him. She was focused on making him well enough to leave and she could not do that if she fell apart at every turn. Pulling herself up, she wiped her face.

"Now," she tried to sound confident and in charge. "Kynan is bringing your medicament bag. How badly are you injured?"

He wriggled his eyebrows. "I have several broken ribs," he said, trying not to make it sound as bad as he felt. "And my right wrist is broken. Other than that, I can move my arms and legs adequately."

Shocked at the assessment, she went immediately for his wrist. It was grossly swollen and she gingerly inspected it. "Can you move your fingers?"

"Barely."

"What can I do to help you?"

He sighed faintly, thinking on how he would treat the injury. "If at all possible, it would do well to find a length of board or a small branch to use as a wrist brace," he told her. "As for my ribs, the only thing to do is wrap my torso tightly until they heal."

"I shall find something to brace your wrist with," she said, bolting up and hunting around for a piece of kindling. But there was no kindling to be found and her focus suddenly fell on the turned-up table. She grasped one of the legs. "Will this do?"

Stephen turned to see what she was looking at. "It should."

Joselyn was about to start bashing the table around when a knock sounded at the door. She raced to it.

"Who is it?" she demanded.

"Open the door," Kynan told her.

Joselyn threw the bolt and Kynan entered, carrying Stephen's familiar black bag. With Joselyn hovering behind him, he laid it down next to Stephen.

"The bag has been strewn about," he informed him. "I tried tae recover what I could but I dunna know if I got it all."

Stephen simply nodded. There was not much he could do about it and tried not to think about the precious ingredients that may have been lost. What mattered now was ingesting something to ease the pain he was feeling. Only then would he be able to think more clearly.

"My thanks," he said, peering at the bag. "Now we shall see how great a physic I truly am if I can heal myself."

Joselyn cocked her head. "But I am here, my angel. I will heal you if you tell me what to do."

He smiled faintly at her, the eager desire to help, the unselfish risks that she had already taken for him. He thought briefly on the horrific tale Kynan had told him, the depth of Alexander Seton's debauchery, but he didn't dwell on it. If anything, it seemed to underscore what a truly amazing woman he had married, her ability to give and love after the horror she had been dealt in life. He didn't think it possible that he could love her any more, but he did.

"Of course, sweetheart," he said softly. "Listen carefully to what I tell you and you will probably be a better physic than I am."

She smiled brightly as the magical process of Stephen's healing began.

❧

BY EVENING, STEPHEN had been cleaned up, wrapped, fed again and plied with mysterious medicaments from his bag. Kynan had lugged down the straw mattress that was on their bed up in the third floor chamber and they lay it on the floor of the solar, moving Stephen onto it so he would be more comfortable. He seemed to breathe better sitting up so they wedged the mattress into the corner and propped him up. Feeling better than he had in days, Stephen ate again when Kynan brought around bread, mutton and beans, and very cheap ale.

As Joselyn snuggled next to her husband propped against the wall, Kynan debated how much to tell of what had occurred on his trip from the kitchen to the keep. He opted for all of it because sooner or later, the situation would take a turn and it would be best if they were both prepared. As Joselyn slowly fed Stephen a slab of bread covered in mutton gravy and beans, Kynan pulled up a stool next to them.

"Ye've done nothing but eat all day, *Sassenach*," he quipped.

Stephen lifted a dark eyebrow. "I have not eaten for three days. I have much to make up for."

"Ye eat enough fer me army."

"Tread carefully. If I am hungry enough, you might find yourself on the menu."

Kynan made a face, sending Joselyn in to fits of giggles. Kynan watched his beautiful cousin, knowing he had never seen her happier. He wanted to make sure she never knew anything else.

"Moray's men know that I have ye," he looked at Stephen. "I saw them as I was bringing ye food and they asked me how ye fared. I told them you were hovering near death and that only time would tell. But they are demanding tae see ye. I told them they could see ye on the morrow after ye'd had time tae sleep."

Stephen's congenial expression faded. "Did they say what they wanted?"

Kynan exhaled sharply and looked at his hands, turning them over and inspecting them. "I have heard talk that they want tae hang ye as Tommy and Willie Seton were hanged," he replied. "But at the moment, they are concerned with fortifying their position at the castle. They fear that Edward will come down around them again, especially with Pembury as a captive."

All humor was gone from Stephen and Joselyn's expressions. Joselyn looked at her husband, her wide-eyed expression on the verge of tears. Then she turned back to Kynan.

"Who has said such ridiculous things?" she hissed.

Kynan cast her a sidelong glance, still picking at his hands. "Moray is in charge," he replied. "I heard it from his men."

Joselyn was growing increasingly livid. "Who?"

"The knight in command," Kynan looked at her, then. "Morgan de Velt."

Joselyn's eyes widened. "De Velt?" she repeated. "He must be our kin, Kynan. My mother and your mother were de Velts. Do you know him?"

Kynan nodded. "I know of him," he replied. "He is more English than Scots, hired by Moray. The man is powerful and deadly and, I believe, well paid fer his service."

"He is a mercenary?"

"Aye."

"I know him," Stephen spoke up.

Both Joselyn and Kynan looked to him. "What do you know of him?" Joselyn wanted to know.

Stephen sighed, puffing out his cheeks. There was resignation in his manner. "Morgan served Roger Mortimer. He is an enemy of Edward, which explains why he is siding with the Scots. And he most definitely knows me. He and I have faced each other before in battle. In fact, that explains how the Scots knew to target me when the walls were breached. Undoubtedly, Morgan described me to them and told them to disable me."

Joselyn was curled up against him, watching him with wide eyes. "He will want to kill you, then?"

Stephen wriggled his eyebrows. "It is possible," he said, looking to Kynan. "I will see de Velt in the morning and get to the heart of this."

"Ye might not like it," Kynan said softly.

"I already do not like it."

"Wait," Joselyn put up her hand to stop them from continuing along that line of conversation. "Ky, we must get Stephen out of here. We cannot think of anything but that."

Kynan nodded. "Ease yerself, lass," he told her. "I have already thought of such things."

"And?" Joselyn demanded.

Kynan grinned, but it was at Stephen. "Perhaps I'm wondering how yer *Sassenach* will look wearin' McCulloch tartan."

CHAPTER EIGHTEEN

I T HADN'T BEEN as simple a trip as they had thought.

When de Lara and his men, including Lady Pembury, had departed Forestburn, Cade and Roman had been ready. They had tried to steal a horse but the grooms kept shooing them away. Their only chance had been in an old nag they found tied up near the kitchens, so they stole the horse and squeezed it out through Forestburn's postern gate. But Forestburn had a moat, so after a very precarious walk around the walls, they were able to urge the horse up onto the drawbridge and plod across it when some traffic from the castle distracted the guards. All in all, they had been lucky. They prayed their luck would hold.

Unfortunately for both boys, they hadn't much experience in navigating travel. They tried to follow de Lara's trail but when it became too muddled up, they had to ask for directions. Three times. They spent two nights sleeping in the woods, too fearful to start a fire. It had been cold, but not too terribly, and in the morning they jumped on the nag and kicked the animal into a bumpy trot.

Somewhere during the second day of travel, they traded clothes with two peasant boys working in a bean field. Cade's clothes had bugs and Roman's were far too small, but they silently endured the tribulations they had brought upon themselves. They considered it the price to pay for their adventure. Rising early on the dawn of the third day, they traveled for several hours before finally reaching the outskirts of Berwick.

The old nag plodded and swayed along the road, heading into the town from the southwest. Cade was itching like crazy and Roman, taking his turn at handling the horse, kept trying to still him. The castle, perched on the edge of the river, eventually came into view.

It looked broken and beaten as the boys pulled the nag to halt, gazing at the fortress in the distance. Roman finally looked back at Cade.

"So what do we do?" he asked. "Do you even have a plan?"

Cade didn't have much of one but he didn't want Roman to know. He was older and, therefore, wiser, and he was determined to hatch a plan that would save Stephen and quite possibly the entire garrison at Berwick.

"We need to sneak in," he told Roman. "If we sneak in and pretend we're servants, then we can find out where Sir Stephen is."

"And then what?"

Cade made a face at him. "And then we rescue him."

Roman looked at the castle and shrugged. "Okay."

Cade was glad he hadn't asked any more questions. They climbed off the horse and led it into a wooded area with a small stream running through it. There was plenty of grass and water, so they tied the horse off and trudged back up to the road. In their peasant clothing, they looked like just another pair of boys roaming the countryside, not the son of an Earl and the son of the Guardian Protector of Berwick. In fact, Roman tried not to think about his mother, knowing she was probably frantic with worry. But this adventure was important. He wished he had been able to tell her. She would have just told him that he couldn't go.

So they marched on towards the castle as the day passed into afternoon, having no idea that Tate and his men were about a quarter of a mile to the northwest. Cade and Roman moved into the town, dodging carts and horses, realizing they were very hungry because the food they had brought with them ran out that morning. They had no money, so Cade thought it would be acceptable to steal what they could since they were on a rescue mission. He was sure God would forgive them. Clever boys that they were, Roman distracted a shop keeper by falling in front of his stall and crying loudly as Cade stole a loaf of bread.

Just about the time Cade disappeared with the bread, Roman's crying miraculously stopped and he fled, meeting up with Cade on the next block and devouring their stolen goods. Half running, half walking as they shoved bread into their mouths, they cleared the town and found the stretch of road that led to the castle.

Their pace picked up.

୧୪

STEPHEN HAD SLEPT all night and well into the morning, his battered body struggling to heal itself from his near-deadly beating. Joselyn, not feeling well in her early pregnancy, was coming to experience some insomnia and hadn't fallen asleep until it was nearly dawn. So when Stephen awoke, it was to the gentle sound of his wife's snoring. She was snuggled up against him, her face pressed into his chest, sleeping like the dead. Stephen didn't move, smiling at the sound of her charming snores. He was so very thankful to be alive and to be with her, regardless of the circumstances. Up until yesterday, he was not sure he would ever experience moments like this again.

He did notice that Kynan was not in the room with them. He was not sure if that was a good or a bad sign. His mind moved to Morgan de Velt, the mercenary knight who pledged his services at a high cost. He had fought with Mortimer because the man had heaped praise and money on him, but his services could have just as easily been bought by Edward. All that mattered to de Velt was where the money was coming from.

Stephen knew that his wife's mother was a de Velt, but there were quite a few of them this far north. Their ancestor, the fierce mercenary Ajax de Velt, had been a warlord back in the time of Henry the Second, in the dark days when England and Scotland and Wales were still places of great turmoil and little organization. He had eventually married well and had several children, branches of the family that were a paradox. Some were reputable and moral while others, like Morgan, carried on their ancestor's mercenary tradition. But Ajax de Velt had also been known as a ruthless killer. Morgan could, from what Stephen knew, be the same way. He wondered how much knightly courtesy would keep Morgan from making an example out of him.

So he lay on the mattress with his wife, holding her close and staring up at the ceiling lost in thought. He didn't even know what time it was, but he knew he was hungry. Perhaps Kynan had gone to get food. As he continued to lay still, relaxed and quiet, the door to the solar creaked opened.

Kynan stood in the doorway, his hand on the latch as he looked at Stephen. Stephen caught sight of him in his peripheral vision and turned slightly to get a better look. When their eyes met, Stephen was put on his guard simply by the expression on Kynan's face.

"Aye," Kynan said with regret. "He's awake."

Stephen knew he was not talking to him. In fact, he gently shook Joselyn awake as bootfalls approached and men began to crowd into the room. Joselyn awoke with a start but he shushed her swiftly.

"I am sorry to wake you," he whispered. "But we have guests. Please help me to sit up."

Rubbing her eyes, Joselyn was instantly full of fear but did as he asked. She was groggy but tried to stay calm, taking hold of Stephen's arm as he sat up, very slowly, and leaned back against the wall. By the time Joselyn turned around, three big men were in the room with Kynan lingering somewhere behind them. She sat down next to Stephen and held his hand tightly, her pale blue eyes wide with fright.

The knight standing in the forefront was not Scots; that much was clear. He was a big man with brown eyes and dark blond hair that fell to his shoulders. Huge hands rested at his sides as his gaze moved over Stephen. So far, he hadn't even bothered looking at Joselyn.

"Pembury," he greeted, his voice deep and quiet.

Stephen lifted an eyebrow. "De Velt, I presume?"

"You presume correctly. I see that you are alive."

"I am, no thanks to you."

De Velt actually grinned. "My apologies," he replied. "I have been very busy trying to secure Berwick. I forgot you were out in the yard."

Stephen had an expression on his face that let the man know without benefit of words that he knew he was lying. "I would not expect you to treat a prisoner with honor."

De Velt's smile faded as he studied Stephen, plotting what to say next. Having only seen Stephen twice in his life, he knew of Pembury by reputation only, knowing he was one of the more powerful knights in the arsenal of King Edward and one of the tallest knights in England. He had been both pleased and surprised to have captured the man called Guardian Protector during the siege of Berwick and his commanders had told him to keep the man alive until they decided what was to be done with him. Now the decision was made and that directive had come this morning, directly from Moray. The news was not good.

After a moment, de Velt exhaled wearily and looked around for a chair. One of his men shoved a stool at him and he pulled it up, seating his big body heavily. Only then did he look at Joselyn, curled up against her husband. He lifted an eyebrow at her.

"What is the wench doing here?" he asked, not kindly.

Stephen replied before Joselyn could voice her outrage. "This is not a wench," he was beginning to sound perturbed. "This is my wife, the Lady Joselyn de Velt Seton Pembury, and her father is Alexander Seton. Perhaps you have heard of him."

De Velt stared at her. Then he looked around to the crowd behind him, jabbing a finger at Joselyn.

"Why did no one tell me that she was here?" he demanded, suddenly bolting up from the stool and using it like a weapon to crown the man nearest him. "Did no one think to tell me that Pembury's wife was here?"

Men were getting smacked around and Joselyn screamed, pressing herself against Stephen and turning her head away as one man took the stool in the mouth and blood sprayed. Stephen put his enormous hand over her head, holding it against his chest to protect her as de Velt swung away. Even Kynan ducked away as de Velt beat his men. But as swiftly as it started, the violence stopped and de Velt set the stool back down, reclaiming his seat.

De Velt exhaled sharply, collecting himself, as he returned his focus to Joselyn. She was still clutched against Stephen's chest, her pale blue eyes peering out of the safety of his protective hand. When her eyes met de Velt's, he smiled at her.

"Lady Pembury," he said, sounding calm. "I was unaware you were here. You were not here during the battle, were you?"

Joselyn looked at Stephen, who removed his hand from her head and answered for her. "Nay," he said quietly.

"Then how did she get here?"

"I rode from Forestburn yesterday," Joselyn found her tongue, thinking that it would be a good time to ask for her husband's freedom now that she had de Velt's attention. "As the daughter of Alexander Seton, I demand that you free my husband. If you release him, the king has promised to release my father."

Stephen looked at her sharply, wondering what in the hell she was doing making that kind of proposal. Edward would surely never agree to anything like that and he cursed under his breath at her bold foolishness. De Velt, however, never took his eyes from her, becoming increasingly interested in the very beautiful young woman before him. If he thought her proposition was ridiculous, he didn't let on.

"You are a de Velt," he said after a moment, completely ignoring her offer.

Joselyn nodded. "My mother was the daughter of Micah de Velt, Lord Carham." She pointed to Kynan, standing over by the door. "Kynan is my cousin. His mother and my mother were sisters."

De Velt nodded, glancing back at Kynan. "Are you the one who admitted her to Berwick without my knowledge?"

Kynan shook his head. "The guards did that. I happened tae see her in the bailey and brought her in here fer her own safety."

De Velt digested that, understanding a little more of the lady's mysterious appearance, before returning his focus to Joselyn. "Micah was my father's brother," he told her. "Micah was the oldest of fourteen children and I am sorry to say that I do not keep track of all of my kin. But It would seem that you and I are related, Lady Pembury."

"And Kynan, too."

He nodded slowly. "And Kynan, too."

Joselyn was not sure if that was a good or bad thing. She pushed herself off of her husband and rose, smoothing her gown and trying to convey a somewhat presentable and collected appearance. She didn't want to come across like a groveling wife, as de Lara had warned her. She wanted to present a strong, determined front.

"Since we are related, I would ask you, as my kin, to please release my husband," she said firmly. "He is injured and I wish to take him someplace safe where he can heal."

De Velt scratched his head, inspecting Lady Pembury's delicious figure beneath her soft yellow surcoat. She had luscious full breasts and he found himself staring at them.

"I am not sure that is possible, lady," he replied. "I understand that Pembury hanged your brothers as you and your family watched from the battlements. Is this true?"

Joselyn looked stricken, struggling not to appear off balance. "My brothers were hanged," she confirmed. "But Stephen did not personally do it. He has, in fact, done many wonderful things for me and my family since the event of our marriage. He is a good man."

De Velt looked at Stephen. "She lives in a dream world where you can do no wrong," he said. "You will tell me the truth, Pembury. Did you personally hang her brothers?"

Stephen sighed faintly, looking up at Joselyn, who was now staring back at him with some fear. He averted his gaze, thinking carefully on his answer.

"I was Thomas' guard the entire time he was Edward's hostage," he replied quietly. "He was a fine young man who never stopped believing that his father would seek his freedom. When Alexander Seton did not honor the terms of the hostage agreement, it was my duty to present the boy to the executioner."

De Velt's gaze was riveted to him. "Ever the obedient knight," he said, bordering on sarcasm. "Did you put the noose over his neck?"

Stephen's blue eyes were intense. "Nay," he replied hoarsely. "Tommy did it himself, weeping as he did so, because his father had failed him. The boy put that noose on his own neck and stepped off the scaffold under his own accord. None of us had to make a move because the boy took his own life."

Joselyn suddenly turned away, weeping softly, and Stephen reached out to put a comforting hand on her. De Velt's gaze was intense on Stephen.

"Many Scots witnessed this hanging," he said. "I have not heard mention of that particular version."

"As if they would tell you," Stephen's gaze was equally intense. "I would not lie to you."

"I believe you," de Velt said in a surprising show of reassurance. "You are a man of honor from what I am told. I would not expect you to lie to me to save yourself."

By this time, Joselyn was wiping her tears away, struggling to put the details of Tommy's death aside. There would be another time to grieve for her little brother. Squaring her shoulders, she faced de Velt with resolve.

"I want my husband released," she told him. "He has told you that he did not hang Tommy or Willie. His only crime is that he fought for the English king. He is Alexander Seton's son-in-law and you will let him go."

De Velt looked at her, the manner in which his eyes drifted over her body causing her skin to crawl. Stephen saw it and he stiffened with outrage but made no move against de Velt. Injured as he was, he knew he would not last long in a fight. If he was going to attack the man, then let it be for something more than a lascivious glance.

"Alas, my lady, I cannot," de Velt replied after a long, lustful moment. "I have come to tell your husband that I received orders from the Earl of Moray this morning. It would seem that the earl is to make an example out of your husband to show the English what will happen if they make another attempt to capture Berwick."

Joselyn's blood ran cold. Her heart began to pound and her body to shake. She could feel Stephen grasping her by the wrist, pulling her over to him. As he put his massive arm around her, she struggled against him. She was not interested in being held at the moment. She wanted de Velt to clarify himself.

"An example?" she repeated, both angry and terrified. "What does that mean? What foolishness is this?"

De Velt shook his head. "No foolishness at all, I assure you," he replied without a hint of distress in his voice. "Your husband is an enemy of Scotland and all enemies of Scotland are harshly dealt with. In two days, at dusk, Pembury is to be drawn and quartered, and parts of his body distributed along the border as an example to all who oppose young David as the king of Scotland. His head will be sent to Edward himself."

Joselyn coiled like a spring, making a lunge for de Velt even as Stephen held on to her. "You cannot make an example of my husband," she screamed. "He belongs to me and I am taking him from this place. I shall kill you if you try to stop me. Do you hear? I will *kill you!*"

It was as much passion and anger as Stephen had ever heard from her. She was all fury and fight. He pulled her back against him, trying to soothe her, as de Velt almost seemed amused.

"I believe you," he said sincerely. "Which is why I will have Kynan remove you. Go home, little lady. Go home and forget you ever had an English husband for soon he will fade into memory."

Joselyn went mad. She screamed angrily and grabbed the nearest thing, which happened to be an empty pitcher from their meal the previous night. She threw it at de Velt, who ducked, allowing it to sail into the man behind him. Kynan was already moving towards her, putting himself between Joselyn and de Velt. He grabbed her by the arms, forcing her down beside Stephen as the weakened man tried to keep a grip on her.

"Stop it," Kynan hissed. "If ye sufficiently anger him, he'll make an example of ye, too!"

Stephen wrapped both his arms around her, pulling her against him. His ribs were screaming with the exertion but he had little choice. Joselyn had turned into a wildcat. He trapped her, forcing her to face him.

"Sweetheart, stop," he murmured. "Stop your fighting. You will listen to me and listen well."

She interrupted him as the angry, terrified tears began to come. "I am not leaving you!"

He put his face into the side of her head, his lips by her ear. "Listen to me," he whispered, making sure that de Velt didn't hear him. "You must return to Tate and tell him what has happened. I need you to take that message to him, do you understand?"

She was weeping fearfully into his neck but she still managed to comprehend what he was saying. "But I do not want to leave you," she whispered, her lips quivering. "Please do not make me leave you."

He smiled sweetly at her, cupping her face between his two massive hands. "You will never leave me, sweetheart," he declared, gazing into her eyes. "You will always be with me, locked deep inside my heart. But I would like to see our son grow up and unless you take a message back to Tate, I am not sure that will happen. Please? It is important."

Joselyn was struggling between hysteria and composure. She wanted to go wild with what de Velt was suggesting yet Stephen's calm words were sinking in. If she wanted to see her husband live, then she must do as he said. She had done all she could and it was clear the Scots would not release Stephen. They were going to punish him for being English. She just was not strong enough to free him herself. She needed help.

Her tears faded as she gazed into his blue eyes. "Oh, Stephen," she breathed. "I am so frightened."

He stroked her cheeks with his thumbs. "I know," he whispered. "But you must force that aside and do as I say. You are my only hope and I need your help, not your tears."

She swallowed hard, wiping her nose and looking hesitantly to

Kynan, who nodded firmly.

"Come along with ye, Jo-Jo," he reached out and grasped her arm. "Let's take ye out of here."

Panic flashed in her eyes but Stephen squeezed her gently, kissing her on the cheek. "Go," he murmured. "I will see you soon."

She threw her arms around his neck, kissing him furiously, painfully. "I love you," she whispered between sniffles and kisses. "I love you more than life, Stephen, and I swear this is not the end. I swear it."

Stephen returned her kisses, tasting her tears. He seriously wondered if this would be his last taste of her. "And I love you," he said. "You are everything to me, Jo-Jo. Never forget that. Now hurry and leave before de Velt alters his decision and keeps you here. I could not bear it if that happened."

She was a mess, sobbing and weeping, but she yanked herself away from Stephen and threw herself against Kynan. Kynan took hold of her and very quickly took her from the room, fearful that de Velt would change his mind and not allow her leave. The man could have just as easily made a whore out of condemned man's wife. Once Kynan and Joselyn had fled the solar, de Velt turned to Stephen.

His dark eyes were cool, appraising. Stephen met his gaze without emotion, not wanting to hasten what was to happen to him by saying the wrong thing. He needed to give Tate time to figure out a plan. He needed to give Joselyn time to get free of Berwick. If he thought about it, he was frightened, but not for himself; death did not hold fear for him. But he was frightened for his wife and unborn child and what would become of them. He very much wanted to see his son.

De Velt chased everyone else from the room after Joselyn and Kynan fled, bolting the door when the chamber had emptied. It was a surprising move and one that had Stephen apprehensive. He watched De Velt closely as the man resumed his seat on the stool and faced Stephen with his cool demeanor.

"Now," he said quietly. "You and I will speak of what Edward's intentions for Berwick are. Why did he station you here, Pembury? Is he planning on launching invasions into Scotland to secure the country for himself?"

Stephen gazed steadily at de Velt, not surprised by the line of questioning. As he had done to Kynan for weeks, now he was to be on the receiving end. As he continued to watch de Velt, a thought suddenly occurred to him. He deduced that he had nothing to lose by pursuing it. Time, and his life, was ticking away.

"I would rather speak of something else," he countered. "You, for instance; everyone knows that your loyalty is to whoever pays you the most. There is no shame in that, of course, but I would like to know how much Moray is paying you to cut my head off."

De Velt's lips twitched. "Does it matter? Do you truly wish to know what you are worth?"

Stephen's eyes fixed on him. "Whatever it is, I will double it plus grant you titles which belong to me. Let me go and it all becomes yours."

De Velt lifted an eyebrow. "You think to bribe me, Pembury?"

"I think to make you a very wealthy man. What does it matter how you acquire it, so long as you do?"

He was not surprised that de Velt was interested in hearing him out. But the conversation did not end well. Stephen found himself back in the stocks by noon.

CHAPTER NINETEEN

A S CADE AND Roman neared the gatehouse, Lady Joselyn Pembury and a strange man suddenly emerged from the gates. Joselyn was on a little gray mare and the Scots was on a big bay steed. Roman and Cade fell flat into the knee-high grass to conceal themselves, watching as the man grabbed hold of the gray mare's bridle and began leading it off to the northwest. The boys' heads came up the further away the pair drew, watching as they headed off towards a distant bridge that crossed the River Tweed. The boys continued to watch until Lady Joselyn and the strange man faded out of sight.

"She came out," Cade popped up, resting on his knees. "Something must be wrong if she came out without Sir Stephen."

Roman's gaze moved between the direction that Lady Pembury had taken and the castle to his right. "Who was that man with her?"

Cade shrugged. "I do not know. Do you suppose he abducted her? Maybe we need to go and save her!"

Roman shook his head. Then he nodded. In truth, he didn't know. "She was not screaming so I do not think he abducted her," he said, looking up at the castle. "We've got to get inside so we can find Sir Stephen and maybe he'll know what is happening. Maybe we'll just have to get him out by ourselves."

Cade's mind was already working furiously, convinced that, with the departure of Lady Pembury, he and Roman were Sir Stephen's only hope. It was puzzling as well as frightening, and his excitement began to surge.

"I shall think of something," he said confidently.

Roman was staring up at the towering castle walls of Berwick. Suddenly, he didn't feel so confident. Maybe they should not have come after all. Their little adventure was turning into something more significant and he was not sure they were prepared. But it was too late to turn back and not look like a coward.

"You'd better," he grumbled.

It was Cade who finally came up with the idea of catching fish from the river and taking them to the castle, pretending they had been ordered to do so. If anyone asked them who ordered them to bring the fish, they were to say a big Scots on a bay steed. That part of it was Roman's idea. Cade figured that the men inside the fortress would not turn down fresh food and would not be suspicious of two small boys. So they scooted down to the river amongst the high summer grass, fashioned a spear out of a branch, and went spear fishing.

The water was freezing as they waded in, managing to catch eleven fish in a two hour period. Roman was better at it than Cade was. He had extraordinary patience for a young boy and was able to stand for long periods of time so the fish would draw close to him. He caught nine out of the eleven, much to Cade's displeasure. They were plump fish and rather large, so the boys gathered them up and ran back towards the road. With wet breeches and chattering teeth, they made it back to the road that led directly to the gatehouse.

Because of the battle several days before, the area surrounding the castle was desolate and pock-marked from the incendiary devices that Stephen and Kenneth had thrown over the walls. There were also several dead bodies thrown into a pile near the wall, awaiting disposal, but they were creepy and smelly, and it was the boys' first experience viewing battle-killed bodies. They remained stoic but Cade didn't want to look too closely. Roman poked them with the fish-spear.

The gates had been burned out during the battle, leaving only the double portcullis that was lowered. Guards milled behind the lowered grate, intimidating the boys, so they lingered back, just out of view as they studied the gatehouse area. It took a significant amount of courage to finally approach the gate. As they drew close, Cade held up the fish on the spear.

"Oy!" he yelled.

It took him two more tries before they were noticed. Scots in dirty tartans lingered at the closed portcullis, eyeing the boys as they stood there, cold and wet, with fish in their hands.

"What do ye want, little man?" one of the guards asked.

Cade pointed in no particular direction. "A man told us to bring these to the castle," he said. "He was a big man on a bay horse. He said he wanted them for his supper."

The guards looked at the boys, each other, and the direction in which the boy was pointing. "Who was the man?" the same guard asked.

Cade shook his head. "I do not know," he replied, sensing that this was not going to be an easy sell. "He... he told us to catch these fish and bring them to the castle for his sup. He said he would be back and would be very angry if the fish were not here."

The guards truly had no idea who they were talking about. They muttered among themselves, not particularly concerned, until one of them reached his hand through the bars.

"Give 'em tae me," he said. "I shall make sure they get eaten."

Cade stepped back, away from the hand. "He said that he wanted these fish and he would kill anyone who tried to eat them," he insisted. "I have to bring them in and take them to the kitchens myself."

"Otherwise, he might kill our families," Roman put in for good measure.

Cade nodded sincerely to confirm Roman's lie. "Aye, he said that," he claimed. "Please, sir, won't you let us in? I do not want this man to kill my mother and father."

The guards chuckled, finally shrugged at each other, and yelled for the portcullis to be lifted. When it was about two feet off the ground, Cade and Roman slipped in and made a mad dash for the bailey beyond.

Having no idea where they were going, however, proved to be a problem, because they ran so fast and so blindly that they ended up over by the keep. Only Cade had been inside of Berwick but he truly didn't remember that much about it. He vaguely recognized the keep as he and Roman ran around to the southeast side, hiding in the shadows until they could figure out where the kitchens were. Berwick, surprisingly, seemed deserted and eerie. Most of the men seemed to be upon the battlements and there was a great deal of noise coming from the great hall. Their eyes moved over the interior of the castle, studying, trying to figure out their next move. And that's when they saw Stephen.

He was chained up to the stocks, his big body beaten and worn. Cade's eyes widened and he poked at Roman, pointing towards the area between the great hall and the kitchens. The section was nearly out of view from the main part of the bailey and easy to overlook. Roman spied Stephen, chained like a beast, and his hazel eyes bulged.

"Look!" he hissed. "There is Stephen! They are torturing him!"

Cade nodded emphatically, sickened at the sight. He was afraid the Scots would do the same thing to him if they caught him. "He looks hurt," he muttered apprehensively.

Roman nodded, studying the man at a distance. He had known Stephen since birth and viewed him as an uncle. It made his little heart very angry to see what the Scots had done to a man he loved. He was so young and naïve, and it hadn't really occurred to him that Stephen would have truly been abused. Although his father was a warlord, it was not something that he had been seriously exposed to during his young life and the sight was something of a shock. He felt very scared but fought it. He pulled on Cade's arm.

"Come on," he said. "Let's go see him."

Cade readily agreed. Still clutching their fish, they looked around to make sure there was not anyone in close proximity before bolting from the shadows, racing across the dusty bailey to where Stephen was chained in partial sun.

Stephen's eyes were closed, his head down, and the boys looked panicked as they visually inspected the heavy chains that secured the man to the wooden stocks. Stephen was sweaty, dirty, bloodied and bruised, and Roman finally reached out and touched the man's nearly-black hair timidly. When Stephen didn't move, Roman tried again. He gently shook Stephen's head.

"Stephen?" Roman whispered. "Can you hear me? Are you alive?"

The boys jumped when Stephen suddenly shifted, lifting his head and groggily blinking his eyes. As the great head came up, the blue eyes struggled to focus. Stephen beheld Roman for a few seconds before his expression changed dramatically.

"Roman?" he rasped, noticing there was another body next to him and recognizing the face. "Cade? What in the … is it truly you?"

Roman nodded emphatically. "It is," he told him. "We've come to save you!"

Stephen's mouth popped open in shock, then shut in outrage. "What in the hell are you doing here?" he hissed. "Roman, where is your father? Did he send you?"

Roman received the impression that Stephen was not too thrilled to see him. "Nay," he shook his head, confused that Stephen was not more grateful. "He does not know we have come. We came to help Lady Pembury rescue you, but we saw her leave a little while ago. Where did she go? Why did she leave?"

Stephen gazed back at the two young, handsome faces, feeling more sickened than he thought possible. "You came to help Joselyn?" he repeated, stunned.

Roman and Cade nodded eagerly. "She is just a lady, after all," Cade finally found his tongue. "We came to help her because the Scots would not suspect us."

"Aye," Roman nodded firmly.

"We're just boys. Nobody pays any attention to us."

"Aye!"

"So we are going to save you!"

Stephen looked between the two of him, his mouth hanging open again. He could hardly believe what he was hearing. "What?" he looked at them as if they were mad. "Roman, what about your mother? Does she know you are here?"

Roman was defiant. "Nay," he told him. "I didn't tell her. She would not have let me come."

"So you traveled all the way from Forestburn by yourselves?"

"It was not so difficult, except we had to steal bread this morning."

"We were hungry," Cade explained helpfully.

"Aye," Roman looked at his companion for moral support. "Do you think we should get money and go back and pay the man once we have rescued you?"

Stephen was dumbfounded. After a moment, he closed his eyes against the vision of Roman and Cade traveling alone on unsafe roads, stealing bread to eat. It was too much for him to take at the moment. "God have mercy," he muttered. "Thieves."

"We are not thieves," Roman said adamantly. "We were hungry. We will pay the man when we get money, I swear it."

Stephen couldn't help it; he snorted. The whole thing was so ridiculous. On one hand, he was so deeply touched that he could not put it into words. That these two young men should risk themselves for him was beyond comprehension. Yet he was so furious with them that he thought, perhaps, fury alone would see him break from the chains just so he could get his hands on them. He was torn, tormented and injured, a volatile combination.

"Boys," he said hoarsely, struggling to stay calm. "While I appreciate your bravery, you should consider yourselves lucky that I am tied up. If I was not, you would suffer the beating of your young lives for this stupidity. You will leave immediately and go find Tate. I am told he is near the Whiteadder Bridge. Get out of here while there is still time."

Roman looked flattered, frightened and indignant at the same time. "But... we cannot leave you," he insisted. "We can find a way to release you!"

Stephen tried to shake his head, restricted by the chains. "Roman de Lara, if you do not leave here immediately, I will break these chains that bind me and beat you within an inch of your life. And when your father finds out what you have done, he will do the same.

Roman was taken aback by the attitude. He looked at Cade, who gazed back at him with equal shock. He looked back at Stephen, baffled, before determination overtook him and he shook his head firmly.

"Nay," he said. "I am not leaving. Cade and I are going to help you."

Stephen began to work himself up into a righteous rage. "So help me," he muttered, "if you do not leave immediately, I will thrash you so soundly that you will not be able to sit, ride or otherwise use your buttocks for an entire month. You will not disobey me."

Roman was intimidated, that was clear. But he was also resolute. "Nay!" he stomped his foot. "I am not leaving. Come on, Cade!"

He grabbed Cade and they dashed off, out of Stephen's line of sight. He could hear their footfalls fading away, panic such as he had never known filling him. He almost shouted at them but didn't want to attract any unwanted attention, so he kept his mouth shut. Exhausted, dehydrated and injured, he could only stand in the stocks and fume, wondering what those two brave, foolish boys were going to do. Tate or no Tate, he was going to blister Roman's backside if he got out of this situation alive. And Cade... it was not such a glorious beginning for him and his new son. But he greatly admired the lad's courage.

After several long and frustrated moments, he suddenly began to laugh. He didn't know why, but he found the entire circumstance humorous. He figured, at that point, he must be losing his mind. Only an idiot would laugh at what the boys had done. But insanity didn't reduce the fear he felt for Cade and Roman.

꩜

"THAT'S WHAT THE man said," Kynan's voice was grim above the sounds of Joselyn's weeping. "At least he allowed me tae remove Jo-Jo. Ye can be grateful fer that small mercy."

Tate stared at Kynan, not particularly surprised at the message the man bore, before turning away to collect himself. He was, frankly, sickened at the news, something he'd feared but had not allowed himself to fully entertain. Kenneth, however, was not done with the interrogation.

"De Velt said that Moray ordered Stephen drawn and quartered?" he repeated, his voice deep and threatening. "That does not make any sense. Stephen is a minor knight. 'Tis not as if he is an earl or viscount and holds any particular significance. He is simply a knight given a duty by the king. It does not make any sense that Moray would want to make an example out of him."

Kynan was wary of the bulldog of a knight with the blond hair and ice-colored eyes. Kenneth had managed to thrash him about fairly well when he was in the vault and the questions Kenneth asked were not properly answered.

"Be that as it may, those were Moray's orders," Kynan kept a distance from him. "At dusk on the day after tomorrow, Stephen is tae be executed and his body scattered throughout the border as a message to all those who oppose David's rule. More than that, it's meant tae scare the English. After what happened tae Tommy and Willie Seton, Moray has prepared shock tactics of his own."

"But Stephen had nothing to do with my brothers' deaths," Joselyn was sobbing. "He said that he was Tommy's guardian until the end. Knowing my husband as I do, I know that he must have been greatly saddened by Tommy's death. He is a man of deep compassion. He does not deserve what Moray plans for him."

She was growing increasingly hysterical and Tate wriggled his eyebrows at Kenneth, who took the hint. He went to her, putting a big arm around her shoulder to comfort her. But she didn't want to be comforted and when she tried to pull away, he grasped her firmly and forced her to look at him.

"Jo-Jo," he said, his voice softening. "Nothing has happened to Stephen yet and as long as I have breath in my body, I swear that nothing will happen to him. I understand that you are upset. We are all upset. But we are also seasoned warriors and if anyone can get Stephen out of this, Tate and I can. Do you understand me?"

Eyes watering and nose red, Joselyn nodded once. "A-Aye."

Kenneth smiled faintly. "Good girl," he murmured. "Do you believe me?"

Again, she nodded, struggling to calm. "I do," she hiccupped. "But… but he was so badly beaten. There is no knowing what they have done to him since I have left. What if…?"

Kenneth shook her gently. "Listen to me," he interrupted. "I learned long ago that it is a waste of time and energy to worry over things you cannot control. As long as Stephen has an execution order, they are more than likely leaving him alone at this time. They would not want him to die before his appointed time and risk upsetting Moray. Therefore, there is no reason for you to be upset right now. In fact, it would be better for Tate and me if you were calm. We are trying to think of a way to free Stephen and cannot think clearly if we are constantly concerned over your mental health."

By this time, Joselyn's tears were gone completely. She swallowed hard, nodding to his words. "I am sorry," she whispered. "I will try to be calm, I promise."

"I know you will," he squeezed her arms gently. "Your bravery helps us face what we must."

She wiped at her nose daintily. "Thank you, Kenneth. Stephen is fortunate to have such a good friend."

Kenneth's smile returned and he patted her gently on the cheek, understanding why Stephen loved this woman so. She was very sweet and definitely beautiful.

"You are welcome," he said softly, giving her a wink before turning to Tate and, when he was sure Joselyn couldn't see him, rolling his eyes with relief.

Tate caught the expression from the normally expressionless man and suppressed the urge to grin. He watched Joselyn a moment as she struggled to compose herself. He was, in truth, wondering how in the world they were going to get Stephen out of Berwick in spite of Kenneth's words of confidence. John Randolph, the third Earl of

Moray, was an extremely powerful man in Scotland. If the orders for Stephen came down from Moray, then there was little chance that someone superseding Moray could counter the command other than the king himself. Unless….

He turned away from Joselyn, his mind whirling with thought. He didn't want her to see his expression, the gleam of an idea in his eye. He caught Kenneth's attention and motioned the man to him.

"Send a messenger escort to Alnwick bearing my colors," he snapped softly.

"Alnwick?" Kenneth repeated, confused. "Why would…?"

"Because Alexander Seton is being held prisoner there," he whispered. "I will send a missive to Henry Percy ordering him to release Seton and send him back to me at Berwick. Send another man back to Forestburn and summon my army. Have them arrive by tomorrow noon and we will begin the bombardment of Berwick. Perhaps if we distract the Scots enough, their attention will be diverted from Stephen's execution and we'll buy the man some time until Seton arrives."

Kenneth was following him but it was clear by his expression that he was not in total agreement. "Bombardment?" he repeated, incredulous. "I thought we agreed that this was not a job for an entire army."

Tate fixed him in the eye. "It was not until Joselyn failed. I do not see where we have any choice now. Besides, you have already sent word to Edward, have you not? If I know the man, and I do, he shall bring his whole damn army, highly angered that Berwick is back in the hands of the Scots again. He is going to want the city back."

Kenneth suspected he had a point. "True enough. He should already be on his way." He crossed his big arms thoughtfully. "But what do you think Seton will be able to do. He is Berwick's defeated commander. They will not listen to him over Moray."

Tate held up a finger. "Perhaps not, but I am willing to wager on the fact that Seton will have the sympathy of every man at Berwick for what happened to his sons," he said. "That could sway the situation in

Stephen's favor if Seton makes a plea on his behalf."

"What makes you think he will?"

Tate's gaze moved to Joselyn, who was standing with Kynan, listening as the man spoke quietly to her. Kenneth looked at her as well, understanding the implication, before puffing out his cheeks in a hissing sigh.

"Stephen told me what her father did to her," he lowered his voice. "I can guarantee that he does not want Joselyn's father near her. We will have to be very careful on the amount of contact we allow between them."

Tate looked at him. "Stephen can thrash me for the rest of his life for my decision if, in fact, he survives the morrow," he snapped softly. "We have made two decisions that Stephen will not agree with so I fully expect the man to ream me the moment he is released."

Kenneth crossed his enormous arms, looking thoughtful. "I intend to run far, far away and hide."

"I may not be far behind you."

"Let us hope we are provided with that chance."

Tate nodded faintly and turned away. Kenneth watched the man pace, his thoughts moving to Stephen and wondering what he would do if, in fact, they were unable to prevent tomorrow's execution. Then his gaze moved to Joselyn, pregnant with Stephen's son. It all seemed so horribly unfair, just when the man had found some happiness.

But Kenneth was not willing to give up, not yet. He ordered four men south to Alnwick, about a day's ride under normal circumstances, with instructions that they were not to stop until they reached Alnwick. Once Seton was retrieved, they were to make all due haste returning. He sent a second set of riders to Forestburn to collect Tate's army with essentially the same instructions. Ride straight through, return with all due haste.

With Kenneth barking orders and men on the move, Tate collected what remained of the escort he had brought from Forestburn and moved them well downriver, concealing them in trees and brush. He gave Kynan some money with the instructions to take Joselyn to town and find her a good room and a decent meal, but after the battles in Berwick recently, he was not so sure something like that was possible. It was made more difficult when Joselyn refused to go until he essentially forced her. In tears, the woman did as she was told. He then sent Kenneth back to the bridge with four men to watch the road and the castle for any activity.

But Kenneth couldn't remain stationary, not when his best friend was fighting for his life inside the pale walls of Berwick Castle. After a few hours of waiting near the bridge with his favored weapon, his crossbow, slung across his shoulders, he gave up the fight completely and took his men down to the river's edge. Very carefully, they made their way upriver, around the castle, and to the southeast side where the postern gate was lodged.

As he watched the castle at closer range, Kenneth was not at all sure he could wait for Seton's arrival from Alnwick. Every second that ticked away was a second closer to Stephen's death. As he hid in the tall river grass and watched the activity on the walls, he began to concoct a plan that would either save them all or see them all dead.

He hoped it was not the latter.

CHAPTER TWENTY

D E VELT HAD not moved Stephen out of the stocks. In fact, it seemed that he didn't want to be bothered with the man, as he was more involved in playing lord and master of Berwick. Stephen's possessions were still in the keep, which de Velt had claimed as his own, including any coinage that was in his bags. The next morning after he had been returned to the stocks, Stephen even saw de Velt wearing one of his tunics. It seemed that Morgan had not been satisfied with the bribe Stephen had presented him with, the reason for Stephen's return to bondage. Stephen was only willing to give him the title of Baron Lamberton, including Ravensdowne Castle. De Velt was very interested, but he wanted the Pembury inheritance as well, which Stephen would not give him. So Stephen found himself back in the stocks and the victim of a spiteful mercenary.

He was miserable and wounded. His back was killing him, his ribs screaming in pain and his arms had long since lost circulation. He couldn't even feel them. But captive as he was, an odd and wonderful thing occurred. A few hours after Roman and Cade had run off, the boys returned under the cover of darkness, and brought Stephen water and some kind of bread that they had stolen from the hall. Stephen had struggled to resume his fury at them but couldn't muster the strength when they were trying so hard to help him. It made his heart ache, these brave little boys who were risking their lives to give him water and food. The sustenance had kept him alive, or at least kept his strength from leaving him completely. It, and they, had been a God-send.

The boys returned to him twice more during the night and when dawn broke, they brought something they had found stored in clay pots in the kitchens. It looked like some kind of pie and when Cade shoved it into Stephen's mouth, he discovered it to be a cold meat concoction. For some reason, it made him think of his wife and her wonderful cooking. God, he missed her.

Roman was giving Stephen the last of the water when they began to hear footfalls. Tucked between the hall and the kitchens as they were, there was a relative amount of privacy that had enabled the boys to come and go on a regular basis. But it also meant that if they were caught by surprise, they would be cornered. The moment they heard the boots, they dropped the cup and nearly crashed into each other in their haste to hide. The entire time, Stephen was hissing at them to hide until they finally managed to wedge themselves in behind a small wall that bordered the kitchens. Just as they ducked behind the stone, a booted man appeared.

Kynan came to a halt when he saw Stephen, his eyes widening. In the early morning, he was swathed in his dusty tartan, partially obscuring his face, and it took Stephen a moment to recognize him. Kynan yanked the tartan off his head, his dark eyes blazing.

"Not again," he growled, moving for the stocks and trying to figure out how they had all of the chains secured. "The bloody bastards tied ye up again, did they? Barbarians!"

He began to rattle the chains, pulling out the iron pegs that held them secure against the wood. He was making enough noise that Cade and Roman heard him, too far away to hear what he was saying but terrified that a Scots had come to remove Stephen from his prison. They were positive that the man was taking Stephen away to kill him. Cade was the first one to grab a big rock.

"Get something," he hissed at Roman, who began looking around furiously for a weapon. "We cannot let him take Sir Stephen away!"

Roman's hands fell on two smaller rocks and he nodded sharply at Cade, who suddenly leapt out from behind the wall with a very acceptable rebel yell. Roman was right behind him and they rushed Kynan, who was startled and stumped by the two young boys charging him. His lack of reaction was his undoing. Cade launched the rock and hit Kynan between the eyes, causing the man to go down. Before Stephen could stop them, the boys jumped on Kynan and began pummeling him with their rocks.

"Cade!" Stephen was trying not to shout. "Roman, cease! Leave the man alone!"

Roman stopped but Cade didn't. He continued to beat Kynan in the chest with a rock. Kynan, however, had only been momentarily stunned by the flying rock. He blinked his eyes to regain his focus before shoving Cade off of him. He struggled to his feet.

"Ye little devils!" he growled, grabbing Roman by the arm because he was the closest. He landed a big palm on Roman's buttocks before Stephen could stop him. "I shall thrash ye both within an inch of yer lives! I shall beat ye senseless! I shall…!"

"Kynan," Stephen snapped over the man's furious chatter. "Leave them alone. They are on our side, believe it or not."

Kynan stopped smacking Roman but he still had him by the arm. "What's this ye say?"

Cade was terrified for his friend and kicked Kynan in the shin when the man's attention was diverted. Kynan howled as Roman broke free and both boys rushed at him, shoving him onto the ground and kicking him.

"Good God," Stephen hissed as a battle once again ensued. "Roman, Cade, cease your abuse. Kynan is not the enemy. Stop kicking him!"

Roman stopped but Cade was slower to react. He kicked Kynan one last time and Kynan grabbed his leg, throwing him on to the ground. Stephen intervened once more before it got ugly.

"Gentlemen," he snapped softly. "Enough fighting. Kynan, those two young boys belong to me. Well, at least one of them does. The taller lad is Cade Alexander, Joselyn's son."

Kynan's furious and confused expression washed with surprise. "Are ye serious?" he looked at the tall, handsome lad who had nearly brained him. "He… he's Jo-Jo's lad?"

"Aye," Stephen said steadily, hoping to impress upon the man that the boy knew little of the circumstances of his birth. "Joselyn and Cade have spent the past week becoming acquainted. He understands that Joselyn was forced to surrender him at birth to the nuns because she had little choice. But she loves him and that is all he need know."

Kynan was not over his astonishment yet but understood not to say too much to the boy regarding his birth. Still, it was a shock to see him. The lad looked a good deal like Joselyn with his dark hair and pale blue eyes and he felt some relief that he did not see Alexander Seton in the little face. Perhaps the man was not the father, after all. Kynan's shock rapidly transformed into something warm, at least as warm as Kynan could manage.

"I'm yer cousin, lad," he pointed at himself with a thumb. "'Tis a proud heritage ye bear."

Cade simply stood and stared at the big Scots, eyeing him with some suspicion. When Kynan didn't get a reaction, he looked at the other boy. "Who is this whelp?" he asked.

Stephen answered. "De Lara's son," he replied. "The boys rode all the way from de Lara's castle to save me."

Kynan was back to being shocked. "Are ye lyin' tae me, man?"

"Not at all. They traveled alone over several miles to reach me."

Kynan looked at each boy, suddenly smacking Roman on the side of the head. "Ye foolish little brutes. What possessed ye?"

Stephen struggled not to grin as Roman rubbed the side of his head and kicked out at Kynan again, who deftly moved aside. In fact, Stephen found the whole circumstance hilarious and it was very difficult for him not to laugh as the boys continued to swipe at Kynan and he continued to dodge them. Finally, Stephen called a halt to the antics. He had to before they attracted attention.

"Kynan," he singled the man out, hoping to distract all of them from their punching game. "What are you doing here? You are supposed to be with Jo-Jo."

Kynan gave Cade a good shove by the forehead and sent the boy to the ground as he moved back to where Stephen was tethered. He resumed unwinding the chains.

"She is safe," he told him. "I took her intae town meself and found her lodgings. She has a good bed and good food and men tae watch over her. She is fine. But ye, on the other hand...."

"Why did you come back?" Stephen demanded quietly.

Kynan lifted an eyebrow. "Because I'm gonna get ye out of here," he said frankly. "Ye may be English and ye may be me enemy, but Jo-Jo is me family and she couldna survive if something happened tae ye. I told ye before, the lass deserves some happiness."

"Has de Velt seen you?"

"Nay," Kynan fumbled with the last iron peg. "But I found some of me men. I told 'em tae gather the rest and meet me near the kitchens."

Stephen sighed heavily as Kynan pulled off the chains and lifted the arm off the stocks that was pressed down over his shoulders. The relief was indescribable as Stephen tried to lift his arms but, due to lack of feeling, he was having difficulty. Cade and Roman rushed to him, helping him move arms that were as big around as they were. But Stephen's size required a bit more strength so Kynan helped him remove his arms completely. Cade and Roman tried to help Stephen rub some feeling into them.

"Ye know this castle, Pembury," Kynan lowered his voice, looking around to make sure no one was watching or focused on them. "We need tae hide ye somewhere until I can get ye out of here."

Stephen shook his head. "Once they discover I am missing, they will lock this place down. It would be better to leave right now before any suspicion arises."

"I canna do it until me men arrive," Kynan replied. "I shall wrap ye in tartan and take ye out with a bunch of Scots so no suspicions can be raised."

Stephen was gazing off into the bailey, his blue eyes fixed on something in the distance. Kynan turned around to see what the man was looking at but having no idea what held his attention. He looked back at Stephen.

"What are ye looking at?" he demanded.

Stephen lifted his chin in a pointing gesture. "The postern gate," he said softly. "I do not see any guards."

Kynan wriggled his brows. "Ye dunna see them because everyone is on the walls or in the hall. The postern gate is easily seen from both of those places so dunna think ye can easily escape from it. They will be on us in a flash."

Stephen grunted in acknowledgement, thankful that they were at least partially hidden between the hall and the kitchens as they were. He was also thankful that he was getting the feeling back in his arms because the first thing he did was grab Roman and swat the boy on the buttocks. As Roman yelped, Stephen did the same thing to Cade. When the boys looked up at him, angry and hurt, he pointed a finger at them.

"I told you not to disobey me," he rumbled. But his harsh stance lasted for a half-second before he reached out and put his arms round the boys, hugging them as much as his weakened state would allow. "But for keeping me alive, I thank you. You are very brave men."

The boys grinned at him and each other, proud they had accomplished something in spite of the risks. Kynan just shook his head.

"Little brutes," he grumbled, eyeing the boys. "But brave. I shall give ye that."

Stephen half-grinned at Kynan, looking at the section of the bailey he could see from their vantage point and feeling even more exposed. He could hear men all around and was becoming increasingly uncomfortable. They had to move.

"We cannot simply stand here," he told Kynan. "Where are your men?"

Kynan looked around, sticking his neck out and peering around the side of the hall for a full view of the bailey. After several long moments, he returned his attention to Stephen.

"I dunna see them," his gaze moved between Stephen and the stocks. "I shall go look for 'em but it might be best if ye returned to the stocks until I return. That way, if anyone sees ye, nothin' will look odd.

You'll still be in the stocks where they left ye."

Stephen knew he had a point. Wearily, he went back to the wooden framed beast and put his head and wrists into the slots. It was excruciatingly painful for him to resume the stance, but he knew it was important. Kynan draped the chains around to make it look like Stephen was still chained down even though he could quite easily break free. When Kynan was satisfied with the illusion, he abruptly waved his hands at the boys.

"Go and hide," he commanded softly. "Stay out o'sight until I return."

The boys did as they were told. As Kynan wrapped the tartan back over his head and slipped away, Stephen stood there in his hunched, uncomfortable position, wondering if he was going to indeed live to see the next few days come to pass. It was not simply himself to worry over. Now there was Cade and Roman, as well meaning as they were. He was far more concerned with getting the boys out safely. He could only pray that Kynan had a workable plan. All of their lives were in the hands of a man once considered the enemy. The seconds were ticking away faster now, ever closer to his date with doom.

Fortunately, it was not too long before Kynan reappeared. Behind him came several men, all of them clad in the same brownish-orange tartan. They were big, dirty men with an unruly way about them. Kynan didn't have to say a word. He simply pointed at Stephen and three burly Scots went to him, pulling the chains off and releasing him from the stocks. Stephen stood with some assistance, his ribs still badly injured and his back injured on top of everything from having been confined in stocks not built for a man his height.

One of the men produced a length of tartan and wrapped it around Stephen's massive shoulders, draping it so it covered most of his battered torso before wrapping the end of it over his head. Stephen nodded his silent thanks to these men he had fought against, killed against, feeling very blessed and guilty that they were willing to assist him. He wondered fleetingly if these men had been part of the ambush weeks ago that had injured Joselyn, or if he had fought against them during the innumerable skirmishes over the past month. They had all been bred since birth to kill and hate one another, but now, he found his life in their hands more than he could have ever imagined.

By this time, Cade and Roman had come out of their hiding place and were watching the activity with big eyes. Kynan saw the boys and beckoned them with a crooked finger. Hesitantly, they went to him, afraid they were going to be slapped in the head again.

"Now," Kynan put a hand on either boy's shoulder. "We're gonna get Sir Stephen out of this place but I need ye tae stay close tae me, do ye hear? Dunna run off."

The boys nodded solemnly. "We won't," Cade assured him. "But can we help?"

"Aye, of course ye can," Kynan assured him. "I would have ye be look-outs. Ye need to keep yer eyes open for anything suspicious."

"Suspicious?" Roman repeated. "Like what?"

Kynan turned the boys around so they were facing the bailey and the postern gate in the distance. "Like men with weapons chargin' for us," he said, pointing. "See that gate? We're gonna make our way tae it. I shall need yer help tae open it."

The boys nodded eagerly, preparing to behave like true warriors. They were terrified and excited. When Kynan made sure the tartan was sufficiently draped over Stephen, he motioned the group to move. They did so, but very quickly realized that Stephen was moving like an injured man. If they were going to move unnoticed, then Stephen would have to make a better attempt at behaving normally. Kynan went to him.

"Ye walk like ye have two broken legs," he said. "I dunna mean tae make yer life more miserable than it already 'tis, but can ye at least stand straight? Ye walk like a cripple."

Stephen grunted, trying to straighten up. The blue eyes were blazing. "I *am* a cripple," he groaned. "But I will do my best."

Kynan nodded, motioning for his men to take the lead as he stayed close to Stephen. He was concerned for the man, concerned for who might be watching, and terrified that they weren't going to make it out of the gate. But their best option was to behave as normally as possible, so he and his men moved in a casual group towards the postern gate, that small opening to freedom that loomed before them.

Stephen could see the gate and never in his life had something meant so much to him. He needed to make it to that small doorway and to the freedom that waited beyond. A wife whom he adored, a son on the way... he needed to get to his family. That one thought alone kept his focus. They made it across the bailey without incident and were within several feet of the gate when a shadow suddenly blocked their path.

Stephen saw the movement and he reflectively flinched, moving for a sword that was not at his side. Kynan's men were armed but they did not move to draw their weapon. They simply came to a halt, facing the figure that stood between them and the postern gate. Kynan saw the figure, the face, and hissed under his breath. He really was not surprised. But he was extremely disheartened.

Morgan de Velt was standing between them and freedom.

☯

HIDDEN BY THE reeds growing by the river's edge, Joselyn gazed up at the massive bastion of Berwick. She could see the familiar postern gate and the path she had taken once from the castle to the river where she had found her fawn. The soft breeze blew the grass around her, folding it to the wind, as she crouched low and watched. She knew she should not have come, but that knowledge had not stopped her. Stephen was inside and she was determined to get to him and to free him.

Tate had meant well. He'd had Kynan take her to the last standing hostel in town, a place called the Sword and Fife. Kynan had procured the best room they had to offer, an abundance of bread, oatcakes and cheese, and had left her there with four men-at-arms as escort. They were Tate's men, seasoned and weary, and had all ended up down in the main room drinking. Joselyn had told the innkeeper to give them as much ale as they could drink. They ended up getting ragingly drunk and she was able to slip out unnoticed.

Now she was here, hidden in the grass as she watched the activity upon Berwick's soaring walls and having no idea what she was going to do to get her husband out. She crept closer on her hands and knees, trying to stay as quiet as possible. At one point she thought she heard the grass moving several feet behind her and she froze, ears cocked, but everything remained still.

Thinking the sound was a figment of her paranoid imagination, she paused and sank to her buttocks, watching the walls and gate that were now closer. The castle loomed above her, a place with the most wonderful and terrible memories for her. She felt as if she had come home again, to a place that did not belong to her yet was a part of her. It was an odd sensation.

She sat for some time, gazing up at the pale stone walls. Everything was quiet and peaceful until a hand suddenly went over her mouth and an enormous arm encircled her waist. Joselyn screamed but the massive gloved hand blocked the sound. She tried to fight, to struggle, but whoever had her was far too strong. She found herself on her back with a big body over her. Panic overtook her until she looked up into ice blue eyes.

Kenneth was gazing down at her, his jaw tight and eyes blazing. Joselyn's eyes widened when she realized who it was.

"I would ask what you are doing here but I already know," Kenneth whispered. "The next thing you feel is going to be the palm of my hand to your buttocks, and your husband be damned. He would do the same thing in my position."

His hand came away from her mouth and she took a big gulp of air. "Please do not be angry," she whispered, fright in her eyes. "I... I simply could not stay away, sitting in a strange room and wondering if my husband is going to live or die. Please do not send me back. If he... if he is going to die, I must be here. I must be close to him. Do you not understand?"

Tears rolled down her temples as Kenneth gazed down at her. He was beginning to feel like a lout, struggling to maintain his fury at finding her at Berwick crawling around in the grass. But he also knew how much Stephen meant to her. He was coming to understand it more and more as the hours passed. Truth be told, he really was not surprised to find her here. With a heavy sigh, he sat up and pulled her with him.

"I understand that you are risking your life and if your husband found out, he would blister your backside," he made a good try at maintaining his firm stance. "Lady, I am here to ensure that your husband does not die but if I have to worry about you as well, Stephen's chances are greatly diminished. If the choice comes down to saving Stephen or saving you, then you know what I will have to do. Stephen would never forgive me if I did not. Do you understand the position you have put me in?"

She looked up at him with her pale, sad eyes and nodded. "I am so scared, Kenneth. I had to come. I could just not sit and wait."

He could see by the look in her eyes that she was not going anywhere. He could send her back to the hostel and she would just find another way to return. After a moment, he simply nodded his head in resignation.

"Then if you are not going to leave, I need for you to stay right here," he said quietly. "Do not make any attempt to get closer to the castle for if you do, you will be within the range of the archers. Is that clear?"

Joselyn nodded seriously. "Aye, Kenneth."

"Good."

His attention suddenly turned back to the castle, the ice-blue eyes intense. He looked as if something had his interest. Joselyn was about to ask him what the trouble was when she heard it, too. It sounded like metal on metal but as she listened more closely, it sounded like a sword fight. Kenneth shoved her down into the grass.

"Stay here," he commanded. "Do not move for any reason."

She watched him crawl away, hidden by the tall green river grass. But the sounds of the sword fight grew more intense and she dared to lift her head, looking towards the source. Movement caught her eye and she could see where it was coming from.

From the between the iron grates of the postern gate, a full-scale battle was in bloom.

CHAPTER TWENTY-ONE

D E VELT JUST stood there and shook his head. He had an amused look on his face that one would have took for a friendly gesture had he not gripped an enormous broadsword. His dark eyes moved between Kynan and Stephen. Even though Stephen's head was covered with the tartan, the blue eyes that blazed beneath it were unmistakable.

"You know," de Velt stroked his chin, "when one of my men came to tell me that he saw Pembury released from the stocks, I almost cut his throat for lying because I know that no one under my command would be that stupid. But I had to come and see for myself if he spoke the truth and look at what I have found."

Kynan was stiff with anticipation, waiting for the broadsword to come flying out at him. "Ye're a hired man, de Velt," he growled. "Ye've no real stake in Berwick other than what ye're paid fer. Ye would carry out orders against a fellow Englishman fer his death? Ye've nothing agin' Pembury. Why would ye kill him?"

De Velt cocked an eyebrow. "Because, as you have said, I am being well paid for my services. Moray wants Pembury dead, so dead he shall be."

Kynan shook his head. "He'll not be dead," he said, more forcefully. "Because I am removin' him from this place. He's beaten and weary, can ye not see? Yer men have done their worst tae him. Now leave him be. He has a wife and child waiting."

De Velt focused on Kynan. "I would not expect this from you, of all people," he said. "Were you not in Berwick's vaults after the siege? Did Pembury not torture you? Tell me the truth and then tell me why you defend him."

Kynan's lips flattened into a hard line. "'Tis none of yer affair, *Sas-*

senach," he hissed. "How would ye know what happened tae me after the siege?"

"Because I was told of your captivity by men who served with you. Is this not true?"

Kynan's frown grew. "Ye dunna belong here," he spat. "Ye're not Scots. We dunna need yer kind here."

De Velt lifted an eyebrow. "Need or not, I am here and here I will stay. But you will give me back my prisoner."

Kynan didn't have a weapon but several of his men did. He reached out to the man closest to him and unsheathed his broadsword, a razor-sharp weapon that was surprisingly well made. He leveled the weapon at de Velt.

"Ye'll have tae fight me fer him," he snarled. "But I warn ye, I shall make it a tough fight."

De Velt shrugged disinterestedly, a move that infuriated Kynan as it insulted his skill. As he lifted the sword and prepared to take the offensive, a big hand suddenly stopped him.

Stephen stood next to him, his hand on the weapon and his eyes on de Velt. The tartan covering his head had fallen to the ground and he was standing tall and proud as if he had never been injured. He looked whole and powerful, and quite ready to kill de Velt.

"Nay," he said softly. "I will do this. It is between de Velt and me."

Morgan might not have cared about fighting Kynan, but he did care about fighting Pembury. His disinterested expression turned to one of curiosity and perhaps approval. He seemed to straighten in the face of the conflict.

"If you can fight me given your present state, then I commend you," he told Stephen. "But it changes nothing. I will subdue you, kill your friends, and tomorrow you shall meet your execution date. Why not make it easy on everyone and simply surrender?"

Stephen took the sword from Kynan, feeling the pommel in his grip, acquainting himself with the feel of it. In truth, he felt better than he had in days. Now with a weapon in his hand, he felt as if he had a fighting chance. Finally, he could defend himself.

"If you were in my position, would you surrender so easily?" he asked.

De Velt smiled faintly. "Nay," he replied. "I would not."

"Then it comes to this."

"I understand completely."

"No mercy will be asked."

"None given."

As Stephen and de Velt faced off, Kynan suddenly shoved Cade and Roman out of the way. They had been hovering behind Stephen in a terrified huddle, but as Stephen uttered those fateful words, Kynan knew what was coming. His own men scattered as several of de Velt's men charged in from the direction of the hall. Swords were unsheathed and men began charging one another. And in the middle of it, Stephen launched a blow against de Velt that sent the man reeling backwards.

The battle had begun.

CB

KENNETH COULD SEE that the men on the walls were facing towards the bailey. The sounds of sword blows grew louder as he crept nearer and nearer, thinking it was an odd blessing indeed that the sentries on duty weren't paying attention to the tall grass beyond the postern gate. The men with Kenneth were also creeping forward, making their way to the wall. Kenneth made it to the edge of the grass, noting that there was about a fifteen foot area between the grass and the walls that had been cleared away. There was absolutely no cover. Glancing upward to ensure that the sentries had not turned around, he bolted to his feet and raced across the cleared area.

Kenneth threw himself up against the wall, noting that the men with him had done the same. Silently, he motioned them to stay in position as he made his way towards the postern gate. The sounds of sword fighting were very loud now and he dared to peer into the iron bars of the gate to see what was going on. What he saw shocked him.

Stephen, beaten and bloodied, was battling for his life with a big knight who was healthy and skilled. As Kenneth watched, horrified, he could see that Stephen was not able to lift the sword with both hands. His right arm was wrapped around his torso, as if holding his guts in, as his left arm did the fighting. This was troubling because Stephen was not left-handed, leading Kenneth to believe that his right hand was injured. No matter how skilled a knight Stephen was, he was obviously at an extreme disadvantage.

Kenneth knew he had to do something. Although the consummate and controlled knight, he was not beyond feeling some panic for his friend at the moment. He rattled the gate but it was clearly bolted. There was no way for him to enter. He went for the blade at his side, knowing even as he grabbed for it that a broadsword could not reach through the grate. But in touching the broadsword, his elbow bumped up against the weapon strapped to his back. And that gave him an idea.

Kenneth ripped off the crossbow and positioned it in the grate, training it on the knight battling against Stephen. He almost let the arrow fly, twice, but both times other men doing battle had moved between him and his target. He could see that there was a rather large battle going on in the bailey of Berwick, Scots against Scots, and Stephen was somehow in the middle of it. It was confusing but there was not time to question. Kenneth kept his eyes trained on the target, praying they would not move out of range, because he could see that Stephen was growing weaker. One blow from his opponent almost took Stephen's head off because he had grown considerably more drained. His reflexes were weakening also.

Kenneth watched with aggravation as Stephen and his opponent shifted positions and suddenly Stephen was between the crossbow and Kenneth's target. He almost yelled with frustration but was distracted when a very recognizable face suddenly appeared, looking back at him through the iron grate. Kenneth nearly fell over when he realized it was Roman de Lara. His mouth flew open in surprise.

"Roman," he hissed. "What are you doing in there?"

"We came to help Stephen," he cried. "He's in trouble! You must help him!"

Roman was terrified, that much was certain. Right next to him, another head popped up and Kenneth recognized Cade. Both boys were inside Berwick and in a great personal danger. Kenneth, feeling more panic as well as a healthy dose of confusion, rattled the gate furiously.

"Open the gate," he tried not to sound as if he was barking. "Throw the bolt and open it."

Cade and Roman struggled with the old iron bolt, edging it further and further out of its socket. Kenneth's attention moved between the boys and Stephen, now greatly struggling as his opponent hacked away at him. It was clear he would not last much longer. Kenneth pressed the boys onward.

"You can do it," he urged. "Just work the bolt out. Quickly, now. Work it quickly."

Roman and Cade were doing their best, grunting and groaning as they tried to throw the bolt. But they had attracted unwanted attention with their efforts and a man suddenly rushed them, sent to the ground as Kenneth put an arrow in his chest.

Terrified and startled, the boys resumed their attempts to throw the old bolt as Kenneth swiftly reloaded. He placed the crossbow through the grate once more, praying that the boys would release the bolt in time. The end was approaching and soon, he would have no choice. He would have to release the arrow whether or not he had an optimum target. It was either that or watch Stephen die, and he simply was not prepared to do that.

As he quietly urged the boys onward, time for Stephen finally came to an end. Kenneth watched with horror as Stephen's opponent managed to disarm him, getting close enough to the injured man to get a foot in behind his knee and toss him to the ground. Kenneth could see the man preparing to deliver the death blow and he lifted his crossbow, preparing to launch it. There was no more time to delay. But a split second before he released the trigger, the old bolt suddenly slipped free and Roman yanked open the gate. Kenneth charged through, raised his crossbow at de Velt's back, and fired.

Dazed and injured on the ground, Stephen was watching de Velt lift his sword in preparation for the death blow. He was in so much pain that there was nothing he could possibly do to stop it. He was unable to fight back. His strength was gone and his body was no longer responding. So he closed his eyes and thought of Joselyn as he waited for the final blow, praying she would forgive him for surrendering. He had tried. God knows he had tried to save himself. But his injuries had gotten the better of him. Yet as he prayed, an odd thing occurred. He suddenly heard de Velt grunt. Opening his eyes, he watched with shock as the man crashed to the ground.

Startled, Stephen looked to see a nasty arrow protruding out of de Velt's back. He was doubly startled when Kenneth suddenly appeared at his side.

"Good God, man, you look terrible," Kenneth slung the crossbow onto one shoulder and reached down to pick Stephen up. "You had better come with me if you ever want to see your wife again."

Stephen was dead weight and even with Kenneth's incredible strength, he needed help. Cade and Roman suddenly appeared, yanking on Stephen's arm with all of their boyish strength but hardly able to move him. Kenneth's men had charged through the gate after him and were now engaged by several Scots. Kenneth looked around in a panic, trying to find someone who would help him, when Kynan suddenly appeared on Stephen's other side. He grabbed Stephen's left arm and between him and Kenneth, they managed to get Stephen to his feet.

"Dunna hang around here, knight," Kynan said to Kenneth. "This place is comin' down around our ears."

Kenneth didn't know where Kynan had come from and he frankly didn't care. Between the two of them, they managed to get Stephen out of the postern gate as an epic battle ensued in the bailey behind them.

Now that de Velt was dead, there was no longer a central commander and the Scot factions, realizing this, began to rapidly deteriorate. Men began bolting out of the postern gate, fleeing the castle, and those on the walls began shouting and rushing around. As Kenneth and Kynan cleared Berwick, everything fell to chaos. Within seconds of de Velt's death and Stephen's escape, the castle deteriorated into madness.

Joselyn saw them coming. She bolted up from her seated position, crying out in horror and joy when she saw her husband. But behind him, she saw Roman and Cade, running furiously, and her elation turned to complete and utter bafflement.

"What in the…?" she cried as the men drew close. She pointed at the boys. "Roman and Cade are here! What are they doing here?"

Stephen, half-conscious, was so glad to see his wife that he was close to tears. All he wanted to do was fall in to her arms and never let her go. But Kenneth and Kynan didn't stop so the couple could be happily reunited. They ran right past her.

"Jo-Jo, grab the boys!" Kenneth called as they dashed by. "Do not let them out of your sight!"

Although Joselyn was supposed to do the grabbing, Cade and Roman turned the tables and grabbed her instead. They yanked her along as they ran after Kenneth and Kynan.

"Run!" Roman hollered, pulling her down the slope towards the river. "We have to get away!"

Joselyn raced between the boys who had her by the wrists. She couldn't figure out if she was really running that fast or if they were just pulling her that fast. By the time they reached the river bed, Kenneth was loading Stephen onto a horse. Then he grabbed Joselyn and took her with him, practically tossing her up onto his charger and leaping on behind her. Kynan grabbed the boys and managed to mount with them.

As the rest of Kenneth's men mounted up, the entire party took off, racing up the embankment and away from Berwick, heading for the safe haven of Tate de Lara's escort nestled on the other side of White-adder Bridge.

CHAPTER TWENTY-TWO

Norham Castle, Northumberland

T HE NIGHT WAS still, dark and peaceful. The only sounds were those of night insects, alive in their nocturnal world as they searched for a meal. Those peaceful and delicious sounds wafted into a dark chamber nestled deep in Norham's massive keep, lit only by two fat tapers and a glowing fire.

Joselyn sat next to the bed, mending her husband's torn tunic because it was the only clothing he had at the moment. Stephen was sleeping the sleep of the dead in a fat and comfortable bed, snoring softly. But he moved in his sleep, causing himself pain, and awoke with a groan. Joselyn's mending fell into her lap as she focused on him.

"Stephen?" she asked softly, touching his cheek. "Are you all right, my angel?"

Stephen's cornflower blue eyes rolled open. He grunted again, softly, as he oriented himself. Then he looked at his wife, her ethereal beauty shining as the firelight illuminated her features, and smiled.

"I am fine so long as you are with me," he whispered. "But I feel as if I have been asleep for days. What time is it?

Joselyn set her mending on the table. While she was there, she collected a cup and poured a measure of wine into it. She took it back to her husband.

"It is very late," she said, helping him lift his head and putting the cup to his lips. "And you have, in fact, been asleep for days. Off and on for three days. How do you feel?"

"As if I have been run over by an ale wagon," he grumbled, wiping an exhausted hand over his face. He looked around the room as much as his stiff neck would allow. "Where are we?"

Joselyn smiled faintly. "Do you not remember?"

Stephen shook his head. "I remember fleeing Berwick but little after that. Why? Where are we?"

"Norham Castle," she told him. "Tate felt that you were too injured to ride straight to Forestburn, so he stopped here and asked for assistance from the garrison commander who is loyal to Edward. The castle physic splinted your right wrist, wrapped your ribs, and we have been here ever since. The commander said we could stay as long as needed."

Stephen was beginning to vaguely recall their arrival. "Where are Kenneth and Tate?"

"Tate returned to Forestburn but Kenneth has remained here," she replied. "The man is as loyal as a dog. He would not leave you no matter what."

Stephen sighed faintly. "He risked his life to rescue me from Berwick," he suddenly lifted an eyebrow at her. "Speaking of risk, where are Roman and Cade?"

Joselyn smiled faintly. "Where do you think?" her eyes twinkled. "They are convinced that they single-handedly rescued you from Berwick and would not leave either, not even when Tate threatened them. So he left them here with Kenneth. The only reason Tate went home was to soothe Toby, who is undoubtedly furious and worried over Roman's disappearance. He said he had to go home and ease her mind so that Roman would live to see another year."

Stephen smiled faintly, reaching out to take her hand. She clutched it tightly as they grinned at each other.

"Cade is quite a boy," he said softly. "I will be proud to call him my son."

"He seems very fond of you as well," she murmured, kissing his good hand. "Oh, Stephen, it is so good to have you back. Those weeks when we were separated were the worst of my life."

"And of mine," he gave a tug and pulled her onto the bed with him, wrapping his big arms around her, reacquainting himself with the feel of her. "I was truthfully not sure if I would ever see you again. God has been merciful."

She lay down against him, careful not to hurt his ribs. But the moment she did so, the tears came. Stephen wrapped her up tightly in his powerful embrace, relishing the feel of her against him. He kissed her dark head.

"Why the tears, sweetheart?" he asked softly. "All is well now. I will heal and we will welcome our son come the spring. There is a good deal to be grateful over."

She nodded, wiping at her nose. "I know," she whispered. "But I came so close to losing you. I do not ever want to feel that fear again, Stephen. It will surely kill me."

He kissed her again. "Do not trouble yourself," he said softly. "As you can see, we have a myriad of friends and family that will always ride to my aid. Tate, Ken, and those two foolish young lads who risked their necks to help me will be around. And let us not forget your cousin, either. He was the greatest God-send of all."

She smiled, wiping the tears from her temples. "Kynan cannot decide if he is a traitor to the Scots now or simply loyal to his family," she said. "He is, in fact, discussing that very thing with my father down in the hall."

Stephen's smile faded. "Alexander is here?"

Joselyn nodded, lifting her head to look at him. "Tate sent for him. He had originally hoped that my father might convince those at Berwick to release you, but Kenneth and Kynan took care of your release before my father could arrive. So he is down in the hall with Kenneth and Kynan. Tate told him to wait here until you decide what's to be done with him."

Stephen stared at his wife. Her sweet, beautiful face, her luscious pale blue eyes. She was so exquisite that he was sure he was gazing upon God's most precious creation. But he was also well aware that the very reason for the woman's horrific past was seated in the hall below him.

Tate had known, eventually, that Stephen would have to confront Alexander for his sins. As Joselyn's husband, it was his right. But gazing into his wife's anxious face, he was not sure any of that was necessary any longer. He had Joselyn and the most wonderful life he could have ever imagined. He was not sure that condemning a sick old man would make it any better. In fact, he was sure it would not.

"What do you want me to do with him?" he asked his wife.

Joselyn appeared thoughtful. She watched Stephen's big fingers play with the ends of her dark hair, her mind lost in thought. It was clear that she was both uncomfortable and surprised by the question.

"He is my father, after all," she said softly.

"I realize that."

"What he did… well, it was long ago. I have long since forgiven him."

Stephen watched her face, the emotions rippling across her brow. "So I will repeat my question; what do you want me to do with him?"

After a moment, she looked up at him. "Send him home, Stephen. Send him back to Allanton and let that be the end of it."

"Is that what you want?"

"Aye," she reached out, stroking his scruffy cheek. "I have you and we have a wonderful life together. I am so blessed that I can hardly believe my fortune. Let no man, not even my father, cast a shadow upon that. Send him home with my forgiveness and with yours. Let that be the end of it."

He kissed her hand as it moved near his mouth. But it was not good enough for him so he pulled her down to him, sweetly kissing her lips.

"With all of the love I have in my heart for you, I did not think it possible that I could feel more, but I do," he conceded, suckling her lower lip gently. "You are a remarkable and gracious woman, Lady Pembury, and I am deeply proud to be your husband."

She smiled faintly, her hands on his face. "Kenneth said that if I ever grow weary of you, then he will gladly take your place."

Stephen's eyebrows flew up. "Is that so?" he grumbled, watching her giggle. He tried to throw the covers off but his ribs made it difficult to move quickly. "Where is he? I will thrash him soundly."

She laughed at him, pushing him back on the bed. "Not to worry, husband," she straddled him, pinning his arms. "I will never grow weary of you, I swear it. Kenneth will have to find another wife."

He gazed up at her, a smile on his lips, once again reflecting on how more rich his life was. He was happier, more content, than he had ever been. The journey to get to this point had been well worth every twist and every turn. His hands came up, even the bandaged one, and cupped her face gently.

"I love you, Lady Pembury," he pulled her down to his seeking lips. "With all that I am, I love you."

Joselyn couldn't even answer him. Her touch said everything he needed to know.

EPILOGUE

December 1337 A.D.
Bayhall Castle, Pembury, England

S TEPHEN WAS A man with his hands full. With all of the battles in all of England that he had fought, there was no battle more harrowing than the one he had on his hands at the moment.

It all started when he had turned his back on his toddlers for a moment to relay the command to open the great iron portcullis of his ancestral home, Bayhall. It was now his seat as Baron Pembury, hereditary home of the Culpepper family, Stephen's family name. His attention could not have been diverted more than a few seconds, something he would be swearing to his wife at some point, but in that time his children ran amuck. When he turned around, both babies had found a section of melted snow that had made muddy soup and had gleefully stepped into it.

Stephen tried to move swiftly to pick the children up before they muddied their clean clothes, but he was not fast enough. His three and a half year old son, Remington, was the leader of the Pembury rebels. He had his father's size, the Pembury cornflower blue eyes, and a natural air of command even at his tiny age. Rem was the first one into mischief and had little sense of making the wrong decision. If he wanted to do it, it must therefore be right. Stephen already had his hands full with him, adoring his son more than words could express.

Following right behind him was his younger sister by thirteen months, the Lady Ashton. A splendidly gorgeous child in the spitting image of her mother, she was, Stephen was sure, the sweetest thing to have ever walked the earth. She was also a very vocal child, much more than her older brother, and spoke in complete sentences with intelligence beyond her years. Stephen was positive he could not have been more in love with her than he already was. Almost more than anyone else, his world revolved around lovely little Ashton and her pale blue eyes.

But she was also a troublemaker like her brother and stomped around in the muddy water even as Stephen swooped down to pick her up. Rem was not thrilled with being pulled out of the mud and screamed like a holy terror as Stephen hauled him and his sister away. With one screaming toddler under each arm, Stephen moved quickly to the keep of Bayhall, hoping to get them inside and cleaned up before their mother discovered that he had let them become filthy just as Christmas guests were arriving.

Yet it was not to be. Mother had heard the screaming and was coming to see what the trouble was. Joselyn met him at the door to the keep, a six month old infant in her arms and her pale blue eyes blazing. She rolled her eyes when she saw the mess on the toddlers.

"Good Heavens," she exclaimed. "Stephen, I told you to keep them out of trouble. What happened?"

Stephen sighed with resignation, setting Rem to his feet because he was kicking so much. "I turned my back on them for a moment," he explained lamely. "I have no other excuse."

Outside, they could hear the commotion as the portcullis lifted and the incoming party began to enter the bailey of Bayhall. The sounds of equipment, animals and the voices of people filled the snowy air. Joselyn peered from the entry door, noting the crimson colors of the Earl of Carlisle. She turned to Stephen with a look to kill.

"They have arrived," she hissed, handing him the baby and taking Ashton from his arms. "Welcome our guests while I clean up your mess."

Stephen took the baby, who gazed up at his father with enormous pale blue eyes. Stephen kissed the dark head of Sebastian, moving to help his wife with Rem when the boy refused to cooperate. Joselyn struggled to haul the fighting three year-old to the stairs until she finally came to a halt and knelt down in front of him.

"Rem," she said with gentle firmness. "Your friends are coming to see you. We must change your clothes so that you can play with them and give them your gifts. Don't you want to give them your gifts?"

Rem was such a handsome young lad with his dark hair and bright blue eyes. He frowned at his mother but had, at least, stop kicking for the moment. "Is Cade here?" he asked.

Joselyn nodded patiently. "He is coming with the Earl. You want to see your brother, don't you? Then we must hurry and change our clothes."

Rem began to scramble up the stairs. Joselyn watched him clamor up the stone, puffing out her cheeks and exhaling sharply as she turned to her husband. She indicated the baby in his arms. "Can you at least manage to keep Sebastian clean while I take care of these two?"

He smiled, moving to kiss her sweetly. "I will endeavor to do my best," he kissed her again. "You had better hurry before Rem tears his room apart looking for clean clothes."

"He will tear his room apart in any case. He is such a terror that I am fearful of what will happen when he grows older."

Stephen wriggled his eyebrows. "I am still bigger than he is. Hopefully I shall be able to hold my own as he grows older."

Joselyn shook her head and grinned, holding her daughter by the hand as she carefully helped the child up the steps. Stephen watched them go before wrapping the swaddling tightly around the baby and taking him out into the cold winter weather.

The bailey was full of horses, men, and three heavily packed wagons. A large carriage was off to the left and Stephen's eyes fixed on it as he descended the stairs from the keep. A smattering of clouds was depositing a dusting of snow crystals into the air, sticking on the ice-cold stone structures. As Stephen walked around one of the big wagons, a shout caught his attention. He turned in time to see Toby heading towards him with several children in tow.

She was wrapped in a heavy fur cloak, smiling from ear to ear. She had three children following her; young Arabella was seven years, holding the youngest child, two year-old Sophie, on her hip while four year-old Dane was lured by the snowy mud puddles like Rem and Ashton had been. Toby grabbed the boy before he could get into trouble. She opened her arms, giving Stephen a warm hug as she focused on the baby in his arms.

"'Tis so good to see you," she told him although she was looking at the infant. "And this must be Sebastian. Stephen, he's beautiful."

Stephen smiled proudly, barely having time to say a word before she was pulling the baby out of his arms. She cradled the infant, rocking him gently and cooing soft baby talk to him. Sebastian rewarded her with a smile and Toby crowed with delight.

"He is wonderful," she declared, smiling up at Stephen. "I believe I will take him home with me."

Stephen lifted an eyebrow. "You will have to take that up with my wife. I am not entirely sure she would be willing to give him up." He watched Toby laugh softly. "Besides, you have your own brood."

He put an enormous hand on Dane's head as the boy came close, mussing the dark hair. Toby cast an affectionate eye over her youngest three children. "Roman, Dylan and Alex are on their way here from Kenilworth," she said. "I have not seen them since the summer. I miss them terribly."

Stephen snorted. "I have heard that they have single-handedly taken over the castle," he laughed. "The earl fears your sons. He says he is going to turn them loose on the Welsh."

Toby lifted an eyebrow. "Beware, Pembury. They will be here in a few days. Be careful that they do not take your castle out from under you."

"At least your husband will be here to help me fend them off," he said, looking around. "Speaking of your husband, where is he? And where is Cade?"

Toby lifted her eyebrows. "They both went to go fetch Cate from

Windsor," she replied. "She is eight years old and already entrenched in the court. Tate misses her so much that he went to retrieve her himself, and you know that Cade is quite fond of her as well. I do believe we will be related in a few years by marriage, Stephen."

Stephen put his hand over his heart and rolled his eyes. "I cannot believe how these children are growing up."

Toby grinned. "Just so you know, Tate is extremely protective over Cate and views your son as a threat. But he loves the boy and approves of him, so he is somewhat torn. Be prepared to receive all manner of lecture from him."

Stephen couldn't pass up the opportunity to jab at Tate, for any reason. "Hmmm," he looked thoughtful. "I do believe that I will bring up the subject of his daughter's dowry. My son will marry no pauper."

"He should be here in another day or so and you can discuss it with him then. But I would be prepared to defend myself if I were you."

Stephen laughed softly, watching Arabella set Sophie to her feet and then snorting as Sophie and Dane did exactly as his youngsters had done. They went straight for the snowy mud puddles. But a firm word from Toby stopped them and Stephen raised his eyebrows.

"I have not yet learned that particular command when it comes to children," he commented. "My children do as they please no matter what I say."

Toby shook her head reproachfully. "Stephen, you command hundreds of men and a powerful empire. Do you mean to tell me that you've not yet learned to control your children?"

He looked ashamed. "My wife does but, unfortunately, they do not seem to listen to me very well. That is why Joselyn did not meet you in the bailey, in fact. I allowed Rem and Ashton near the mud puddles and, well...."

Toby shook her head, laughing at his sheepishness. "Do not feel so badly," she told him. "Kenneth is the same way with his boys and I never thought I'd see the day when the mighty Earl of Wrexham would lose control of any man."

Stephen grinned, thinking of Kenneth, having gained an earldom by marriage, and his two blond-headed sons, Brennan and Evan. "Aye, but the difference is that his boys are polite and well behaved and he need not worry. I fear I am raising a pack of wild animals."

"Do you not remember how Dylan and Alex were at that age?" Toby reminded him. "Though they are no longer uncontrollable, they still get into mischief. I cannot tell you of the countless missives Tate receives from Kenilworth on the subject. All he asks is that they not beat the boys. Other than that, the punishment is up to the knights."

Stephen shrugged in agreement, knowing he would probably be facing the same thing with Rem. As if on cue, his eldest suddenly bolted from the keep, racing down the stairs as much as his baby legs would allow as Joselyn suddenly appeared behind him. She admonished him to be careful as she held Ashton's hand, helping the little girl down. Toby and Stephen watched as Rem ran right for his playmate, Dane, and promptly shoved him into the mud. The boys began tussling and Joselyn moved to intervene before she even said a word of greeting to her guests. But she waved at Toby apologetically and Toby laughed.

"Do you remember those years ago at Cartingdon when I first met you and Tate and Kenneth?" she asked softly.

Stephen nodded, thinking back. It was eleven years ago but seemed like a lifetime ago. "Aye," he replied. "I remember entering the church in Cartingdon and watching you argue with your father in front of the townsfolk because he wanted to support young Edward's fight against Mortimer and you did not want to get involved. I remember thinking what Tate was thinking; that you were the most beautiful woman I'd ever seen but with insufferable manners."

Toby pursed her lips angrily at him while he snorted. Then she grew serious. "Did you ever imagine your life would turn out as it has?" she asked.

Stephen's humor faded as he watched Joselyn deal patiently with Rem and Dane. His heart softened at the sight of her, the woman he loved with his entire being. He couldn't imagine his life without her.

"Nay," he said softly. "It is beyond my wildest dreams."

"Happy?"

"Ecstatic, and then some."

With Sebastian still in one arm, Toby slipped her hand into the crook of Stephen's elbow. "Shall we go and greet your entire reason for living, then?"

Stephen looked into Toby's almond-shaped eyes, twinkling up at him. He suddenly felt very emotional although he did not know why. "There are no words, Toby. No words at all to describe the joy of these days."

She nodded with understanding. "I know, Stephen. I know."

Tate, Cade and Cate arrived the next day, followed shortly by Kenneth, his lovely wife Bella, and their two young sons, Brennan and Evan. Roman, Alex and Dylan arrived last, big boys ready for their holiday celebration away from their training at Kenilworth.

The night of the great Christmas feast, Stephen sat in the hall with Tate and Kenneth, watching Roman, Alex and Dylan play with the younger children while Cade and Cate sat in a corner in private but proper conversation. Toby, Joselyn and Bella sat near the hearth, fussing over baby Sebastian, their laughter filling the hall now and again.

Stephen glanced over at his friends, men he loved like brothers. He was so content, so overjoyed with the blessings in his life, that he could not describe his elation. As he was thinking on his good fortune, Rem suddenly broke off from the group of children, being chased by Brennan and Dane. Brennan managed to tackle Rem, sending him to the ground as Dane fell on top of them. The boys were rolling around like puppies fighting and Stephen looked at Tate and Kenneth, who merely shrugged in succession with the resignation that fathers tended to show when their boys rough-housed.

As the mothers rose from their seats to break up the fight, Stephen lifted his cup to his friends. Tate and Kenneth lifted theirs as well, knowing instinctively what the man was thinking because they were all thinking the same thing.

"To the next generation," Stephen said softly.

As the years passed, more children were added to their collective families. The years to come saw Stephen add two more sons, Seton and Brenton, who, along with their brothers Rem and Bastian, grew up to serve Edward the Black Prince and his son Richard the Second while their sister, the lovely Lady Ashton, became one of the most sought-after women in England and eventually married the commander of Northumberland's armies.

Kenneth had one more child, daughter Witney St. Héver, who married a great Welsh warlord. Brothers Bren and Evan became two of the more powerful knights along the Marches, following in their father's footsteps as fair and wise men. But it was Tate de Lara's legacy that had the greatest impact. As the man who should have been king, his progeny followed great and prominent paths.

Roman became the next Earl of Carlisle and gained a reputation for wisdom and generosity. Cade Pembury served as the commander of Roman's armies and the two remained lifelong friends as well as brothers when Cade married Catherine de Lara.

Dylan and Alex de Lara, the troublemakers of the bunch, ended up serving the hot-headed Black Prince as his most trusted knights, with Dylan unfortunately losing his life at the Battle of Poitier. It had been Alex, Brennan and all five Pembury brothers who had escorted him home for burial.

Arabella de Lara married into the English royal family while Dane de Lara became a powerful garrison commander for Tate's brother, the great marcher lord Liam de Lara, along the Welsh border, eventually taking a Welsh wife and gaining lands and titles of his own. Sophie de Lara married a prince of Denmark and became mother to a future king.

As Stephen had once said on that wintery night in the year 1337; *to the next generation*. It was Tate who added the rest; *and to the generations to follow*.

The legacy of Dragonblade and his knights lived on.

☙ THE END ❧

THE DRAGONBLADE TRILOGY SERIES

The Dragonblade Trilogy Series contains the following novels:

Dragonblade

Island of Glass

Fragments of Grace

The Fallen One

Stephen of Pembury's great-grandfather is Bose de Moray, the hero of The Gorgon:

The Gorgon

The Dragonblade novel is also grouped in the Marcher Lords of de Lara. Tate's brother, Sean de Lara, is the main character in Lord of the Shadows.

Lord of the Shadows

For more information on other series and family groups, as well as a list of all of Kathryn's novels, please visit her website at www.kathrynleveque. com.

Bonus Chapters of the exciting Medieval Romance **THE FALLEN ONE**, a prequel to the Dragonblade Trilogy, to follow.

1332 A.D. – As the premier commander for Roger Mortimer, Earl of March, when he commandeered the throne from a young Edward III, Sir Mathias de Reyne is the type of knight that all men aspire to be; fair, powerful, intelligent, and bold. Men on both sides of the Mortimer/Edward lines respect and admire de Reyne for his outstanding character, including Dragonblade himself, Tate de Lara. Before the war separated men into two groups – those that supported Mortimer and those that supported the rightful king – Mathias, Tate, Kenneth St. Hever and Stephen of Pembury were inseparable friends. But then, sides were chose and lines were drawn. When Roger Mortimer lost his head, Mathias de Reyne was spared because of his great and fair reputation. Stripped of his lands and titles, however, he was forced into obscurity. He became known in legend as The Fallen One.

More than a year after being stripped of his knighthood, Mathias now makes his living as a blacksmith in the north Cumbrian town of Brampton. One morning, he hears cries for help and, being an innately brave and helpful man, follows the cries and comes upon a terrible scene. Rescuing a young woman from a fiend, he very quickly realizes that the young woman is the most beautiful he has ever lain eyes upon. The Lady Cathlina de Lara is a lush beauty with dark hair and flashing dark eyes, and the attraction between the pair is immediate. But she is also a de Lara, related to the man who took Mathias' titles from him… his former best friend.

Still, he cannot forget the dark-eyed beauty and soon finds himself swept up in a wildly passionate love affair, breaking his promise to never bear arms again by resuming his knighthood without the permission of the king and fleeing to Scotland. From the brutal Scots borderlands to the fields of Dupplin Moor and a historic battle, join Mathias and Cathlina as their journey in life takes them on a passionate adventure of love, life, learning, and the redemption of the man once known as The Fallen One.

CHAPTER ONE

May, 1332 A.D.
Carlisle, England

"Gazing at people, some hand in hand,
Just what I'm going through, they cannot understand.
Some try to tell me in thoughts they cannot defend,
Just what you want to be... you will be in the end."
~ 13th Century Minstrel Lyrics

ଔ

"NAY!" THE YOUNG woman screamed. "Let her go!"

It was the middle of a busy marketplace in the middle of the day, with hundreds of people bustling to and fro. The sun was shining, birds were singing, and clouds darted across the sky in the brisk breeze. But in the middle of the busy avenue, no one seemed to be paying attention to the young woman in a panic.

She was pulling on the tunic of a rather burly man with one eye who had a young girl in his arms. The young girl was screaming and kicking as the young woman fought him for all she was worth.

"Let her go!" she demanded again, hitting him on the arm and trying to grab at the girl in his arms. "Put her down, do you hear me? *Put her down!*"

The man tried to ignore her. He was drooling, his clothing torn and stained. He had grabbed the young girl from the back of the wagon she had been sitting in and now he was trying to make off with her but her sister had other ideas. He was moving away from the wagon with his quarry squirming in his arms as the sister beat on him.

"Nay!" The sister screamed again, realizing the man wasn't about to release his prey so she grabbed hold of her sister's arms and dug her heels into the mud, trying to pull her sister free. "Release her, you animal! Father, *help me!*"

The young woman knew she needed assistance. The brute that was trying to make off with her sister was big and strong. The young woman was in a panic, struggling to keep her head. Her father and sister were down the street with the spice merchant, running errands for their mother, and she had been left with the wagon and her younger sister. The young woman had been admiring a dress merchant across the busy avenue when she heard her younger sister scream. A man had grabbed her. And the fight began.

Her young sister was crying hysterically, grabbing on to the young woman's arms by digging her nails into the flesh as she fought against her abductor. But the young woman saw that she wasn't making any headway against the man, determined as he was, so she kicked him in the knees. It was a hard kick. When he faltered, she grabbed his dirty, vermin-filled hair and yanked as hard as she could.

The man roared and tried to hit her. As he released one arm around the young girl, she slipped and ended up hanging almost upside down. The older sister, down on one knee to avoid the strike from the brute, grabbed her hanging sister with both hands and pulled as hard as she could. Her sister slipped free and landed in the mud.

But the brute wasn't giving up so easily. He grabbed the young girl by the legs and pulled, drawing more screams from both women. People were noticing now, seeing the brutal struggle and wondering what it was all about.

Down the avenue in the midst of the bustle stood a smithy shop; they had heard the screaming, too, and a dark head poked out from the enormous shop that was blazing with fires and hammering anvils. Steam and heat rose through the thatched roof.

Mathias had heard the screaming but all he could see was people. Being that it was a very busy day in spring when farmers brought their spring harvest into town, there were more people than usual. Horses, wagons, women, children, and a few knights who had arrived for next week's local tournament... they were all here. Moreover, it was a bright day with good weather, but that would change as the sun grew warmer and the smell from the sewers began to fill the air. The flies would be bad, too. Not seeing the source of the screams, he was about to turn back to his business when the cries of panic caught his attention again. Then, he saw it.

A big bear of a man had the legs of a girl in his grip, but an older girl had her arms and they were tugging her apart. Both girls were screaming and the older one was calling for help. No one seemed to be coming to her aid and Mathias thought it was a family squabble until the man let go of one of the legs he held firm and punched the young woman who had hold of the girl's arms. The blow to the shoulder sent the young woman reeling.

But she was tough. The woman was stunned but she didn't lose her grip. She continued to hold, shaking the bells out of her head before resuming her death grip on the young girl and screaming once again for help. Meanwhile, Justus, pausing in shoeing a horse, noticed where Mathias' attention was. He could hear the girl screaming, too, but it was none of his business. Besides, he'd been banned from that kind of thing. There was no more chivalry left in his veins. That had died along with his permission to bear a sword.

"Mathias," he called quietly. "Lad, do not...."

It was too late. Mathias was already tossing off his leather apron and moving towards the struggle. Sebastian, pounding out a chorus of sparks on a piece of steel destined to be a sword for a local baron, saw his brother heading towards the struggle and thought he wanted a piece of it, too. Unlike his father, he missed the thrill of a fight and the exhilaration of a kill. Mathias, on the other hand, never spoke about it one way or the other, but Sebastian knew that his brother's sense of chivalry certainly wasn't dead. He just kept it buried.

As Mathias approached the fight, he could see that the young girl in contention between the young woman and the beefy man had been twisted around so violently that she had vomited. She had it in her hair. The young woman who had hold of the girl's arms was losing her fight. Defeat was written all over her face. The man was winning simply because he was much stronger and the young woman was trying not to collapse because of it. She was holding on until the bloody end. It was a puzzling and violent scuffle and as it raged, Mathias walked to within a few feet of the fracas.

"What goes on here?" he asked evenly. "Why do you hurt these women?"

The brawling came to a startled halt and the woman with the weakening grip on the girl turned to Mathias with wide and terrified eyes.

"He is trying to abduct my sister," she gushed, her voice trembling. "Please help me."

Mathias cocked an eyebrow, looking at the hairy and filthy man. "Is this true?"

The man bared his teeth at him and roared. That was as much of an answer as he could give. Then he gave one hard yank and pulled the girl free of the young woman's grasp. He turned to run away with his prize but Mathias moved quickly.

Reaching out, he threw his arm across the man's neck and jerked him back so hard that the young girl tumbled out of his arms. As the brute fell to the ground, it was enough of a break for the young woman to grab the child and pull her to safety. Meanwhile, the fight had now moved from the scruffy man against two small women to the scruffy man against an extremely formidable opponent.

Mathias was more than ready to go to battle against the filthy man who seemed to be covered in lice and sores. Upon closer inspection, it was a fairly disgusting sight. But he made no move against the man, instead, waiting for him to throw the first punch. Poised, fists balled, Mathias stared down his opponent, waiting. As he stood there, primed and ready, a flash of red hair moved past him and Sebastian charged the dirty man, getting his kicks by grabbing him by the face and throwing him to the ground.

"Bastard!" Sebastian spat, kicking the man in the ribs. "Do you go around taking your fists to women, then? You should be taught a lesson."

Mathias reached out and grabbed his ruffian brother by the arm. "Wait," he told him, pulling him back. His focus was on the brute, now wallowing in the mud. "Were you trying to abduct that girl? Answer me or I shall turn my brother loose on you. It is better now to speak than suffer his wrath, I assure you. Answer me."

The brute, now covered in mud, only grunted as he rolled to his knees and attempted to crawl away. Mathias and Sebastian looked at each other, shrugged, and Sebastian went after the man as Mathias turned to the two terrified women. As Mathias approached the pair, Sebastian leapt on the man's back as he dragged himself through the mud and began to ride him as one would a wild horse. He grabbed the man by the hair and rode him right into the muck, laughing all the way.

Mathias heard his brother but he didn't pay any attention. He was looking at the two panic-stricken women in front of him.

"Did he hurt you?" he asked the older woman. "I saw him strike you."

The older of the pair, a young woman of exquisite beauty, gazed up at him with an amalgam of fear and gratitude. It was difficult to decipher her expression. Mathias, in fact, didn't try. All he could see was beautiful brown hair, rich with a hint of red to it, and enormous brown eyes. Her skin was pale, like fresh cream, and her features were petite and pixyish. He was momentarily taken aback by all of her beauty, none of which he had noticed until that moment. Now, he felt as if he'd been slapped in the face with it.

"He did not hurt me," she replied, her voice quaking.

"The younger girl, then. Is she well?"

The young woman looked at the sobbing child in her arms. "I... I believe she is well," she said. "I do not think he hurt her overly."

Satisfied with the answer, Mathias looked around. "Is there someone here for you?" he asked. "Surely you are not alone."

The young woman shook her head. "My father and older sister are in town," she replied. "They are on errands for my mother. My youngest sister and I were sitting in our wagon – that is our wagon over there – when that man suddenly grabbed my baby sister and tried to run away. My lord, I can never thank you enough for coming to our aid. No one else seemed to be willing to help but you and... dear God, I cannot possibly thank you enough."

Mathias was fairly swept up in her sweet voice and doe-like eyes. He found himself clearing his throat nervously.

"I am glad I could be of assistance, my lady," he said.

The young woman peered around him to get a look at the big red-haired man as he jumped up and down on the brute. "What will you do to him?"

Mathias turned in time to see his brother roll his burly quarry over onto his back and leap on his stomach. "I am not sure," he said casually. "I will leave the punishment to my brother because he seems to enjoy it so much."

There was a touch of humor in what could have been a deadly serious statement. It helped alleviate some of the abject terror the women were still feeling. In fact, the tension seemed to have lifted a great deal now that the young girl was safe and the culprit being taken away. There was no longer any reason for him to remain.

With a polite nod, Mathias turned away because he was unsure what more to say to her and furthermore found himself just the slightest bit giddy. In fact, he was fairly unbalanced but a word from her stopped him.

"My lord," she called. "I do not even know your name."

Mathias came to a halt, turning to face her. He thought perhaps she was more beautiful at second glance.

"Mathias," he said after a moment.

The young woman smiled and Mathias heard himself sigh with satisfaction. Even her teeth were beautiful. In fact, everything about her was beautiful and he was quickly succumbing to her very presence. With a mere glance or soft words, she was a siren luring him to his doom.

"Mathias," she repeated softly. "I am the Lady Cathlina de Lara and this is my sister, the Lady Abechail."

Mathias felt as if he had been struck, lifting the delirium of giddy fog he had been feeling. *De Lara*, he thought. He knew that name all too well. He tried not to linger on the name, that powerful and consequential name, as his attention shifted to the slender girl in Cathlina's arms, plastered up against her sister.

The child was dark-haired, pale, and very frail looking. When she saw that Mathias was looking at her, she buried her face in her sister's torso.

"Greetings, my lady," Mathias said to Abechail, somewhat gently. She looked as if a louder tone would cause her to shatter. "I sincerely pray you were not injured in the struggle."

Abechail was pressed as close to her sister as she could go. When Mathias spoke to her, she closed her eyes tightly and tried to block him out but her sister shook her gently.

"Abbie?" she said softly. "Will you thank this man for helping you?"

Abechail turned slightly, peeping an eye open from the safe haven of her sister's embrace. Instead of her sister's doe-eyed gaze, she had blue eyes that were red-rimmed and frightened. She had tears all over her face and remnants of dried vomit on her neck.

"My... my thanks," she stammered.

Mathias cracked a smile. "It was my pleasure, my lady."

Abechail's gaze lingered on him a moment before smiling timidly. She still looked horribly pale and terrified, however, and it occurred to Mathias that until the brute was properly restrained or imprisoned, the poor young girl might never feel safe. In fact, neither lady would feel completely safe. He turned to his brother.

"Sebastian," he said. "Take that animal over to our stall. There are some old stocks back behind it. Put him there."

Sebastian's ruddy face lit up. "The old binders?" he repeated gleeful-ly. "One of them is broken, I think. I believe that is why they no longer use it."

"Then chain him to it," Mathias said. "That fool will not be free to roam as long as these ladies are in town. See to it."

With a smile on his face, Sebastian picked the muddy, lice-ridden brute up by the neck and dragged the man across the avenue towards the smithy shop down the way. People were dodging to get out of his way as he hauled the man behind him, singing a song very loudly about bearded women and knights with no libido. It was a song better suited for a tavern but Sebastian didn't care. He was happier than he had been in a long while, beating up on someone.

Mathias watched him go, fighting off a grin when he saw his father stick his head out of their smithy stall at the sound of Sebastian's voice. The shock registering on the man's face was priceless. Justus was, physically, the toughest man in England but he had a habit of showing his thoughts plainly on his face. That could make him rather vulnera-ble, but it also made him very humorous. Mathias had to turn away before his father saw him grinning. His expression was straight by the time he turned back to the women.

"He will no longer be a threat, I promise," he said, his gaze moving over Cathlina's features but trying not to be obvious about it. "Mayhap I should wait with you until your father returns to ensure your safety."

Cathlina shook her head. "I am sure that will not be necessary, my lord. You have already done so much for us. I do not wish to keep you from your duties."

Mathias essentially ignored her. He gestured in the direction of the wagon, a few dozen feet away. "Allow me to escort you to your wagon."

Cathlina eyed the man who was not only their savior but now de-termined to play their escort. He was enormously built and several inches over six feet with shaggy dark hair that had a bit of curl to it. His features were even, very handsome, and his square jaw was set with determination. But it was his eyes, rather large orbs of dark green that conveyed… something. She wasn't quite sure what she saw within the guarded green sea, but there was something there lingering just below the surface. She sensed great mystery in the searingly masculine depths.

"You are too kind, my lord," she said, pulling her clinging sister with her. "We owe you a great deal of thanks for the regard you have shown us."

Mathias herded the pair across the busy avenue, stopping short of touching her in any way, as a polite escort would have. A proper attendant would have taken the lady's elbow to show both protectiveness and guidance, but given the circumstances of their meeting, Mathias didn't think they would have taken any manner of physical contact too kindly. Therefore, he basically shepherded them to the wagon and watched Cathlina, who was hardly larger than a child herself, lift her sister up into the wagon bed.

Abechail crawled up underneath the bench seat and rolled up in a dusty oil cloth that was there. It was evident that she wanted to hide away from what had just happened. Cathlina watched her sister as the girl pulled the blanket over her head. She shook her head sadly.

"She was so excited to come to town," she said with quiet sorrow. "More excited than the rest of us. After this happening, she will never want to leave home again."

Mathias folded his big arms across his chest, his gaze moving from the swaddle-bound child on the wagon to the exquisite creature standing next to him. He wasn't one for idle chatter. In fact, he kept to himself most of the time. He was rather quiet and introspective. But something about that lovely face made him want to engage in conversation. He hadn't done that with a woman in years.

"Did you come far?" he asked politely.

Cathlina shook her head. "Not really," she replied as she looked up at him. "We live at Kirklinton Castle. Have you heard of it?"

Mathias nodded. "It is a well-regarded fortress," he replied. "It is to the north if I recall correctly."

Cathlina nodded. "It is," she confirmed. "It belongs to the Earl of

Carlisle. My father, who is the earl's cousin on his father's side, was appointed the garrison commander last year. Before that, we lived in a small tower near the Roman wall further north. In fact, our home was a Roman castle hundreds of years ago and before I was born, my mother was told about a local legend that bespoke of a Roman commander and his Saxon love, the Lady Cathlina Lavinia. My mother named me for the Saxon lady of legend. She thought it would bring me good fortune."

So... she is de Lara's cousin, he thought. He was wondering how, precisely, she was related to the great Tate de Lara and now he knew. It was a sad thought, indeed, but something he wouldn't waste the energy to dwell on. He'd never had a real romantic interest in his life and realized he wasn't in danger of having one now, not with the knowledge that she was a de Lara. It was too bad, too, but he pushed the disappointment aside to focus on her sweet voice, husky and honeyed. That was a much more pleasant thought.

"Has your name brought you good fortune, then?" he asked.

"Up until today it has."

It was a cute turn of humor and they shared a small chuckle. Mathias thought he might actually be blushing but he wasn't about to touch his face to see if it was warm. He could only pray it wasn't. He'd never in his life met a lady that so easily extracted emotion from him in so short amount of time. He labored to keep his control and not look like a giddy fool in front of her.

"I am sure the events of today will not sour your good fortune," he said. "I suspect you still have many years of blessings before you."

Cathlina was still smiling at him but as she lingered on her sister's near-abduction again, her smile began to fade. She was still quite shaken by the whole thing.

"What do you suppose he wanted with my sister?" she asked hesitantly. "I have never heard of a man simply walking up to a woman and trying to steal her."

Mathias shrugged, trying to make light of the situation because it had ended well when it could have ended so tragically. He thought it was perhaps best not to dwell on what could have been before he had intervened.

"Mayhap he wanted someone to come home with him and cook him a meal," he said, mildly teasing as he skirted the subject. "Or mayhap he simply wanted a wife."

Cathlina turned to him, rather surprised. "Steal a wife?" she repeated. "I have never heard of such a thing."

"'Tis true. Those things happen."

She could sense his humored manner and it was difficult not to give in to the mood in spite of the serious subject matter. "Do you speak from experience, then?"

Mathias looked at her, full-on. His lips twitched with a smile. "I do not need to steal a wife."

"Is that so?"

"It is."

She cocked an eyebrow. "I see," she said with feigned seriousness. "I suppose women simply fall at your feet wherever you go and you can have your pick of them."

He was trying very hard not to grin. Her humor was charming, and rather mocking of him, but he wasn't offended in the least.

"Something like that," he teased. "Women are always eager to marry a smithy."

Cathlina laughed softly, glancing towards the smithy stalls down the avenue. "Is that your trade over there?"

She was pointing and he followed the direction of her finger. "Aye," he replied. "My father, my brother, and me; we are the largest smithy operation in Brampton."

Cathlina dropped her finger and looked at him. "You were very brave to come as you did," she said. "I would not believe a smithy to be so brave."

He was amused. "Why not?"

She cocked her head as if cornered by the question. "Because that is not your vocation," she said, trying to explain. "You shoe horses and make weapons. You do not answer the call to arms as brave men do."

His amusement faded. *As brave men do.* He had been a brave man, once. Her comment hammered home the fact that he was no longer among the privileged, no longer in command of thousands of men who looked to him for guidance and strength. It seemed like an eternity ago when he last held a sword. Truth was, he hadn't thought much about it since the day he had been stripped of his weapons and lands and titles. There was no use dwelling on what he could not change. But at the moment, he was thinking on that very fact. He felt very useless.

"It was not a matter of answering the call to arms," he said quietly. "It was simply a matter of doing what was right."

Before Cathlina could respond, she caught sight of her father and sister coming down the avenue towards them, weaving through the crowds of people. Cathlina waved frantically at them.

"Father!" she called. "Roxane! Thank the Lord you have returned!"

Cathlina's father was a big man, muscular in his younger days but had now gone mostly to fat. He was balding and with a growth of beard, focusing curiously on his middle daughter as she called out to him.

"What is it?" he asked, depositing a burlap-wrapped bundle into the back of the wagon. "What is amiss?"

Cathlina didn't hold back. She told her father the entire sordid tale, watching the man's face turn red with anger and fright. Upon hearing the horrible story, the older sister, a dark-haired young woman who had a mere shadow of her middle sister's beauty, leapt into the back of the wagon to comfort Abechail. When Cathlina came to the part in the story where Abechail was so wonderfully saved, she pointed right at Mathias.

"This brave man came to our aid when no one else would," she told her father. "He was wonderful. He and his brother saved us. You *must* reward him."

Mathias was uncomfortable now that they were all focused on him. The father, his features still flushed with shock, made his way to him.

"Is this true?" he asked Mathias, as if he didn't quite believe his daughter's fantastic tale. "Was there truly a man to take my youngest daughter?"

Mathias could see the look of panic on the man's face. "It is true," he said. "But she is safe now. Lady Cathlina was quite brave. She fought him valiantly."

The father was stunned. He turned swiftly to Cathlina, inspecting her hands and arms for bruises before kissing her palms and turning his attention to Abechail.

The youngest daughter, who had managed to calm down somewhat since her brush with violence, was now weeping and quivering again as her eldest sister and father fussed over her. Mathias could see how shaken they all were. It was, in fact, quite touching to see how much they all cared about one another. That kind of devotion was rare.

Feeling rather as if he were viewing something intensely private, he turned to leave but was halted by Cathlina. She called his name, stopping him, and by the time he turned around, she was running at him. Her soft hands grasped his arm and those big brown eyes were shining up at him.

"Please," she begged softly. "You cannot leave before my father has had an opportunity to reward you."

Mathias had been touched by many women. He had also touched women from time to time, purely innocent gestures that meant nothing more than polite attentiveness. But he had never felt such fire from a touch as he felt now. Cathlina's soft hands were searing his flesh like brands. He could feel the heat all the way down to his toes.

"A reward is not necessary," he assured her. "It was my pleasure to assist."

"Will you at least come to Kirklinton and dine with us?" she pleaded softly. "Please allow us to show our thanks for your bravery. Do not deny us an opportunity to show you how grateful we are."

Gazing down into that sweet face, he knew he shouldn't agree. It wasn't a good idea, on so many levels. As much as he wanted to accept her invitation if only to bask in Cathlina's beauty for the evening, it simply wasn't wise. She was a de Lara and he wanted to stay far away from anything de Lara. But as he stood there with her, having her on his arm, he felt more like a man than he had in over a year. Odd how such a gesture fortified him. *She* fortified him. But he was forced to refuse.

"Your offer is very kind but I must decline, my lady," he said, trying not to sound cruel. "I can live the rest of my life on the gratitude you have already shown me. Anything more would seem greedy and excessive. I wish you and your family well."

He would never forget the look on Cathlina's face as he turned to walk away from her. It was a very difficult thing not to relent because he certainly didn't want to cause her such disappointment, but it couldn't be helped. He had done his good deed and would leave it at that.

He had work to do.

CHAPTER TWO

"**I**S THE BASKET packed?" Cathlina asked.

"It is, my lady," the red-faced cook replied. "I just put the bread in. That should be all of it."

In the small, cluttered kitchen of Kirklinton, she was peering into a basket laden with goodies; pear and cinnamon compote in an earthenware jar sealed with beeswax, cherries soaked in honey and wine, pickled onions, two loaves of bread baked with cheese and garlic, and small cakes that Cathlina had made herself – a little flour, lard, eggs, butter, honey, walnuts, nutmeg and cloves made delicious little bread-like cakes. Satisfied her basket was packed to her specifications, Cathlina carefully covered it with an embroidered piece of cloth. It was her own kerchief with the elaborate letters "*CLM*", for Cathlina Lavinia Mary, stitched in the shape of vines.

"Excellent," she said, lifting the basket off of the massive, scarred butcher table. "Thank you for your assistance"

The cook waved her off and returned to the suckling pig she had just killed. Hands wrapped around the moderately heavy basket, Cathlina headed out of the kitchen and into the yard beyond.

It was early morning in Kirklinton. In late May, the weather was warmer and they hadn't had rain for several days, which meant the ground had dried up somewhat and the mud wasn't what it usually was. In fact, it was rather dry and pleasant. Pleasant enough for a trip back to Brampton.

That was her plan, in any case. Dressed in a yellow linen surcoat with a matching linen cloak, the surcoat had lacings in the front of the bodice that, when tightened, emphasized her curvy figure to a fault. It was her favorite dress, given to her by her mother because the color had been so striking against her pale skin and dark hair. Cathlina's mother, the Lady Rosalund, was rather partial to her middle daughter. She reminded her of a sister she'd had in her youth, now long dead. Therefore, Cathlina usually had the pick of the wardrobe.

Even with the favoritism of her sometimes flighty mother, she was still remarkably unselfish or spoilt. She was, however, quite head-strong, and knew that she would not be punished for whatever she decided to do because her parents could never bring themselves to discipline her. Cathlina knew, therefore, that she would not be punished for her latest scheme. It was simply something she had to do and her parents would have to understand that.

Kirklinton's bailey was relatively small, as the castle itself wasn't particularly large. A big, square keep constructed of bumpy gray stone sat in the middle of the complex on a slightly raised motte. There was an enclosed entry and then four rooms of various sizes on the ground floor while the second floor had three sleeping chambers and a smaller chamber used for bathing and other personal needs. On the ground floor, a trap door in the largest room, which served as a smaller great hall, led down into a dungeon-like basement for storage.

The great hall was a separate structure as was the kitchen, both of them built into the curtain wall on the north side of the complex. Cathlina headed away from the kitchen and towards the stables built against the east wall. She could smell the hay and the smells of animals, and hear the braying and bleating as the beasts were fed by the stable workers.

Clutching her basket tightly, she kept looking around to make sure no one noticed that she was dressed for travel. She did not want to be stopped before she could accomplish her mission. Fortunately, everyone seemed too busy to notice.

Cathlina's horse, a lovely dapple gray mare that was part Belgian warm blood and part Spanish Jennet, was tearing at her hay when Cathlina entered the dark confines of the stables. A litter of kittens nestled near the stash of hay up against the rear of the stall and she had to take the time to pet each tiny furry creature. She set the basket down so she could cuddle the babies. As she put the last kitten down and turned for the horse, she caught sight of a figure standing next to her.

Startled, she gasped with fright until she realized it was her older sister. The Lady Roxane Marietta Anna de Lara was eighteen months older than her middle sister, a plain-looking girl with long features and frizzy dark hair. She was rather silly and not particularly bright, and she had a dreamy manner about her. With Roxane, other people's concerns or quarrels didn't interest her in the least. She was mostly focused on what made her happy. She was also quite jealous of Cathlina and often followed her, which is how she ended up in the stable.

Cathlina knew the way her sister's mind worked. Roxane was very nosy. She was the one person who couldn't know what she was doing. Cathlina's heart began to race with apprehension, wondering how she was going to prevent her sister from running for their parents when she discovered her plan to leave Kirklinton. The best way to deal with Roxane was to go on the offensive and hope to bully her into submission.

"What are you doing here?" Cathlina demanded.

Roxane cocked a thin eyebrow. "I saw you come from the kitchen," she said. "What are you doing?"

"That is none of your affair," Cathlina hissed. "Go back to the keep."

Roxane's eyes narrowed. "Tell me where you are going."

"Nay."

"Tell me or I shall tell Mother."

Cathlina's expression twisted angrily. "If you tell her anything at all, I shall tell her that you were the one who stole her store of fine wine and used it to ply Beauson so that he would kiss you!"

"You would not dare!"

"If you do not leave me alone, I most certainly will!"

"Oooh!"

"*Oooooh!*"

They shrieked and pointed at each other, furious and outraged. The next step was usually pulling hair but fortunately that didn't occur. Still, there was agitated posturing going on that eventually settled with Roxane backing down first. She was still making faces, however.

"I will not tell her," she finally grumbled. "But tell me where you are going. What is in your basket?"

Cathlina settled down as well, though she was still eyeing her sister with some anger. Roxane had a way of getting under her skin.

"Breads and treats," she finally said, returning her attention to her mare as she began to saddle the animal. "I am going to Brampton to bring them to the man who saved me and Abechail from the attacker yesterday. It is the least I can do."

Roxane followed her sister to the horse and actually began helping her tack the animal. "The man?" she repeated, thinking back to the day before and the events surrounding Abechail's near abduction. "The big man with the dark hair?"

Cathlina nodded as she strapped on the saddle. "Aye," she said. "He said he would not take a reward but I feel strongly that I must do something for him. Had he not intervened, surely Abechail would now be lost. He would not even come to dine with us so I thought to bring him some manner of treats to show our gratitude."

Roxane pulled the bridle off the nail on the wall above the mare's head, her manner thoughtful. "What was his name again?"

"Mathias."

"Mathias? What was his surname?"

"He did not say."

Roxane fussed with the straps on the bridle, her mind drifting to the very big, very handsome man who had saved her sisters from tragedy. He had delightful dark hair and a sculpted face.

"Mathias," she repeated, somewhat dreamily. "He was quite handsome, don't you think?"

Cathlina could hear the hopeful tone and she was irritated by it. Her sister had an eye for men, *any* man, and she could already tell that

Roxane's easily-won affections were about to shift to yesterday's hero.

Cathlina had spent most of the evening thinking about the dark-haired stranger, pondering his beauteous face and deep, gentle voice. The massive arms, the unruly hair, the twinkle in the green eyes… she was smitten by the picture. The mysterious Mathias was her private joy and no one else's, and certainly not her fickle sister. She would not share a secret fantasy that would surely never be fulfilled. It was but a dream, but it was *her* dream. She turned swiftly to Roxane, a finger in her face.

"You will not think of him," she hissed. "If anyone is to show affection towards him, it will be me, do you hear? I was the one he saved, you little fool. You have Beauson and Dunstan to occupy your affections. Leave Mathias alone."

Roxane looked rather surprised. Her sister never spoke of a man, so this was a rare occurrence. It also made Roxane very jealous because as the eldest, she felt it her birthright to have first right of refusal on any man that crossed the sisters' path.

"Beauson and Dunstan are merely father's knights," she said. "They are not men I intend to marry."

"Why not?"

Roxane shrugged her slender shoulders. "Because they are mere knights," she repeated. "I will marry a lord."

"Then you will put Mathias from your mind because he is not a lord. He is a smithy."

Roxane's brow furrowed, just as quickly lifting in realization when she became aware that her sister was right. "You are correct," she declared. "He is not a lord. We are de Laras and therefore must marry well. Mayhap Father will convince Cousin Tate to find us wealthy husbands. Do you recall when we visited last Christmas and the fine men that were gathered at Carlisle?"

"You mean when you first beheld Kenneth St. Héver?"

"I do."

"He is a mere knight, Roxy," Cathlina said, somewhat gently, although she was thankful that Roxane was off Mathias' scent. "He is not a lord. But I am sure there are many other men of standing that Cousin Tate can align us with."

"I hope so," Roxane said wistfully. "I am growing rather weary of kissing knights."

Cathlina lifted an eyebrow at her. "You should not be kissing them at all."

Roxane shrugged with a half-hearted attempt at defiance. "I do not kiss Dunstan anymore," she said, "merely Beauson. I do believe Dunstan has a fondness for you so he is unresponsive to my charms as of late."

Cathlina finished with the bridle. "Dunstan is a nice enough man, big and strong, but he is not what I would call a smart man," she said. "Besides, he is too old. I am not interested in him as a romantic prospect. He will have to seek affection elsewhere."

With that, Cathlina finished the last strap on the bridle and moved to secure the basket on the back of the saddle. Roxane assisted her and between the two of them, they managed to tie it down securely.

"Mayhap you should ask Dunstan or Beauson to escort you to town," Roxane said. "It is a long ride to Brampton and there are dangers about. You know you should not go alone."

Cathlina shook her head as she gathered her mare's reins and turned to lead the horse from the stable. "I do not need an escort," she said. "The ride to town will take an hour or two at the most. It is a fine day for travel and I shall return in good time."

Roxane didn't argue with her, mostly because she knew it wouldn't do any good. Cathlina was stubborn and determined and Roxane was never strong enough to take a stand against her. She didn't think the ride into town was a good idea but she had already voiced her objections. Now there was nothing to do but wait until her sister returned.

The wind was picking up as they moved into the stable yard. Bits of chaff blew about as Cathlina mounted her mare and adjusted her cloak, gathering the reins. Once she was settled, she turned to her sister.

"I should be back before the evening meal," she said. "If Mother or Father is looking for me, tell them that you have not seen me. Swear it?"

"I swear it."

"Good."

"Can I have your clothing if you do not return?"

Cathlina made a face at her sister to let her know exactly what she thought of that question. Kicking her mare in the ribs, she trotted out of the bailey quite simply, losing herself in the peasants and farmers milling in and out of the open gates. Being the only castle within a several mile radius, many of the locals came here to do business with each other. It was easy to get lost in the masses of the small and crowded bailey.

Soon enough, Cathlina was on the road south towards Brampton.

CHAPTER THREE

"**I** AM GOING to marry her," Sebastian said firmly. "Did you see the way she looked at me? She *wants* me."

Mathias was in the midst of shoeing a massive charger with a nasty temper. He was trying to concentrate as his brother, propped on the edge of a table, chewed loudly of his nooning meal, a large bird leg. Food flew about as Sebastian chomped and spoke.

"Could you see how attracted she was to me?" he asked enthusiastically. "Mark my words, I have found my future wife."

Mathias avoided a thrown horse-head. "You never came even remotely close to her," he said. "How can you know anything about her?"

Sebastian tore at the bird. "It was the *way* she looked at me."

"Is that so?"

"It 'tis. It was the look of love."

"How would you know? You have never seen such a look."

Sebastian snorted, pieces of food falling from his lips. "I have indeed, my fine lad," he informed him. "Every time I step foot in The Buck's Head down the street, those women give me the look. They want me."

He was deeply self-assured and Mathias couldn't resist taking a swipe at his arrogance. "They will give anyone the look that they think will pay for the privilege," he said.

Sebastian shrugged, unwilling to admit that only whores were throwing him expressions of passion. "Sometimes I do not have to pay them."

Mathias fought off a grin at his brother's damaged ego. Letting go of the horse's hoof, he went back over to the fire and pumped it hard as the flames sparked and roared.

"I would guess that Lady Cathlina does not even know you are alive," he said as he removed the red-hot shoe. "Besides, she is a de Lara. I told you that."

Sebastian was back to snorting as his brother transferred the shoe to an anvil and began to hammer. "What would the great Earl of Carlisle say if one of his lovely relatives ended up married to me?" he wondered. "It would make us family."

Mathias put the shoe into a barrel of rainwater, watching the steam hiss up into the air. "I am sure that would not excite him half as much as it would excite you," he said, eyeing his brother. "De Lara would not want us in the family."

"Why not?" Sebastian demanded. "You served with him and St. Héver and Pembury. You were all as thick as thieves."

"I was Tate's squire when he was a young knight," Mathias muttered. "I am not sure that makes us blood brothers."

"He loved you and you know it," Sebastian pointed out. "Besides, there is only a few years difference between you two."

"Seven years."

"He still knighted you at nineteen," Sebastian pointed out. "Two full years before most knights receive their spurs."

"That is because there was a war going on. He needed my sword."

"And I would wager he has missed it long enough this year past," Sebastian said. Then he looked thoughtful. "In fact, I do believe you even saved his life once. He owes you everything."

"Sparing his life and saving it are two different things," Mathias said quietly. He didn't want to talk about that particular incident. In fact, he didn't want to discuss that part of his life at all. Politics had separated him from his friends. A king had stripped him of all that he was. Nay, he didn't want to talk about it in the least and Sebastian knew it, but Sebastian had jelly for brains sometimes.

But Sebastian didn't have so much jelly for brains that he didn't know he had broached a sore subject with his brother. Mathias kept himself so bottled up, however, that sometimes Sebastian wondered if the man cared about anything at all. But he knew, deep down, that he cared a great deal.

"He would be honored to have a de Reyne in the family," he said confidently. "De Lara views you as an equal, Mat. You know he does. Ken and Stephen view you as a brother. Mayhap it is time to speak of such things again. Mayhap… mayhap it is even time to contact them again."

Mathias kept his mouth shut as he removed the shoe from the water and moved to the horse. Bending over, he pulled the horse's hoof between his legs and fitted the shoe. The horse tried to move around a bit and tried to kick at him but Sebastian set his food down and went to help his brother. He held the horse firm as Mathias hammered on the shoe.

Dropping the hoof to the ground, he wiped the sweat off his brow and moved back to the fire where the remaining shoe was being heated.

"Mat?" Sebastian said quietly. "Did you hear me?"

"I heard you."

"What say you?

Mathias pulled the shoe out of the fire, his face red from the heat and exertion of wrestling with the horse. "What would you have me say?"

"Tell me your thoughts," Sebastian pushed. He could see that he wasn't getting anywhere with his brother so he ventured onward in an attempt to prompt him. "I heard something the other day that might be of interest."

Mathias was only half-listening to him. "What is that?"

Sebastian reclaimed his food and chewed on the last of the meat. "Henry de Beaumont is trying to put Edward Balliol on the throne of Scotland instead of the infant David," he said. "I heard some men speaking of it the other day. De Beaumont will need knights, Mat. Mayhap this will be an opportunity for us."

Mathias looked at his brother. "De Beaumont is allied with our king," he said frankly. "If we take up arms for de Beaumont, do you not think that Edward will catch wind of that? Nay, brother, I will not lose my head for a Scots rebellion."

Sebastian knew that would be his brother's response but he wasn't pleased with it. He tossed aside the stripped bird bone and stood up, his manner growing agitated as it so often did.

"I do not want to be a smithy the rest of my life," he hissed. "Mayhap you find comfort in swinging a hammer instead of a sword, but I do not. I will be a knight again someday, I swear it, and if it is without your support, then so be it."

Mathias wiped the sweat off his brow. "Patience was never one of your virtues."

"What is that supposed to mean?"

"It means that times change. Tides and the flow of power change. You must be patient, little brother. We will not be like this forever, but for now, it is what we must do to survive."

Sebastian wasn't satisfied with that. He was about to fire off a volley of insults at his brother's lack of courage when a soft voice interrupted him.

"Excuse me?"

It was a gentle female voice. Startled, Mathias and Sebastian turned to see Cathlina standing at the entrance to their stall. Lit from behind by the nooning sun, her silhouette gave off an ethereal glow as she stood at the threshold. Wrapped in a yellow linen cloak, her dark hair was braided and draped over her right shoulder and her dark eyes glimmered as she fixed on Mathias.

"I am so sorry to interrupt," she said politely. "Do you remember me? You saved my sister and me yesterday from a brute, right out there on the avenue. I do hope you…."

Mathias cut her off, gently done. "Of course I remember you," he said, realizing in a rush that he was both surprised and glad to see her again. "Are you and your sister well?"

Cathlina smiled warmly at him, thrilled that he remembered her. "We are very well, thanks to you," she said. Then her gaze passed between Mathias and his brother. "I did not mean to intrude. I will only beg a moment of your time and then I promise I shall be gone."

Sebastian was the first one to move towards her, his enormous red-headed presence overwhelming. "Lady Cathlina," he said, a smile on his lips. "'Tis a welcome interruption, you are."

Cathlina looked at the big, ruddy-faced brother and couldn't help but be a bit put-off by him. He was smelling and sweaty and large. She instinctively took a step back as he came close.

"Thank you," she said, eyeing him. "How do you know my name?"

Sebastian pointed to Mathias. "My brother told me," he said. "I am glad to hear that you and your sister are faring well after yesterday's fracas."

Cathlina nodded. "Well indeed," she replied. "Thank you again for coming to our aid. In fact, that is why I have come. I have brought you something in the hopes of emphasizing our gratitude."

She lifted the basket in her hands and both men looked at it as if only just noticing it. Both of them had been looking at her face, mesmerized by the unexpected appearance of such beauty. Sebastian looked at the basket with interest but Mathias was on the move. He didn't want his brother frightening her, or worse. The man could offend easily.

"Your thanks yesterday was quite enough," he said, his deep voice soft. "You did not need to bring us anything."

"I realize that, but I wanted to," she said, once again completely focused on Mathias as if Sebastian did not exist at all. She couldn't seem to do much more than stare at him. "You would not take a reward and you would not sup with us, so I took it upon myself to bring you a few tokens of my appreciation. I hope you will accept them."

Mathias was genuinely touched. More than that, he was coming to realize that every time he saw the woman, she seemed to grow increasingly more beautiful. He was still apprehensive about her being a de Lara but truth be told, every second that he gazed at her saw that resistance taking a beating. Looking at her hopeful face, he knew he could not refuse her.

"Of course we will accept whatever you have brought," he said, his eyes glimmering at her. "You did not have to go to the trouble."

She smiled brightly and he was enchanted. "It was no trouble at all," she said, moving to the nearest table surface, which happened to be littered with a mixture of tools and scraps of food. Setting the basket down, she peeled back the embroidered cloth. "I brought you pear and cinnamon compote, and different types of bread, cherries soaked in honey, and – oh! – pickled onions. Have you ever had them? They are quite delicious. The cook pickles them with vinegar and herbs."

Sebastian was extremely interested in the contents of the basket, pulling things out to smell them, while Mathias tried to control his boorish brother by putting things back where they belonged.

"I have had them, aye," he replied, smacking Sebastian's hand when the man tried to stick his fingers in the cherries. "This is most kind and generous of you, my lady. This is truly an unexpected treat."

Cathlina beamed happily, thrilled by Mathias' response but rather peeved at his brother's uncouth manners. She had the little cakes she had made tucked down in the corner of the basket and she pulled them out before Sebastian could stick his fingers in them, handing them over to Mathias.

"Here," she said. "I made these just for you. I do hope you like them."

Sebastian was busy with the bread and wasn't paying much attention to the cakes Cathlina had presented to Mathias. But Mathias was acutely aware that she seemed to be speaking only to him. His eyes were on her as he unwrapped the cakes, hit in the nose by the clove and nutmeg smell. The gesture of bringing him gifts coupled with the delight of her lovely face had his careful control slipping.

"They smell wonderful," he said quietly. "It was very kind of you to do this."

She picked one out of the bundle and held it up to him. "Would you try one?"

He did. It was a marvelous bit of culinary achievement. "Did you make these yourself?" he asked.

"I did."

"Then they are the most wonderful gift I have ever received," he said. "No one has ever made treats for me before."

Cathlina was smiling so broadly that her face threatened to split in half. "Then I am happy to be the first," she said, noticing that Sebastian was tearing into the onions. She sighed at the sight. "Mayhap I should have made two baskets – one for you and one for your brother. It would seem he is going to eat everything before you have the opportunity to taste it."

Mathias cocked an eyebrow as he snatched the basket away from his brother, shoving the man back by the chest when he tried to pursue. Sebastian balled a fist but Mathias held up a finger.

"You have already shown Lady Cathlina what an animal you are," he said. "Would you show her that you are a brute as well? Show some manners in front of the lady, Sebastian. You are shaming me."

Sebastian tried to throw the punch but couldn't bring himself to do it. His brother was right; moreover, if he had any chance of wooing the woman, he would have to behave himself.

Lowering his balled fist, he forced a smile at Cathlina and sought to apologize for whatever brutish manners he had thus far shown when Justus entered the stall with a customer, bellowing for Sebastian. Disgruntled, Sebastian was forced away from his brother and the lovely lady.

"Good," Mathias snorted as he watched his unhappy brother stomp away. "That should keep him occupied for a while."

Cathlina watched Sebastian move away. "Your brother is quite... lively? Friendly? I am searching for the correct word that will not offend you."

Mathias laughed softly. "He is aggressive and he is a boor," he said. "But he is also fiercely loyal and strangely compassionate. It is an odd combination."

Cathlina grinned at him. "Mayhap you should hide this food from him. I have a feeling he will eat it all given the opportunity."

"He will," Mathias agreed, his gaze drifting over her delicate features. "Truly, it was quite kind of you to bring this. Where is your father so that I may thank him also?"

Cathlina's grin faded. "He is at home," she replied. "He did not come with me."

Mathias looked over her shoulder, back in the direction she had come from. "Where is your escort?"

"I do not have one."

His brow furrowed. "Did you come here alone?"

"It was not a long ride and the day was fine."

Now both eyebrows lifted in a mixture of concern and disapproval. "It is not safe for a lady to travel alone," he said as mildly as he could. "Does your father know you have come?"

"He does not."

Mathias wasn't sure what to say to that, but one thing was for certain; he was very flattered that she should risk her personal safety to deliver what she considered a reward for assisting her. In fact, he was rather stunned.

"Would you allow me to escort you home, then?" he asked softly. "I cannot allow you to return home unattended now that I know you have no escort. I hope you understand."

"It is truly not necessary. I can find my own way home."

"I am sorry, but I must insist. If you will not give me permission to escort you, then know that I will follow you all of the way home to ensure you do not run into any trouble. I can either ride with you or as your shadow. It is your choice."

Cathlina very nearly refused him again but she quickly realized that if he escorted her home, they would have more of a chance to talk. Perhaps she could come to know him better. Clearly, she was attracted to the man. Now that she had seen him again, it served to reinforce her initial opinion of him. He was handsome, gentle mannered, and undoubtedly brave. There was much to be attracted to.

Unlike her sister, Cathlina didn't particularly care if he was a lord or not. Roxanne was the one with lofty goals. Cathlina had, since she could recall, merely wanted a man she liked a great deal no matter what status he held in life. She'd heard of many lords who were selfish, vain, and immoral. Being a lord didn't mean one was automatically of good character. Cathlina would rather have good character and love over wealth and status. The man in front of her was of good character. She could sense it.

"Very well," she said after a moment's deliberation. "I would be honored with your company. Are you certain you can spare the time?"

Mathias looked around the stall, at the big charger he needed to finish. Taking the basket in one hand and the lady by the other, he gently escorted her over to a stool near the wall and helped her to sit. He set the basket down next to her.

"I must finish with this Son of Lucifer," he said, throwing a thumb in the direction of the big black charger. "When I am finished, I will be happy to escort you home. Is that acceptable?"

"It is."

Their eyes met, brown against green, and for a moment, the pull between them was stronger than they could grasp. It was difficult to describe, this attraction between two people who had no expectations or obligations to their brief association. Up until a few minutes ago, all Mathias knew of the Lady Cathlina de Lara was that she was incredibly beautiful but, unfortunately, she was also a de Lara. He had warned his brother against her. Now, he was not so apt to heed his own warning. There was something about the woman that was very, very special. He couldn't seem to take his eyes off of her because she muddled his mind. She was bewitching. He finally had to force himself away.

"I will not be long," he said as he made his way back over to the horse, who tried to bite him. He frowned at the animal. "These animals are sometimes quite difficult to handle for those they are not familiar with."

Cathlina watched him with interest as he pulled another red-hot shoe out of the fire and began hammering at it.

"It is a very big horse," she said. "A war horse?"

Mathias nodded as he pounded. "This nasty boy has seen several battles."

Cathlina eyed the scarred horse. "We saw several knights in town yesterday when we arrived," she said. "My father says there is to be a tournament in a few days."

Mathias nodded as he put the shoe back into the fire. "So it would seem."

Cathlina studied the man as he stirred the fire. He was wearing leather breeches and a leather apron, and a rather worn linen tunic that in greater days had probably been a bright shade of red. It was very worn and the neckline was torn just enough so she could see portions of his muscular chest. The man had the biggest arms she had ever seen, muscular to a fault, and his chest seemed to match that particular pattern. She'd never thought much about men's chests before but in peeking at Mathias', she thought his rather attractive. The man was purely big and beautiful, and her cheeks began to flush. She averted her gaze and sought to divert her innately passionate thoughts.

"Where… where were you born, Mathias?" she asked, struggling to think on something else to speak of.

He continued to stoke the fire, his face and body riddled with lusty, oozy sweat, causing his inky hair to kink up in small curls around his neck.

"Throston Castle in Northumbria," he said. "It is near the eastern coast."

"I see," Cathlina said, cocking her head as she tried to imagine where he was from. "You must have learned your trade from a very young age. Did you ever think to become anything other than a smithy?"

He pulled the red-hot shoe out of the fire again and set it on the anvil. He didn't want to tell her his deepest, darkest secret for many reasons, not the least of which was the fact that she was a de Lara. Therefore, for all she knew, he was what she saw: a smithy. There was no reason to tell her any differently because it would have been far too complicated to explain anyway, and it might possibly frighten her away. He didn't want to frighten her away.

"Like what?" he asked, glancing up at her with a twinkle in his eye. "A farmer? A sailor?"

Cathlina took the question seriously. "You are big and brave and intelligent," she said. "Perhaps you could have found someone to sponsor you as a page or squire at a young age. You could have been a fighting man. You said you were born at Throston Castle? Who is the lord at Throston?"

My grandfather, he thought. They were heading deeper into a subject he wanted to avoid. He pounded on the shoe.

"An old man by the name of Lenox," he replied, then shifted the course of questions back onto her and away from secrets he did not wish to divulge. "Your father is a knight, is he not? Allied with the Earl of Carlisle, you said?"

Successfully diverted, she nodded. "My father is a cousin to the earl," she replied. "During the wars between the king and Roger Mortimer, my father served the earl and the king. But he sustained a very bad injury in the battle at Stanhope a few years ago and resigned from fighting. He simply administers the garrison at Kirklinton now and has knights and other men who do the fighting for him."

"What is your father's name?"

"Sir Saer de Lara. Have you ever heard of him?"

"I am sorry, I have not. I am sure he was a great knight."

"They used to call him The Axe. Father did not fight with a sword. He liked his axe much better."

The Axe. Now, Mathias had heard *that* name. De Lara's Axe had been a feared fighter, indeed. More and more, Mathias was sure he would never divulge his past to Cathlina. Or at least, never divulge it to her father. He was coming to wonder if his attraction to her would lead him down paths he was trying very hard to avoid. If their attraction grew and he eventually pledged for her, somehow, someway, he would have to be truthful. To lie about who, and what, he was then have the truth come from someone else's lips to Cathlina's ears would have devastating consequences. Truth be told, lying was not in his blood. Truth and honor meant everything to him.

"I could make him an excellent axe," he teased softly, watching her giggle. She had the most beautiful smile. "Mayhap you will want to give your father a gift someday and employ me to make it."

She laughed softly. "I am sure you would do a very good job."

He grinned, swept up in her charm, when a pair of knights entered the stall. They didn't see Cathlina, sitting against the wall, as they sauntered into the shop, knocking over a hammer and hardly caring. They were young, arrogant, and full of entitlement. The taller of the pair, a young knight with bristly red hair, approached Mathias.

"Have you finished with my horse yet?" he demanded.

Mathias picked up an enormous steel file and bent over, pulling a hoof between his legs. "Almost," he said. "A moment longer."

"A moment longer?" the knight repeated, incredulous and outraged. "He has been here all morning."

Mathias was filing the front left hoof. "He has been here not yet two hours," he said steadily. "These shoes were specially prepared, as you requested. That takes time. I am almost finished."

The young knight pursed his lips angrily, eyeing the big smithy. "You are incompetent," he announced. "This job should have been completed an hour ago."

"I will be finished in a moment."

"I will not pay you, then. You did not finish on time."

Surprisingly, Mathias kept his composure. "I told you when you brought him in that he would be finished by early afternoon," he said. "I have finished him sooner than I estimated and you will indeed pay me the full price or I will pull every one of these shoes off of him and you can find someone else to shoe this bad-tempered beast. Do I make myself clear?"

The young knight was looking for a confrontation. He was too arrogant to back down from what he considered a challenge. "You will do no such thing," he said. "I will not let you. I will take my horse now and I will not pay you for being lazy and slow."

Mathias kept filing. "You will pay me or the horse stays here and I will sell him to the highest bidder to recoup my losses."

The young knight was outraged. "He is my horse and I am taking him."

"Not until you pay me what you owe me."

The young knight marched over to Mathias and lifted a hand to strike him, but Mathias grabbed the knight's wrist before he could follow through with the action. The knight yelped as Mathias shoved him away and tumbled over a bucket near the anvil.

This brought the knight's companion charging forward, unsheathing his sword. Mathias dropped the charger's hoof, preparing to defend himself against the armed knight, when a stool suddenly sailed into the knight's feet and the man went down. With both knights on the ground, Mathias was rather dumbfounded when Cathlina rushed up and kicked the armed knight in the shoulder. It was a hard enough kick that the man's entire body rattled.

"Shame on you!" she scolded angrily. "You foolish whelps! By what right do you try to cheat a man out of his earnings? You are a dishonor to the knighthood, both of you!"

Mathias' eyebrows lifted at her furious manner and brave tactic of throwing the stool she had been sitting on in order to disable the armed knight, but in truth, he wasn't surprised. She had shown remarkable bravery the day before whilst fighting with a man three times her size. If he thought about it, his respect for her had sprouted at that moment. She was a strong and courageous woman. Now, with this latest show of courage, his respect for her had gone from a sprout to a healthy bloom.

"'Tis all right," he soothed her, trying to steer her away from the men who were trying to gain their feet. "Please go and sit down. Do not trouble yourself over this."

Lured by the commotion, Sebastian appeared from outside the stall. His brow furrowed at the men on the ground.

"What goes on here?" he demanded.

Mathias merely shook his head but Cathlina spoke. "These men were trying to cheat your brother out of his earnings for shoeing this horse," she pointed angrily. "They tried to attack him."

Sebastian's red eyebrows flew up in outrage. "Is that so?" he said, going to stand over the young knight who had started it all. He was just starting to sit up as Sebastian loomed over him and glared. "You were trying to cheat us?"

The young knight rolled to his knees, attempting to stand up and keep a distance from the enormous red-haired knight. "He... he was slow and lazy," he stammered, his arrogance gone now that he was being challenged by two very big men. "It is within my right not to pay him for a job he did not complete when he said he would."

Sebastian reached out and grabbed the man by the neck as Justus, lured from the opposite side of the stall by all of the scuffling going on, came around to see both of his sons standing and two armed knights in various positions on the ground. The big old man with the long gray hair went straight to Sebastian.

"What are you doing?" he hissed, pointing fingers at the man in Sebastian's grip. "I have warned you against harassing our customers."

Sebastian didn't let the young knight go. "He is trying to cheat us out of paying what he owes," he told his father. "He tried to attack Mathias."

Justus looked at his eldest son. "Is this true, Mat?"

Mathias had positioned himself between Cathlina and the men tussling, including his brother.

"He tried," he confirmed. "But it is of no matter. His horse is finished and he owes a crown. If he refuses to pay, as he has declared to be his intention, then we keep the horse. Hopefully he has reconsidered, as a knight without a horse is a sorry sight indeed."

The young knight had managed to yank himself away from Sebastian and was fumbling angrily for his purse. Mathias untethered the charger and held out a hand, refusing to hand the reins over until the young knight paid him in full. By the time the young knight got the reins in his hand, he was so angry that he yanked at them and the horse took offense. A big head swung at the young knight, nearly knocking him over, as the young knight and his companion stumbled from the stall.

When they were gone, Mathias went about his business cleaning up as if nothing was amiss. Sebastian, however, followed them out and stood in the entry to the stall, watching them walk down the street with an expression that dared them to turn around and look at him. He would have liked nothing better than to go charging after them.

With the situation settling down, Justus eyed his two boys before realizing that Cathlina was standing back in the shadows. Surprise filled his expression as his gaze beheld her lingering on the fringe.

"A lady?" he said, pointing to her. "God's blood, there is a lady here. Does she have business with us?"

Mathias put his hammer on the anvil and began to remove his leather apron. "This is the Lady Cathlina de Lara," he said. "It 'twas her and her sister that we did a good turn for yesterday. Lady Cathlina has come bearing gifts to thank us."

"Good turn?" Justus was still confused. "What do you mean?"

Mathias had a half-grin on his face, his eyes on Cathlina as he spoke. "The lady's sister was nearly abducted yesterday," he said, trying not to be thankful for such an event but it was the reason that had introduced him to the lovely young woman. "Sebastian put their accoster in the stocks back behind the stall."

Justus was aware of that particular circumstance. "The animal with one eye who will not speak?"

"The same."

"He was still there last I saw."

"He will be there for a few days or until Sebastian has had his fun with him and decides to let him go." He set his leather apron down and pulled a leather vest off a nail. "I will be gone for a few hours, Father. I must escort Lady Cathlina home."

Justus' gaze was still lingering on Cathlina, thinking on the events of yesterday as Sebastian had told them. He and Mathias had all but swooped out of the sky like avenging angels. Mathias was a bit more modest, but in looking at the beauty of the lady before him, he began to suspect that one or more smitten sons were on the horizon. It would be hard to look at all of that beauty and not be bewitched by it. That spelled trouble.

"I am sure she has her own escort," Justus said. "Your presence is needed here. With the tournament beginning tomorrow, we have more business than we can handle. I cannot lose you, even for a few hours."

Mathias put the leather vest on over his rough tunic, securing the fastens that held it snug to his body. It was, in truth, a measure of protection against sharp objects, like swords or daggers, because the leather was heavily woven and fit his enormous torso like a glove; tight against his broad chest and snug against his slender waist. Since he was disallowed armor, the vest was the next best thing.

"I will not be gone long," he assured his father. "And Lady Cathlina has no escort. She bravely rode here alone but I certainly cannot let her return alone."

Justus could see the glimmer in Mathias' eyes when speaking of Lady Cathlina and he knew the man was already infatuated. It hadn't taken long at all, but he hardly blamed him. Still, he had to discourage it quickly.

"Then I will send Sebastian to escort her," he said. "You are needed here."

The glimmer vanished from Mathias' eyes when he looked at his father. "*Not* Sebastian," he growled, leaving no room for discussion. In fact, the last time his father heard that tone, they were in battle. "I will return in a few hours and do not let Sebastian touch anything in that basket. If he does, I will put *him* in the stocks. You will tell him that."

Justus sighed heavily, realizing there was no way to discourage his eldest. Strangely enough, he was rather glad for the lady's appearance when it came to Mathias. The man hadn't shown so much interest or concern about anything in well over a year. The Mathias that had lumbered around the smithy stall since that dark January day had been morose and sullen, quiet. A mere shell of his former self. But this Mathias was much more like the Mathias of old; humorous, concerned, and interested in what was going on around him. Aye, the lady had done that much, at least. Justus had no choice but to relent.

"Return as quickly as you can," he said, with reluctance. "We shall be working long into the night as it is."

The glimmer was back in Mathias' eyes. "I will, I swear it."

When Sebastian found out where Mathias was going, he tried to follow until Mathias slugged the man in the chest so hard that he fell into a big puddle of horse urine and got covered in the stuff.

As Mathias and Cathlina walked off, Sebastian vowed to get even.

Read the rest of **THE FALLEN ONE**,
a prequel to the Dragonblade Trilogy,
in eBook or in paperback.

ABOUT KATHRYN LE VEQUE

Medieval Just Got Real.

KATHRYN LE VEQUE is a USA TODAY Bestselling author, an Amazon All-Star author, and a #1 bestselling, award-winning, multi-published author in Medieval Historical Romance and Historical Fiction. She has been featured in the NEW YORK TIMES and on USA TODAY's HEA blog. In March 2015, Kathryn was the featured cover story for the March issue of InD'Tale Magazine, the premier Indie author magazine. She was also a quadruple nominee (a record!) for the prestigious RONE awards for 2015.

Kathryn's Medieval Romance novels have been called 'detailed', 'highly romantic', and 'character-rich'. She crafts great adventures of love, battles, passion, and romance in the High Middle Ages. More than that, she writes for both women AND men – an unusual crossover for a romance author – and Kathryn has many male readers who enjoy her stories because of the male perspective, the action, and the adventure.

On October 29, 2015, Amazon launched Kathryn's Kindle Worlds Fan Fiction site WORLD OF DE WOLFE PACK. Please visit Kindle Worlds for Kathryn Le Veque's World of de Wolfe Pack and find many action-packed adventures written by some of the top authors in their genre using Kathryn's characters from the de Wolfe Pack series. As Kindle World's FIRST Historical Romance fan fiction world, Kathryn Le Veque's World of de Wolfe Pack will contain all of the great story-telling you have come to expect.

Kathryn loves to hear from her readers. Please find Kathryn on Facebook at Kathryn Le Veque, Author, or join her on Twitter @kathrynleveque, and don't forget to visit her website at www. kathrynleveque.com.

48705993R00216

Made in the USA
Middletown, DE
25 September 2017